THE PARENT KILLER

A portion of the proceeds from this book will go to
the national organization, Prevent Child Abuse America.

Ashley Blake

THE PARENT KILLER

RĀ PUBLISHING

new york   nashville   jackson   los angeles

Published by RĀ Publishing, Inc.
300 Park Avenue, Suite 1700, New York, New York 10022
1207 17th Avenue South, Suite 303, Nashville, Tennessee 37212
385 Highland Colony Parkway, Suite 100, Ridgeland, Mississippi 39157-3500
West Olive Avenue, Suite 770, Burbank, California 91505

This novel is a work of fiction. Names, characters, places, and incidents either
are the product of the author's imagination or are used fictitiously. Any resemblance
to actual persons, living or dead, events, or locales is entirely coincidental.

Cover design by George Otvos
Text design and layout by Mary Ann Casler
Edited by Margrett M. Bess Ed. D

Library of Congress Control Number: 2001119736

ISBN 0-9706983-2-1

©2001 by RĀ Publishing, Inc.
Printed in Canada
November, 2001
First Edition

10 9 8 7 6 5 4 3 2 1

Acknowledgements

---ⱲⱲⱲ---

Outside, it's dark, and America rests. Since the recent shock to our nation, I want to take this opportunity to say I am proud of her. She will endure.

Thank you for spending your time and money on a novel written in the early months of 2000, with an equal anger.

Ashley Blake

I would like to extend my thanks to the following people:

To Almighty God, for every blessing and a wonderful life. You are my way.

To my mom, Reba, for your understanding and your adventurous drive to achieve. You are so special to me and make life so much more fun. You are unlike any other mother, and I love you for it. Thanks for helping me with my writing at such a young age.

To my dad, John, for your patience and generosity, and those talks we had on that front porch swing back home, which seemed to come around way too often. I still use the advice, man. I have the highest respect for you, and the deepest love.

To my sister, Julie, the best Rock drummer in the world! You're the most energetic person I know and have a lust for life few people possess. You are a beautiful woman, and you're always yourself. Thanks for always being there. I love you so much.

To Burns McFarland, for your faith, your excitement, and lighting the fire. I cannot fully express in words how much it means to me. You are truly an impressive man and have become a great friend. Thank you.

To Anna McFarland, Robert McFarland, John Sexton, and Justin Boykin—new young guns of the publishing world. Thanks for your enthusiasm and performing such a fantastic job.

To my editors, for your honesty and having no mercy.

To Bobby McFarland Gower, for being a wonderful employer and generous enough to allow me to do what I love for a living.

To Mary Ann Casler, for your creative imagery and your diligent work on the manuscript.

A special thanks to George Otvos and David Johnson for the incredible book jacket.

And to everyone at RĀ Publishing who gave of their time and effort and worked so hard to produce this book and guide it to bookshelves. I consider myself blessed to be working with such professionals. Thank you all, from the bottom of my heart.

To two powerful creative writing teachers—Dr. Dan Skelton and Patty Stanford—for telling me to fill up a blank page, and for giving me the encouragement to keep going. Also, I'd like to thank Penny Richards for taking that call in '91 and agreeing to show me the ropes and read my stuff.

To all my family and friends, here and now, and those who live on in memories.

Dedication

—ﾟﾟﾟ—

There's a sad thing going on here that I'd like to share with you before you turn the page. Though this is fiction, it would not have been written if a little girl I've never met, had not died. She's in Heaven, that precious world where there is no pain, no grief–the place we all want to call home once we live a long, prosperous life into ripe old age. But unlike us, she didn't have that chance. She will never know what it's like to take a family vacation, walk proudly down the aisle with her graduating class, experience a first kiss, marry, begin a family, or simply travel that path you and I are on to reach success, love and happiness that the American Dream promises.

Child abuse is an ongoing problem, and she's not the only one who has suffered. There are many children who cry themselves to sleep at night, who wake the next morning in the dark, who are extremely afraid of the people they call "Mommy" and "Daddy." This is a handicap that our society tucks under the sheets, and doesn't hold as a top priority in the effort to make this country a safer, more beautiful land in which to live. I did not write this book from experience. The research involved was sobering. I researched several child abuse cases and couldn't imagine the things people do to their children. I even felt for the parents. What burned inside them so, that would make them hurt their kids? And that's the saddest thing of all. Where does it end?

In my heart, I know that sweet girl is in a better place. This book is a statement against child abuse—a lie, based on true events, and nothing more.

When it's all said and done, whether a convicted child abuser is jailed or given the death penalty, it comes down to an eye for an eye and a tooth for a tooth.

For those of you who don't know, for those of you who don't care, and for those of you who have been waiting, this story is dedicated to the memory of:

—∙∙—

Heather Alexandria White-Alford
December 23, 1992 - December 15, 1999

God bless.

—∙∙—

For the thing which I greatly feared has come upon me, and that which I was afraid of has come unto me. I was not in safety; neither had I rest; neither was I quiet. Yet trouble came.

Job 3.25

Prologue

—◊—

I saw her last night in the moonlight haze. Her skin was ripped away from bone, the muscles deteriorated to hair-like fragments, the dents sunken in her forehead purple, black, and slick. A long gash that ran the length of her cheek melted into and over her eye like a dried red worm in summer heat. Her face was pale and bluish, her lips cracked and peeled from lying in a coffin. She looked at me, through me, and I knew that I had done wrong. She smelled of death, and I felt cold and empty. For the first time in my life, I felt wrong. Should I have allowed her to live? To see another day? I saw my dad there, too. His neck was lacerated so severely, his head was leaning onto his right arm, one ear touching the side of his throat. When the car went off the road, he flew through the windshield and slammed face first into a cypress tree. In the dream, his body crumpled to the ground like a bag of ice and I wondered if that was how it really happened. The coroner said the impact was so goddamn hard, it forced the hinge of his jawbone through his brain and into the back of his skull.

The haze moved on and I went with it. I was thirteen again, standing at the morgue. Looking at them. Lifeless bodies on cold slabs of steel.

I should have felt something. Regret. Pity. Sorrow. Something. But I didn't. They had hurt me for the last time. The anger in me then was too deep. It had flowed through me for way too long, a glowing flame that would not fade, and *when they died, I sat at the police station and watched the men in blue drink coffee and cram powdered donuts into their mouths. I listened to their questions, nodded, shed tears to act like I gave a fuck, and beyond the whole scene, I felt a load being lifted from my chest.*

I looked at Sheriff Combs. He was younger then, with only a shade of gray instead of a full head. I saw in his face a picture of sadness. He knew by my behavior that I didn't know what really happened to my parents. I could have been one hell of an actor. He touched my shoulder, told me it would be all right. Then, he walked away to get another cup of coffee.

I just sat there. Inside, I grinned.

—m—

The Sutter Springs Press. June 5, 1997.
Continued from cover:

Local Sheriff T.R. Combs heads the search of the slaying last Thursday night, without any suspects at this time.

Bobby "Champ" Rampart was found dead at his home on 138 King Street, the morning of June 4. Injuries to the head and neck proved fatal.

In view of this, authorities suspect foul play.

Sheriff Combs stated this is by far the most brutal murder the region has witnessed since Johnny Gilroy's killing spree in the mid-Eighties.

Rampart's son, Danny (10) is still missing. The search also remains to find the other children: Melissa Giles (10) and Sadie Bellis (11).

"We're dealing with a disturbed individual," Sheriff Combs said at a press conference held yesterday at the Sutter Springs Civic Center. "He's very dangerous and I advise folks to take precautions. Bolt your doors and lock your windows. We have no leads at this time on who is responsible for committing this horrible crime, but the Sheriff's Department will not call off the search until someone is in custody, and until the kids, wherever they may be, are safe at home."

Mayor Darabont has called for a nine o'clock curfew until a suspect is apprehended. Parents are advised to keep watch on their children, as the perpetrator is believed to still be in the area. We at the Press are particularly interested in the pieces of this puzzle and are concerned for the welfare of all. If you have any information, please call us at (318) 555-3270.

Terry Robert Combs, formally known as Sheriff Combs (a.k.a. "Fats"), ran his fingers through his short gray hair and stared at the news article as if it had been printed yesterday. It had been a year since he was on the killer's trail. A year since he caught him. A year since he wore his badge and loved his job.

He spent his days on a forced retirement that paid enough, but missed the thrill, the challenge of being in the respected position he reached as Sheriff of Milan Parish in Sutter Springs—the small, sleepy town nestled in the woodlands of northern Louisiana that had only one thing going for it before the murders.

Peace.

Rain wrestled the wind, rushing to the black earth in heavy, fat bullets. It hurled and slammed into the windows and pelted the rooftop. The sound was a reminder of the emptiness he'd felt the day he found Bobby Rampart's slaughtered body hunched over a table-saw in his garage where he worked as an auto mechanic.

Terry's face crumpled as the vivid image took shape in his mind, every detail vibrant and fresh, bringing him back to the crime-scene tape, to those questions he couldn't answer, to the scene of death, sight of blood, smell of rusted tools in the garage. He could see the tattered patches of skin and split bone before the paramedics zipped up the body bag and hauled Bobby off to the parish morgue. After the autopsy proved he'd been murdered, Bobby was then dumped six feet into the earth.

Terry swore by looking at the man's huge body bitten in half by the saw blade, he could hear his screams somewhere far off in a black world he never wanted to visit.

He rubbed his eyes and checked the clock. 8:05 a.m. His wife Monica left only minutes ago. She had her rounds to make. Pick up a few items at the grocery store, stop off by the children's shelter at the edge of town to deliver a case of donated books from the library, and, most importantly, refill his medication. Ever since the murders he'd suffered massive headaches, an ongoing pain game without the promise of an end. He thanked God each and every day that he had Monica by his side, to help him through the nightmares that came and went like girlfriends and boyfriends in a journey through adolescent puppy love.

The days slipped away slow and easy, leaving him searching for things to occupy his once busy mind. On weekends he'd load up his bass boat and journey to Toledo Bend. He'd rake 'em in and stuff them on crushed ice in a large cooler, gut and clean them, and finally either stir up the fryer on the patio or stack the catch with the other pounds frozen in plastic bags at the bottom of his freezer.

Through the week, he worked in the yard, drank coffee with the guys down at Joe's Coffee House, and cruised the back roads like he did when he was a teenager: a cold beer between his legs, a cigar between his lips, the radio tuned to Outlaw Country 105.3—the only station within fifty miles that played nothing but Haggard, Nelson, and Jones—without all that cliché, sugar-coated music pumping out of Nashville every other month.

Life was now carefree, a vacuum of endless freedom. The drawback was that he suffered painful migraines. When he had these attacks, he couldn't sleep without a Valium or his medicine, or both.

He picked up the paper and scanned the article again. Since he couldn't dream, he allowed his mind to drift off. Back to those days, to the time that would prove to make him or break him. It did both, in a sense, but he had his regrets.

He'd never forget that summer.

It was the summer of death. The summer of forgiveness. As the press labeled it, that was the summer of *The Parent Killer*.

Chapter 1

May 23, 1997. 4:35 p.m. The day before freedom.

Sadie Bellis poured a glass of sweetened tea and took a sip. Upstairs, the shower ran full blast, nailing the tile walls of the empty bathtub. She thanked God she was alone in the house. At last, a moment of peace. These moments had grown few and far between over the years even though she prayed for them every single night. She was afraid, she was always afraid. Every day she held her breath and hoped they'd leave her alone, that they wouldn't hurt her, but every day she saw that nothing had changed. Just the realization of another day in hell.

She tightened the corner of the towel wrapped around her petite, light-skinned body and padded into the living room, leaving dampened footprints on the polished hardwood flooring.

Sadie snuggled into a fetal position on the couch and placed a throw pillow between her knees to keep them from knocking together. She clicked on the TV and caught the last few minutes of a *Seinfeld* rerun to pass the time.

Eleven years old. Today was her birthday and she'd turned the Big Eleven. She imagined having a party like an ordinary kid. The scene was so clear and perfect in her mind, it made her smile. Her friends gathered around a decorated table piled high with colorful gifts and pretty cards she could save and look back on to reminisce as the years rolled by. Balloons, laughter, cake and ice cream, and tiny plastic forks set on tiny paper plates.

Nice thoughts. But it wasn't reality, it wasn't her world, and she knew it. Her parents probably forgot her birthday altogether. She was nothing to them. Sadie knew that, too.

It hurt. The feeling doubled up inside and flexed her muscles, pounded her brain it hurt so much. She was convinced her mother hated her.

Hated her.

She still loved her mother. Or thought she did. Wanted to. Longed to. Why? She didn't have the answer. The world around her was crumbling, and there was no one to turn to, no one who seemed to care, no one out there who could save her.

That in itself was scary as hell.

She bent her legs underneath her butt. The pain from her most recent bruise on her hip came alive, sending a troubled wave through her midsection. She'd been spanked with a two-inch wooden board for being late coming to dinner last weekend. Big deal, but . . . .

Won't do that again. I'll be on time. I won't listen to my music in my room so loud that I can't hear Momma call me down to dinner. It won't happen again. No way. She's always catching me do the wrong things, and the next time I leave the house, I will tell her where I'm going so she won't have to get the belt. She's gonna hurt me no matter what I do.

She thought about Danny Rampart and Melissa Giles, her only friends in the world.

Danny was ten years old. He lived the same unimaginable horror. Trapped in the same cage like a wingless bird.

He's exactly like me, Sadie thought. Living under a roof with a maniac who doesn't care for him, who beats him.

Was he punished like me? Did his father make him spurt glue on his tongue and force him to swallow it? Or balance two heavy textbooks in each hand while holding his arms out lengthwise for talking back? Or slap his face for making a C on an assignment instead of an A?

Sadie knew how strict her parents were, and what they were capable of. Knew the pain, lived with it. Knew that if this was the case and if Danny dropped those books, or didn't make the grade, there'd be trouble, maybe even a broken nose or a bruised eye.

She shivered at the thought. It wasn't fair.

Melissa. Her parents treated her the same way. It just wasn't fair.

Outside, a car door slammed. They were here.

She punched the remote, and the TV went black. Her heart pounded. She jumped from the couch and took the stairs two at a time, hurried to the end of the hall past her parents' bedroom and shut herself in the bathroom. The air was fogged, tight, making it difficult to catch her breath.

Sadie dropped the towel to the floor, stepped into warm water, and whipped the blue and white flower-print curtain across the rod. The sharp shower spray dug into her naked back and legs. Her long blonde hair soaked up the water, turning it to a slick, stringy mass.

The bar of soap melted in her palm as she pressed it.

She waited. Straining to hear outside the door, her face contorted into a blank mask of patient eyes and lips.

A knock sounded to break her concentration.

The soap hit the side of the tub with a hard thud and slipped into the water at her feet.

"Sadie?" called Anne Mase. It was her fat mother with short dark hair, an evil grin, and arms and butt as wide as a trailer.

Sadie opened the curtain and peeked around through the steamy air. The door was locked. Thank God. She'd remembered to lock it.

"Yes?" she said over the spray's noisy splashes.

"When you get out of there, I want you to help me in the kitchen. Those dishes should've been washed already. What've you been doing since we've been gone?"

"I can't hear you!" Sadie lied, not wanting to dive headfirst into another argument. "I'll be out in a minute." She stayed in the shower for twenty more minutes, going over the story in her mind, the lie she'd tell her mother when she got dressed and went downstairs.

I vacuumed your precious carpet, did my homework, took out the trash, swept the house, and polished Quitman's shoes. His dress shoes. I polished his dress shoes. I didn't answer any phone calls, and I didn't watch TV. You hate it when I watch TV. Only you and Quitman are allowed, you ugly fat hog.

After drying off, she grabbed a pair of pajamas out of her closet and pulled on a pair of socks. She smelled seared ground beef in the air. Her mother was cooking Mexican casserole again. *Great.*

Sadie gathered her nerve and readied herself for the worst, then went downstairs.

In the living room, her stepfather, Quitman Mase, drank beer in his usual position on the couch. He was focused on the weather channel, where a meteorologist was pointing out thunderstorms in London.

Quitman said nothing when she passed by, headed for the kitchen.

Her mother stood over the stove, stirring the meat. White smoke billowed up in curls from a cast iron skillet. She added salt and pepper and tore open a package of fajita mix. Anne spoke up and Sadie never made a sound. She always wondered if God had installed eyes in the back of the woman's head.

"Look in the refrigerator and get me those peppers."

Sadie opened the door. Her eyes immediately fell on the bottom shelf where a large white box took up most of the space. The middle of the box was constructed of a flimsy see-through plastic strip, and she blinked twice, surprised, as she looked through it and made out her own name.

"It's yours," Anne said tightly, leaning down. She pecked Sadie on the cheek. "Happy Birthday." She paused, put her hands on her hips. "Well, don't just stand there, take it out. We'll cut it now and eat some after dinner."

Sadie managed a shaky smile. "Thanks." She picked up the huge white cake with blue and red icing. Across the top read "Happy Birthday Sadie" and eleven candles were pushed into the soft, creamy icing. She placed it on the counter and lifted the top.

Anne handed her a carving knife. "Cut it lengthwise three times, then go back over it to make solid squares. Even squares."

"Okay, Momma."

From the living room, Quitman yelled, "Beer!"

Anne wiped her hands on a small towel. "Go get your father a beer. You can finish this later."

Sulking, not wanting to even look at the man, Sadie took this opportunity to complicate her already disheveled relationship with her mother. "He's not my father. He might be married to you, but he's still, like, your boyfri—"

Anne backhanded her. The girl fell to the linoleum.

Towering over her—a living, breathing skyscraper, shadowing out her features—Anne's face swelled. A beet red color flooded her cheeks and her eyes shrunk to small, beady coals. "Don't you talk about him that way, you little shit! As long as you're living under my roof, and as long as Quitman is around, you will recognize him as your father. He's the only one you have, the only one you'll ever have! That sorry son of a bitch who put you in my stomach for nine months left the minute you were born. Stop crying. Do you hear me? Stop it." Anne grabbed a cold Budweiser out of the freezer. "Now, get up and carry your ass in there before I give you something to cry about."

Sadie got to her feet, holding the side of her face, trying with all her strength to stop the warm tears from sneaking out the corners of her eyes. She took the bottle and crept away, feeling stupid, behaving like a hurt little puppy.

I hate her, I hate him, I hate this.

Quitman took the drink from her and handed it back. "It's not open."

"It's a twist-off, stupid," she wanted to say, but didn't. She pursed her lips, opened it and returned to the kitchen. Her mother had put the casserole into the stove. In thirty minutes they would eat.

Anne took off the apron and hung it beside the door. "Did you take out the trash?" she asked with no mercy to her voice.

"Yes."

"Polish your *father's* shoes?"

"Yes."

"What about this carpet?"

"Vacuumed. I swept up in here, too."

"What about your homework?"

"Finished it. Tomorrow's the last day, then it's summer. Didn't have much."

"Good. Now, wash these dishes. We can't eat off dirty plates. It's a sin."

Anne was not really religious. She never went to church, she didn't read the Bible (she liked to think she did) and the only time she spoke God's name was not in prayer or in conversation, it was in cursing, like when she stubbed her toe on the couch's leg the other night while roaming through the darkened living room and woke Sadie with her ferocious screams and shouts. Anne Mase was more superstitious. Not rabbit's foot and upside-down horseshoe superstitious, but "quit that, something bad will happen if" superstitious. If things weren't going right, if things weren't as they were supposed to be, she called it a sin. Dirty dishes, for example. Going a week without dusting the house. And if you didn't leave your shoes at the front door before stepping on her precious carpet, or eat anywhere else in the house but at the dinner table . . . Jesus! She would go ballistic. It was ridiculous. Just like her. Miss Fat, Stupid, and Ridiculous.

But she was pretty. She had a pretty face and nice skin. Sadie had her features, but the girl was yet to get chunky in the waist and heavy in the chest. Of course, she hoped that would never happen.

Sadie scrubbed away and by the time she finished washing and drying the cups and glasses, plates and silverware, it was time to eat. She looked around where the table was set with the Mexican casserole along with her birthday cake, her belly groaning in its empty cell.

Whose idea was it to buy her a birthday cake, anyway? Anne's? Quitman's? Did God make her mother finally do something nice? This was the first time they'd ever bought her a cake for this special day. She couldn't remember a time when she got gifts, for that matter, and the thought made her sad.

She dried her hands and sat across from her mother.

There was no blessing. The two adults dug into the food without first offering her a scoop or helping her fill her plate, so she waited until the spatula was resting on the glass container and cut herself a corner. She dabbed it with hot sauce and drank her tea. The adults discussed bills and when and where Quitman would go to work, maybe they should buy a new ceiling fan for the living room since the present one was broken and the air conditioner only worked half the time, how about let's watch that eight o'clock movie, no we can't afford you another truck, just get that one fixed, and tomorrow I'm gonna get my hair done 'cause it's getting too long, just look at these frickin' split ends.

Sadie paid no attention to their conversation. Same old thing. She eyed Quitman and wondered how and why her mother would marry such a freeloader.

Look at him, Mom, she wanted to say. He's only with you because he can eat and sleep here, that's it.

Quitman Mase was a construction worker, a tall and lanky redneck with long, greasy dark hair, a skinny nose, thin cheeks, and bulging blue eyes laced with sharp, upturned brows. He always looked angry, and he had only brought home five paychecks since they were married last September. Up and down, up and down. Wasn't the way of the construction business, it was the way of the construction worker. They had to find the jobs, go where the pay was, even if it meant leaving town for awhile. There were only a few things going on in Sutter Springs that Quitman had jumped in to, and the work was short. About a month, tops. Brick-laying, roofing, pouring concrete, setting rebar and laying pipe was about it. Anything beyond these little jobs was out-of-towners, and Quitman hated to travel. Besides, his truck was on the brink. It needed a new transmission, but he'd been hounding Anne for a new one. Still, ride or no ride (and that went for a job, too) he liked the fact that Anne supported him. All he had to do was sit back and keep promising to find that next job soon—wherever it was and whenever he'd get there.

"Could you pass the salt?" Sadie asked.

Quitman placed it in front of her. "How does it feel to be eleven?" he asked her. "Believe you me, you'll never be that age again. Have fun while you can."

Thanks, ya big dummy. She giggled to herself.

"What is it? What's so funny?" Anne said.

"Nothing . . . just a joke I heard at school today."

"Tell us."

Sadie thought, utilizing her wit. "Um . . . how do you circumcise a redneck?"

"Where'd you hear that word?" Anne said, shocked at her daughter.

"How?" Quitman asked, interested in the question. He forked the food, shoved it into his mouth that was presently surrounded by a day's worth of dark stubble, and sniffed.

"What word?" Sadie asked her mother.

"Circumcise."

"I heard it at school. Why? What's it mean?"

"If you don't know, then why're you telling the joke?" Anne said matter-of-factly. Her face twitched as she stared hard at her daughter.

"It's when a doctor cuts off your cock," Quitman offered. Sadie laughed into a napkin. "So, what's the answer? How do you circumcise a redneck?"

Sadie avoided her mother's heated eyes boring into her. "Punch his sister in the chin."

Quitman laughed out loud. Sadie joined in.

Her mother didn't think it was funny at all.

$\mathcal{M}$ason Xavier stretched out on the couch, his feet propped up on the arm. The log house was quiet. Too quiet, even with Rachel showering in the back room.

With the ease of an old man, he got to his feet and headed to the refrigerator for a beer. He downed half and with remote control in hand, turned on the stereo from across the room. Jimi Hendrix—"Little Wing." He set the system on repeat, finished the beer, and grabbed another. His faded jeans were ripped at the knees and his sharp-tipped black cowboy boots were polished to a brilliant shine. Bare-chested, he stared at the oval mirror hanging from the east wall. His blond hair had gotten longer seemingly overnight, cascading down over his ears and eyes.

Rachel loved it. She'd been wanting him to grow it out since their last trip to New Orleans. It would have been a magical weekend had they not decided to show up in the Big Easy in the middle of Mardi Gras. The entire trip had been a daze. They walked and stumbled along the alcohol-soaked streets illuminated by neon lights that lined the Quarter, shoulder to shoulder, breath against skin, the mystic, almost sexual scent of gardenias and mint alive in the air, and perfume lifting from the skin of every possible type of girl you'd ever want to meet, from every corner of the world, their hair streaked with sweat from dancing and drinking hard liquor at open-air bars. Quite a sight. Groups of bankers and lawyers and doctors gave up their morals, and yelled out "Show us your tits!" as spit flew from their lips; frat boys spilled cupfuls of beer on their shoes, or someone else's, but no one cared, as the city hid behind the façade of electricity and excitement of the celebration. It had been a weekend full of bourbon and shouts and screams where the beauty and sleaziness of New Orleans joined together. A weekend filled with laughter, dancing, and the drunken haze of kissing a stranger you'd never see again—letting rip your secret desires and hidden passions on a night you secretly hoped would never end.

"There's something about it," Rachel told him on the ride home, combing her fingers through his then short mop. Her voice was husky, recouping from three nights spent hounding Bourbon Street and the Garden District and every blues club they could cram inside. "I think it's sexy. Very."

Mason had it all. Money, freedom, and Rachel Borello's love. He'd met her when he was fifteen, she eighteen. They were the odd couple around town, but paid no attention to those who thought it would never last.

After nine years, they were still in love, still together, and happier than they'd ever been.

He was medium-built, muscle-toned with hard hazel eyes, a breezy smile, and a smooth appearance. At twenty-four, the kid had the world in his hands.

But it hadn't always been this easy.

Growing up with his parents had been pure hell. They beat him and fussed and argued with him all the time. His father had been a pipe welder at the plywood plant before it shut down, a hard drinking Arkansan from Little Rock, with ash-gray hair that feathered his head, near-black eyes, a strong jaw, and a body that seemed to have been molded from a barrel. His arms and hands knotted with muscles and veins that raised the skin. William "Billy" Cole met Mason's mother, Janet, at a Crawfish Festival in Abbey while he was working as a journeyman with Wade Construction and staying at a shabby motel that provided vibrating beds and showed triple-X movies twenty-four, seven.

Janet had always been a lean woman, her face clear, her eyes a soft green, with a smile that punctured your deepest frown. To this day, Mason had no idea how she could have done those awful things to him when, at first glance, you would've taken her for a good-hearted Baptist, the kind of woman you'd be proud to take home to Momma.

They married two months later in the city park gazebo, her friends and family present, William's best man his boss, who fired him for smoking dope in a "cherry picker" a year later. Janet told him her dad had connections and could probably get him a job at the paper mill. The connections worked fine, William landed the job, and the couple moved into a white A-frame house on Dalton Street near "Thrill Hill"—a sloping dagger of road where teens punched the gas pedal and soared over to get the feeling, for only a second, that they were on a roller coaster at Six Flags and not in some one-horse town built around forests and cow shit.

William would come home, park his dented Chevy by the garage, slip off his stained work boots on the porch, hang his hard hat on the hook, and walk in with the smell of oil and rosin fuming from his navy blue coveralls, grab a beer and kick back in the recliner. There were times when Mason would be in his room and he'd hear them doing it on the couch, his mother cheering his father to "pound it harder" and saying things like, "yeah, that's it, do it, do it!" And Mason would stare out his bedroom window and be grateful the pigs were wrestling in the mud and not hurting him at that moment. Other nights were filled with his father's harsh tone, yelling at him for just being in the room. "Get outta the damn way! Cain't see the TV." His mother would try to start an argument just for the talk, provoking him so that she could get off a good slap on his young skin. It was in those days that Mason learned to be quiet and stay out of their path.

Education of an abused child. He'd have done anything to have lived with his grandfather during those years.

Janet didn't mention her father too often. It was almost as if the name Tillman Xavier was unknown to her lips. Mason later found out Tillman had disowned her, cut her from the will, at first as a threat so that she'd quit her whoring, a rumor that gelled into truth as time crawled by. He perse-cuted her for her drug use, which she denied, but the worm-like lines and pits and bruised veins at the dent of her elbows and on the backs of her legs told a different story, and when she became nothing more than a two-dollar piece of ass with bad hygiene, her father made his decision final, and shut the door on her.

It was never easy for Mason, that's for sure. All the screaming and yelling. He'd been hit with everything within his parent's reach: hollow lead pipe, extension cords, wire hangers. At the age of thirteen, after years of pain, he thought about committing suicide. Simple way out.

Yeah, just take the gun, put it to your forehead and pull the trigger.

He wouldn't have felt a thing. He'd be dead and free. But suicide was for pussies, those who couldn't take what life dealt them. So, he'd been given a bad hand. Why should he punish himself? They were the ones who should pay.

That was his way of looking at it. Instead of ending his own life, he ended theirs.

A month after his thirteenth birthday, he cut the brake line on his mother's Buick LeSabre. It was a Saturday night. Every weekend, his parents drove to the Chickie House Bar and Grill on the outskirts of town to get drunk and search for the next hookup. That night, his parents never returned home. The car was found in Bouvoir River, and the next day, police equipped with a search party found their bodies at the murky bottom.

Mason never felt regret for what he did. It was either them or himself. He decided he made the right choice.

"Whatcha doin', babe?"

Rachel strolled into the kitchen with a towel bundled around her long brown hair and one secured around her body. She was sexy and beautiful, the type of woman your eyes followed even when you were walking hand and hand with your wife. From her deep dark eyes to the top of her tanned feet. She caught his gaze.

"You all right?"

Mason sipped the beer and plopped down in a chair at the table. He rubbed his eyes. "Yeah, just thinking."

About my mom, my dad, the screams I never heard.

"You look tense." She straddled the barstool behind him, her feet hooked under the holds, took the towel off her head and placed it before him. "Lay your head down. I'll make you feel better." Her professional hands were like magic. She began at his lower back and kneaded her way over his spine to his tight neck. Certified Massage Therapist. When she got out of school Mason had put up the money to start her own business downtown. And business was doing well, but the locals didn't think much of it at first. Like one elderly man said to another, overheard in a grocery store when Rachel had gone shopping after it first opened: "It's like something outta the damned city. You seen 'em. Know what they do in those places? Have sex. Yessir, that's right. I ain't lyin' to ya!"

Rachel was offended by the comment, and was so distraught that she left her cart-full of items in line and left. Hers was a professional business. She didn't have to work if she didn't want to, but she wanted to work, she wanted something to call her own, and Rachel's Massage on Third and Main was that something. Where did people get off saying things like that? "Dumb old fart," Rachel said in retribution.

Her fingers pressed into Mason's muscled skin, breaking the claws that gripped him. "Feel better?"

He moaned his approval. Rachel was half-Italian, which blessed her with smooth, toned skin as pure as spring water. She had an angelic face and a shapely body. Mason knew everything about her, and though Rachel might think she knew all about him, there was one secret he'd kept from her. He'd told her that his parents had gotten in a car wreck when he was thirteen, but he never mentioned his role in that wreck off Highway 109.

After the "accident" Mason was sent to live with his grandfather, Tillman Xavier, owner of Xavier Oil Company. It was there he learned the true meaning of freedom. It wasn't the endless summer days of doing nothing that promoted this feeling (nice, but that wasn't it) or the money given to him for movies and for passes to amusement parks that opened in early fall and late spring. It wasn't any little treat his heart desired: his four-wheeler, the .22 Rifle, the clothes, his motorcycle, all the video games, or the countless other wonderful things that made life a play land for a teenager with the means.

None of these gifts from Tillman could rise to the level of feeling the freedom he held deep within his heart for simply being away from his parents—dead as they were.

He had no regrets.

All that other stuff was grand, it put a smile on his face, but it was material. The real freedom came from knowing that yes, his parents who hurt him all those times were six feet under ground, and no, they would never return, they'd never hurt him again, and truth be known, that's all he ever wished for.

His grandfather passed on and in his will, he'd appointed Mason, then only twenty, the sole heir to his oil empire. When Tillman took his last breath of this life, Mason became an instant millionaire. The shock to know he'd never have to bust ass from nine to five was enormous. He was ecstatic, to say the least. The problem was that he had no idea how to run the business, so he sold his grandfather's empire for seventy million to a big-league corporation in Houston.

At first it was great. He and Rachel took trips all over the world. Paris, Hong Kong, the Bahamas. Two-week cruises. Vegas. Boy, he had fun there. In the two-car garage was a key-cabinet. It held the keys to his most valuable possessions: his black Porsche 911 Cabriolet, his jet-skis, his lake house overlooking Red Lake, and a convertible Mercedes coupe. He bought a chalet in Colorado, a condominium in Miami, and a beach house in Palm Springs. But he built his log house in his hometown of Sutter Springs, Louisiana. This was home.

After some time of living the good life, however, challenges became few and far between. He took up snow skiing in Colorado, scuba diving off the Florida coast, and even skydiving from the Texas horizon. It was fun and exhilarating, yet something was missing.

Nowadays, he stayed at home more often, and took late-night drives in his Porsche or Mercedes, and loved Rachel. Though he hadn't done it all, he'd done enough.

"Are you hungry, baby? I bought some lemon-pepper chicken. I'll put them on if you want some."

"Sounds delicious." Mason opened the newspaper, lit a cigarette.

Rachel took out the marinated breasts and heated the stovetop.

"Whatcha reading?"

He kept his eyes on the paper. "The personals. I'm looking for a new girlfriend. Wanna help?"

"Give it up. No one else would be able to put up with you."

He laughed and traced his finger over the opposite page, pin-pointing the Alternate Lifestyles section. "Look at all these fags. This page is chock full. They're all over in Summerset. Probably some here in Sutter Springs." He chuckled. "Men wanting men, women wanting women."

"Rachel wanting Mason."

He looked up, his cheeks pink.

She loosened the towel around her waist and it fell to the floor. Her damp skin glistened under the kitchen light. Her lips pursed into a naughty pout. "I'll give you a new girlfriend, baby."

Mason moved his eyes over her naked body, feeling the stir in his crotch, the heat rising in his chest.

She stepped to him and kissed him. Her hand slipped down his pumped chest to the button of his jeans. Lazy bedroom eyes lifted to his, held them, and her mouth parted slightly from the thin film of saliva that lined her lips like watery glue, and she unsnapped it.

They paid no attention to the meat frying in the skillet. Strong lemon-and-pepper flavored smoke filled the air, the meat sizzled.

Mason took in her sweet scent, his hands following the curves to her warmth. He placed his palm over the one clean strip of pubic hair and felt her heat, the insides of her thighs framed with shower water and sweat.

She flicked out her tongue, touched the tip to his ear. "Now it's your turn to massage me," she whispered.

Within seconds, they were on the couch. Rachel guided him inside her, leaned back her head, and closed her eyes. Mason moved his hands over her ripe breasts and felt her hot breath wash over his neck, cool his shoulders.

"That's it, baby. C'mon. Give it to me."

Mason reached out and touched the lamp, felt for the switch. When he found it, he clicked it, and the living room fell to darkness.

Chapter 3

Someday it's going to be all right and I won't get mad no more.

Danny Rampart
Notebook entry #23.

The three kids met as often as they could. Sadie Bellis was the oldest and she assumed the responsibility of their "leader."

There was Danny Rampart, the only boy. At ten years old, he had innocent blue eyes and a calm face, his black hair uneven and shaggy. A scar ran from his temple to the base of his chin where, two months ago in a drunken rage, his father had struck him with a leather strap used to sharpen hunting knives. He'd told his homeroom teacher he'd fallen down the porch steps at his house and scraped his face across a screw that protruded from the woodwork. She had nodded her head, the expression on her face numb. Ms. Hail didn't believe him.

There was Melissa Giles, the same age as Danny, younger by only a few months, with pale white skin, and honesty in a set of pure green eyes. She was tiny and had flaming red hair that made her stand out in a crowd. A thousand freckles covered the middle of her face. She thought they made her look ugly. That's what her mother told her. "Look at those things! You look like you just fell in the mud!" Her friends promised she looked cute, and though their compliments made her feel good, she wore make-up to camouflage her skin. Her mother was always on her about that. "You're too young to be wearing lipstick and goddamn eye-shadow," she'd say, and curse her daughter off and on throughout an entire day so that Melissa would get the point. But the girl was always back into the make-up bag, in front of the mirror dabbing her eyes with black liner and covering up her little imperfections with coat after coat of base.

Their meeting ground was a treehouse built in an eerie grove of pine trees near the border that separated northern Louisiana and southern Arkansas. A bench was positioned in the middle of it, atop it a collection of reading material from comic books to *People* magazine. Candles in glass holders sat high on shelves among an array of candy in plastic bowls they bought at Pop's Grocery. Folding chairs they had stolen from the back of a pickup truck after a little league game last spring were positioned against the walls and Melissa added a homey feel to the place by bringing flowers from her mother's rose garden, set in cheap, curved vases.

They called it a club because they met in a tree house and the way Danny explained it, if you meet in a tree house, you're supposed to call it that. He sure as hell wasn't going to be part of a group, or session, or some kind of girl's organization without the word "club" somewhere in the mix. Their purpose was to talk about what went on behind closed doors. A blue notebook on one of the shelves chronicled meeting times and dates. It was in that notebook where the bad things were written.

Sadie spent the half-hour at the dinner table thinking about the club, and when she finished eating she returned to her room. She brainstormed the possibility of running away as she had every night for several months. Leave the place behind. Forever.

It was almost seven-thirty, and she was supposed to meet her friends in thirty minutes. This was always an "iffy" situation, depending on whether they could sneak away or not. Asking permission to leave the house for an hour was a "no no." They just left, and if their parents found out, well, they had to face the consequences. "We'd get in trouble for something anyway," Sadie had once told them. "Might as well get in trouble for something worth the time." It made sense, but they'd only gotten caught a few times.

The orange sun was fading fast. Sadie opened her bedroom door and peeked down the empty hallway. Quitman and Anne were downstairs talking to each other. Good. It was one of those days when her mother didn't even know she existed. Better than Anne jumping down her throat and squeezing a lung. When she left, they would think she's in bed as always. They never bothered her at night. They usually got high and drunk and passed out on the couch.

Sadie crawled out of the window, grabbed hold of the drainage pipe and slid to the ground. In the open garage was Anne's car, Quitman's motorcycle, and her bicycle. She pedaled north to the state line, a solid mile away, and when she arrived, she looked over her shoulder to see if she'd been followed, as always.

She loved this time of year. Tomorrow was the last day of school and summer was so close she could taste it. She stopped her bike beside the other two—Danny's was on the ground, handlebars facing the sky—and she dropped the kick-stand. She climbed the sturdy boards nailed to the tree and heard her friends inside engaged in one of their usual light-hearted arguments.

"Danny, quit it! You're so stupid! Gimme that thing, it's nasty!" Melissa.

Danny continued poking her with a blue fly-swatter, giggling uncontrollably. He looked up as Sadie entered, the orange and pink rays from the setting sun blazed across his excited face. "Hey, Sadie!" He went for her with the floppy thing, forcing her against the wall.

Resentment grew on her face. "Danny, gimme that!" She grabbed the end and pulled it away from him. It took a moment for Danny to realize he was no longer holding it, his eyes focused on the ground. Sadie smiled. "How does it feel?" she teased, slapping his bare arms and hips.

"Augh!" Danny jumped over the coffee table. "Stop!"

Melissa finger-combed her fiery red hair from over her eyes and stared hard at Danny. *"Idiot."*

Sadie got the notebook from the shelf, opened it to page fifty-six. She sat in a yellow and white folding chair, crossed her legs. "So, how long have you guys been here?"

"All damn night!" Danny joked.

"Watch your mouth," Melissa scolded.

"Oh yeah, like you've never heard that word."

"Okay, you guys." Sadie slapped the chair's plastic arm, gaining attention. "The meeting has started."

"'Scuse me, Miss Judge?" Danny raised his hand high in the air. "I gotta take a leak. A big one!"

"God, you're gross," Melissa said.

"Settle down, Danny."

"But I do!"

"Well, I'm not stoppin' you. Go outside." Sadie clicked a pen and dated the top of the page. Danny left.

Melissa stood, hands at her sides, and paced the room, the boards creaking underneath her. "He is so annoying."

Sadie crossed one leg over the other. "Yeah, but he's one of us." She lifted her head. "He has to put up with the same crap we do, so chill out."

"Happy Birthday, Sadie."

Her face was soft in the light, and she had a lost gleam in her eyes as though she didn't know how to react. "Thank you." She looked down.

The notebook stretched back as far as October when the thrio began coming together to talk about their seemingly endless battle within their dark worlds.

Danny returned shuffling a deck of cards. He bent them, letting them flutter out of his hand and into Melissa's face.

Melissa let out a sigh.

Sadie pointed at him with her ink pen. "Siddown, Danny. We can have fun time later. Missy? Everything goin' okay at home?"

Melissa's instant smile was erased by a straight line. She looked at her feet, picked at her nails. "No. Like always."

"Did she hit you again?" Danny asked, his voice slow and soft, each word clearly tattooed with apology for his earlier actions. He leaned back on the bench beside her, clasped his hands around his knees, his body now a short, stubby ball.

"I was in my room playin' PlayStation and Momma came in with a plate in her hand. I had put it in the sink and it still had some salsa on it. I was eatin' chips and salsa before she got home and she told me I should have cleaned it. I mean, my God, it was just a little bit. It was my fault I didn't go ahead and put it in the dishwasher so she couldn't see it. So, she just goes nuts." Melissa lifted her shirt and pulled her shorts down over her hip. "She got a belt. Doubled up." She touched a fresh, dark bruise that appeared on the verge of bursting with blood. "The buckle hit me here on the side, and right across my stomach. It hurt at first, but now it's not that bad."

As her friend spoke, Sadie wrote like a doctor filling out a prescription for a waiting patient. She shook her head and kicked the floor. "We've gotta do something."

"What *can* we do?" Melissa asked. "We've been saying that forever."

Sadie dug into the candy bowl, got a piece and unwrapped it. She took in a deep breath. A light wind coursed through the window and attacked her hair. "I don't know. I just don't know."

"Let's call the cops!" Danny almost screamed.

"Shh! No, Danny, we can't. It'd be a great idea if it'd work, but we can't. The cops won't do anything." Sadie licked her lips, lowered her eyebrows. "I've heard stories about kids calling the cops on their parents. After that, they were in bigger trouble than before because they tried to get help. The cops won't help us, okay? What're they gonna do? Come by, ask questions, and leave. That's what. You'll still be in the same place, under the same roof, living in the same mess."

"Same shit," Danny whispered, struck funny.

"This isn't a joke!" Melissa exploded. She jumped to her feet, her hands balled into angry fists. "Sadie's right. Until we're old enough to leave home, we've got to put up with our parents, and the cops are out of the question!"

"Melissa, chill out. Don't yell, remember? We get enough of that anyway."

"Sorry."

"I hate my dad," said Danny, watching the sun sink behind bulbous, purple clouds.

"You don't hate him. Danny, don't say that." It was Sadie's comforting voice that forced him to rethink his statement. She was the last person he'd argue with, but he believed his own words. He did hate his father. "You might not like him a whole lot," she continued. "I don't think anybody here likes our parents a whole lot, but we don't hate them." She got out of the chair and hugged Melissa. "I'm sorry that happened to you last night, Missy. Remember what I told you. Do whatever they say to avoid a fight. Don't argue with them, don't smart off. I know you want to. *I* want to, but it won't help. It'll only make things worse."

"That's the problem!" Melissa blurted. "I didn't do anything, I just forgot to clean a plate good and she, she came in and hit me. Bitch!"

Sadie held her hand and beckoned Danny. He walked to the girls, the fear on his face beating.

"It's okay, Danny. Everybody hold hands."

"It's time to pray, isn't it?" he asked.

"Yeah, it's time to pray," she answered. "Bow your heads." They did, and Sadie began. "Dear Lord, Our God, we pray that you will keep us safe from the things we see and hear at home. Please guide us and direct us, show us you care because we believe in you and know that you are our Savior. Help us every day. We pray for kids like us everywhere. Please help them." A pause. Sadie again licked her dry lips and fought the urge to cry. "But most of all, Lord, keep the three of us safe from our parents. Amen."

The group gathered their bicycles and departed, heading their separate ways.

As she watched her friends pedal off into the coming night streaked with blue and gold hues, Sadie whispered a final prayer to herself. It may have been selfish, but it was basically a wish.

Sadie Bellis wished her parents were dead.

Chapter 4

R̲achel lay on Mason's lap, her legs stretched to the end of the couch. A hand-crafted Italian throw covered half her body and sweat glistened on her forehead in the early moonlight. She snuggled against him, mumbled something, and drifted off.

The chicken burned to a black crisp while they made love and afterwards they ate frozen lasagna in paper trays. It was not until they both climaxed that Mason turned the smoke alarm off.

The Cranberries played at low volume on the radio. He stared at the wall, his third whiskey sour in his hand. Rachel's bare feet jutted out from underneath the cover and he methodically ran his finger over the top of one foot, combed his fingers through her long brown hair with the other hand. He kissed her hot, wet skin and took in her sweet scent.

The drapes were drawn, the living room dim. It was comforting being here with the one he loved, hidden from the world and without a care. He watched Rachel sleep. Beautiful. Through the curtains, he caught a glimpse of a hawk soaring over the pines. This was his life. He could stay at home for a solid month and do absolutely nothing every day if he wished. He had the freedom, the money, and though these were two elements of what he called the American Dream, there was something missing. When he was a teenager, he had an afternoon job at a mechanic's shop and there was something to be said for bringing home a paycheck. It felt good to use that money to buy baseball cards, a new glove, go to the movies, or fill the tank on his motorbike. It was a sense of security, a test of boy growing into man. It showed independence and proved values instilled in him by his grandfather. Earning money was wonderful, even if he hadn't inherited millions, he believed some way, somehow, he would have made a fortune on his own.

He could feel Rachel's heartbeat against his thigh. Her breath came in soft throws on his bare stomach. In the far corner of the room, he stared at a grandfather clock he'd purchased at an antique shop in Virginia for twelve hundred dollars. Lost in the silence, drained of energy and nearly drunk, his eyelids grew to bricks. He sipped the tart drink, forced it down his numbed throat.

His mother's face appeared before him. Short blonde hair and ghostly eyes. The withered skin and wicked, lopsided eye.

I gave her death.

Scars lined her face, a gash opened her scalp revealing the moist gray mass of her brain, and another dug down to a circle of white bone.

Mason remembered when he escaped from them. The brake line on the Buick, the mangled metal, smoke, and blood. The night they left for Chickie's. It happened two miles from where he grew up. The Devil's Elbow was a dangerous curve positioned west of Beauvoir River that immediately switched back. If you weren't a local who knew of its awesome power, you'd fly off the road and smash into the tree line at the riverbank. A clump of small wooden crosses had been set up to remember those who failed to complete the turn: speeding teenagers, drunkards, innocent joy-riders who were careless at the last moment of their lives. And if you weren't careful, if you lost control and humped a pine tree, the area would be in need of clearing to make room for a brand new cross wrapped in a bright red ribbon and surrounded at the base by silk flowers that could withstand the weather.

That night, his parents didn't make that curve. That night, they wrapped the car around a tree. It was smashed and looked as if a giant fist had gripped it, crumpled its body into a pile of ugly brown metal. His mother's face stared hard at him. Her mouth moved.

I know what you did, I know it was you, you killed us, you killed your parents, you killed, Mason.

"Jesus!"

Rachel stirred awake, her voice groggy. "What is it baby?" Her spiky nails caressed his neck.

His chest pumped hard and fast. He set the drink on the coffee table, felt the back of his neck where his muscles cramped. He touched her hand.

"Get up, Honey. My stomach hurts."

She moved and he hurried down the hall.

He closed the bathroom door and washed his hands and face. Staring at himself in the mirror, water dripped down his cheeks, hit the sink's side. He took in a deep breath. What the hell was going on? He'd never had nightmares—none that he remembered, especially those where his parents were the star attraction. Could it be that his past was catching up to him?

Rachel knocked on the door. "Are you okay? Want some ice water?"

Mason flushed the toilet. "Yeah." He scratched the back of his head and caught his face in the mirror. His skin itched and he scratched, a habit Rachel was trying to cure him of. "What's wrong with you, Mason? Don't fall apart," he told himself. "Don't you fall apart now. That was a long time ago, and they deserved what they got. Remember what they did to you. Remember what they did to you!" He opened the door.

Rachel handed him a tall glass and two aspirin. "Hangover already?"

"Nightmare." He cupped her clear face in his strong hand. "I didn't mean to wake you."

"Honey, you don't look so good."

"I don't feel so good, either." He grasped his stomach, turned away from her, and vomited in the bathtub. The smooth yellow stream splattered against the sides and jumped to the tile.

Rachel put her hand on his back and pulled off a long strip of toilet tissue. "Ohmygod, baby. Here, wipe your mouth." She turned on the hot water. The waste swirled to the drain, disappeared. She put her arm around his hip and lead him to the toilet, dropped the seat. "Sit down." He did and lowered his head in shame. She took a wash rag from the shelf and wiped the tub clean. "C'mon," she said, holding the bulky rag. "Let's get you to bed. The weather's changing, so you might be coming down with a summer cold. I'll get some antibiotics from Lynn tomorrow." Lynn was her uncle, a pharmacist at a Walgreen's in Abbey.

She helped him to the bedroom and turned off the ceiling fan. He stripped his boxers, now fully naked. The bedside lamp cast a ray on his body. Elaborate artwork specifically designed to hide his imperfections colored his back. The wingspan of a red and green dragon stretched between his shoulder blades. Its knotted body curled downward, riding Mason's spine, the diamond tail whipped up over his right kidney. A long prehistoric snout blasted orange flames. Yellow, cat-like eyes. Broken chains were clenched in thick claws. The tattoo covered that hanger. The broken bottle. Cigarette burns. A claw hammer. The belt buckle that chipped out a divot the night before he found the gardening shears. He slipped under the heavy blankets. A shiver passed through him.

A few minutes later, Rachel joined him, snuggled up to his backside, and pulled him close to her body.

He kissed her fingers and she gently placed her palm against his heartbeat. He wouldn't know what he'd do without her. It was as simple as that. She was his everything. If his millions were taken away tomorrow, at least he'd have her. When he first saw her, he fell hard. She was eighteen with long legs, bronzed by the sun. Her hair hung past her shoulders and curved to a wave in the middle of her back. Her smile did everything a country song wails: it lit up the room, made people feel good, and her eyes glowed like an angel's. God, how he wanted her. His friends told him that he was a fool, that he could never have her. She was too good, out of his league, they said, so he'd better search somewhere else for the love of his life. "Man, she wouldn't give you the time of day," they teased. But Mason was hardheaded, strong at heart, and had more confidence than his friends. If all they could do was cop a feel on a first date, that was their problem. Mason had his sights set on bigger plans.

So, he had to have Rachel. If it was love, he would stop at nothing.

Funny. Surprises came in many shapes and sizes. Sometimes, they just popped into your life and changed everything. The first time Mason asked Rachel out to his grandfather's corporate office party, she gladly accepted. She arrived in her mother's 1990 Volkswagen dressed in white jeans and a blue blouse tied in a knot at her washboard stomach that fit tight around the curve of her breasts.

The picnic was held at Red Lake on a hot July afternoon, the orange sun peeling skin and sizzling the concrete walks that wound throughout the trail toward the water's edge.

Mason was never shy. He walked hand in hand with her along the bank. They talked, laughed, and just got to know one another. He discovered that her mother was an LPN at Abbey Hospital, taking night courses to become certified as a Registered Nurse. Her father was in advertising with a Dallas firm, but he worked out of his home. "He designs billboards for Franklin," she'd told him. "He's in charge of the final product and stuff."

He loved to hear her voice, and when she talked, he watched her mouth move—those pouty, pink lips he wished he could kiss.

As dusk fell on what would be the first date for the rest of their lives, Mason told her that since his parents were in a terrible car accident, he was sent to live with his grandfather. At the time, that was all the information she needed.

"I like your car," he lied, at the end of day.

She thanked him, held his hands, stared at her reflection in his sunglasses, and politely asked if he'd take them off.

"My eyes, they're really sensitive. The sun hurts them," he told her, adjusting the plastic-coated handle over one ear.

She faced west. "The sun's going down. It'll be gone real soon."

He lifted his head, searching his mind for a way out, a way to change the subject, and when he had it, the words caught in his throat. "Can I ask you a question?"

She nodded, hummed, "Mm-hmm."

"Can I kiss you?"

She leaned forward without warning and pressed her lips to his before he could make another move. It was the warmest, sweetest kiss he'd ever had—and probably, if he counted all the kisses he'd actually given, this was the fifth one, and he loved it. Boy, did he ever love it. Stupidly, his heart went into overdrive, rising past the point of puppy-love and all that "we'll be together forever" crap, and knew then and there that he was truly in love, real love. Rachel was his soul mate.

"Mason?" She was awake and he didn't even know it. She raised her hand, her smooth skin shiny under the lamp's light, turned her fingers down to target her engagement ring. "When are we gonna turn this into a wedding band?"

His eyes fell to the outline of her swollen breasts, the nipples protruding against the thin fabric of her tee-shirt as if drawn there with a dark marker. "Are you sure you want to marry a redneck?"

"Better than a bastard redneck," she said, her eyes alight and soft.

He held her tight, moved his hand over her hip and back up again, the tips of his fingers gliding over the microscopic hairs, his heartbeat a roll of snakes in his chest. "How big do you want it?"

"The wedding or the ring?"

"Both."

"Large enough to fill a back yard and big enough to weigh me down." She giggled, the sound like that of a child chasing fireflies on a hot July evening.

He touched her nose with his finger. Amazing. If she only knew that at one point in his life, he couldn't even afford a pack of gum at the neighborhood grocery store. Rachel had this view that since his grandfather had been rich, that in turn, his entire family was rich. But if he told her how that wasn't the case, he might have to tell her everything, including spilling the beans on his criminal efforts to dispose of his very own parents. What would she think then? He didn't want to brood over it. They weren't nice thoughts.

He was thankful his life had turned out this well. He didn't need to complicate it any further. When he thought about his childhood, he knew the old saying about going through hell to get to heaven. He had his heaven. The hell was now behind him. Best to leave it there.

He hugged her. "Someday we will."

"I love you, Mason," Rachel whispered, and kissed his cheek.

Chapter 5

$\mathcal{S}$adie used the spare key under the welcome mat to open the carport door. The only sound was the clock ticking in the kitchen and the ceiling fan whirling at low speed in the living room. Quitman was passed out on the couch, empty beer bottles lined the floor at his feet. She took the stairway to her room. Her mother was asleep, and knowing this made Sadie feel better. Anne didn't know she'd left.

She stripped to her underwear and slipped under the covers. Her left hip was bruised and hurt, so she had to lie on her back, not her side. Anne had whacked her several times with a wooden spoon four nights ago for talking back. Her face still throbbed when she swallowed from today's most recent slap. Sadie closed her eyes, thankful that she'd made it to her room without crossing her mother's awful path.

She drifted off to sleep and in her dream, she saw him. She called him the "stranger." He wore a starched midnight black dress shirt that danced with the oncoming wind, his striking blond hair something out of a fairy tale. He wore sunglasses and his mouth was one straight line—no emotion in his features, no regret behind the dark shades. He stood in a lush green field, where the background of trees rose to meet the metallic sky. The sun fell, crashed and burned the ground, and gushes of wind thrashed over the hard earth. The night's stars lifted from weed patches and healthy grass. All the images blasted away, backward and tangled in her subconscious mind. Clouds dropped rain and ice and snow in unison.

Still, throughout the craziness, the man never moved an inch. He remained rooted in the middle of the scene, that look on his face, seemingly empowered by the cold hell in the black orbs of his shades—the black things that made him evil. His mouth did not move, but the wind snatched his words and she heard them.

"Some things you won't understand, but they will happen, they must happen."

This wasn't the first time she'd seen him. He'd been here in other dreams (or nightmares) on other sleepless nights. Always standing there. But he had never threatened her. There was no smile on his lips, no frown, just the line, that "no emotion," and it was more frightening than any sharp-toothed lion's grin.

Another voice came to her, sent from somewhere else, neither good nor evil, just a warning. "He's bad . . . real bad . . . safe, be safe, watch, don't look in his . . . ." But the stranger stayed frozen, an entity, in all black and producing a menacing, unruly attraction, and fear. A world of ruthless fear.

He stood. Watching. Waiting.

Sadie's bedroom door flung open, banged the wall. The sound snapped her awake. She tasted salt and bad breath in her mouth. Her eyes were full of crust, her sight instantly filled with white dots as she tried to adjust to the darkened room.

The light flicked on. Was this part of the dream?

Nightmare, it's a nightmare, it's always been a nightmare.

She took in a sharp, quick breath when she heard Anne's voice.

"Where did you go tonight? Do you think you can just get up and go whenever you feel like it, girl? You think this is some kinda goddamn half-way house where you've got a right to leave without telling someone? Well, I got news for you, Miss Priss!"

Sadie was deaf in her left ear, a scar from when Anne once slammed her head onto the stovetop, and her mother's voice was barely audible. She leaned her head forward. "Huh?" she said in her sleep-induced voice. The light stung her eyes. She rubbed them with her fingers. "I was sleepin', Momma. I didn't go any—"

"Do I look like a fuckin' idiot to you? C'mere!" Anne moved toward her, a belt doubled up in her hand to thicken and strengthen it.

Sadie instinctively jumped back and slammed the top of her head against the headboard, then fully alert.

Yanking away the blankets, Anne swung the belt and attacked the young girl's flesh. "Don't you ever! Sneak out! Of this house! Again!"

"Momma! Quit it!" Sadie yelled. She raised her arms to protect herself, but it was no use.

Anne swung. The metal buckle came down and made contact with Sadie's crotch. She cried out in explosive pain. Tears fell from her swollen eyes, her mouth opened to a silent scream. Saliva seeped out in a long, clear string.

"And that's for telling that dirty joke! Don't ever let me hear you say things like that again!" This time Anne slapped her face, then left the room as unexpectedly as she'd entered, making it a point to slam the door in her wake.

Sadie paid no attention. Her crotch throbbed and she reached for the panty waistline, for now ignoring the red abrasions that cropped her legs. She lifted the thin material and peeked inside. Blood crept out from the top of her vagina, and it pulsated with extraordinary pain. She felt like dying. She touched herself and winced. On the bedside table, she plucked tissue from the box and wiped herself clean, the small cut a reminder of the world she lived in.

But wasn't there a way out? Shouldn't there be a way out? She convinced herself she did not have to live like this.

You can get away, Sadie. You could run away, get as far away from this place as possible, and be safe, you can go where you'll be safe.

Her tears dried on her cheeks, chapped her face. She gathered more tissue. Her big toe bled from under the nail and she dabbed it. Shit. She'd have to wear jeans tomorrow in order to cover the bruises that would form overnight.

Sadie pulled her knees into her chest, folded her arms around her battered legs, shoved her head between her arms, and cried. She prayed God would save her. The clock in the corner ticked its solemn tone. The night turned, kept on, and she made a promise to herself that this would be the very last time her mother would ever touch her.

—◆—

Sheriff T.R. Combs had recently endured a painful divorce. His ex-wife took everything but his badge. He was living with his girlfriend, Monica Wise, and getting used to this new way of life. She comforted him when he was down, whispered sweet nothings in his ear to put a smile on his face, and tried to lift him out of the deep blue funk he'd delved into. Lord, he was trying his best. But it was difficult. The only thing that kept him happy was Monica's unconditional love. "It'll be all right, Terry," she told him time and again. "Just wait it out. You'll be fine." He could see it in her eyes. Monica would marry him in a second. All he had to do was ask.

But that was the least of his worries. Call him selfish, call him an ass-hole. The man planned to win the reelection in November come hell or high water, and his girlfriend, the divorce—anything that walled his path—would become second issue.

Terry Robert was always busy with his work. Lately there had only been the misdemeanors: traffic tickets, simple battery, public drunkenness. Small things to keep him occupied.

The last big news that hit Sutter Springs was when Rodney Simmons, an out of work diesel fabrication welder, plowed through the Go-Go Truck Stop out on Highway 109 in his renovated '67 Chevy. He'd been drunk, had the Stones cranked up on his radio, and had nothing to lose, man. He killed an elderly couple at a four-top eating a late Saturday lunch and wounded a teenager, who had been inside to buy a pack of smokes. The story was that Rodney's girlfriend, a cashier, had been screwing the bus-boy in the storage room in back of the truck stop on cigarette breaks. In a vengeful rage, Rodney drove through the entrance doors with a steel hood. The state gave him ten years in the pen, but he only served three for good conduct, and when he was paroled, he moved to Florida for another job.

Terry headed that investigation. When it was all said and done, April, the cashier, lost her job for selling tobacco to a minor. She was last seen running the roads from town to town. Just another truck-stop lot lizard who gave blow-jobs at night and counted her money by day.

The story made the local news and showed Sutter Springs in its criminal light. Terry had been busy with that one. He enjoyed law enforcement. He believed the crime should fit the punishment. Since Rodney's joy ride, there hadn't been that much excitement around, and he was getting edgy. He wanted something big. As sadistic as it sounded, he needed it.

He left Monica's house for another one of his evening drives. Every once in a while he needed time alone to think. What if he didn't get re-elected? What then? Crucial decisions. If he was not Sheriff of Sutter Springs, he was nothing. It wasn't only a job. It was a hunger.

Maybe something would happen, he thought, taking his usual route to town. Maybe soon.

—⁂—

Melissa squirted a dab of toothpaste on her toothbrush and held it underneath the running water. She stood before the sink in shorts and a flimsy tank-top. She brushed her teeth, listening to her parents argue in the next room. It was times like this that she wished she lived on the other side of the house. You could hear everything through the walls. Their screaming and yelling, their sex, the TV, the radio. Sometimes she heard her father fart, and that was gross, or it could have been her mother, and that was more gross.

Her father, Brady Giles, was a respected man in town. He was a Deacon at the First Baptist Church of Sutter Springs and participated in charity work throughout the northern Louisiana region. His name appeared in more than one newspaper or was posted on a business wall for "acknowledgement of giving hands" from some hippie organization that used the money to save the trees in the area. But that was a crock, and Melissa knew it. Lumber was one of the state's most lucrative revenues, and even she knew you couldn't save the world. Her father didn't give a crap about what charity did what with the money. He used that as a medium to make sales. People knew him and would buy from him. He was the manager of Sedwick's Furniture Emporium, with a handsome office in the rear of the store where he worked, where he bought and sold stock over the Internet when business moved slow. When people walked in, he usually knew them by name, and they usually left with a new couch, a dining set, a love seat, or a lamp. An expensive lamp.

Tall, with light brown hair and brooding brown eyes, always clean-shaven and dressed in khakis with a pressed white shirt and a clip-on tie, he was business-oriented. Anyone could tell from his white-collar appearance that he was a family man. Loved his weekends at home and his evenings in the back yard doing some little job. Type of man who enjoyed relaxing in front of the TV with a bowl of French vanilla ice cream. He was wealthy. A happy man.

"He don't sound too happy tonight," Melissa said out loud. She stared into the mirror and counted the freckles across her nose. She washed her face and dried her hands. Damn Mr. Rolle. He was her arithmetic teacher and had assigned his class to work three pages of problems by tomorrow. Melissa thought he was a butthole. She was tired and didn't feel like doing homework tonight. Tomorrow was the last day of school. To hell with thinking.

She put the heavy book on her night-stand and grabbed the remote. Stuffed animals and pillows her grandmother had stitched for her before her death adorned the tiny TV set in the corner of the room. The news came on. She hated the news. Boring. Blah, blah, blah. She switched channels and settled on *Baywatch*, wishing she looked like the sexy, bikini-clad girls on the show. She'd heard those actresses just slept their way to the top. Whether it was true or false, and though she might have only been ten years old, she heard things, she surfed the Internet. It was difficult to hide the real world from children. There was just too much out there. And most of what she saw and heard was bad. "Bad news travels fast," her mother once said.

She looked over at her computer. She could go to a chat room, but it was late, and she was tired, and besides, the Net now frightened her. After she'd seen what her father was doing last Halloween, after she puked up her guts and called him every curse word she could think of, she'd been fearful of the Information Superhighway. And fearful of Brady. The image of him lying face down on his desk at work with the white powder under both nostrils as if a make-up artist had applied it perfectly was too much to bear. What he had been looking at on his computer, what he'd done to her—his own daughter—it was just too much.

Melissa knew what kind of man hid behind those eyes. Not the nice, "how-ya-doin'-come-in-to-see-me-sometime" man, or the peaceful, guilt-free Deacon who shook everyone's hand and smiled and kissed old ladies on the cheek and babies on the forehead. He was evil. A maniac. Sorry excuse for a father. Melissa hated him for who he was and hated him for making her feel this way. She deserved better.

Brady Giles had evil pumping through his veins. Melissa had seen it. Last year, a week before Halloween.

She hadn't told Sadie and she felt bad about that. It wasn't written in the notebook, either. No one knew what had happened except her and her father.

The thought came quickly, but she saw and heard and smelled every detail. That evening was here again. Vivid and crisp as if it were happening now. She closed her eyes, hoping it would go away, tried to think of something else, but it was unveiled nonetheless.

She had knocked on his office door. It was late and all the employees had gone home for the day. No one answered, so she walked inside.

Brady was hunched over in his chair at his desk against the wall. A layer of crinkled aluminum foil lay beside his face. His nose and mouth were covered in cocaine, the white powder wet from saliva and perspiration. His eyes were closed, his chest pumped heavy.

Melissa saw the photos on the computer screen, and gasped. No. It couldn't be. It was pornography, but not ordinary porn with big-busted women in vulgar positions. There were children on the screen. Children her age. Some younger.

They're kids. They're only kids!

She began breathing as fast and as hard as her father. Melissa touched his shoulder and felt his hot skin through the thin fabric. Shook him. No movement.

"Dad?" she said, her voice weak and far off. She had only dropped by to get five dollars so that she could go to the movies with her friends. It was Friday, they were waiting for her outside, they were in a hurry. She only wanted five measly dollars.

"Huh!" Brady jarred awake. His eyes drooped, his mouth hung open. He focused on her and reached for her, grabbed the waistline of her jeans.

"Dad, what's wrong?" she asked on impulse.

Brady said nothing. He jumped up and staggered toward her. The swivel chair rolled back into the wall. His actions were blurred, as was his speech because he said something she could not understand, and pushed Melissa to the door. Large hands gripped her frail arms.

"Daddy! What! What're you doing? Daddy, wake up!"

Brady was awake. He wasn't himself, but he was awake, and he knew who he was holding, he knew what he was doing. He turned her around, reached for his daughter's stomach and placed his fingers over the jean's button.

Melissa wiggled. "Dad, stop it!" She elbowed him in the side, struggled to get away.

His hand plunged into her armpit and he held her tight. "Shutup, Honey." As he spoke, he unbuttoned her jeans, pulled down the zipper—"don't you say a word"—shucked her underwear—"if you tell, I'll kill you, I will kill you"—he moved his hand over her vagina and slipped one finger inside.

Melissa shrieked.

Brady grabbed her hair, pulled her head so that her face pointed skyward. His breath stank of whiskey, and the cocaine mixed with sweat rubbed off onto Melissa's neck. She felt the wetness on his brow and face while he kissed and licked her skin. Her ear, her shoulder. Touching, feeling, cursing her.

Hot tears fell over her cheeks, dropped to the floor. "Please stop," she whimpered.

He pulled his finger out of her and sniffed it. Licked it.

Melissa screamed.

There was a shuffling sound, and then a loud crash. Melissa turned around. Brady was sprawled on the floor. A small filing cabinet had slammed to the ground inches from his right leg. Files and paper were scattered about, outlining his unmoving body.

She pulled in a deep breath and tried to gather herself. She dressed and left, half her face and neck filthy with flecks of cocaine and his spit.

That night she never made it to the movies. She told her friends that she'd walk home, and walk home she did, spaced out all the way. Dirty, angry, sad.

Though it was the single most horrible experience of her young life, Melissa obeyed her father. She didn't tell anyone. She didn't know whom to trust. The man threatened to kill her and fried out of his mind or not, he meant it. She knew that. From that moment on, she viewed her father in an awful, dark light. To her, Brady Giles was nothing but a sick pervert.

Even when she became a member of the club, that time was still a part of her, that day had remained a secret. Sadie and Danny knew nothing about it, but sooner or later, as the memories came to her more frequently nowadays, she would have to tell someone or she'd burst.

She was awake, staring at the ceiling, her thoughts scrambled, her feelings hurt just by thinking of that awful day. Sadie was right, oh she was so right. They had to do something. Cops were out. "What're the cops gonna do?" she remembered. True. How would they help? Calling them was out of the question.

Melissa pulled the covers up over her shoulder and closed her eyes, thinking of a way out.

Chapter 6

Thursday night a storm tore through the town, bringing with it golf ball sized hail and splintering rain in hard, sharp torrents. Lightning broke the sky in gangs of spider webs. A jagged bolt touched down, and like a knife, split a live oak at the edge of Mason's property and the throw of thunder rumbled across the hillside at the Witching Hour with the sound of a hungry monster on the prowl.

Strong gusts of wind shook the treehouse on the other side of the ballpark. Floorboards creaked and snapped, fell to the ground one by one. The notebook on the top shelf flipped rapidly as if a ghost thumbed through it. The awesome wind lifted it up and slammed it to the wall. Pages fluttered. It fell between the space where the boards had been nailed, slid alongside the tree's wet bark, and rode the air, hit the diamond fence, then toppled over it, doing cartwheels to second base, past the pitcher's mound, on to the dugout. It snagged the underside of the fence, lay there, its pages fanning, shielded from the rain by the tin roof.

A half mile away, Sadie woke to the thunder. Her face was lit by brilliant lightning. She pulled the covers to her chin and rolled over, situating the pillow under her neck. The clock on the night stand read 3:06.

She lifted her head, eyed the door. There was no light underneath; Anne and Quitman were asleep. She clicked on the lamp and threw off the covers, saw that the sheet was colored a faded pink, and gently, sucking in a breath, touched herself. The blood had stopped, but the pain was still there, still throbbing.

It's okay, she told herself. Tomorrow, you'll be gone. After tomorrow, it'll never happen again.

Her bedroom lit up in silver flashes. She turned her pillow onto the cool side and switched off the light, watching the lightning dance to the roll of booming thunder.

—⁂—

The moon's pale glow fell in wide slants like smooth wine through the open bedroom windows, and the ceiling fan moved slowly, giving off a lonesome creak on every rotation. Two vanilla beeswax candles burned on the end table in hand-carved wooden bases, the bullet-shaped flames tossing shadows along the walls.

The storm faded, leaving in its rage broken limbs and leaves scattered across neighborhoods and fence posts lying on their earthen graves; curbs and ditches were bundled with clumps of glassy bits of hail next to family drives where lawn chairs had rolled over blades of grass in the grayish light; in town, streets were littered with acorns, weeds, and trash, its hardened surface slicked with rain reflecting the dull, yellow lamps that lined Berry Avenue and Main.

Mason lay awake, unable to sleep. He licked his fingers and extinguished the candle flames, rolled over, shuffled the covers off the end to let his feet breathe, and kissed Rachel's finely lined back that arched to the effect of a model posing for the cover of a glamour magazine. She smelled of the purity and sweetness only women possess, her long brown hair curled to show her black widow tattoo. His hand crawled over her curved hip to her exposed stomach, his touch excited by her silky skin.

She snored softly, the air rushing out of her mouth in mouse-like rasps. He pulled her close, chest to back, ran his hand to her right breast, and let it lay there like a feather soaked in oil. She woke, blinked her eyes into focus, and faced him, cradled his head in the crook of her arm. Like a mother caring for her child, she brushed a sheen of sweat from his forehead and pulled in a deep breath, her chest expanding into his face.

"They're still on your mind, aren't they?"

"Who?" he mumbled, feeling the red pain tighten into a knotted fist behind his eyes.

"Your parents."

A dot of sweat dropped from his brow. "You always know what I'm thinking, don't you? I wonder if you're psychic."

"I know you. You always get sick when you think about that night. It must've been a pretty awful dream to make you throw up."

"Just something I ate."

She planted a soft kiss on the top of his head. "It wasn't your fault."

Yes it was. I killed them. Me. A little boy who got beat up at school by the bigger guys and who couldn't ride the thrill rides at the fair because he was too short. The one they hurt and yelled at and laughed at. I killed them. That's right. Never regretted it. Never will.

"G'nite, Hon."

"Goodnight, baby."

—⁂—

The next morning on the back porch, they ate fried eggs, crisp bacon, and fresh biscuits with butter and strawberry jam. The log house overlooked vast hills kissed by the sun. It was picture-perfect, a greeting card scene. A gentle breeze rose from the tall weeds near the catfish pond and greeted them. A woodpecker in a live oak drove its beak into the bark, the sound like that of bones cracking.

Mason had taken his Porsche out of the garage and parked it underneath the tree after an early wax-job, fearing now that a gang of blackbirds would soon drop by for a visit. He'd been awake since five o'clock, crediting his insomnia, or newborn energy, to the prospect of a new day, the arrival of different challenges. Yeah, just another rider removing the drape of last night's bad vibe to refill his cup of life with a fresh shot of whiskey. And whiskey he drank. Gentleman Jack. Two shots in his coffee across from Rachel's glass of milk.

"Are you starting a trend? I've never known you to drink this early in the day."

He speared a piece of egg, dabbed it in steak sauce, and ate. "Wrong. Remember that time we were in New Orleans and I bought that pen for eight hundred dollars? The one with the gold trim?" She nodded. He wiped a bit of egg from his lip. "I was drunk that morning, otherwise I wouldn't have bought it." He chuckled dryly. "I mean, it was a pen. A fucking ink pen."

She snickered at him and collected their plates, took them inside.

"Bring me some ice," he called.

"What's the magic word?"

"Now."

"Try again."

"Pleeeeeze, my lovely, exotic Italian angel of love and lust and everything good."

"Better. Much better."

He wore his shirt unbuttoned to show his defined chest, the sleeves rolled up his forearms, cleaned, pressed blue jeans, and steel-toed work boots his grandfather once owned. "I got a feelin' today's gonna be nice," he announced when she returned carrying two burnt-glass tumblers. "Wanna help me finish off this bottle?" He grinned, showing his teeth, the lower set just off by a bit.

"Sure. I can hang with the big dogs, boy. I've never been kicked off the porch, but I do think a fifth before noon is what causes fights, and infinitely damaged libidos." She winked.

"No problem on this side of the world. I'm always horny."

She cupped her chin in her palm. "So I've noticed."

He poured her a shot and lifted his drink. "To us. Every day. Again. For the rest of our lives."

She clinked his glass and downed the whiskey, her lips burning with satisfaction. Her eyes wandered to his. "The rest of our lives, baby."

—◊—

The last day of school was typical. Young faces beamed. Each second that clicked away relieved the pressure of actually having to be cooped up in a classroom. They wandered through the day filled with excitement and nervous energy. All they could do was wait.

Shooting spitballs at the ceiling was a favorite way to pass the time.

Groups huddled up and played tic-tac-toe on scraps of paper and used PE as time for a game of three-on-three instead of laps around the track.

Sadie sat a row across from Danny in Ms. Faye's English class. Their teacher had instructed them to write in five hundred words or less their plans for the coming summer. Ms. Faye was an ex-college professor who sometimes talked over the kids' heads, called them "guys," and she didn't think it was a big deal to give too much homework at times. She wore her hair in a bun, tinted glasses, pink lip gloss, and a tight skirt. On her desk was a small handbook purse like the ones Danny had seen on an episode of *COPS*, shouldered by prostitutes cruising the streets of New Orleans.

She stood in front of the blackboard and used her finger as a pointer.

"Ladies and gentlemen, learning is an art. When you fell off your bike the first time you tried to ride it, you got back on. Swimming lessons. You stayed with it until your head no longer dipped under and you were treading water alone. What if you didn't hop back on that bike? What if you got out of the pool too soon? I'll tell you. You would have denied yourself one of the greatest character-building components in life.

"Challenges. You must remember that challenges test us in everything we desire to achieve." She pushed her glasses up onto the bridge of her nose. "To deny yourself taking chances in life is as rigorous as watching paint dry on a lone wall somewhere in the Sahara Desert, and as sad as wasted talent, or even wasted food for that matter." She noticed their confused faces and quickly regrouped. "In a few words, guys, be true to yourself. Know what you want and go after it."

Aware of Ms. Faye's hawk eyes, Sadie tore a corner off the top of her blue-lined notebook and wrote.

"Meet me outside when the bell rings. We need to talk — Sadie."

She reached across the row and dropped it on Danny's desk.

He read it, crumpled it in his hands and shoved it in his front pocket. The late afternoon sun spread a flat wave of orange, dusty light into the room. The clock above the chalkboard showed one minute 'til three. Danny craned his neck, caught Sadie's stare, and nodded.

"So this summer, your time in front of the TV could easily be replaced by more intellectual pursuits," Ms. Faye announced, circling the air with a ballpoint pen. "Take a hike in the woods, pick a bouquet of flowers for your grandmother, read a book, get up early one morning and watch the sun rise. Live and breathe the next three months as if it were your last three months on this earth." She looked off as the last bell rang. Students scattered. "Be careful, children. Turn your papers in on my desk when you go out. Have a safe summer!"

Sadie was one of the first to lay her paper on the desk. On the top line, under the xeroxed theme that read "Summer Plans," she wrote only one sentence: "I plan to be happy."

Outside she joined Danny and walked to the nearest exit. Kids ran amuck, threw their books in the air, clawed and dug out their lockers, littered the halls with paper and pencils and miscellaneous school materials. They screamed and yelled and whooped all the way to the bus stop, while Sadie and Danny walked quietly away.

"What'd you want to see me about?" Danny asked. He looked across the dirt lot behind the metal shop where four juniors were sharing a joint.

Sadie stopped, her book bag slung over one shoulder. A breeze took the loose golden strands from her face, her lips a bright red in the sunlight. Behind her, a Chevy roared its throaty exhaust, and its wide tires scraped up dust in fat curls. The sound made her flinch. A hand appeared outside the truck window and sent a beer bottle flying into the skeletal woods, whoops and yells coming from inside the cab. Sadie waited until the noise stopped and the truck merged onto the highway and drove off. She licked her dry lips. "Meet me at the clubhouse at five. I haven't told Melissa yet, but I'm goin' to."

"Why're we meetin' today?" Danny asked. He knelt to tie his shoes, looked up, his eyebrows raised high. The smell of burnt rubber hit his senses and he winced.

"School might be out for everybody else, but it's just startin' for us."

"What do you mean?"

"We're gonna do it, Danny. We're gonna run away."

"Where we gonna go?" he asked, scratching his nose.

Sadie peered up at the brick building. "Here."

"What? Are you crazy?"

"What do you want to do? Danny, if we don't take this chance, we'll be mad at ourselves. Remember what Ms. Faye said: 'Know what you want and go after it.' Well, I want to run away. You with me? C'mon, you've gotta."

"I'll try, but my dad, he wants me to mow the yard when I get home. Don't know if I can get away from that. What time you want me there anyway?"

"Five o'clock. Don't try, Danny. Just do it. Bring some extra clothes, too."

—⁓—

At three-thirty, the inside of his head numbed with alcohol's swirling comfort. Mason drove to the state line ballpark alone. The afternoon was pleasant, a totally different picture than the storm had painted last night.

He parked his Porsche behind the announcer's box, set up a pitching machine on the pitcher's mound, knocked the dust off his cleats with the end of a Louisville Slugger, and took his stance at home plate.

A fast ball came and he missed. "Shit!" He tipped his bat to the plate, readied his arm. Another. He swung and caught it in the sweet spot and smashed it into a real estate billboard at left field. For the next twenty minutes, he practiced his swings and follow-through, landing a few good home-runs.

It was when he knocked a curve ball off the edge of the bat that shot straight up and rolled into the dugout, that he knew his game was not the best it could have been had he been out here doing this since March. The machine was empty.

He wiped the sweat from his hands and went for the foul ball. When he found it, it lay on top of a blue notebook with "The Club" written on the cover. He nudged the ball out of the way and reached for the notebook. The blue cardboard cover was stained with water, the pages damp and slippery. He opened to the first page. It was dated October 21, 1996.

Tiny print appeared to be a boy's stick figure handwriting. On the top line was scrawled MEMBERS, and underneath were the names of three people he'd never met.

Sadie Bellis, Melissa Giles, Danny Rampart.

He flipped through the pages and found that every one had been dated. Some were filled with paragraphs, some were only two or three lines. He read one paragraph, his lips moving silently.

Yesterday, momma ran after me with a iron.
She pushed the end of it on my back. I was
naked and I was taking a shower. She got
mad at me because I told her she drinks
too much. Momma doesn't like me to say
that. She says I got a smart mouth. That's
what she calls it. I went to my room and put
some cream on the burn. I didn't want to
go to the hospital. Momma wouldn't
take me to the hospital anyway because she said
the doctor would ask questions and that was bad.
I slept with the light on all night and lockd
my room. She can't get in when it's like that
and I feel a wole lot better. Sadie.

His eyes narrowed, and what he read brought on a hard edge to them. He wet his thumb, flipped to the next page.

I hate my dad. He's mean. He hits me a lot
but only when he can catch me. Last nite, he
threw me against the wall and picked me up off
my feet. His hand was on my throat. It hurt a lot.
I hate him. I wish he could leeve me alone. I
don't ever want to go to the shed ever again,
for as long as I live. Danny.

The paragraph had been written by the same person. Same lettering, same misspelled words, only it told of someone else. "The Club." He knew exactly what he held in his hands. In a strange way, he was proud that kids who were obviously abused would have the guts to write down what their parents had done to them. As a child, he would have never dreamed of doing something like this. Maybe he wasn't as smart at that age. The notebook in his hands was a testament, a cry for help. Something, he wished, looking back, he'd had at his disposal.

He caught the reflection of his own eyeball in the sunglasses as he stood, and in it, he saw himself as that angry kid who'd been physically abused by his parents; there, in his eye, he found the temper he once had, felt that innocent kid who had endured so much pain, saw the killer who had been created from a hell he wished he'd never known.

The hate had been buried for years. Buried but not dead. It was still with him, still breathing, lying in the back of his mind like a rattlesnake waiting to strike.

Mason folded the notebook lengthwise, leaned the bat against his shoulder, and went to his Porsche.

Chapter 7

Bobby "Champ" Rampart was one of the boys. He hunted deer with a high-powered rifle, drank liquor straight from the bottle, and smoked weed from a one-hitter that had a skull carved into the wood. He lived in a cramped brick house in the country near the Arkansas line, and the front yard was overgrown and disheveled. The opened garage where he worked as a mechanic stayed full of other folks' cars or trucks, tools scattered everywhere, oil stains the size of welcome mats colored into the concrete.

Two years ago he had planned to divorce his wife. She was flighty, disconnected from the real world at times, a spendthrift hooked on over-the-counter drugs, who cheated on him with every dick from here to the Texas border. Fate, or bad luck as it was, beat him to it. At a friendly fish-fry for the local Fireman's Charity Fund Raiser, she choked to death on a sharp piece of rib bone. The autopsy proved that she inhaled it. There had been no hope. When she breathed and coughed, the bone ripped through her lung's air sacs. Like killing yourself while trying to live. The coroner stated to Sheriff T.R. Combs that she might as well have swallowed a butcher's knife. "Cut up the fabric of her lungs like a bulldog through toilet tissue, Terry. Damndest thing I ever seen."

After the accident, Bobby was left to raise Danny alone. It was all the same. She had never brought home a paycheck.

He was a grotesque, big man, with a thick black beard and hard blue eyes. His work made him sweat like a dog in heat and his huge beer belly protruded out from his six-foot-three frame. The man lived in coveralls.

Originally from Texas, Bobby moved to Sutter Springs twelve years ago when he'd met his wife. Since he was good with cars, he had hopes of finding work as an auto mechanic. He worked for Redd's Pay-N-Go for three months and when he was denied more money, told the old timer to shove it. Running his own business wasn't exactly his dream come true, either. The pay wasn't great, but he didn't have a foreman breathing down his neck or a boss yelling orders at him; he was his own boss, and that made it all worthwhile. He kept bills paid, they got by. Earlier on, to make ends meet while still working at Redd's, he competed in local "Tough Man" contests. Bobby placed in several events, including boxing and wrestling, which ultimately earned him the nickname "Champ." The name stuck like a coke habit.

In the garage he wiped his dirty hands on a red oil-stained rag, and wet his lips with his fat tongue. Classic Rock blared from an old, worn radio without an antenna. The evening heat beat down on him without mercy. It bronzed his skin and baked the earth around him. He shut the hood to a Toyota pickup and reached for a lukewarm beer on the top of his six-drawer tool chest. He watched the yellow school bus come to a stop at the end of his drive and swallowed the last sip, tossed the can into the corner.

Danny stepped off, his school bag slung over his shoulder, and walked toward him, his head down.

"Hey, Dad."

Bobby pointed to the shed. "Mower's fixed. Get to it, boy."

Danny frowned, tried to hide his disgust, but wasn't doing a very good job. He opened the back door to the house.

"Okay." He patted the bag. "Lemme put this up." He went into the hot house, the air stout at his skin. Dishes were stacked in the kitchen sink. An elephant magnet had fallen to the linoleum some time during the day. Box fans were set in three corners of the living room. They were all powered to high and aimed in the direction of his father's recliner. Bobby was so cheap, he didn't even bother to repair the air conditioner.

Danny went into his room and dressed in cut-off jeans and a white tank-top with Puff Daddy emblazoned on the front. He emptied his notebooks on the bed and peeled back the mini-blinds. Spying on his dad gave him a sense of power. He was watching, and Bobby didn't know. His dad didn't know what he was doing. It was a small thrill, but a thrill nonetheless. In the garage, Bobby scratched his crotch, popped a loud burp, and moved around the Toyota, one thumb hooked into his jean pocket.

"Don't try, Danny," he heard Sadie's voice in his head. "Just do it."

"And bring some extra clothes," he said to himself. He liked the sound of that, looked forward to the possibilities. If he had his way, he'd pack up his entire damn closet and never come back to this place. That way, he wouldn't have to face Bobby. He wouldn't have to face the shed.

He dug into his dresser, got two pairs of jeans and two pairs of shorts, some underwear and socks, and his tooth brush from the bathroom, then stuffed them all in the book bag. He unlatched the bedroom window and dropped it into a crop of bushes.

Outside, he got behind the push-mower and with sweat already forming on his brow, went to work. The yard was huge, in need of cutting, but all he could think about was five o'clock. That was over an hour away. He'd be with Sadie and Melissa. And far, far from here.

—⁂—

"Meet at the clubhouse at five and bring some clothes," Sadie told Melissa. "I don't have time to talk right now. I'll tell you what's up when you get there." Done deal. They were going to run away. She'd had enough of her mother, and she was positive her friends felt the same about their own parents.

She was alone in the house and was ready to go. This was it. This was what she'd been waiting to do for so long.

Downstairs, the front door slammed.

Sadie cursed under her breath. Damn it. Everything was fine, and now she'd have to sneak away. She walked through the living room, holding the bag tight, and saw Quitman relaxed in his recliner, one leg hung over the arm. The television was on, a commercial for the new Dodge 4x4 airing. The blinds were drawn, darkening the place that much more. Leaning against his crotch was an opened can of Busch Light, his fingers held loosely around it. By the look on his face, and the heavy alcohol smell in the air, Sadie didn't think it was his first beer.

He looked up, his head weighty. His eyes were red, his cheeks flushed. He lifted the remote control and with a press of a button, the television went black.

"Hey . . . where's yer momma? Ain't she was supposed to pick you up at school?"

"I took the bus."

"Well, where the hell is she?"

"I don't know."

Quitman shifted in the seat. He smacked his lips, crossed her with those faint red eyes. "Where you think you're goin'?"

"To a friend's house."

"Bullshit. You ain't goin' a goddamn place 'less she says so. That woman'd kill me if I let you go off somewheres and she didn't know."

"I'm not askin' you."

"Hey! Who's the adult here, smartass?"

Sadie messed up her face. "You're not my dad."

"Watch your mouth, girl. I'll slap it and you know it."

"When did you get here, anyway? I thought you were gone to get your truck fixed."

"Well, it ain't fixed. It's behind the house. Mind ya business." Quitman took a sip of beer.

Sadie remained silent, rooted in place a few feet from the couch. She wished she had just gone to the tree house instead of coming home. She would have rather worn the clothes on her back for the next three months and allow them to stick to her body and smell than to be here with her stepdad. Quitman wasn't supposed to be home until late. The man was now a wall obstructing her way.

He sniffed, moved his tongue around inside his mouth. "C'mere for a sec."

"What?"

"C'mon. I ain't gonna hurtcha. Come over here for a sec. I wanna talk to ya."

Sadie hesitated. A voice told her to turn around and run out the back door and get away from him. She took three steps, stopped.

Quitman reached between his legs and adjusted himself.

She was close enough for him to reach out and touch her and the urge to do as the voice instructed was becoming more and more like a demand with every step toward the recliner.

"Did you get the job?" she asked, trying in desperation to change the subject.

"What'd I tell you, girl? Mind ya business!" His upper body moved forward and he reached out with his long, hairy arm. His skinny fingers touched her shirt over her belly, jerked to her hip, found the belt loop, and pulled.

Sadie resisted. "Quitman, stop it."

"Nice. You gotta real nice body, yessir." He turned her easily as if handling a stuffed doll, focused on her pear-shaped rear. "Cute little ass."

He ran his massive hand up her shirt, his opened palm covering her warm belly.

Sadie held her head low, her breath coming in heated shots.

Why is he doing this? Oh, God, why?

She slapped his hand away. "Stop it!"

Quitman ignored her request. "Shit! Got me a live one here." He pinched her belly button. "Take off your shirt."

"No."

"Do it!" He pulled at the Buck knife clipped to his hip, clicked it open. "I'll cut you if ya don't."

Sadie averted her eyes. She didn't want to look at him. He'd tried this before. He'd never gotten farther than seeing her chest, but she knew if he had the chance, he would try more, much more, probably even hurt her and she wanted so badly to tell him to take that knife and pound it up his ass. Better yet, she wanted to perform the act herself.

Standing before him prompted a memory of what Melissa once told her: how her father, Brady, had sneaked into her room late one night, crawled into her bed, and forced her to kiss his penis. Melissa had been ashamed and made Sadie promise never to tell a soul.

She took off her shirt, revealing a white cotton bra, size double A. At that precise moment, she knew exactly how Melissa had felt.

Quitman folded the knife, snapped it on the side of his jeans. He scooted forward, rocking the recliner. His hand drifted up her stomach, slid underneath the bra cup, and came to rest on her left breast.

Sadie closed her eyes. *Oh God, please help me.*

He grunted. With his left hand, he brought the can to his lips and took a healthy drink, his eyes not once leaving her soft, white skin.

"Please," Sadie begged. "Stop."

He rubbed her puffed skin. "Take off your jeans. Don't ask questions, just do it." With one finger he lifted her head, eyed her face. "Look at me."

Sadie stared at the ceiling.

"Look at me," he repeated.

A tear rolled down her cheek, dropped to the carpet and spread in an invisible spot. She tightened her hands at her sides.

"Don't you tell your momma or I'll kill you. You try me if you think I'm kiddin'. Now take off those jeans."

Sadie felt for the button, unsnapped it. She unzipped, revealed pink panties, let them fall to her ankles.

Quitman craned his head in satisfaction. He touched the soft garment, excited from looking at the few sprigs of light blonde pubic hair, then stood and slid his hand farther past the hair patch.

Sadie trembled.

He smiled, moved closer and that's when she punched him in the crotch.

"I said quit it!" she screamed at the top of her lungs.

Quitman let out a yell of excruciating pain and crumbled to his knees.

Sadie quickly pulled on her jeans and kicked this time. Her foot connected with the side of his head. He dropped. She grabbed her shirt and book bag, ran for the door and hurried into the sunlight.

His moans and curses made her feel in charge. She hopped on her bicycle, heeled the kick-stand.

"You little shit! C'mere!"

"Go to hell! Go straight to hell!" She pedaled toward the state line, her heart pounding in her temples.

It was happening. She was really doing it. Nothing would stop her. She was running away from home, running from the darkness. Sadie took it all in. From now on, things were going to change.

Chapter 8

It was almost five o'clock and Danny had only cut half the yard. Sweat clung to his face. His shirt stuck to his body. He took a break and got a drink of water from inside the garage where his dad was working underneath the hood of a Ford pickup. The room smelled of metal and grease. Crushed beer cans were piled in the corner, and he saw a few empty liquor bottles poking out from the mess as if to add color to his dad's alcohol problem.

Danny never understood why the man drank so much. It couldn't have been because he'd lost his wife. When she was here, Bobby seldom drank at all, and he still beat the hell out of her. Danny's guess was that Bobby needed some kind of human punching bag around. The drinking was probably a new hobby. Since his mother died, he'd become the new bag. Before then, the man never touched him. The closest Bobby had come to hitting him was when he lost a Buck knife on a camping trip in Texas. He spanked him, told him not to touch things that didn't belong to him, but his dad didn't pull a fist and ram it into his stomach, or slap his face until blood reddened his cheek as he would now if he made a similar mistake.

He looked across the gravel drive as a semi roared by. Though he felt guilty about it, he wished his mother were still around to be the recipient of those curse words and those punches.

"Hand me that wrench," Bobby said, the tool just out of his reach.

Danny did as he was told. He got another drink of water. The heat that possessed his skin began to ease off. He felt better, but he did not want to finish the remainder of the yard. He was late for the meeting at the club and it was stupid, he knew, but he feared that Sadie and Melissa might leave without him and that would rip his soul. He had to go. Had to think of a lie to tell his dad to get out of here. He had even been given the freedom of the last two hours to think of that lie, but his mind was blank.

"What're you doin' standin' there? Get back on the got-damn yard."

A drop of sweat crept into his eye and Danny peered out of the smelly garage and saw the work that lay ahead, his face contorted in hesitation.

He hated this. Why wouldn't his dad let him use the riding lawnmower? "It's broken, get the push," Bobby told him when he asked earlier. Bullshit it was broken. One day when Bobby was gone, Danny had cranked it and even turned the blades. It worked fine. He was sure his dad just wanted to see him sweat.

"Go on now, you ain't got all day. Sun'll be gone shortly."

"Can I finish the yard tomorrow? I was thinkin' about goin' to Pop's store and gettin' some ice cream." Good, he told himself. That was a good one. "I can get you some beer while I'm there—if you want." It wasn't an unusual request. Old Pop himself knew Bobby well. He didn't check ID's, and when Danny walked into the store, the old man knew he was there for either ice cream or a sixer of suds for his father. Damn the law.

Bobby slid out from beneath the truck, his hands grasping the front bumper. "To hell with tomorrow. I got enough beer. Finish up, boy. Get to it."

"Dad, I'm tired. Please lemme do it in the morning." He wouldn't be here come morning, but Bobby didn't have to know that, and he wasn't about to tell him.

Bobby slid farther out and stood. He was a giant, ugly monster of a man and grabbed the kid's arm with his big, knobby hand. "You talkin' back to me, boy?"

"No, Dad. I'm just tired, s'all. My arms are hurtin'."

"You think they hurt now?" Bobby struck his small bicep with an angry fist.

Danny recoiled, held his throbbing arm. His eyes crinkled into tiny sponges, quickly wet with tears. "Ow," he whispered.

"How 'bout now? They hurt now? Get to work." He turned and placed a crescent wrench on the wooden bench, pulled out a Phillips screwdriver from the red toolbox. "Craziest thing I ever saw, kids these days. Don't care to do shit, lazy buncha—"

"No!" Danny cried. "I won't! I'm leavin'! I'm gonna run away from here and get away from you. You're mean and I hate you! I hate you, Dad!"

Bobby snatched him away from the bench by the back of his head, grasping his long hair between his knuckles. "Why, you little sombitch. C'mere! I'll teach you to talk to me like that. You must think you're a man now. Huh? That it?"

He pulled and jerked Danny toward the shed. The small white, crusty shed. Inside, it was dark. Even in the middle of the day.

Danny hated the shed more than anything. He squirmed, tried to get away.

Bobby gripped him tighter. "Is that right? You a man now?" He opened the door and walked inside.

Danny wriggled in his arms. "No! No, Dad! No! Don't put me in here, lemme go! Please, Dad! Please! Let! Me! Go!"

Bobby slapped him quick. Hard.

A clean shot of blood trickled in one hot line from the kid's nose. He fell, hit the concrete floor. Pain surged through his butt cheeks.

Bobby picked him up with one hand. Danny's shoes rose two feet off the concrete.

"Just for that, you're gonna stay the night in here. You hear me, boy? Hey! You hear me?"

"I'm sorry. I'll mow the yard. Please don't make me, make me stay in here, please, Dad, it's dark. I'm scared."

"I know you're scared! That's why your little ass is stayin', and the next time you'll think fuckin' twice before you say somethin' like that to your old man. You listenin' boy?"

Danny nodded, sniffed, tried to hold back tears. "Yes-sur."

Bobby slapped him again. "Do you hear me!"

Danny's face turned a bright red, as if his entire left cheek had exploded with blood. "Yes!"

"You are one stupid little fuck. I'll show you a thing or two, you just watch."

When the door closed, the room fell dark. Two windows were spray-painted black and Danny heard the latch click outside, locking him in. Through the half-inch gap of the door and the wall, he saw his dad walk through the grass and into the garage. He hadn't been locked inside the shed since Christmas. That was the last time he'd smarted off to Bobby.

He sat on the blade guard of the riding lawnmower and buried his head in his hands. It was all he could do to keep from going insane then and there. He knew damn well that if he did, he'd only end up banging his head against the wall, and if he was truly lucky, he might slam it into a protruding nail and damage his brain enough to faint or bleed to death.

"Please don't leave, Sadie," he said to the stuffy room. "I'll be there." His red, wet eyes fixed on the door that kept him from his freedom, and he pictured his dad in the garage sitting on the bench in the sunlight, drinking a beer. "Asshole." He put his head between his arms, feeling the sweat stick to his skin and the pain throb through his face.

—⁓—

"Jeez. What happened to the floor?" Melissa said, watching her step around the fallen boards of the tree house.

"That storm was bad last night. Prol'y hit this place pretty hard."

Melissa sat on the bench, popped the top to a Coke and drank. "Where's Danny?"

"He'll be here," Sadie said, disregarding the doubt in her own voice. She hadn't told Melissa what Quitman did to her. There was an urgency to speak of it, to let her friend know how she felt, but at the same time she was unable to summon the words for fear of embarrassment.

"So, do you think this is gonna work?"

"Why wouldn't it?" Sadie opened her book bag and dug through the folded clothes. She retrieved a watch without a band and flipped it in her hands. "It's only five-ten. Give him some time. He'll make it."

Sadie did have a good idea. Run away from home and hide out at the school for the summer.

"It's perfect," she told Melissa. "School's out, there won't be anybody there. We've got food in the cafeteria, bathrooms, showers, a TV. It'll be like a great big house for three months. Our house." She smiled, proud of such genius.

Melissa liked the idea, too, but she asked the one question Sadie could not yet answer: "What about after summer? What'll we do then?"

"We've got a lotta time to think about that. Until then, we need to worry about not gettin' caught."

Sadie reached onto the shelf where they kept the notebook. Her fingers clawed the area, but she couldn't find it.

"What the?" She searched again, fear crowding her veins.

It's not here. Where is it? Oh God, where is it!

"Melissa!" She whirled around, faced her friend.

Melissa brushed her red hair. "What?"

"Have you seen the notebook?"

"No."

"It's not here."

"Where is it?"

"I don't know. That's why I'm asking you. Have you seen it?"

"I told you, no."

"Shit!"

"Where'd ju have it last?"

"Uh-oh." A knowing expression came over her face. "I think I took it to school."

"It might have blew away in that storm."

"No. I think it's at the school."

"What if somebody finds it?"

Sadie reeled in a deep breath. She wasn't sure that she'd taken it to class, but she was known to do so sometimes to go through and look over their entries. Her hands fell to her side and she exhaled an equally big sigh, the color in her face drained a ghostly gray. "If somebody finds it, we're in trouble. Big trouble."

—⁂—

Danny sat on the concrete floor, wiped his face clean of blood, and stared up at the A-frame rafters. His skin still hurt, the muscles beating. He didn't try to reason why his dad treated him so cruelly. He felt unloved and it sucked. Only two years ago, the man would have never done this and he couldn't make sense of it. He'd cried and wished for a way out, tried to understand. Maybe he was screwing up, and maybe this was the way to get him to do right. What bothered him is that he didn't know what he'd done wrong. Just because Bobby locked him in the shed, the man thought he was going to stay there and take it.

The sun was going down. Losing daylight and time. He had to get out of there.

In the corner was an assortment of tools Bobby never used. A rake, a circle-saw blade, a small crowbar, and rusted coffee cans overfilled with nails and bolts and screws. He reached for the crowbar, and wondered if—had this been a half hour ago—he'd picked it up, would he have used it against his own father? No. Either he wouldn't have had the guts to swing, or Bobby would have snatched it out of his hands, and the very thought of thick steel bashing into his own skull frightened him to the bone.

He peered out the window, his face a red mask of sweat and dirt. Bobby wasn't in the garage and his truck was gone. He probably went to Lilly's Lounge to drink and chase women like he always did on Thursday nights. These were the nights he'd return home with or without someone, but always stone drunk and unable to walk or complete a sentence. The same nights Danny stayed in his room under the false safety of his covers where he shivered in bed and prayed to God his dad would not come into his room and tear into him for something as trivial as leaving an empty glass on the porch, or not sweeping the kitchen—one of his many chores and one that he hated. He jabbed the window with the crowbar's hook-end. Harder. A crisp crash sounded. Glass fell to the fresh-cut grass. The sun was still high and burning, it seemed closer to the earth as it touched his skin and heated his face. He sucked in his stomach and slid through the gap. Holding his breath, he dropped face-first to the ground.

Danny sprinted to the bushes outside his bedroom as excitement rushed through him. He grabbed his book bag, slung it over his shoulder, and ran for his bicycle, jumped on, and pedaled down the drive to the street, then headed north. He was going to make it.

Be there, Sadie, he thought. Be there for me.

The words echoed through his mind, it was all he could think about. He pedaled uphill, then coasted down a winding road past cow pastures and the vast landscape cropped with tall pines. To the west, the sky was golden, and a breeze flushed over his face and made him smile. This was great. He was doing it.

He was running away.

Chapter 9

When Anne got home, she found Quitman passed out in the recliner, a string of drool creeping out the corner of his mouth. She put away a few groceries and inspected the house. There was laundry that needed washing in the bathroom and trash that needed to be taken out in the back. The place smelled like cigarettes soaked in water and she sprayed potpourri around the room.

She called upstairs for Sadie. There was no answer. When she reached the top, her chest heaved as she tried to catch her breath. She opened the bedroom door. "Sadie?" Empty.

Anne went back down, stormed into the living room. Quitman snored loud, his mouth hung open. She looked at him and noticed the area around his nose had been bruised. His jeans were bunched around his ankles and between his crotch he'd placed a plastic bag filled with ice.

She shook him, spoke his name.

"What!" He jumped, saw her. "Damn, woman!"

"What happened to you?"

"Your smartass daughter did this. Cracked my balls right open."

"Where is she?"

"She left. Don't know where she went."

"Why'd she leave? Why didn't you stop her?"

"Hey, Anne, I don't need your shit right now. I'm hurtin'. Who knows where she went."

Her face dropped, turned red. Sadie was gone.

She couldn't have run away. It wasn't possible. They had discussed the rules. No talking about what went on in their house and no running away.

Her mother's instinct, though it was buried and seldom alerted, advised her to call the police. But if she did that, they would ask questions, and she had no reasonable answers for them.

Sadie knew the consequences if she went to the police.

"I asked where she was goin' and she started arguin' with me." Quitman pointed down. "Kicked me right here in the balls! Took off on her bike."

Anne didn't pay attention to him. She was worried about what Sadie might do, whom she would tell outside their home, and how it would reflect on her. She could have ridden her bike around the block, or gone to a friend's house. But both privileges called for Anne's permission, so why would she go without asking?

She *knew* it was wrong.

She'd be back, Anne convinced herself. She rode her bike to cool off. There's no need to get the police involved. She realized it was the last day of school. Sadie wanted to see her friends. They were probably downtown at Ye Olde Ice Cream Shoppe eating chocolate yogurt topped with whipped cream and those little multicolored sprinkles. That's it. She'd be back. No need to overreact.

She decided to give her until nightfall and if Sadie hadn't returned, she'd go on the search. Calling the police was the last thing on her mind.

Going to jail for what she'd done to her daughter, if anyone discovered the truth, was the first.

—⁂—

Danny made it. There was a new light in his eyes and on his face. His friends noticed.

Freedom.

They didn't have to say it. The way he smiled and the spark in his eyes were proof enough.

The first thing Sadie did was make it clear that they would not do this unless they did it as a group, as a team. "There's no goin' back, guys," she told them. "It's now or never. Everybody with me?" They nodded. She was happy now that the three of them were here, but in the back of her mind, all she could think about was the notebook. Where the hell was it? Was some kid reading it? It could be a teacher, or worse yet, a bully, or somebody they didn't get along with. What if people were reading it right now and laughing at them? It wasn't in her book bag, wasn't at her house.

She convinced herself she'd taken it to school, so it had to be there. Melissa told her not to worry. "It'll show up, Sadie. Chill." But her words didn't help. Her friend obviously didn't know the absolute power someone would possess if they found the blue notebook with all their secrets in it, nor did she know the trouble that would come their way like a bullet to the heart. Sadie could see it now. A media explosion on the search of three children, their parents on TV, in the newspaper, the lies that would be told to hide the truth, the truth that would be told to hide the lies. It would be a tornado. Their lives would never be the same. They would become figurines on a media game board, and they would be robbed of what dignity and innocence they had left within.

"What took you so long?" Melissa asked. She was hunched on the bench, her arms on her knees, looking at him.

"My dad got mad at me and locked me in the shed for punishment. I broke the window with a crowbar. I got it, too. Wanna see it?"

"No. I say we stay here tonight," Sadie said.

"Where're we goin' again?"

"You didn't tell him?" Melissa asked Sadie.

"I did, he just forgot. Danny, the school? Remember?"

"Oh, yeah!"

"We're gonna hide there all summer."

"Cool!" Danny unzipped his bag and got a sucker, popped it in his mouth. "So, why're we stayin' here tonight?"

"When I passed by earlier, there were still a lot of people there. There's prol'y gonna be people in and out of there for the next few weeks, so we've gotta be careful, take it easy. There's plenty of time. Besides, getting away from home was a big step. We've all done enough today."

"Let's play the Wishing Game!" Danny said.

Sadie smiled. The Wishing Game had been her idea. When they first came together for support, she asked them to make a wish, just one wish, and believe that some day that wish would come true. Danny wished for a million dollars. Melissa wished she could meet Nick from the Backstreet Boys. Sadie wished she could live another life. Though none of their wishes had come true, the game stuck. They told elaborate stories of what they would be doing ten years from now, the places they would go, the people they would meet, the things they would see and do. Another glorious outlet they shared for escape.

"Okay, Danny. You wanna start?"

"I wanna start," Melissa announced, and walked to the window. She looked outside, felt her heart thump in her temples, and heard the hum of passing cars on the highway. "I wish," she said in a weak, mellow voice, "that my parents knew how I felt. Wish they knew what it was like to hurt like this. I think they'd stop hurting me if they only knew how it felt." She turned to Sadie. "That's not so much to ask. Is it?"

—⁂—

Melissa's mother was frantic, pacing the kitchen floor, and she wanted to call the police, had the phone in her hand, a finger poised on speed-dial, but Brady snatched it away from her and placed it in the cradle, his hair clean-cut, face empty.

"What're you doing?!"

"Lisa, let's wait. Missy'll be home. She's just off somewhere with her friends," he told her, holding her face in his large hands. These were the same hands that had touched Melissa in the wrong way, those he extended to welcoming faces in order to make the sale at the furniture store, the same ones he used to slap Lisa when she got smart. "It's all right."

"It's not all right! Missy has never done this. And when she does get home, I'll make it clear to her never to do it again. I'm not like you, Brady Giles. I don't have this calm demeanor with problems such as this. We're talking about our daughter here. You act as though it's not a big deal. Well, it is a big—"

He rotated the clustered diamond ring on his finger and slapped her.

She jerked against the light, gripped the counter top. Her fingers touched her cheek where her skin split open in a white, red slit. She eased onto a barstool, like a trained pet.

"You will not talk to me like that." Brady turned his wedding ring to its normal setting. "I demand respect and you had better give it or I'll divorce you so quick, you'll be back living with Mom and Dad in the trailer I found you in. Here." He tore off some paper napkins, threw them at her. "Wipe that shit off your face."

"What if she goes to the cops?" Lisa asked through her tears.

"I hope she does. At least she'll be safe, we can bring her home," Brady said, his back to her. He sucked on a tooth and stared at the carpet.

Lisa stepped off the stool, spun her husband around. "No. What if she goes to the cops and tells them?"

"You mean?"

"Yes, about the time I burned her with a cigarette, or the other things." She'd beaten Melissa with a metal spatula for talking back and had once used an extension cord on her naked thighs when her daughter had come home late from school. Lisa's fears would come true if Melissa told the police. The tears she cried were not for Melissa's sake, they were from fear the police would discover the truth. Nasty rumors would spread like wildfire through the town. They'd be blacklisted. Lives over.

Brady didn't say it, didn't think Lisa knew it, but he was also afraid Melissa would talk about those nights when he went into her room and lay beside her, told her he loved her, that if she loved him, she would show it, and show it she did, against her will. Someone other than the two of them may know that now, and that unnerved him.

He and Lisa stood in the kitchen holding one another, silent, comfortable at the moment in their belief that Melissa had only left school with friends, and that their little girl would be home soon.

Chapter 10

The last day of school was an eye-opener, a surreal world full of emptiness and a sadness that Ardon Wells felt, apart from the nine months filled with students and books and ball games and life. Every year at this time, he did the same thing. Made his rounds through the classes, thought of how to spend his summer days, anticipated the unseen joy that he'd find when leaves covered the earth and the air turned a shade cooler and the place was bustling with hype of a new school term.

He peered down the desolate halls at the opened lockers and remembered a discussion beside the water fountain. It was with a math teacher about a problem kid named Rudy Jenkins, who chased girls around the playground and grabbed their butts and pulled at their underwear. They had to put the poor bastard in after-school detention with six other fuck-ups until, finally, when he licked his finger and jabbed it into a live electrical socket in the janitorial closet and nearly killed himself, he was transferred to another school. Ardon thought the school would be sued over that one, but no legal action dented the faculty. At the foot of the stairs near the water fountain, he remembered the time he pulled a bully off a smaller kid and had to raise his voice above fifty children to show his authority.

He scratched his chin, strolled by the water fountain where no one stood, gazed at the steps where no one was fighting.

At forty-six, with a balding scalp and black hair slicked back with gel and hair-spray, his eyes welcoming, his face clear of the effects of smoking or alcohol, Ardon was one of the most respected school officials in the region. He'd begun his career as an English teacher and was promoted to principal only a few years later; not a difficult feat in a small town, but he was nonetheless proud of his accomplishments.

Dressed in pressed blue jeans and a short-sleeve button-up, he went on down the hall. Outside, blackbirds lit into the courtyard, and across the way, through the long, slanted windows, he saw cafeteria workers stock meats and vegetables in the walk-in freezer.

Harold "Jazz" Williams, known for his twelve-string riffs onstage in local blues clubs, came around the corner, pulling a plastic trash barrel on wheels. He was black with light-toned skin. It was rumored that white blood flowed in his veins, but he argued that such a man couldn't play so good.

"Lemme tell ya. Them white boys can't play no twelve-strang, 'les they drunk in a dream, no suh! Them nigga's smokin' dope on front porches out in the bottoms tell ya that. My skin's white 'cause I ain't too fond of the sun too much. No friend of mine, uh-uh." Harold had smooth lips and a shaved head with gray-hair sprigs over his ears and around the crown. He was full of energy, always ready to talk and give free advice. The brown hat over his head was set sideways, his trademark appearance.

He noticed Ardon and flashed a gleaming smile with one gold tooth.

"Hey, Mistah Wells. How ya doin'?"

Ardon returned the smile, shoved his hands in his pockets. "Fine, Jazz. You?"

"Oh, jus' cleanin' up a bit. Hancock should be in here sometime this mornin' and hep me."

Hancock was the other janitor, a quiet man who was forever pissed off, with a red face and short black hair and bulging sinister eyes. It had happened more than once that Ardon sent him home for being drunk on school premises. Hancock thought he'd lose his job, which he didn't care for anyway; but Ardon never mentioned it to the superintendent. He viewed Hancock as the type of man who would love to gain unemployment until he cried to the state and received welfare checks. Then he could sit at home, drink and not work, like a grown kid. So, Ardon always did the opposite. He didn't fire Hancock, and that was a worse punishment.

"Place looks lonely, doesn't it?" Ardon asked.

"You know it. All those kids off for the break. They out swimmin' and fishin' and just bein' kids. Wish I was that lucky."

Ardon coughed into his fist, massaged the corner of his thin black mustache. "It's a shame we can't go back. But kids today are lucky, anyway. A year out of high school I was dropped off of a helicopter in the middle of Vietnam. Young, naïve, a million miles away from home with a rifle in my hands and surrounded by war."

Jazz let rip a deep laugh and clapped him on the shoulder. "Aww, it's jus' as well, Mistah Wells. The country's still a mess. We got our own wars to fight. They's drugs, racism, crimes all over the place. These kids, they gonna be our age one day, good Lord willin'. You lucky you got outta that 'Nam walkin' straight and thinkin' good."

A white light opened in Ardon's eyes and he pursed his lips, forced air through his nostrils. He'd killed men in the bush and drank bottled beer at night with the moonlight and a company of men from all over the United States. He never saw them again after that flight home. For two long tours, Death tapped on his back, whispered in his ear. It made a cameo appearance when a bullet sawed off his friend's arm and pronounced its presence with a grenade that took out three boys from Georgia. He'd seen more darkness in those years than criminals would in a lifetime.

Then there was the girl. She was twelve years old. A skinny Vietnamese kid with black eyes and black hair, an angel's face and brown skin tattooed with sun spots. She'd been wearing a white dress the night he spied her in the village eating a bowl of soup in the dirt. Ardon was drunk. But he knew what he was doing. He knew damn well what he was doing.

"Yeah, I guess I am lucky I got out of there with all my senses," Ardon said, almost as an afterthought.

Jazz motioned to the trash barrel packed high with paper and wire notebook rings. "Look here what I got. They didn't waste a sheet of paper, Mistah Wells. Tore it out of they lockers and hightailed it outta here like little to-nado's." Along the barrel hung various cleaning products and throw-away towels. "I was just fixin' to check the middle grades, Ms. Faye's room an' all. You ain't doin' nothin', you wanna hep?" His grin widened and he flexed one callused hand around the barrel's handle.

"Not a problem, Jazz. I don't have much of an agenda today." The sunlight glinted off the waxed floor as they walked to Ms. Faye's sixth grade class. "Come to think of it, I don't have an agenda for the summer. Might go to New Orleans, fish off the gulf in Mississippi. Take the wife to Vegas."

"I'm gonna fish all summer and drink wine every day. That's it, that's my plan," Jazz said, another big grin forming on his face.

"Now, that is a plan, my man."

Jazz stopped short of the water fountain at the end of the hall to pick up pens and pencils, sheets of blank paper, a ripped poster of the Backstreet Boys, and other trash.

Ardon went into Ms. Faye's classroom. The desktops were empty and lifted for inspection. He strolled up an aisle, peered into them at random. There were tic-tac-toe diagrams with C's crossed over them, drawings, and "Hilary loves Tommy" and "Mizz Fay's a Big Fat Idiot" written into the wood grains.

Inside one particular desk on the far aisle, close to the window where daydreamers usually sat, a signature had been scribed in the wood with the tip of a pocket knife. Below it was a date, its life untouched by other markings, and the inscription brought back a certain student's face, his character, his cold stare and soft voice that didn't seem it should have come from such a face or such a boy.

"Mason Xavier/1987."

Looking at that carving, the many times Ardon had sat across from his outcast student, the secret came back, like an old friend dropping by, and the secret grew in his mind, and he could hear Mason's words: "Don't tell anybody. Please. I trust you. Don't tell anybody what I did." The thirteen-year-old boy's eyes and nose were wet, his right hand shook at the arm of the office chair on that cold January day a week after he'd murdered his parents.

"Hey, Mistah Wells!"

Ardon took his eyes off the desk, turned to the door.

"I ain't gonna need no help! Hancock, he's here."

"Thanks, Jazz." Ardon folded his hands inside the pockets of his jeans.

He listened to the wind top the pine trees near the loading ramp and wondered what Mason had been doing since he saw him last fall. As he passed Hancock, he greeted him with a friendly nod.

Wide dust-broom in hand, the man grunted, stared at the floor. Ardon smelled whiskey on his breath, but said nothing. He went through the double metal doors, the hardened dirt crunching under his feet as he got in his 1996 Malibu. He left a trail of dust that floated over the school grounds in a widespread balloon and disappeared in the air like cinnamon smoke.

—⁓—

Dusk fell, a gray ghost over the land, while the kids ate strawberry Pop-Tarts in the tree house. When they finished the box, they kept to themselves, the loss of the notebook in their minds.

Melissa toyed with a portable stereo that had a static reception and the only clear wave she could receive was a sports channel in southern Arkansas. "I hate sports," she griped, and clicked it off, kicked out her feet, and pushed herself against the wall, folded her arms over her chest. Danny read an X-Men comic on the bench and smacked on bubble gum. Loud, to annoy Melissa. Sadie was slouched in her usual chair, one finger hung in her mouth, the look on her face dumb, as if she could see something striking far off in the wood line, hypnotized.

Finally, she broke the silence. "We've got to find the notebook!"

"I don't have it," Danny said without taking his eyes off the comic. "You ever thought maybe someone stole it?"

"Who's gonna climb up here and steal it?" Melissa asked, her face screwed up as though her intestinal tubes were full of gas. "Stupid."

"I left it at school!" Sadie put her face in her hands. "I did, that's where it is."

The cloudless sky allowed the silver-tinged moonlight to beat down on the tree house and the evening's oppressive heat snaked its way to their bodies. Sweat masked their skin and they took out three Dr Peppers and flicked the tops across the room. One hit Danny in the nose.

"Quit it, Missy!"

Melissa laughed, got up, and went to her suitcase and unzipped it. She pulled out a pair of shorts. "Turn around and close your eyes, Danny," she said, and flipped Sadie a pair of shorts.

"I don't wanna see you nekked, stupid. You either, Sadie."

"Then turn around and don't turn around again 'til we say so."

Danny obeyed, but peeked through his fingers regardless and received a well-deserved cursing.

"Turn around!" they chimed.

"I'm not kidding. We'll leave you here if you look," Sadie threatened, her face red as a beet.

They had planned to stay the entire night, wake early before dawn, and get to the school, but their nervous energy kept them restless and unable to sleep. Melissa had brought a small cooler packed with potato chips, another box of strawberry Pop-Tarts, crackers, string cheese and canned drinks.

She flicked her red hair from her cheek and checked her watch. "I say we go now, while it's dark. Whaddaya think?"

"Yeah, Sadie! Let's get out of here. I'm hot." Danny pumped a fist in the air. "Let's go to the school!" He opened the canteen and poured luke-warm water onto his head. The stream fell over his cheeks in staggered lines, dropped to the rickety floor. Or what was left of it.

The notebook, Sadie thought. I have got to find the notebook.

She'd made a promise to herself that once they were inside Sutter Springs High, the first classroom they would investigate would be Ms. Faye's, her homeroom. It had to be in her desk. It just had to be. She couldn't imagine anyone reading their deepest, darkest secrets, and further-more, didn't want to know what they thought about those secrets. Not having the notebook in her possession, not being able to hold it and read it and appreciate it, pricked her nerves like a dentist's needle.

"Okay, let's do it. We'll take the back way," Sadie told them. She twisted a curl out of the end of her hair and spit chewed bubble gum out the make-shift window.

They shouldered their book bags and stepped out into a space of humidity that had the same thickness and heat of diesel exhaust after a twelve-hour run.

Sadie unbuttoned the top two buttons on her shirt, slipped her hand over her skin and fluffed it out. She led them east. The sky was dark as tar at the horizon, and the outline of flat land cropped with forests and lakes touched its edge. One car passed, slowed, turned into a drive, and cut its lights.

"Let's hurry up!" Danny pedaled past Sadie. "My dad might come down this road."

Sadie followed suit, topped a hill and lifted her legs and cruised downward through a stop sign, and trudged up another incline keeping pace with her friends. Mixed emotions filled her and she figured her friends felt the same. Running away from home was not easy. She feared being caught, or hurt, or both, but there was no way she was going back.

Fifteen minutes southeast of the Arkansas state line, they arrived at the school. Sadie's legs and feet ached and her angry heart pumped against her chest.

The building overlooked vast pastures where cows grazed and horses ran wild. The beautiful, rugged country sprawled for miles, infested with pine groves and giant oaks, painted now by the pale moon. The school had been built in the 1930s and all grades gathered in the gray, ghostly place from kindergarten to high school. On nights like this, it gave off a passive, mysterious quality, like a living entity.

Danny braked and slid in the gravel. He stared up at the huge building. The gray brick was weather-worn to a moist black color and areas were covered with thin ivy that resembled green jagged lightning. It was different now that no buses were loading and unloading kids, since there were no people around, no cars parked in front of the office.

"Looks scary," Danny said, and jabbed Sadie's arm. "Boo!"

"Boy, I will knock you off that bike if you don't quit."

"Are ya scared?" he teased.

Sadie paused a moment and licked the sweat from her lips, gripped the rubber handle bars tight. "I'm not scared anymore," she said, and pedaled up the gravel, into the half-moon drive, through the Administration parking lot, and around the corner toward the gym and cafeteria that were separated by a wide breezeway.

Highway 109 stretched past the school in a sharp curve and wound to an intersection where a small post office and a convenience store were located. Off school property, but in sight, an oil rig drove its mighty steel muscle into the earth behind the shadow of an old, shoddy building that had once been a slaughterhouse.

Sadie caught her breath in her throat. "Okay, you guys. Let's hide our bikes and get in."

They stowed away their bicycles in the greenhouse behind the gym and walked past the wood shop. Danny and Melissa followed Sadie across the courtyard, their faces white, eyes clicking to the high outer walls of the connected buildings. The trio turned as a car cruised through the S-shaped road that wound around the school grounds. They stopped and watched the light pass.

They won't find me, Sadie thought. The police can look forever. I won't go back 'cause Momma don't care and I don't either. Now, when she gets drunk and comes into my room I won't be there and that's fine with me.

I won't get caught for what I'm doing. No way. I'll never go back home.

Melissa stubbed her toe on a waterspout that jutted out of the ground. "Ow! Dammit."

Sadie pressed one finger against her lips, her eyebrows furrowed to dark, straight lines. "Shh!"

Near the Junior High wing, they checked the double entrance and side doors.

"Locked, great. What now?"

"You give up too easy, Missy." Sadie brushed against Melissa's ribs, pushed at a window. Her fingers turned peanut white. "Danny, gimme that crowbar."

He pulled it from his bag and handed it to her.

She placed it under the window's lip, pressed down, and her feet lifted off the grass for a second. The latch broke free with a loud click. The hinges creaked as she bent it toward the classroom. "You first, Danny."

"Me? Why me? You go."

"You're the man around here. You first."

The silver light illuminated their faces and the courtyard looked like a square of water. The classroom was pitch black.

"Hey, this was your idea," he persisted. "You go!"

"C'mon, you two." Melissa wiped her sweaty palms on her shorts and shuffled her feet, shifted her hip. "One of y'all go. I don't like it out here."

"Get outta the way." Sadie clicked a small flashlight, poked the yellow beam into the room, and pushed Danny aside. She pulled herself up and made it in halfway. The windowsill pressed against her stomach. A wave of blood entered her face and gripped at such a fast rate, it felt like her head would explode. She moved her hands and knocked over a line of books. The *smack* sound on the floor made her jump.

"What was that?" Melissa asked. "You okay?"

"My shirt's stuck!" Sadie whispered, and felt the seam where she ripped it on the top of a flat-head screw.

"Hold on. I'll push ya." Danny put his hands on her butt.

"Wait!" she yelled, but it was too late.

He sent Sadie into the black room, her arms flailing.

Beside the book shelf, a puffy red beanbag broke her fall. She stared up at her friends. "Well? Are y'all comin' or not?"

Melissa was next, Danny last. Sadie closed the window and aimed the flashlight around the room. They were in Mr. Griffin's eighth grade biology class. Desk tops were up, emptied, and the floors were waxed and clean.

Danny and Melissa huddled close behind Sadie. They walked through the opened door at the far end of the room to the empty hallway. Moonlight poured through the slanted windows above the locker rows and the shadows of tree limbs wavered across the walls and floor like tangled snakes.

"Where're we goin' first?" Danny asked.

"Ms. Faye's class to see if the notebook's in my desk. Then we'll check the kindy-garden rooms for more beanbags to sleep on and get some blankets. This book bag's hurtin' my shoulder."

Melissa stepped to her. "Do you think it's a good idea to have that flashlight on?"

Sadie clicked it off and they walked the hall.

She smiled, but neither Danny nor Melissa saw it. It was a smile of knowing. Knowing that none of them was going to return home.

—◊◊◊—

Rachel fell asleep on the couch and didn't hear his key at the door. Her hair ruffled from the air conditioner's vent and goosebumps had popped up over her arms and legs.

Mason looked at her for a moment and wanted to touch her skin, but decided not to wake her. He poured whiskey over ice and went out onto the back porch with the notebook. A calm breeze wrapped around his face as he sat on top of the picnic table under a lamp bouncing with moths and gnats. He slapped one into a red line on his skin and crossed his legs, flipped to page three, and read a night in the life of Sadie Bellis, aware all the same, that he was peering through a porthole into his own past.

> My mom doesn't smoke, but my stepdad does. She got mad at me one night for droping a plate on the floor. She went to the kitchen and stepped on a piece and cut her foot. She puled the glass out of her foot and yeled at me al night. I thought that was it, but quitman was smoking a cigerete and she puled it out of his mouth and came after me with it. she got the tip real hot like she was smoking it herself and pushed me up to the wal and then pushed the cig on my arm. I got a scar now. That's never happined to Danny. Missy's mom did it like that to her one time with a cigar and that was on her neck, too. My momma did it to me and said I was lucky I didn't have a piece of that glass down my throte by now and I need be lucky to have the burn. The burn stil hurt me a lot though.   Sadie

"Studying for an exam?"

Mason lowered the notebook. Rachel stood in the doorway, her fingers curled around the screen.

"Did I wake you?"

"With all this noise you're making out here I couldn't get a wink."

He closed the notebook, tucked it underneath his butt and picked up the sweating glass of whiskey, took a quick sip.

"What's that?"

"I found it at the baseball park. It's some kind of journal."

"You're reading other people's thoughts?" She placed her palm on his head and messed up his hair. "You're a bad boy. You need to find out who it belongs to and return it."

"It's nothing, really. Just some girl's recollection of last summer when she went to Six Flags. Nothin' juicy," he lied.

Rachel pulled his head to her breasts and slowly moved it from side to side between them. She cradled his face in her hands and caught his hazel eyes. "Come to bed, baby. It's late. Do you even know what tonight is?"

His first thought was that he'd forgotten her birthday, then he scanned his mind for their anniversary date, and when that didn't come, he shook his head in the manner of a man who knew he'd fucked up. "I don't know. What's tonight?"

"The day we try again. I'm off my period."

"Baby time?"

"Baby time," she repeated, and took his hand in hers and led him into the house.

They had been trying to get pregnant for months and it seemed their efforts were in vain, but they kept hoping one day Rachel would come to him with a smile and tears and tell him the good news.

He lay her on the bed with the grace of a father holding an infant, kissed her perfumed neck and found her lips. Stitch by stitch they discarded each other's clothing. Mason's penis pressed hard against his underwear and the heat from Rachel's crotch burned at his hand like a red flame on a sultry August evening.

He grabbed her thighs and spread them, then pulled away, as if someone called his name.

Rachel lifted her head, puzzled. "What is it, Mason?"

He thought about the notebook and the things he had read. Somewhere kids were being hurt by their parents, the very people who gave them life. He knew somehow he had to stop it and no foster home or 800 help line would be able to do what came to him in the darkness of his bedroom as he lay crooked between his girlfriend's legs.

It didn't make much sense to give a child life if you spend your time trying to destroy it, he thought.

Rachel put her palm on his cheek, felt the light stubble that shaded his face. "Mason, are you all right?"

"Do you trust me?" he asked.

"Yes, I do. Why are—"

Kill them.

"You love me, too, don't you?"

"Yes."

Tear out their heart and stuff it in their mouth.

"No matter what happens from here on out, I want us to be together," he said. "If you ever left me, I'd still be with you, I'd still love you. Every night as I fall asleep, I'd still feel you beside me and every morning as I wake up, you'd still kiss me. Even if you're not in the room."

Bury them like you buried your parents.

She swallowed hard and her eyes gleamed with wetness. "I'd never leave you. For anything or anybody."

He hugged her and they made love on the edge of the bed, her arms crossed over his back, her head tilted to the moonlight, and her mouth opened in an ecstasy only few lovers achieve.

Chapter 11

—ⵊ—Thursday.

Ten minutes before noon, the blistering sun high in the clear sky, Brady and Lisa Giles walked into the police station at the end of Main Street. The office was filled with filing cabinets, a fax machine, a water cooler, and three hard-backed chairs at a wooden desk. The air conditioning was on the brink again. T.R. had set up an oscillating fan on a folding card table and opened all windows, allowing the summer wind to move in.

Brady was relaxed, his wife a little nervous. She had recently formed the habit of pinching her earlobes when she talked and the bags under her eyes revealed at least one night of sleeplessness.

Lisa touched her husband's hairy arm. "I don't know, do you think she was, surely not kidnapped, what if she never, if she comes back, she'll be back for sure, don't you know that?"

"Have a seat," Brady told her, and pulled out the chair.

She sat across from Sheriff Combs, snapped at her ears. Brady stood behind her, his hands on her shoulders.

Terry clicked an ink pen and flipped open a yellow legal pad. "When was the last time you two saw Melissa?" His face was chapped red and sweat peppered his forehead and brow. He was a big man. Six foot one, two-hundred and-fifty pounds. His gut was his most prominent feature, the rest of his body chubby with stout muscles, and his hairy arms were like small cannons, attached to large, fat hands. His friends had nicknamed him "Fats" and he didn't mind it so much, but those jokes did get old. "Where does T.R. iron his shirt? On an airstrip." Ha, ha, very funny boys.

Brady thought a minute and pressed his fingers gently into his wife's bare skin. "We last saw her yesterday morning, before she went to school."

Lisa dabbed tissue at her crinkled eyes. "We waited 'til six o'clock, then drove around town. We thought she was out with friends. We asked the kids uptown if they'd seen her, and then stopped by the ice cream place, but nobody had seen her. Drove around 'til about ten, ten-thirty I think it was?" She shook her head, the light wrinkles in her neck punctuated with her gentle movements. "We didn't find her. Of course we didn't find her. We wouldn't be here talkin' to you if we'd found her!"

"Calm down, Lees," Brady said, and patted her shoulder.

Terry wrote on the pad. From his desk drawer he retrieved a fat brown cigar and stuck it between his lips. He bit down on the rolled tobacco and the corner of his mouth opened like a fish hook had caught there and pulled. The fan rotated and hummed behind him, curling the hairs on his neck. "Do you have any idea who she might have been with? Friends of hers you might know?"

"We don't keep tabs on her friends, Sheriff Combs," Brady said. "We sent her off to school and she never came home. That's it."

"Did you notice anything missing from her room?"

"Like what?"

Terry hunched his thick shoulders. Sweat padded his underarms, showing through the brown work shirt. He fiddled with his badge.

"Clothes?"

"Are you suggesting she might have run away?" Brady shifted his lean body to one side.

Terry lifted his hands. "It happens. Teenagers could shoot off for any reason."

"She's not a teenager. She's ten," Lisa said.

Terry moved his soft blue eyes to Brady. "Answer the question."

"We haven't thoroughly checked her room, but—" His voice drifted off and his face caught a hint of red. Melissa's bike. Had she taken it? He didn't remember seeing it parked underneath the garage this morning. "Lisa, did you see Missy's bike?"

"Huh? No. I don't know, I don't remember. Brady, why would she run away?"

"I tell ya what, I'll put out the call," Terry said. "But you've got to call me and let me know if her bike's missing. Do you have a recent picture of her?"

Lisa dug into her leather purse and flipped through a long wallet lined with clip-in photos. She pulled out two and handed them over. "One is about a year old, the other was taken out on the patio in the spring." Her pretty, stressed face begged. "You will find my little girl, won't you, Sheriff?"

"We'll do our best, ma'am. Don't worry yourself. I'm sure she's fine."

They left their home phone and cell phone numbers where they could be reached.

When the door closed, Terry chewed on the cigar with the impatience of a kid trying to crunch into the middle of hard candy. He stretched out his arms, leaned into the desk and scooted his chair forward. The screeching sound echoed off the four walls. "Hanna!"

Deputy Steve Hanna, the youngest officer on the force at twenty-three, rushed into his office, his black baton banging against his leg. He was short, stout, with clean-cut black hair, and a baby-face. "Sir?"

Terry slid the most recent photo of Melissa across the desk. "Go on down to the photo shop at the state line and have 'em enlarge that. Make a hundred copies, post 'em around town. We'll need it printed for tomorrow's paper. It's short notice, so if McGraw gives you any shit, tell him to call me. A girl's missing. Her name's Melissa Giles. Ten years old. Last seen yesterday. Got it?"

Hanna scribbled feverishly in a pocket-size notepad. "Yessir. Anything else?"

Terry pulled the cigar out of his mouth and placed it on the edge of the desk, the tip wet and flattened. He reclined in his chair and stared out the window at the passing cars, the fan in the corner losing its battle with the hot wind that flooded the room. "Pick me up one of those crawfish plates at Lilly's. Extra sauce. Large Coke, Diet."

—〰—

Mason ate a fried ham sandwich in a hand crafted glider on the back of his wraparound porch, looking out over the hills that surrounded his house. His grandfather's friend in Beaux River had carved the swing out of an oak trunk and gave it to him for his twenty-first birthday, not too long after he'd sold his inheritance. The day's yellow light streamed over the brilliant green forest a mile away, the smell of barbecue and pine coming to him in the southbound breeze. Near the city limits, a train blared its lonesome cry. He wore jeans and no shirt, barefoot, sliding the ball of his foot along the smooth cypress flooring. He thought of the note Rachel had left on the kitchen table this morning before she took her jog: "Remember to take movies back. Love ya." Three days ago, they rented a romance, a comedy, and his favorite Clint Eastwood film, *Sudden Impact*. Now that he thought about it, the idea of vigilance crossed with his movie selection struck him as ironic.

You're not a killer, an inner voice told him.

"I was," he argued aloud.

I used a pair of gardening shears, slid underneath the car while they were getting ready to go out. Cut the brake line halfway. Got brake fluid all over my face and hands and on the grass. Used the water hose behind the house to clean up. Went to my room, read a comic book. I don't remember the name of the comic book. I do remember the door slamming as they headed out to the car and to the bar. They didn't even say goodbye. They never said that. I watched television for ten minutes before a policeman showed up and asked if I was their son. He sat down on the front steps with me and told me my mom and dad got in a car wreck, that they were gone. It could have happened anywhere between my house and the bar. They lost control around the Devil's Elbow. The policeman took me to the station and that's where I met Sheriff Combs for the first time. He was younger. He didn't smoke cigars, either. I looked at him. I was fidgety, excited, but had to keep my cool. I looked at him and wanted to tell him that I had killed them, that no one knew exactly how happy I was, that no one could take that away from me, but I had to be cool.

I was a killer.

I can be one again.

He finished the sandwich and opened the notebook, having to squint even behind the sunglasses to block the sun's stinging rays. He read slowly, taking in each word. Again, he noticed the stick-like lettering, the mis-spelled words. A boy's handwriting for sure. Danny. The short descriptions of what the three kids had endured, the way they were wrongfully treated, burned into his mind like a branding iron to a cow's smooth, wet coat.

It reminded him of himself as a child. The beatings. The horror. The pain. Oh God, the pain.

Without warning, the memories rushed back with the ferocity of a tidal wave crashing down on a sand-swept coast.

He was again twelve years old. A clear August night, the wind hot, the scent of whiskey at his skin.

He stood before his father, a short man with a potbelly and patches of gray sprouted on his reddened, lopsided face.

Mason's hair curled slightly just above his innocent, gleaming eyes that reflected the madness he witnessed. The hand wrapped around his throat, lifted him off his feet. The muscle slammed him to the wall. A family por-trait fell and cracked on the floor.

The old house creaked with heavy footfalls. His mother ran into the room. "William!" Janet screamed, her hands on her hips. "What's he done now?"

"Stole five dollars out of my wallet, the little son of a bitch did." Then came the sweet whiskey scent, the grinding of teeth. "Didn't you!"

Mason kept silent. He learned early in life not to argue with his parents. They always won. This aspect especially concerned his father, a man without patience, and a short fuse to a temper that raged and boiled day in and day out, his fury usually carried out through the physical infliction upon his own son.

He stared off aimlessly, the blood flow collecting in his face and turning it the color of fresh roses. He sniffed, tried to catch his breath, coughed, and blinked. Two lines of tears escaped his eyes and fell to the portrait's glass pieces sprayed on the carpet at his father's heavy work boots.

"Whaddaya think oughta teach him a lesson?" his dad asked.

Janet turned swift and left the room.

"Whaddaya think, son?" he said. The evil in his eyes was hollow and alive, the lines on his face deep from a hard life, and his jugular vein throbbed mechanically against thick, leathery skin. "You ain't never far from

learnin' right if you're fuckin' up the roost. I'll show you to steal from me."
He swung and the back of his closed fist struck Mason's eye.

His mother returned. In her hand, she held a plastic cord cut from a
lamp. "I'll hold him down."

William eased off.

Mason crumpled to his chest, face down in the dirty carpet. He sucked
in dust and sweat from feet within the fibers. In a lame attempt to feel his
throat, he loosened his arm from the twisted anchor of his mother's shoe. A
violent cough erupted from his lungs and a mixture of blood and saliva
seeped out the corner of his mouth and soaked into the carpet in a sticky,
spotted pool.

He struggled beneath his mother's weight as she pressed her knee into
the nape of his neck. She covered the side of his head with her fingers. Her
spiky red nails dug into his scalp. "Stay still." She ripped off his favorite
white shirt, displaying his bare back covered with scars from years past.

The cord came down quick and hard, broke the skin. He let out a
squeal. William was relentless. His mother cheered him on. "Harder!" she
yelled. "Teach him a lesson!" The cord slammed against him and cut into
skin and muscle.

Mason screamed out once more, his throat gone numb. His eyes fluttered, the room tilted. He saw shards of white light around him. He was in
shock, let out a breath and passed out.

He woke screaming the next morning with bandages dabbed with table
salt over his wounds. Woke again to the nightmare without a promise of an
end.

But he finally woke from the hell. He ended it.

"I can kill," he said to the wind. As immature and unrealistic as it
sounded, he nodded in affirmation. "I can." He got to his feet and carried
the paper plate and notebook into the cool house. He dropped the plate into
a trash can under the key rack where he saw her new car keys. In the
kitchen, he heard her singing to a song on the radio. Rachel was happy and
Mason loved to keep her that way. He'd bought her a Lexus SC400, white.
"You look good in it," Mason told her when she sat in it at the dealership.
She'd pooched her lips, kissed the air, her silver sunglasses blocking the
morning's sun. "I look cooool, baby." Her excitement alone was worth every

dime.

She was now wrapping up their leftovers and placing them in a covered dish. He watched her from the end of the hall and did not make a sound. She'd dressed in a sports bra, laced up her tennis shoes, and went into the weight room full of free-weights, a bench press, a stair-master, and mats. The room was surrounded by wall-to-wall mirrors. She put on an aerobics CD and began exercising.

Mason leaned his head into the room, fingered his sunglasses down so that she saw him looking. "Have I told you I love you today?"

She stretched, the side of her face brushing the top of her bare thigh that flexed into a hardened cone. Strands of her hair touched the carpet and her lips peeled back at her teeth as she grinned. "Not today."

"I just did."

"I'm going to stop by the parlor after awhile. Did you need anything at the store while I'm out?" She flexed her arms, twisted them behind her arched back.

"Nothing I can think of."

"Let's get kinky tonight," she said.

"What'd you have in mind? Handcuffs?"

"And a whip. You know, the kind with the straps like a mop?"

"Do you have a chest filled with all that stuff or do you expect me to buy it?" He tapped the sides of the door jamb, his crotch burning from her words, his face pink from embarrassment.

"I might. I'm not tellin'. I've got secrets. Everybody's got secrets."

"You don't know how right you are," he said, and left, the words written in the notebook on his mind.

—m—

Terry Robert steepled his fingers at his forehead and blew air through his palms. Another missing child. He set a steaming cup of coffee on his desk blotter, raised his head, his eyes big and puffy.

"Mrs. Mase, you say the last time you saw Sadie was yesterday morning?"

"That's right. I got home late, but my husband saw her that evening. He said she just got on her bike and rode off. Didn't tell him where she was goin' and nobody's seen her since." Anne stood at the desk in a dress with flower prints. Her hands clutched the leather strap of her purse and as she breathed, her massive breasts expanded the dress.

"You say she left on her own? Do you think she stayed the night with a friend?"

"Who knows? I haven't called around. Besides, she wouldn't do anything like that without asking for permission."

"Will you check?"

"Yes, but if she did run away, she's not going to be holed up at a friend's house."

Terry propped his arms on the legal pad and his elbow nudged the styrofoam carton that held scraps of crawfish tails and dirty rice. The spicy stink floated on the hot air, so he closed the lid and picked up his black pen.

"Why do you think she'd run away?"

Anne's eyes focused on the filing cabinet beside the door. The area of crow's feet along her left eye twitched. "Sheriff, my daughter's missing. Her bike is gone. I don't think she's been kidnapped."

Terry bit the tip of the pen, clicked it open against his front teeth and gave her a look.

"I have no idea why'd she'd run away. You never know about kids these days, ya know? Just find her!" Anne left a picture of Sadie in a scarlet blouse and a black skirt she wore last Valentine's Day.

Terry dispatched Deputy Hanna. "Get to the station. We got another missing girl." He went to the window and looked at the park across the road. Kids ran wild at play and parents sat on blankets under thick, green pines eating sandwiches from plastic wrap. The sky bled a soft blue, the sun glinted off pine leaves in tiny spiked beads.

He massaged his chin with his finger and thumb. Sadie Bellis and Melissa Giles were out there somewhere and it was up to him to find them.

The phone rang and he shifted his stance, looked at it, thought about answering it, didn't, then exhaled, and picked up the receiver. "Sheriff Combs."

"T. R.? There's somethin' wrong."

"Who is this?" he asked the rough voice.

"Bobby Rampart. My son Danny's gone. You know. I brought him to that barbecue y'all had a few weeks ago out at the Harper Place. I ain't seen him since yesterday, about five o'clock. He was in his room when I left, then this morning, I looked in there and he wasn't there. Thought maybe you could help me out."

Three. Terry marked the number down on the yellow paper and circled it. He gripped the handset tight. "Yeah, Bobby, I remember him. Have you checked to see if his bicycle's missin'?"

"Huh?"

Terry shook his head. He picked up the cigar and bit the end, struck a match on the hardwood desk, and lit it.

Chapter 12

*S*adie woke staring at the sky with her head pressed down on the floor. The lower half of her body was positioned on a beanbag that was exhausted of stuffing. She cleaned the wetness around her mouth with the collar of her shirt and moved out of the sunlight, into the shadows of the classroom. It had been almost two days since she'd taken a bath and her skin was dry, her hair matted, and she smelled musty. In her book bag, she took out a change of clothes, careful not to wake her friends. She walked to the end of the hall, through the breezeway, and to the gymnasium.

She showered and washed her hair with a bar of soap she'd brought from home and on the way back to the kindergarten wing, she checked the cafeteria door. Their food supply was running low. Nothing left but three Pop-Tarts, two Dr Peppers, and a bag of chips. The door was locked. She thought about breaking a window, but the risk was too high. If anyone noticed, the police would launch an investigation, and their plans would be ruined.

Wearing a loose white shirt, blue jean shorts with stringy edges, and sandals that showed off her eggshell-colored toenails, she met up with Danny and Melissa in the hall. Danny rubbed sleep out of his eyes with his knuckles and Melissa was tugging at her shorts as if the material didn't fit as well as it did last night.

"Who's hungry?" Sadie asked.

"If I eat another Pop-Tart, I'll puke," Melissa said, and stuck out her tongue. Her hand fell to her growling stomach. "Things're makin' me sick."

"Same here." Danny yawned, stretched his arms. "I want real food. A steak!"

"The lunch room's locked."

"Let's break a window," Melissa said.

Sadie waved her hand. "Bad idea. If someone sees it, they might find us." She put her finger in her mouth, bit at the nail. "We might get lucky and find one opened, though."

"I gotta piss." Danny got up and left.

"Thanks for the info," Melissa said, and stuck out her tongue.

"We'll be in the lunch room," Sadie called.

Sunlight fell through the windows above the rows of blue lockers, and the black and white clock near the principal's office read 7:21.

"It's early," Melissa said, her voice groggy. "Still sleepy."

"Go take a shower."

"I needa eat first and then I'll—"

"Did you hear that?" Sadie stopped, stretched her arm across Melissa's chest. They listened. Voices.

"Stay behind me," Sadie whispered. She leaned her shoulder against the gray wall and stepped to where the wall branched off between the principal's office and the lobby. To their left, the hall led to another section of the school, and ahead lay the cafeteria. Sadie peered her head around the corner, saw two men, and jumped back. As she did, she bumped Melissa and stepped on her toes.

Melissa breathed in a quick flow of saliva and air.

Sadie's finger flew to her lips, gesturing to keep quiet. "It's Jazz and that son of a bitch Hancock," she whispered.

The girls saw the men's reflection in the lobby's glass wall and froze.

Jazz wrung a mop in a yellow bucket. "I'm tellin' ya! Muddy Waters was the greatest Blues singer ever lived, tried and true, it's the damn truth!"

Hancock took his time placing a trash bag in the gray barrel between them. He shook his head with confidence, the corners of his mouth moving up in two curls. "Elvis. Elvis was the greatest Blues singer."

Jazz applied pressure to the bucket's loose handle, his black hands as large as a boxer's glove. Water splashed into water. His eyebrows dipped. "Elvis?" He let out a ragged, throaty laugh as if his vocal cords had been burned with acid. "You cain't be serious. Dat white boy couldn't sang the Blues. He sang everything else but!"

"Shit. He sang the Blues."

"Not like Muddy Waters. My man, lemme tell ya."

"Elvis was a legend in his own time."

"Yeah, and Elvis died his white ass on the taw-let in his own time, too. My man Muddy Waters could out-sang Elvis when it comes to da Blues like nobody's business." He hunched his shoulders, shook his head again, the crocodile smile appeared in his face.

Hancock jabbed the sides of the trash barrel with his hands and positioned the bag in place at the corners. "Jerkoff."

Sadie poked her head around the corner and waited until both men returned to the room they were busy cleaning up.

On the side of the barrel was a ring of keys hooked to a clip. One of those keys had to unlock the cafeteria. She hoped another might open the teacher's lounge where they could watch television and get access to the candy machine.

"See those keys?" she asked Melissa.

"Yeah."

"Watch my back."

Melissa grabbed her arm. "Sadie, no. They'll see us. Let's hide."

"Stay here and don't move." She stepped around the corner to go for the keys when Danny appeared beside the water fountain at the end of the hall.

His head was down, one thumb hooked in his pocket. He ran his fingers over the lockers, making loud *clack-clack-clacks*. Sadie motioned to him, waved, her voice barely audible. "Danny." *Don't let them hear me.* "Hide, Danny!"

He looked up, stopped in his tracks, his hair over his eyes, face pinched.

Sadie dashed behind the door to the classroom, squeezed in tight and fell into the wall.

Danny ducked behind the water fountain.

Jazz stepped into the hallway. "You hear dat?"

Hancock showed up with a dust broom. "Hear what?"

"Sound like somebody off in here somewhere."

"You're crazier than a got-damn billy goat."

"You didn't hear the sound out here?"

"Let's get back to work so I can go home. I need a drink."

Sadie took her chance. She cradled the key ring with both hands so they wouldn't jangle, unclipped them, and crept behind the wall to Melissa. They made it back to the classroom without being noticed and hid in an empty coat closet.

"Do you think they'll find Danny?" Melissa asked.

"No, but when they find out those keys are missin', they'll search the whole school. If we're lucky, they won't find us at the same time."

Danny had lucked out. The water fountain hummed and ticked beside him. He peeked through the space between the wall and the back of the machine, through the metal-encased wiring, and saw the janitors move the trash barrel to the lobby, place it in the closet.

"Where the hell're my keys?" Hancock checked the barrel over.

"What you talkin'?"

"My keys. I clipped 'em on the side of the barrel."

"I'll check in here."

"I didn't take 'em in there. Had 'em on that barrel, now. If I lose those keys, I'll lose my job."

"So? If Mistah Wells fires you, you can draw unemployment and sit at home and drink ev-ree day. Heck, it's what you been wantin', anyways. It'd give me a break, too."

Hancock shoved his hands in his pockets. "I don't like you, but you're right."

"I can lock up. You just go on vacation."

"Deal," Hancock said.

Jazz locked the closet, checked the front doors and they retreated into the cloudless day.

Warm piss streamed down Danny's leg, soaked into dark lines through his jeans. The liquid fell into his shoe and collected beneath the sole of his bare foot. He was so nervous and scared, he wanted to cry. It wasn't the toughest thing to do in a time like this, but he couldn't help it. Without dwelling on his weak bladder, he put his legs in gear and ran to the classroom they'd designated as their sleeping quarters. The room was empty.

"Sadie? Missy? Y'all here? Sadie!" He went to his book bag and pulled out a pair of jeans. Shucked his shorts and underwear, then stuffed them underneath one of the desks. "Sadie?"

Danny unfolded a dry pair of jeans and slapped them out as if he were about to fold a towel. He was naked from the waist down, his skinny legs pasty white.

The closet door opened and the girls stepped out.

"Oh my God." Melissa cupped her hand over her mouth.

Danny looked up. There he was, showing off.

Sadie giggled. "Jeez, Danny. Don't just stand there. Get dressed!"

Melissa pointed. "Look at it, Sadie. See it? Looks like a tiny mushroom."

His face went red and he turned away, pulled on his jeans.

"It's as big as my pinky toe!" Melissa wailed.

"Shutup, stupid!" Danny trudged off.

"Y'all settle down. Danny, she's just kiddin'." Sadie jangled the keys. "C'mon, let's eat."

Chapter 13

Mason sat at a round table in the back of the library and searched through Sutter Springs High's most recent yearbook. He folded the double-sided black and white page that showed the three kids' photos and stuffed it down the back of his jeans with discretion. The librarian was an older, soft-spoken woman in her sixties who had been a widow for over twenty years. She shuffled silently, almost ghost like, through the building.

On his way out, he paid a late fee for an overdue Bentley Little novel, and passed a rack which held several magazines and today's copy of the Sutter Springs Press. He picked it up. The pages bent like wet hair in his hands, and he popped them out, scanned the header: "Kids Missing, Police Search Ensues."

Photos of the three kids were positioned across the top. Danny—his eyes innocent and calm, a shock of mop hair, the smile off, his young face giddy. Melissa—her features meek, homely, the expression giving off the gesture that the world had done her wrong, her eyes white, hair darkened and removed from its usual red flame. Sadie—her face serious, the look of self-assurance, her eyes penetrating, the hair not so blonde, but milk-white in the inset.

Mason scanned the article and read a quote from Sheriff T.R. Combs.

"They were last seen May twenty-fourth. We're investigating accordingly and believe this is a runaway situation." He dropped the paper on the rack, turned and tipped his head toward the librarian who was busy stacking books on a rolling cart. He walked into the scorching sun's wrath, his sunglasses slipping at his nose from pearls of newborn sweat.

"Mason!"

The hard-nosed voice split the silence. He spun on his heels and found himself a drug store away from Principal Ardon Wells.

"How've you been?" Ardon extended his hand.

Mason shook and the feel of his friend's hand was soft, gentle, not at all the grasp you would expect from a man who had once split open skulls in Vietnam or hiked up a twelve year old girl's skirt and forced himself inside her.

"Ardon Wells. What's going on?" The yearbook page rubbed against his lower spine. He scratched the area. Across the street, teenagers cruised the sidewalks on rollerblades and he wished he felt their age again.

"Fine, just fine. This summer, I transform from principal to carpenter. The wife wants a guest room, so we're addin' on." He wore a sun hat the color of wheat, a short-sleeve button-up, khakis and loafers, his face speckled with sunlight that tunneled through the tall, wind-blown pines. Over his shoulder, he carried a shirt hooked to a hanger.

"Sounds like a big job," Mason said, and pulled out a cigarette, lit it with a silver Zippo.

Ardon looked at the library and back at Mason, his eyes closed by the sun. "Catchin' up on your reading?"

"Took some overdues back," Mason said. His stomach growled, a twirling sound like that of worms jiggling through his empty gut.

"I was about to eat at Lilly's. Gotta drop off this shirt at the cleaners first, so how about I meet you there? My treat."

It was a quarter after one when Ardon showed. Mason had his third beer before his friend arrived and he took the liberty of ordering two crawfish platters with corn and potatoes at a four-top. They sat underneath a green canopy on the back of Lilly's Lounge that overlooked Main Street, the lunch hour traffic backed up all around them.

Ardon broke the tail off a bright red crawfish, peeled back the shell, ripped out the vein, wiped it through the house's homemade red sauce, and held it on the tip of his finger, as if pin pointing some urgent thought. "It's good to see you again, Mason. It really is." He nudged the tail into his mouth, cleaned his hands on a dampened cloth, and drank iced tea with lemon. "How's life been treating you?"

"Gets better every day. Rachel's twisting my arm to marry her, and I think she'd be worth sacrificing the rest of my life for. She's a good person. Real alive."

A hole was routed out in the middle of the table and a lined trash barrel had been installed there for customers to discard shells. The odor on the porch was that of boiled, seasoned meat.

Mason dropped his styrofoam plate in the hole and ordered another beer, twisting the lime between his lips from the previous one. A cigarette and lighter appeared in his hands as if by magic, and he tilted his head into the sunlight, struck the flame, caught the tip.

"Did you hear about those kids running away?" Ardon asked.

"Just read it in the paper. They went to your school, huh?"

"Yeah. Danny and Melissa are in the fifth grade. Sandy, I think she's in the sixth. Maybe fifth, too. Not sure."

"Sadie," Mason corrected. He shifted his butt in the chair, moved closer, and thumped ashes onto the wooden-planked floor. His voice dived to a slow, drawn-out whisper. "Why do you think they'd run away?"

"Those kids—" Ardon coughed, swallowed, sipped the tea, and set it on a wet napkin, holding up his hand for Mason to wait. "Those kids, nowadays, it don't take much for kids to do something like that. They'll discover quickly the value of a warm bed, food ready at the table, a roof over their heads, and they'll go home. A matter of time." He scratched the corner of his nose, clasped his hands together and tapped one finger atop a fat vein. "In all my years as an educator, I've seen this type of behavior more than once. I tried the same thing when I was thirteen. I asked for a BB gun and my dad, always the joker, said that Santa already bought me a puppy and couldn't take it back to the pet store because they don't take refunds. Said he was short of cash that year."

"Who? Your dad or Santa?"

"Funny. I got mad and stood at the end of the drive with a laundry sack full of fruit and an extra shirt. Stood there for an hour, looking down that stretch of road and scared of what was around the corner, or where the road led. It was cold, I began to shiver, so I went back inside the house, stoked the fire, and told my dad, 'Forget the gun, I'll take the dang dog.'" He spread his hands. "Kids."

"I never tried to run away from home, but I thought about it many . . . many times."

"I'm sure you did," said Ardon, and turned toward the purple clouds along the skyline, his hands together as if praying.

Mason had hated school. It was miserable, almost as miserable as living with his parents. Bad luck tagged his heels for years. He got in trouble for fighting, smarting off, skipping class, and pulling gags like setting off M-80's in the toilet of the teacher's lounge. Once he was expelled when a boy twice his size called him a "white-trash piece of shit" and Mason had arrived at school the following day with a crescent wrench and taken the tool to his head. The assault left the bully with a dislocated jaw, eleven missing teeth, a flattened nose, and a bruised eye that had swollen shut for two weeks. William, his dad, had taken the hospital bill out of his son's flesh with a board he brought home from the plywood plant. "It'll take me three months to pay for that boy's face, you little bastard!" His dad lashed at him so badly that Mason had wished for death. Tears streamed down his young face. His backside, thighs, and stomach were thrashed with bright red welts and he'd yelled out at the top of his lungs in the darkness of that A-frame house on Dalton Street: "Kill me! God!"

Other cutesy antics landed him across from Ardon's desk during those years, too. He'd hot-box cigarettes behind the metal shop, flirt with his teachers, take joy rides on the school lawn mower.

Those heart-to-heart sessions did not make enemies of principal and student. Ardon saw in Mason a little bit of himself. A lost, scared boy living behind the mask of a tough guy.

He knew Mason was tough, and that he'd deliver, if he wanted, and if you pushed him too far.

They had formed a strong bond. Mason told Ardon about his life in hell. How his parents cursed him. How they beat him. Scarred him.

It wasn't until the car wreck that he unveiled the truth behind the matter.

One day, Mason approached him and they sat in the stands at the high school's stadium and watched the cheerleading squad, dressed down in black and orange, practice on the fifty-yard line.

"I've got a secret," Mason said.

"What?"

"Swear to God you won't tell."

Ardon swiped his fingers across his chest, the October chill running a course over his pale face. "Promise."

"I killed them. I killed my parents and they can't hurt me anymore." Mason scissored his fingers. "Cut the brake line on their car. They just flew off the road. Dead."

They were sworn to secrecy never to reveal the truth. Years rolled by and things stayed quiet. But when Mason inherited his grandfather's fortune, he lived in fear that Ardon would betray him, try to blackmail him with the information. Mason was ready. He had no problem putting a bullet in Ardon's head if he talked. Still, his friend stayed true. In fact, one night they went out for a drink and Ardon told him about the Vietnam girl. Told of how he raped her; how good and tight her crotch felt; how he creamed on her face and threatened to snap her neck if she talked. Mason had dirt on his friend, so now things were even.

"Question." Mason squished the lime between his fingers and dropped it into the table's hole.

"Yes?"

"Do you remember what happened to Hailey Carpenter?" Mason asked, his voice earnest. He tapped a ring of salt onto the mouth of his bottled beer and drank.

A stiff shadow appeared over Ardon's face. "The little girl who died two years ago, last Christmas? What about her?" He scratched the corner of his mustache that looked like it had been drawn onto his face with a Magic Marker, averted his eyes. The streets were bright with sunlight that fell through a gap in the sky. They could hear the currents in the black river that flowed behind the building. The expression on his face said it all. Confused, a bit nervous, curious to where the story was going.

Mason crushed his cigarette with the heel of his boot, shot smoke through both nostrils, and folded his arms over his cotton shirt, leaned back in the chair. "She was six years old. Months went by and for some unknown reason—maybe drugs, maybe hysteria, fuck knows—her parents physically abused her. Want me to paint a better picture for you? They spanked her with pieces of plywood, beat the shit out of her with a strap from a Thirty-Ought-Six. Oh, I forgot to mention the time her mother tried to drown her in a dirty toilet." He paused, clicked the Zippo's lid up and down with his thumb. "One night, she stopped breathing. They rushed her to Abbey Medical. Doctors tried everything, but the lacerations were too deep, the hits had come too hard. Hailey Carpenter died that night, two days before her seventh birthday."

Ardon rubbed his forehead. "Why are you telling me this?"

"Rachel used to babysit for the Carpenters. It was before I set her up the massage business. That girl always had to be workin'. It's all she's ever known. She said she wanted to go to college, and I told her I'd send her, but she never pursued it. Her friends told her she didn't need an education since she was dating a millionaire, and that idea just stuck with her, I guess. So, she helped out at the library for awhile, pulled the graveyard shift at the radio station for a year. Then, on her off days, she'd babysit. People around town knew her and trusted her." Somewhere beyond the rough thicket and widespread forest, a car alarm went off, and Mason turned his head toward the sound as if his action would cut the power to the system.

"Rachel was taking care of Hailey the night that little girl died. She told me the Carpenters came home, tried to pay her twenty dollars that she wouldn't accept, and then she left. She got about halfway down the block when she remembered she left her purse. When she went back for it, she told me she heard a lot of shuffling around inside, like running, and Mr. Carpenter yelled 'Shut that kid up!' Rachel found her purse on the front porch swing and looked in the side window. She saw Ms. Carpenter wiping jam off Hailey's mouth with a wash rag. The kid was crying. Rachel just left." The cold, sweet smell from the ice cream stand below them shifted in the wind and an eerie blue tint swallowed the sky as he talked, his eyes now squint and dark. "It wasn't until she got home that she thought it might have been blood on the girl's face, not jam. But she didn't even tell me that part of the story until news of Hailey's death hit the papers the next day." Mason bit his bottom lip, blew air out of his mouth. "It's like when you see the right numbers on the lotto ticket and you're pissed at yourself and say, damn it, I could've picked those numbers. That's how I felt. If Rachel would've told me what she saw, let me know of her suspicion, that that could have been blood on the girl's face, then Hailey Carpenter would have lived."

"It was a sad thing. What ever came of her parents?"

"Her father was sentenced to death down at Angola. The mother got life. I went to the funeral and never even knew her. She was buried in a pink and white casket. In her arms, she was hugging her favorite stuffed animal, a Scooby-Doo doll. It broke me, man. It did."

Ardon moved his hands over the blue and white checked tablecloth. "You know, that puppy Santa brought me got run over by a diesel."

"Figures."

"Mason, if you had known about the abuse, what would you have done?" he asked in an even tone.

The yearbook page crinkled and folded against Mason's back. He stood abrupt, the chair's legs creaking over the planks with the hard sound of wood on wood. He dropped a twenty on the table, set his beer bottle on it. "That crawfish was seasoned just right, wasn't it, Ardon?"

He walked away.

Chapter 14

Sadie got a package of bacon and a half carton of eggs from the walk-in freezer, set the items on a stainless steel table and heated the stove range. It was weird to fry bacon and scramble eggs in the school cafeteria of all places. The whole thing seemed unreal, like a dream.

Melissa sorted out silverware and green plastic trays and got a package of dinner rolls off the lower rack of a free standing bread rack and placed them on a pizza tray to warm in the oven.

Danny set the table and kept watch at the door for any unexpected visitors. Luck smiled on them. Jazz and Hancock had not returned.

When the food was prepared, they sat in the high school section, the same section where they wondered what it felt like to sit where the popular kids ate lunch during those dragging school days. They intruded new area where jocks, cheerleaders, and the rich kids sat. And there was no one here to shoo them away or tell them they weren't good enough, to rant and rave for them to run along and sit with their teacher.

The day had become warm, the golden sun a shiny penny in the sky. Black birds skittered in the courtyard and the wind came in soft, gentle tones, swayed the pines that fenced the cafeteria.

Danny raised a hip off the seat and farted as if to mark his spot.

"Gross, Danny!" Melissa said, her face crumpled into a wince.

"Yuck! I'm tryin' to eat over here," Sadie wailed.

Breakfast was the first thing they had eaten since a shared bag of chips at two a.m. Their trays were empty and the best part was that they didn't have to clean up their mess just yet. If they wanted, they could wait all day and do it when dark settled in.

Melissa lay on her back on the long metal table between Sadie and Danny, with her hands over her stomach, the heel of one shoe on the toe of the other. Her feet swayed from side to side.

Danny buried his head on his arms. "I'm sleepy."

Sadie held her head up by both hands, stared out the huge windows without blinds, into the enclosed courtyard.

"I wonder if they're looking for us," Melissa said.

It was the first time any of them had spoken of the possibility. Had their parents yet noticed they were gone? Were the cops combing the area?

"My mom and Quitman're probably happy about it." Sadie threw one leg over the bench, grasped the hard plastic with her palms. Her leg danced nervously on the ball of her foot.

"My dad's probably throwin' a party for all his friends and thinks I'm still in the tool shed," Danny muttered.

"Why'd he do that to you, anyway?" Sadie asked. "What'd you do?"

"Just didn't feel like mowin' the yard and I told him that. There ya go." Danny stood. He didn't enjoy taking baths. If he had his way, he'd never take them, but he knew he needed one. His clothes stank of his father's cigarette smoke, his skin fumed with sweat, and after eating two servings of scrambled eggs with hot sauce, his breath was rank. "Guys, I'll be back. I need to go to use the bathroom."

Melissa watched him leave, then turned to Sadie. She touched her friend's hand and pulled.

"What're you doin'?" Sadie asked.

"I haven't told you this yet because I can't say in front of Danny." Melissa scooted on her butt across the table's surface and now perched over Sadie like a salivating vulture. "He's a boy. I don't want to say this in front of a boy."

"Does it have something to do with us?" asked Sadie.

"Yes."

"You know the rules."

She did. The rules were that they shared everything. No matter how horrible or disgusting, they shared with each other what happened underneath their parents' roof. No lies, no holding back. Sadie learned that some things that happened between them when they were at home were never spoken of again.

"I know the rules, but I can't say this around him, okay? Do you wanna hear it or not?"

"Do you want to tell me?"

"Promise me you won't tell Danny, and I will. Okay?" She held out her hand. Sadie shook. "It happened last Halloween. Okay? That's how long it's been, that's how long I've kept this to myself. I just couldn't, couldn't say at the time."

Sadie saw the tears wet her friend's eyes and touched her hand. "It doesn't matter, Missy. Take your time, tell me what happened."

Melissa brought her hands from her face, wiped the corner of one eye with the back of her wrist. "So I—I went to my father's office, you know, at work, about a week ago and just bein' in that room lookin' at him made me feel the way I did when he, when that stuff happened in October. The same feeling came over me. I thought he was going to do it again." She suspended her legs in the air, swung them. "I thought I'd forget, or hoped I'd forget, and that's why I never told you because I didn't want you to write it in the notebook, so I kept it to myself and—"

"What the hell happened?" Sadie interrupted, her voice stern.

Melissa's eyes narrowed, her skin flushed with the color of a cherry. She blew a breath upwards that lifted her red bangs. She eyed the door to check if Danny had returned. "It was bad, Sadie. Gina Mackie, she dropped me off at his office. She borrowed her mom's Firebird for the night. It was her thirteenth birthday, so she got to take it out. She was with that guy who picks his nose all the time, what's his name? Ricky Something. Anyway, they wanted me to go to the movies with them, so I went in to get five dollars from my dad and that's when I knew something was bad wrong.

"His door was locked. At least I thought it was. I knocked. I kept knocking 'cause nobody answered, but his light was on and I could hear music playing. Probably off the Internet. He likes to listen to radio stations in Washington and New York just because he can and he makes fun of the DJ's accents, but I tell him they don't have accents, they just talk fast, and he laughed about that, and well, I—I just walked in."

She told Sadie everything. Even threw in the fact that her father had been viewing child pornography.

"That's sick!" Sadie said.

Though Melissa hated Brady for what he'd done to her that day, she still loved him, or wanted to love him, but couldn't help that he was a madman, a depressive, dirty soul living behind a pack of lies that he showed to the world.

"I won't tell, Missy. I won't put it in the notebook, either. Can't even find the thing."

Danny leaned around the opened door. "Hey, y'all! Come check this out."

They went into the hall to find a large, flat dolly. Its surface was decorated with nicks and cuts and drops of paint. Danny sat on it, turned to the girls, his face hyped, smile wide. He pointed down the hall. "I found it in that closet over there. Somebody push me!"

Sadie placed her hands on his back. "Hold tight." She ran with him and pushed off. Danny rolled fast, rotated and dipped down a slight incline between the lobby and principal's office, then slammed into the wall, flew sideways to the hard floor. He jumped up, energetic and happier than they'd seen him in days.

"Whew! That's some fun right there." He waved at them. "C'mon, Sadie. You try it. Hold on to the sides, but watch your fingers. Don't let it get close to the little wheels. It hurts!"

Melissa giggled. "Go on, Sadie. I'll push ya."

For the next hour, they took turns riding the dolly, laughing away the time, and oblivious that a killer was about to rise and hunt down their parents.

Chapter 15

~m~ Rachel got home at four. Mason was in the weight room doing curls with twenty-five pound chrome weights. He felt her footfalls vibrate through the floors at the opposite end of the house and he stood from the bench, his arms tense and throbbing from the work-out. He reached for a towel off a wall hook and wiped the sweat from his face.

In the hallway, he saw her body silhouetted by the late afternoon's pale light. His eyes went from her head to toe and up again, taking in her tanned skin and toned legs, the hourglass shape of her hips, the slight crookedness of her nose, and the swell of her breasts. He touched the tip of his tongue to his lips.

He'd left the notebook on the couch beside two lavender-colored throw pillows and walked over and hid it beneath the marble coffee table before she faced him.

"Hey, baby. Workin' out for me?" Her hips swayed gently in the tight white stretch-pants that punctuated the definition of her body. She kissed his mouth and tasted a salty film of sweat. Her finger curled around his nipple and the indention of his chest. "I like it."

"You do, huh?"

"Oh yeah." She moved her hands around his back, trailed her fingers up his neck, and gripped the sides of his head with both hands, pushed her tongue farther into his mouth. She pulled back. "I hope you don't think you're finished with your workout." She unbuttoned her shirt and pulled it over her head. Her hair fell over her shoulders in a wave, and she shook her head as if she'd just stepped out of the shower. "You're about to sweat some more, cowboy."

Mason touched her stomach, dug his finger into her pants, and pulled them down to her white panties, touched her bare hip. "I've been waiting for you to get here. Why don't you just quit that job and stay home and fuck me all day, every day?"

"I do." Rachel removed her bra and stepped out of the pants. She flicked her tongue across Mason's chest and buried her head in his neck, kissed his skin. "Besides," she said, her breath hot on him, "I don't care how much money you've got. I like to work especially on you."

They dropped on the floor and Mason discarded his shorts, hugged her close, and lay her on the kitchen table. He spread her legs and leaned into her scent and wetness, kissed her. From over the patch of pubic hair, he winked, then stood and put himself inside. They moved slow, rocked back and forth, when Rachel pushed him away.

"What's wrong?"

She forced him to the kitchen floor, straddled him. "Don't say a word until I'm finished." She pouted her lips. "Shhh, baby. Let mommy do her job." Her nails clawed into his chest, and she lowered her head, her hair blocking her face in the motion, and rode him.

Ten minutes later, Mason dressed and plopped down hard on the couch. "Buy groceries?" He put a pillow under his neck.

Wearing panties, she set a plastic bag on the bar that separated the living room from the kitchen and unloaded fresh fruit and canned goods. "I got some of that clam chowder you like so much. Bananas, apples." She picked up a small green basket of strawberries and a pressured can of whipped cream. Lifting both items like a poster girl for a Fifties advertisement, she flashed a winning smile. "Strawberries n' cream for later tonight, you vicious animal you. Didn't feel like cooking, so I thought we'd brown bag it. No onion, no pickle." She threw him a cheeseburger wrapped in crinkled white paper.

He set the food on the coffee table. "Thanks, but I'm not hungry. Ate at Lilly's."

"Oh? By yourself?"

"With Ardon Wells."

"Principal Wells? How's he doing?" Rachel dropped the grocery bag in the trash can, swiped her hands together. The heat of the day had melted away most of her make-up, leaving her face only touched by simple beauty. She sat at the end of the couch and propped her feet in his lap.

"He's fine."

"Mason, did you hear what happened?"

"What?" His voice was absent of emotion. He rubbed the underside of her bare foot.

"Ms. Reba Myers, you know, the lady who owns that women's suit shop? She came in today and said that these three kids were missing. I saw it in the paper, too. Two girls and a boy. Oh yeah, one of the girls? Her father's the manager of that furniture store up past the shopping center in town. Sedwick's."

"Sounds like big news for a small town."

"I hope they're okay. But the cops'll find them." She spread her arms. "I mean, just how far can a few kids get? You know?"

His eyes dropped to the corner of the notebook underneath the pillow and he stopped the argument crawling up his throat.

—⁂—

The abandoned gray halls were eerie tunnels illuminated by the moonlight bleeding through the windows at the end of the corridors that branched off like the invisible arms of a monster.

Sadie smelled faded perfume on her hands, old textbooks stacked in the library, the scent of chalk dust and erasers in the classrooms she passed, coupled with the lingering fumes of disinfectant and window cleaner from Jazz's earlier work.

On either side of her, allowing her to take the lead, were Danny and Melissa, their steps silent, their eyes watchful of each exit door they left behind.

Sadie clicked on the flashlight, flung out the key-ring in her hand, and aimed the beam on the door to the teacher's lounge. She tried several keys before finding the one that worked, then pushed it open. For some reason, she thought an alarm would sound.

They stepped inside. The air in the small room felt different, lighter. It was furnished with a dull green sofa, two winged-backed chairs, a water cooler, a solid block coffee table, and a foldable table nudged against the far wall reserved for fresh-baked foil-wrapped cookies and meat and cheese trays on Friday evenings. It reeked of day-old coffee grains that were piled in a soft, blackened clump in the machine to their left. A wall-mounted television set was bolted high above their heads and a silver portable radio with the name "Glen" written across it in a black marker sat on the hard, multi-colored floor that was tightly knotted and resembled a million curled maggots attached at the sides.

Danny removed his cap and his hair fell out with the lazy motion of wet, black string. "Whoa. The teacher's lounge. I never thought I'd come in here. This is cool!" He wrung drops of water from the cap his mother had given him the morning she'd come home after spending the night in a Peterbilt truck on a shallow dirt road somewhere between Abbey and New Orleans. He smoothed back his hair and turned the cap around on his head, the plastic band etching into his forehead as if he'd been strapped to the electric chair.

On the coffee table, he spotted a change bowl. "Hey, look at the money!" His greedy hands dug into the quarters and dimes. "I'm gonna get a Coke." He hurdled the couch and stood before the glowing red and white machine that gave off a bright glare that fell across the carpet like fresh cream.

"I'm not thirsty," Melissa said. She plopped down on the couch, the stuffed cushions exhaling her weight, and laced her fingers behind her head, crossed her legs.

"Me, neither," Sadie answered, and walked to the metal blinds. She bent a blade with a finger and stared out. The night was clear as tinted glass, the sky the color of chrome flecked with stars. Tree tops danced in a wave of breeze. She placed her palm against the glass and felt the season's warmth, its ferocity seeping into her skin.

Melissa pressed the red button on the remote and the TV flicked to life, its blue/white glare throwing shadows along the corner walls and ceiling.

Danny finished his drink and bought another.

Channel 3 Action News was on. Sadie turned, folded her arms across her chest, and looked up at the screen, her mouth parted slightly as if to issue words, but none came, and her eyes stayed wide, fearful, and for a brief moment, she wanted to avert her gaze, but couldn't.

The brunette reporter had thin lips, a tiny nose, pale cheeks, and too much make-up, her hands trembling as she shuffled papers and eyed the camera as if she were only talking to the kids and no one else in the world. "Three children have been missing since yesterday evening. Eleven-year-old Sadie Bellis, ten-year-old Danny Rampart, and ten-year-old Melissa Giles were last seen leaving school grounds in Sutter Springs yesterday afternoon. Sheriff Combs has devised a search party, but their whereabouts still remain unknown." She clasped her hands before her, hunched her shoulders. In the corner of the screen were their photos.

Sadie mumbled, "Look at that."

The brunette continued: "It is believed that the kids ran away, instead of criminal intrusion as first predicted by investigators. Our thoughts are with the parents."

Danny slapped his hands on the arms of the chair. "Wow! We were on TV! Can you believe it?"

—m—

Rachel slept in pajama bottoms under the ceiling fan, her mouth moving out streams of air.

Mason rolled out of bed, careful not to wake her. The carpet was cold to his feet, the coolness from the vent flow in the center of the room raised his hair. At the dresser he grabbed a pair of jeans, and carried his boots into the bathroom at the end of the hall. He washed his face, dressed, and went to the hall closet, reached onto the middle shelf and pulled down a navy blue towel. Inside lay a nine-millimeter Glock, snug in a black nylon holster. He loaded brass-tipped hollow points into the magazine, pushed it gently into the handle, and shoved it down the back of his waist, the feel at his skin heavy, cold, and brutal. The gun gave him a sense of power that he hadn't felt since he had those garden shears.

Moonlight poured in. Block window shadows crossed the walls as he found his way to the living room and picked up a tight-fitting shirt, put it on. He hurried into his office opposite the exercise room, dropped the local telephone directory on the desk, and fanned through the R's.

He wrote Bobby Rampart's address on a scrap piece of paper.

Outside, he slid his car into neutral, walked it out of the garage. At the end of the drive he hopped in, engaged the engine, hit the lights, and sped off into the green blackness.

He clicked on the radio, turned it up. Shifted into high gear as The Offspring pounded out "Self Esteem." The road was a gray snake that curved and dipped and he couldn't help but smile at the monotonous hum underneath the machine. The vibration sank comfortably into his back and thighs. His mouth was dry and pasty, so he opened a hot Dr Pepper sitting in the cup-holder and downed half the can.

An inner voice told him that he was doing the right thing. The little fucking monster conditioned his mind that Bobby Rampart—the first parent on his list—had to die.

Tonight.

The stereo's digital clock read ten-forty. He gave himself an hour to do the job. He'd be home in bed with Rachel before she knew he'd disappeared.

Turn back now or you never will.

He parked on a dirt road in front of a cattle fence, the road rutted by tractor tires the sun had baked hard into the earth. The Porsche looked like a lopsided Hot Wheels. He put on leather gloves and pulled the gun from his jeans. It seemed to mold to his hands as if it had always been there.

Mason crossed the road and took the sidewalk east toward King Street where the road bent and edged brown garbage bins set up for locals. A cool breeze came in short gusts to his face, slapping the shirt outward as if pushed by invisible hands. His boots crunched on gravel and slid onto smooth concrete. Through the inky black, crickets chirped and fireflies snapped in the silver sheet that enveloped the forests surrounding the only house at the turn.

He stopped at the mailbox, checked the address, then pursed his lips and breathed through his nose. Perched on a tree somewhere behind the house, a hoot-owl rolled off a fluttered call to the night, and when he faced the street, it resembled the slicked, wet skin of a serpent. He pulled back the gun's slide and loaded the chamber.

Inside the A-frame house the living room light burned and the darkened figure of a man strolled through, passing the opened windows, his shadow falling quickly to the shiny grass blades.

Mason moved to the window, kept his distance. A wrestling match was on the TV and Bobby Rampart drank bottled beer in a carpeted recliner straight out of the Seventies.

I broke a glass when I was washing dishes and my dad cut my back with a piece. It was a long cut and I used some Power Ranger band-aids to cover it up. I didn't go to school for two days. Daddy said I was sorry and couldn't do a dam thing right and should never should have been born. He didn't let me sleep in my bed that night. He told me to go out to the garage and sleep with the tools. It was cold and I covered up with a newspaper and some dirty magazines he got hiden in a big box in there. He didn't keep me shut up in the shed. I hate the shed.   Danny

Mason swallowed a hard knot down his throat, his eyes like liquid glass transfixed on the huge man through the tweaked window blinds. He folded his free hand tight into a fist, white knuckles pressing against thick skin. A dot of sweat fell, swam over his temple and the side of his face in a clear line.

So this was the thing he'd read about in the notebook. Danny Rampart's nightmare.

Bobby snacked from a bag of chips. He lifted the bag and munched, bits falling into his full black beard. He twisted off the top of a longneck and took a sip, the hulk of his body like three stacks of tires in the chair.

Mason bypassed the edge of brick, turned, and walked the dirt drive to the side yard. His movement was stealth, a smooth, even motion. He unlatched the gate. It creaked back and tapped the honeycomb fence where a faded "Beware of Dog" sign had been tacked with a staple gun. In the middle of the yard sat a lawnmower, the tool shed he'd read about, and a

1937 Ford pickup without wheels, rusted and overgrown with weeds. On the back porch a fern had fallen from its hanger and overturned, the wood covered with potting soil. A temperature scale read seventy degrees, but Mason felt hotter in his skin. The screen door was secured with a string tied to a hook screwed into the wall. A draft inflated his shirt as he quietly stepped over the threshold, aware of the hard sound his boots would make if he scuffed them just once. It was an old house, but he walked on tile, not hardwood floors, into the dimly lit kitchen. Yesterday's newspaper lay in sections on the bar, the sink was full, the coffee pot empty, but the red light was on, and the air smelled of dirty socks and heat. When he turned the corner he came upon a view of the back of the recliner and the bulk of Bobby's arms, his sight fixed on the bald spot in the center of the man's head. A deer head adorned with Mardi Gras beads hung above the air-conditioner unit and a gun rack on the opposite wall held a .30/06 rifle and a 12-gauge pump.

Mason's hand twitched. The gun now felt heavy in his palm, suddenly a dead, dull weight, pulling at his fingers and bones. He wondered which gun had brought down the buck.

This was one big son of a bitch. Mason remembered seeing the likes of Bobby "Champ" Rampart on TV, cheered on by regional fans every Saturday night during "Tough Man" competitions held in Baton Rouge. He'd never seen him in the flesh.

The man sat lazily in the recliner, one hand on the remote, the other digging at scraps in the chip bag.

Mason's mind went blank.

Leave, don't do it . . . think of sex. It's good, isn't it? Go home. Get some sex from Rachel. You don't have to do this. You can forget about those kids and their problems and go on with your life as if you never found that notebook. You've never done this.

But, he had done this before. Hadn't he?

When he rigged his mother's car so many years ago, it dawned on him that he wasn't there when the actual death took place. It wasn't until he begged Sheriff Combs to take him to the city morgue that he saw their faces and the blood and the gashes in their skin. He wasn't there when they swerved off the road and slammed into a line of trees; didn't see his mother's face split the steering wheel into two pieces on impact; didn't know the pain his father experienced when the man sailed through the windshield and sliced open his neck on a cypress as thick and round as a stone column.

Mason Xavier—abused child turned vigilante—had never really killed.

Sweat coated his hands. His nerves stood on end. He opened his mouth and breathed. It felt good to breathe.

Then he remembered why he was standing in a stranger's house, why he was doing this, and knew there was no turning back.

Danny's pain had brought him here. His own suffering had brought the gun.

Remember what happened to that boy, a voice said. He needs help, he needs escape. He'll never know freedom if he comes back here.

Mason hadn't thought about committing murder since he was thirteen. Over ten years ago. No, that was wrong. There had been the old man and the little girl. That drink two years ago, in 1995. Couldn't forget about them.

Standing in the shadows for what seemed like an eternity, he became jittery. Afraid. Bobby hadn't noticed he was so close, that a stranger was in the house, and he watched the man, deciding where to place a bullet in his body.

A boxing match was now showing on TV, and Bobby was into it, rooting for the fighter in the red shorts.

"Kick some ass," Bobby cheered. He finished off the bag of chips and reached into a small red cooler for another cold one.

Mason reached the living room's border, touched down on the carpet. Swallowed. In a world only he knew, he pushed away the angels in his mind and conjured up the demons from their burial grounds, hardened his stare, and tapped the side of the gun with the tip of his finger, felt the adrenaline pump through his veins, the calmness thrive from his heart that churned into hate, opened the window to his soul—a soul that was black and hollow, the soul he'd had when he was thirteen, the time when he experienced the smell of his own blood, the wickedness of his mother, the terror of his father, and the evil within himself—and he welcomed the rage once again.

You're helping Danny, not hurting him. Remember his face, remember what he wrote. He needs your help. You've got to set him free, or there's no pur-

pose for you. You're his god.

He lifted the cannon and screwed the cold barrel into the man's fat hairy neck. Bobby flinched forward. Mason thumb-cocked the hammer, the sound making an unnerving click that chilled him to the bone.

Bobby dropped his full beer. It landed, fell to the side, and chugged urine-colored liquid into the white carpet, leaving a thick, frothy puddle.

"Stand up," Mason said.

Bobby lifted his arms. "What the—?" He tried to peek over his shoulder.

"Don't look."

"Mister, you don't know who you're fuckin' with."

"Put your hands behind your back."

"I'm gonna make you wish you never walked in here."

Mason pushed his head forward with the gun. "I'll splatter the right side of your face to the left side of that deer head if you don't put your goddamn hands behind your back."

Bobby dropped his arms, moved them into place. "Hey, look, I don't know what you want, but you can take anything in this house. If it's money, I'll give you all I have. Just put the piece down, man. I've got a son for Chrissakes."

Mason said nothing. He bound Bobby with a pair of handcuffs Rachel had gotten from a sex shop in Dallas.

"There," Mason said. "Now we can talk." Bobby was a huge man, towering over him like a giant. "Is there anybody else in the house?" A pause. "Answer me. Is there anybody else in the house!"

"Just me."

Mason unloaded two bullets into the TV screen, the sound a direct and explosive *pop! pop!*, leaving the box nothing but a rumpled hunk of plastic and metal. "Don't talk, do what I say, or I'll bury you," he said.

He led Bobby through the screen door and into the night air. They reached the back porch steps. At that moment, Mason realized with his first step onto the concrete walk to the garage that he'd underestimated his victim. Bobby slammed into him with all his weight. Mason fell in the sun-dried grass and Bobby kicked him in the side with his bare foot. The gun fumbled from his hands, went *clickety-clack* across the concrete. He doubled up in pain. The man knelt, maneuvered into an awkward position to pick it up with his handcuffed hands. Mason tackled him and punched his face. Bones cracked and blood poured from both nostrils. Bobby grunted, stumbled back. Mason retrieved the gun, grabbed his head from behind, positioned the barrel on his earlobe and squeezed off a shot. His ear exploded in a mess of ragged flesh.

Bobby leaned the wounded part of his head onto his shoulder, tried to stop the blood flow. "You . . . motherfuc—!"

"Get up! Walk!" Mason aimed the gun at his face. "Get in that garage and turn on the light."

The place smelled of oil and grease and rust. Bobby dropped to his knees on the oil-stained floor. What was that? What was that sound? Mason listened. Big Bad Bobby Rampart was crying.

Mason lowered the pistol. He lit a cigarette and sat on a red bench in the middle of the room. "You say you got a son, huh?"

Bobby spit up blood. "Go fuck yourself."

"Pretty tough. Guy like you beatin' the shit outta your own son."

"What? You got my son, you son of a bitch?"

"Listen to me. I know what you've done to that boy. Do you think he likes your fist in his face every time he messes up? By his own father?" He waved. "Don't answer that." He sucked on the smoke. "I don't know where he is."

"I ain't never laid a hand on him! Who are you?!"

"Mason Xavier," he answered. "I used to own Xavier Oil Company." He picked up a full can of oil from a nearby shelf, held it in his hands. "Looks like you used to be one of my customers."

Bobby licked his lips with a fat tongue, his head turned downward as if in shame of being under the control of someone else.

"Man, I gotta tell ya. I'm kinda pissed off tonight. I've had a headache all day long to start. Been tired lately. My girlfriend and I are trying to have a baby, and we haven't had any luck there. She wants to get married and just the word scares me. She's a wonderful person, though, ya know? What do you think? Think I should marry her?" He poked his pinky in his ear and pulled out wax flakes, flicked them away. "Yeah, I think I will." He thumbed the gun's safety on and off as though he were bored, moved from the bench and sat on a stool with a cushion secured with gray duct tape. "I admit I'm a little disappointed in you, Bobby. You struck me as more of a man, not some jerk-off who gets off on abusing his son."

"What do you want, mister?"

Mason dropped the cigarette, crushed it with his boot, and stood. "I heard you usually lock Danny in the shed for punishment. I'd do that to you, but you'd bust your way out. You're bigger, you're stronger than him. That shed wouldn't hold you for one minute. It'd be like I never showed up tonight, and I've got to do something. I hate to sound like a spokesman for a child abuse foundation, but I've got to make you understand that you're not supposed to hurt . . . little kids. I've put a lot of thought into this, Bobby. It's not right what I'm gonna do, but it doesn't look like you're capable of learning from your mistakes. You don't seem to understand that hurting your son is wrong. If Danny comes back, I'm sure you're gonna bitch at him for something, hit him when he doesn't deserve it, hurt him. Hurt him bad." Mason made a smacking sound with his lips, pinched the sweat along the bridge of his nose. He might as well have been playing a hand of poker. "So, here's what I thought about doin'." He grabbed the back of Bobby's head, twisted him around. "How about I look inside your head and see what makes sick motherfuckers like you tick? I'll just put your face on that table saw over there and split your skull wide open."

Bobby's chest pumped, his eyes widened, his breath shot out in short, fast gasps. "I'll give you anything. Anything."

Mason snapped his fingers. "Stay with me Bobby. C'mon, you with me on this?"

"This can't be—you can't do this. You can't do this! You can't do this!"

Mason looked at the man's face pierced with sweat and etched with fright. "Which gun did you use to kill that deer in your living room?"

"Huh?"

"I saw a Thirty-Ought-Six and a 12-gauge shotgun in there. Which one did you use to kill the deer?"

"I—I didn't use a gun. Bow. Killed it with a Mathews Bow."

"What kind of arrow?

"What?"

"What kind of arrow did you use?"

"Uh, it was uh, a Beaman ICS Carbon arrow."

"Impressive."

Mason whacked him in the head with the butt of the gun, and the big man was down.

Chapter 16

Dawn broke over the town in a pink splash, the sky streaked with flames when, at six-fifteen, authorities were dispatched to the Rampart residence.

Sheriff Combs stood behind the yellow crime tape at the murder scene. A light breeze shuffled his crew cut, massaged his scalp. He stole a glance at the body, the neck cut to white bone, blood and bits of muscle splattered in hair, within the clothing, along the ground, gathered on the tips of the table saw in a black circular stain. The pungent smell coasted on a cool wind, causing others to cover their noses with their shirt collars.

When paramedics covered Bobby's mutilated body with a white sheet, it resembled raspberry swirls in vanilla ice cream. They loaded him onto a gurney and placed him in the back of the ambulance like a piece of furniture.

Without having to turn and face him, Terry saw in his peripheral vision the town's coroner, Gary D. Self, approach—a thin man with long hands corded with blue veins, a flat face, sunken dark eyes, with the lame, hunched walk of a bull rider after being thrown onto a dusty arena floor.

A toothpick hung out of the middle of his mouth and he moved it with his unseen tongue. "Awful thing, ain't it?" Gary said.

"It's big," Terry answered. "Real big." He folded his arms over his chest and his badge tilted against his sleeve. The paramedics closed the ambulance doors, and drove away, red and white lights flashing, the siren rising to a high moan.

"Whaddaya got so far, Fats?"

"From what I gather, there weren't no witnesses. Some kid, Kyle Fergusen, came out this mornin' to let Bobby work on his truck, then called us. Said he puked twice before he reached the phone." He spit on the gravel and the saliva string whiplashed against his chin. He wiped it off with the front of his wrist. "This ain't good at all, lemme tell ya."

"Who do you think would do such a thing, Terry?"

"Bobby did have his enemies. Drug runners, panty chasers. Who knows, he could've owed money. But if I know anything about a drug ring, if they want your debt, and you ain't willin' to pay it, they'll just put a bullet through your chest and call it even." He motioned with his opened hand at the garage. "They wouldn't have done this. Cuttin' a man's head damn near off takes too much time and effort. Screen door's kinda battered. There's spots of blood on the walk over there and his shirt's torn at the sleeve. That tells me he was forced out of the house. Somebody just yanked him into the garage. Two, maybe three somebodys at that because ol' Bobby ain't no Boy Scout. In the livin' room, we found a glass frame busted where it looked like a picture was taken out."

"Sweet Jesus. His son's still missin' on top of that. I can't believe it."

"Forensics'll finish up," Terry said, and ducked under the yellow tape. He dusted his Stetson and walked to his patrol car. "Thanks for comin' out, Gary."

The coroner gave him a friendly salute, turned to the blood on the metal walls and dirty concrete, then shook his head.

—⁂—

Bobby Rampart's murder made all the news and the front page of the Sutter Springs Press. The header read "Local Man Slain, Killer Unknown." His photo stared out ominously from the cover, his full black beard needled with silver, his cold, hard eyes staring into space, his crooked nose that had been broken in a barroom brawl during his youth dotted with wide acne scars.

Mason folded the newspaper and tucked it underneath the champagne leather seat. He held another photo of Bobby in his hands that he swiped last night. The big man stood beside the gutted deer he'd stuffed and hung on his wall, the bow in one hand, a satisfied look on his face. Mason lifted it into the sunlight, bent it with his fingers, and tore it in half, the smooth paper making a cutting sound. He lay the two pieces under the seat, then stepped out of his Porsche, hooked the key ring around his middle finger and flipped the set in his hands as he entered a room full of spiced steam.

Rachel stood over a skillet frying turkey bacon, a rather healthy choice as opposed to their usual diet of medium rare rib-eye steaks and cheeseburgers loaded with grilled onions and sliced peppers. She flipped the strips with a fork and greeted him with a wet kiss.

"Hungry for a late breakfast?" she asked. Barefoot, she shifted her hips to the sound of Bush's "Glycerine" on the stereo. She wore a white exercise bra that heaved her bubbled chest into a tempting display and her gray sweat shorts were cut off at the tops of her thighs to show muscle definition.

"I'm starvin', I'll eat anything." He placed the flat of his hand on the small of her back and moved to the bra's strap, stretched it with two fingers, and let it fly.

"Ow! You butt." She elbowed his side.

He planted his lips on the Black Widow tattoo etched into her bare shoulder and tasted her salty skin. On the counter he grabbed a handful of day-old popcorn that hadn't been discarded, and popped a piece in his mouth.

Restless. *You took a life.*

He opened the back door to the afternoon air. The smell of pine and distant wood smoke drifted through the open porch to greet his nostrils. The day was golden bright, the orange sun encased in a dark red ribbon blanketing the woodlands at the edge of his property, the light glinting off the treetops in lines. Rachel had left the cordless phone on the porch swing and he sat beside it, picked it up. Maybe he'd call the movie listings in Abbey and take Rachel out tonight.

He munched from his hand and thought of Danny Rampart. The kid would be happy now. His life, normal. He remembered the expression of agony on Bobby's face. It was a result of the darkness that was his mind that had erupted in the night that was his friend.

The phone rang. He answered it.

"Hello?" He pushed off and lifted his feet.

"I know what you've done."

He touched the hardwood floor with the tips of his shoes to brake the swing's glide. His eyes transfixed on a hawk soaring through the puffed, milk-white clouds, as if, for a moment, to forget what he'd heard, or pretend he didn't hear it at all. "Who is this?"

"You killed Bobby Rampart," the voice said.

Mason's brow dipped to a straight line. He turned to see Rachel patting the grease off the bacon strips with a paper towel. His tone grounded to a harsh, solid wave. "Who is this?"

"Meet me underneath the Sandstone Bridge at ten o'clock. Be alone."

He pulled the handset away from his ear and stepped down the porch. A hollow shiver ran up his back to his neck. He knelt at a blooming rose bush Rachel had planted in the spring. He cut a stem with his pocketknife and carried it inside.

"What's this for?" she asked, placing a grease-splattered spatula on a paper napkin.

"You're beautiful. You deserve beautiful things."

"You're sweet, baby." She pecked his cheek that was now crisscrossed with light red lashes where it looked like he'd been slapped by broom whiskers. Her fingers caressed his skin. "Are you okay? Is there something the matter?"

Nerve rashes, baby. Don't worry your pretty little head over it.

He went into the laundry room and dug his black shirt out of the dirty hamper.

Who had called? And why?

Rachel stopped him at the door, her hand on his arm. "Where're you going? Mason? Don't you want to eat?"

His foot just outside, without facing her, he said, "I'll eat when I get back, Hon. Keep it warm."

He got in the Porsche and drove seventy miles-an-hour to the city's limit, then slowed, tried to collect his thoughts. He didn't recognize the voice on the other end of the line. Who could it have been? He was careful.

No one had seen him. At least he didn't think so. He'd been in and out, quick and safe—a ghost. No one knew of his little visit to Bobby's house last night and the thought of someone discovering the truth made him uneasy, even scared, and he wished he had the name of the person who threatened him.

He drove around for three hours, thinking. He did his best thinking when he was behind the wheel–couldn't think when Rachel was home. He had to be alone, sort things out, weigh the odds against him, fully understand his actions and how it would affect his life, and hers.

Whoever had called had not asked for money, so why the late-night visit? He decided it'd be best to carry his gun, just in case.

At six o'clock, he returned home. He exercised in the weight room, standing directly under a vent that shot out slabs of fresh, cool air. In the mirror, he watched his skin and muscles contract as he curled five sets of sixty pounds, sweat and heat rolling into his right eye.

Rachel walked in to the sound of Stevie Ray Vaughan blasting from the portable radio in the corner, folded her arms at her chest, and leaned against the wall.

"So, where'd you go, or should I ask where you're going? The casinos? Fly off to LA and visit your thirty-six-year-old cousin who's still tryin' to get that big break for the next Spielberg movie?" Again, she wore no makeup and in the white light, her tanned face took on a natural flare. "Talk to me."

"Rachel, what's your problem?"

"My problem? Look at you. Every time you take off like that, you stay gone for two or three days. So which is it? The casinos? LA? Colorado? You know, you could ask me to tag along. Is there someone else?" She pushed herself from the wall, her entire body telling him that play-time had come to an end as she swung one hip to the right and froze. "Well? Is there?"

He set the barbells on the floor, downed a cup of water, sent a sweat-soaked towel wrapped around his neck sailing to the other end of the room, and stopped before her, his eyes to hers, his face only inches away. "Why would you say something like that?"

"I have to know. Is there? Are you seeing someone else?"

"No. I'm not, okay?"

"I worry, baby. I can't help it."

"You on the rag?"

"Don't be such an asshole."

"We've talked about this, Rachel."

"I don't mean to be like this. If you say you're not, I believe you."

"Then why do you keep doubtin' me? Why keep bringin' it up? I've got friends in town. Ever thought I might be out drinkin' with the boys? Just takin' a drive to relax? Why is it when I stay gone, you think I'm bangin' some girl?"

She fidgeted with her hands, her lips quivered. "I don't know, it just comes to me. That you want somebody else a little prettier, a little less crazy at times. I think about it a lot, and I know I shouldn't, but it's there. What can I say? I get these feelings. I don't want to lose you."

Her eyes still caught in his hold, he placed his hands on her hips. "Rachel? I love you. Look at me, please. And listen. Don't hear, listen." He lifted her chin with one finger. "I love you. You are everything to me and nothing or no one's gonna come between that. I don't know how I can explain it better than to show you. We'll get married as soon as you want, baby. I do love you and I want to be yours for the rest of my life. You have got to know that, and believe it. There's no one else, okay?"

She closed her eyes and hugged his neck, kissed his lips, and held him close as if he could walk out of her life at any minute. "Thank you, Mason."

—m—

The sun was still blazing when the kids retreated to the teacher's lounge to watch television. Sadie and Danny had eaten corndogs with mustard out of a microwave, but Melissa claimed she was sick to her stomach, and spent half the afternoon in the bathroom. When they asked what was wrong, Melissa replied, "Something I ate," which was a lie.

Sadie could see it in her face. "You're worried about what your folks might do to you if you get caught and the police send you back home, huh?"

"Is it bad to think that?" Melissa asked. "I'm not worried, Sadie. I'm scared to death. My momma, she might hit me again, and my dad, I don't even want to think about what he'd do."

"Don't think about it. Let's watch some TV."

Danny plopped down hard on the winged-back chair, remote in hand, and turned it on the same channel from last night—*Action 3 News*.

The brunette was there again, a touch of rouge on her cheeks this evening, her lips glossy in the camera light's brilliance. "Tonight's top story is that of a slaughtered man found at his home earlier this morning where Casey Darrel takes us now." The picture transformed its view to Danny's front yard, the honey combed fence, the rear of his dad's truck, and the white garage outlined in yellow tape. A small inset of Bobby appeared on screen to the right of the reporter's head. He was a perfect picture of a menace to society in a black muscle shirt, his armpit hair like copper wire curling up to his red, freckled biceps, and zombie eyes that stared at nothing.

"Thanks, Sheryl. In addition to the missing child, Danny Rampart, it seems another hardship has befallen those who reside at 138 King Street. Bobby Rampart, father of the child, was found dead at approximately six o'clock this morning. Authorities say his body had been badly injured with severe lacerations, and that there is possibility of criminal activity. However, there are no suspects at this time."

Danny clicked it off. The room fell silent.

Melissa took in a fast breath that sounded like air being let out of a tire peg with the tip of a knife, and her hands flew to her mouth, covered it, as she dropped her feet to the ground and hunched forward into her own lap.

"Danny?" Sadie asked, her voice warm. She reached out, touched his shoulder.

"My dad," he whispered. "My dad's gone." His face leaked of all energy, the color turning to a light pink. Splotches of red grew into the skin of his neck and cheeks. He behaved indifferently, as if he'd been told he could not go on the class field trip to Six Flags because he didn't get a signed permission slip and had to sit with the freaks in Mr. Kindell's class and read comic books he'd read before, and listen to the kids talk about the way he dressed, how poor he was, why his neck hair looked like baby duck feathers, and how come his breath always smelled awful.

His heart rolled and dropped, then jogged into a frenzy that was familiar when he got scared. "I gotta go," he choked, and dashed into the hall, hooked his hand around the corner, and drove his legs as fast as he could, his sneakers squeaking on the buffed floor—the way he did when he tried to outrun his dad before a trip to the old tool shed.

He disappeared into the darkness, and Sadie's voice trailed him like a lost, frightened child's in a windstorm. "Danny!"

He ran from his fear, from his dad, from himself.

—⁂—

For dinner, Terry and Monica ordered take-out from Paul's Pit Barbecue. The day's activities showed on his face. His eyes had grown tired and red, his head bombarded with questions.

Who killed Bobby Rampart? Where were the kids? Was there a connection? He didn't think so. Forensics came back with nothing. The murder had been messy, but their man had been clean, having left no prints, no clues.

Night fell, and stars blinked in the onyx pool. They sat in Monica's white Monte Carlo at the end of her drive listening to bullfrogs croak on Bayou Sans.

Terry leaned his elbow on the armrest, drumming his fingers on the rubber that lined the door. His button-up was opened at the neck and a flurry of chest hair peeked out. In the passenger seat Monica admired her nails, rotating her hand in the carport's yellow light.

"You haven't said much since dinner. It's what happened to that guy, isn't it? It's getting to you."

"It doesn't make sense why the man had to *die* the way he did, or even die for that matter." He cut the engine and peered through the windshield at the gate that bordered her back yard and swimming pool illuminated with phosphorous light. "The people in this town will expect me to bring someone to justice and they don't care if it's the wrong person. They just want to see something done. Those kids are still missin'. Haven't had any luck there." He shook his head and bit his bottom lip, ran a finger over the steering wheel. "Can't find a duck when it dives under water. When and where this guy pops up again, who knows? That's what's so hard for me to understand. No one saw this coming. There were no witnesses, so I don't have a suspect. Next time, though, I'll be ready."

"You're serious? You think it'll happen again?"

"It's a feelin'. You do this as long as I have, that feeling comes like a hurricane out of nowhere. Slaps you in the face. I'm almost sure it'll happen again. You see, Bobby dealt in illicit drugs. Meth, Mary-Jane, coke. There could be a number of people who wanted him dead. But not like that. A junkie would've just shot him in the back of the head, not tear his spine out with a saw blade. That's why I think it's someone else."

"Okay, Terry, that's enough. I just ate." Monica placed her hand over her stomach.

Inside, she poured two cups of coffee. They sat at the kitchen table under a lamp with a burned bulb, the dimness covering Terry's face. She took a sip. "Is this what it was like with Linda? The cop life?"

"What do you mean?" he asked, the mention of his ex-wife's name generating a picture of her in his mind and a secret hurt he couldn't place.

She shrugged. "I see how you push everything away in order to follow through an investigation. Like that time with Rodney Simmons a few years back. You were up to your chin with that one. No time for anything else."

"I wasn't even with you then, Monica. Besides, this is different."

"No it isn't."

"I've got a killer on my hands. And we're not talking about your garden-variety hold-up man who accidentally shot the clerk for fifty bucks cash outta the register. This man is a thing. Cold. Ruthless. Like something out of a horror movie. Rodney Simmons was a drunk bent on revenge. There is a difference."

"Linda felt ignored, Terry. She was alone and—"

"You don't have to say that. I know why she divorced me. No use pulling off the scab with one hand and dancing with table salt in the other."

"I didn't mean it that way."

"What did you mean? That I cared for the job more than her?"

"I don't want to argue." She picked up her coffee and moved to the counter, set the cup on a saucer.

"Monica, Linda's a part of my past. She couldn't handle my job and sometimes, I didn't think I could. The late nights, the fact that I could be put underground just by pulling a routine traffic stop, or that I wasn't getting the best pay—those were things she couldn't adjust to." He pushed his palms out. "But I was elected to this position, and it's the only thing in my life that I know I can do well."

She held the coffee cup with both hands, gazed over the rim. "Are you sayin' a man must have an identity?"

"That's exactly what I'm sayin'. A real man doesn't go through life wondering why he's here, or what he's supposed to do. They just know."

Monica moved her finger to her chin. "Want to know what I see? I see a man who's suffered a long, flustered relationship. A man who does the best that he can in whatever life throws his way. I see a man who loves me." She smiled, her lips faded a ripe red. "But I also see a man who needs to put his priorities in place."

"Like what?"

"T. R., we're not getting any younger, ya know. I understand why Linda worried so much. She loved you. I do, too. A lot. You're almost at retirement age. So, come re-election time, whatever decision you make, I'll back you up. If you give it up to go fishing every day, then so be it. If you stay in, if you believe you must have that title because a man's got to have an identity, well, just be careful. For me."

"You're a good woman, Monica, with a big heart. For the next few weeks, this whole thing'll swallow me." He covered her soft hand with his, and squeezed. "I just pray you'll hold out longer than Linda did."

Chapter 17

They found Danny huddled and shivering behind the same water fountain he used to hide from the janitors earlier this morning, his knees pulled into his chest, arms locked around them. His face was red and dirty, his eyes soaked. He wiped one eye with the heel of his hand as the girls gathered beside him.

"Danny, we're so sorry. It'll be okay," Sadie said, fingering a long wave of hair from his cheek. "Do you need something? Maybe to eat?"

"Just go away. Leave me alone." He gulped, turned his face, and stared at the gray-painted cinder blocks that formed the wall, trying with all his strength to control the fear inside.

"We'll be in the teacher's lounge if you need anything."

Danny remained silent, his only defense. Melissa stormed away, her footfalls echoing throughout the main hall. Sadie followed.

At the corner, she caught up to her friend, and pinched the back of her shirt. "Where're you going?" She hooked a thumb over her shoulder. "The TV's back there."

"I'm gettin' my bike. I wanna go home."

"Missy, do you hear what you're saying?"

Her voice was weak, but direct. "Someone killed Danny's dad. What if the same thing happens to my parents? To yours?"

"Why in the world would you think that?"

"I don't know, I really don't. I've got this feelin' somethin' bad's gonna happen to them is all." She walked toward the metal doors.

"Melissa, wait! Don't leave."

"Why should I stay?"

"We're all in this together. C'mon! Don't break up the team."

"What team? Me, a boy who wets his bed, and a best friend who bosses me around? I can't believe you talked me into this. Runnin' away from home was a dumb idea." She pushed open the door.

The muggy air fell to their faces, lifted their hair, as they took the steps two at a time to the graveled lot.

"If you think it was so dumb, then why'd you come along?" Sadie asked, keeping with her friend's hurried steps.

Melissa walked on, her arms swinging in the fashion of a business-woman late for an appointment.

"Then go on! Go back home and let 'em beat ya up. Hitcha with belts and let your dad come in your room and let him do what he likes! We don't need you!"

The breeze ceased on the low ground and rose to the treetops, its sound rhythmic and calming. Melissa retreated up the sidewalk, her hands opening and closing at her sides. Her face was pinched, tightened, the result of quick anger.

"Take that back, Sadie!"

"I ain't takin' it back." She popped at the gum in her jaw and spit it out as a farmer would a wad of black chew.

"Take it back!" Melissa's demand shot through the shadowed hillside painted by the blue neon moon. She pushed Sadie's chest.

Sadie stumbled back, caught her balance, and rushed into the darkness, grabbed Missy's hair, and yanked. Melissa screamed, clawed at her arms, tried to pry the vice-grip hands from her scalp. She spun around, swung, and caught Sadie's tender cheek with an opened palm.

"Stop it!"

The girls froze, Melissa's hand underneath Sadie's thigh, and Sadie's hand laced through a mop of red hair.

Danny stood on the top step, his hair blowing away from his eyes.

"Don't fight. I'm okay now, okay?"

They exchanged glances, set each other free. In that moment between holding their breath and lashing out once again for the last hit, they averted their gaze, looked at Danny, and didn't speak as they returned inside the building.

An hour later, Sadie lay awake spoon-shaped on a beanbag. Danny slept beside her, but Melissa had chosen to stay on the other side of the room, underneath the chalkboard, deep in dreamland. She didn't think Melissa had been serious about leaving, but the more she thought about it, the more she accepted the possibility, and with one of them gone, especially if one of them talked, these beginning days of freedom would be no more.

—ɷ—

A light mist rode the air, whirling to the earth in light bags of spray. Oak branches hung overhead preventing the moon's light from fully penetrating the silver tongue of slicked road, and in the distance where the town touched the horizon, forked lightening split the sky.

Mason hit his high beams and took the Devil's Elbow, headed west toward the Sandstone Bridge.

He straightened the wheel, shifted down to fourth, and pulled off onto a red dirt road cropped with tall weeds that spiraled down to the muddy bank of the river. Spanish moss sagged on a cypress tree at the bank, and tied to a limb that stretched over the water hung a fat knotted rope kids used to swing out into the Beauvoir River during summer. He bypassed the tree and all the memories that came with it. Those were the days when he and his friends would throw tailgate parties and light bonfires using wooden crates and gasoline; the sound of southern Rock streamed out of car door speakers, and truck beds held chests filled with crushed ice and canned beer; there had been whiskey and tightly rolled joints; country girls gathered 'round, the kind who wore Daisy Dukes and spit without wiping their mouths and didn't care if you rubbed on their tits before you drove them home after curfew.

It was before Rachel, before the money. He smiled for memory's sake, then put it out of his mind and drove underneath the bridge.

Principal Ardon Wells's white Malibu was parked on the embankment where graffiti and "FUCK YOU" and "I Love Jaime Forever" were spray painted on the time-worn concrete.

Mason engaged the emergency brake. The Porsche bobbed forward, crunched the gravel beneath the wide tires.

Headlights covered Ardon's face, blinding him, and he raised his hand in an effort to shield his eyes.

The river was a dark sheet of rippled glass. Crickets sang out and bull-frogs hiccuped in the brush. Mason dragged his cowboy boots over the salty ground. A coarse wind rose and fell around them, pushing the currents flapping into the bank down the boat launch to their left. Half of Mason's face was lit by the concord of yellow and white light from the moon and his car. He drew on the cigarette, the fiery tip reddening his hardened yet childlike features. Those midnight black sunglasses spoke only one word, a word Ardon could not see but could definitely feel in the air between them.

"You're angry," Ardon said.

Somewhere off in the distance, lurking in the woods, a panther cried out, splitting the night, penetrating their ears with its intensity. Neither flinched.

Was it so difficult a puzzle, such a surprise that Ardon had discovered his plight? After all, at yesterday's lunch, the way Mason had discussed the kids' disappearances and then Hailey Carpenter's short life, he might as well have written his plans on an interstate's billboard.

Ardon stood still, his head cocked up, the pleated khakis shaking with a light breeze. Overhead, a diesel rolled across, rattling the bridge's beams and physical structure, the sound like a thunderstorm in their heads. He did not offer his hand. Instead, he kicked a bed of rocks with his loafers, scattered them over naked dirt, thinned his lips and stared at his shoes, hands hanging on his hips. "Why'd you do it, Mason?"

He licked his lips, feeling the rough edge of them, faced an empty trailer on the boat launch across the river. If he'd planned to use his gun, that idea was gone. Someone on the river would hear it. "Ardon, you know I've never had any regrets for anything I've ever done. You're one of my closest friends, almost like a father figure. But you know this. It's no surprise."

"I know your past. There's no need to dig up a dead horse, and that horse is dead like Elvis." He lifted his arm, moved the sleeve over his wrist and checked his watch. "It's just after ten. I should be asleep right now. At home in bed with my wife, comfortable. But I called you out. I must have your reasoning on this. You have got to tell me why you did this."

"Do you have a tape recorder? Are you recording our conversation?" He spread his arms wide. "This is a secluded place, but my trust is thin. Trust, as far as I'm concerned, is a four-letter word. Could be fuck. You wired?"

"That's an insult. If I wanted to turn you over to the cops, then to a judge who would do anything in his power to put you behind bars, and then finally to a jury who would love to barbecue your ass, I would've done it years ago!" Ardon's face jiggled as he talked, the knob of muscles moving within his cheeks, a red sheet embedded underneath the skin that became brighter with the raise in his voice. "You murdered Bobby Rampart in cold blood. You've got more than two deaths on your hands now, son."

"Don't call me son."

"Why'd you do it?"

He pulled out the notebook from under the driver's seat, threw it at the car. It slid across the hood, came to rest under the tip of a windshield wiper. "Take a look. Speaks for itself." A tight, curled smile stretched the corners of Mason's lips. He stared at the ground, brought his fingers in sight and picked at a nail. "Seems like I'll be busy for the next few weeks."

Ardon scanned the entries, looked at the three photos from the newspaper taped inside the cover. Shuffled his feet. "I see. These kids have written down all the things their parents have done to them, you found it, and now you're taking justice in your own hands." He slapped the notebook on the hood, lifted his hands. "Jesus, man! Are you crazy? Who do you think you are? Charles Bronson? Didn't our talks all those years ago feed your brain some leveled amount of intelligence?"

"What, now I'm a fool? You gonna turn me in?" He got the notebook, pitched it through the Porsche's opened window.

"Don't be so defensive."

"Then don't lecture me."

"I'm not gonna argue here," Ardon said.

"Remember when you told me about how you killed all those gooks in Vietnam? Men, women, children, it didn't matter. You were there for blood.

Nothing to you but warm bodies with no names, no faces. Just another target. Don't tell me about murder. You are a murderer."

"If it's one thing I don't have to do, it's having to explain my military duties to my country because you think it may justify what you did to that man."

"In the notebook, read page four. It's when Danny comes home, goes to sleep, and his dad wakes him with a beer bottle. Exciting scene. Only wish it was a movie. It's not. It's real. Those kids are real and so is the pain they went through. Yeah, I killed Bobby Rampart. The man deserved it." He thumped the cigarette into the river.

"I only wish what you did wasn't real." Ardon shook his head, his eyes the color of stars. "It's got to stop. The cops have no leads, you can get away. Don't pursue this because you think you owe these kids something, like some kind of make-believe hero you wished you had when you were their age. Don't you see, Mason? I'm trying to help you. What you're doing is too big of a risk. You've got too much to live for, all the money in the world, a beautiful girl. Why would you want to make a crap shoot out of your life? The cops'll catch you, and when they do, all that's gone. And for what? For doing something that doesn't need the attention. Social services, adoption agencies. With enough proof, those kids can live in a safer environment. Their parents will be sitting ducks. They won't be able to do anything once the state intervenes. Let the authorities handle this. Don't become a vigilante, and man, God in Heaven, you killed him. Don't you have any regret? Aren't you feeling anything?"

Mason lifted his head, took off his sunglasses, wiped them with the bottom of his shirt, and replaced them. "I feel tired right now. Didn't get much sleep last night."

"I'm serious."

"Satisfied. Is that what you want to hear? I'm satisfied that I released a kid who lived in fear of his dad. I'm glad I put that man's head on that saw blade. I'm glad I beat him in the face with a crescent wrench and kicked him in the balls with these boots. I'm glad I ran his skull into the blade like plywood." His face opened, alert. "I'm gonna do it again. There are more people on my list and when I find them, they're gone. If you're my friend, if you're my true friend, you'll agree that something has to be done. Just keep quiet until I'm finished."

"Is that a threat?"

"It's whatever you want it to be." He opened the car door, sat, and started the engine, a clear puff of exhaust pumping out the twin pipes as he shifted into reverse.

"You're not normal, Mason. I thought after your parents' death, the hate you felt was gone. Why is it still there?"

"Hate stays with you," he said, looking through the opened window that framed his head, the line of his mouth hard and straight, his facial expression black as rain in a thunderstorm. "Love takes work."

"Don't leave, Mason. I'm not finished talking!"

The Porsche left a wide dust cloud in its wake. It crawled up the slanted road to the highway, leaving Ardon standing in the gravel lot, his thoughts jumbled and tossed in his mind.

It had come to this. The student he'd once tried to help had again summoned a certain evil that haunted his childhood, and he was using it to shed the blood of strangers.

Chapter 18

The following morning, Lisa Giles burst through her husband's office door in a puffy blue blouse, black jeans, and turquoise sandals that wrapped around the top of her feet and ankles, her hair brushed back in a long brown wave. She opened a newspaper, held it up to show him the front cover.

"Have you seen this?"

Brady took off his reading glasses, lay them on a manila folder on top of the cleaned desk, rubbed his eyes with a finger and thumb. Sleep deprived, irritable, and having gone two weeks without making love to her—because she didn't want it—he looked vaguely like the people represented in alcohol abuse commercials; the skin flared, cheeks sand-papered, eyes droopy, the whites cut with plump red veins. "Yes. I heard about it."

"Why didn't you tell me?"

"I stayed here the night."

"I can see that. I tried to call, you couldn't answer?" Her fists automatically rose to her hips and the muscles in her neck twitched. She even pinched her earlobe. "Brady, if you're going to stay on the Internet all the time, the least you can do is get service at home. At least I'll know where you are." She pointed to the newspaper, pinpointed Bobby Rampart's photo.

Brady sipped at a cup of coffee that had lost its steam, and stared at the far wall.

"That man's son is one of the missing children. This might have something to do with Melissa. Haven't you even thought about the welfare of your own daughter? She's out there. Someone has her, something's happened to her, and it doesn't look good from where I'm standing."

He wiped his mouth with his hand, leaned back in the chair, and crossed one pleated pant leg over the other. "I have thought about her. What do you suggest? What can we do? Sit and pray is the only thing I can think of. I was out last night. I drove around looking for her again while you were at home wondering what should be done. And, as you can plainly see, I didn't find our daughter. Hopefully the cops will have better luck."

"These small-town cops couldn't find their head if it was buried in their ass."

"Lisa!"

"Brady, I am angry. I'm having PMS and I haven't eaten a decent meal since Missy's disappearance. I don't know what to do anymore." Her eyes filled with tears, her voice a mere squeak. "Where is she? Where's our little girl?"

He went to her, wrapped her in his arms, and hugged her close, ran his hand through her hair. His fingers massaged her neck, tapping a flat sponge of muscle. His chest expanded, his heartbeat in rhythm with hers. "I know you're scared and I don't know what to say to make you feel better. What happened to that guy they found yesterday, he was a bad man, Lisa. Don't let your mind go overboard. It has nothing to do with Missy. I have a feeling she's fine." He pressed his head to hers, kissed her skin and smelled a heavy coat of base. "Let's get breakfast. You need your energy."

They walked out of the office, past furniture-filled boxes stacked to the ceiling, a forklift, empty wooden crates, under the high air ducts, to the plastic flaps that led into the showroom, and out the door to her car.

He opened the passenger door for her, helped her in, got behind the wheel, and before he started the engine, somewhere, far off, he thought he heard the sound of police sirens, and a gang of chill bumps exploded across his skin.

—∽—

Anne Mase called in sick to work, dressed, and called Terry at his office. "Sheriff Combs speakin'."

"Sheriff? This is Anne Mase. Have you found out anything?" She looked out a window at blackbirds playing in freshly planted grass.

"We're working on it ma'am. Haven't come up with nothin' yet, but you'll know when we do."

She shook her head, shot Quitman a disgusted look. Empty beer cans were strewn at his feet, his legs hanging over the couch's arm. She picked up two of the cans, angry with his lack of cleanliness. "Sheriff, this can't go on. I gotta know what's happened to my daughter. She could be dead for all I know and this sittin' around waitin' shit ain't helpin' me none. I gotta know somethin'."

"I know you're frustrated, Ms. Mase, but we've got units searchin' the whole town."

"That guy Bobby Rampart—his son's one of them. Did you know that, Sheriff? Look what happened to that man. Somebody cut off his head, and where does that leave me? What am I supposed to think? This is a lotta crap. You find my daughter!" She threw the phone against the wall. It thumped, sounded off a list of beeps, went dead. She slapped Quitman's leg. "Get your ass up. We're goin' to look for Sadie."

He opened his mouth, lifted his heavy lids, and placed his hands over his face. "What time is it?"

"Get dressed." She threw him a pair of faded Levi's. "Sadie's out there somewhere and we're gonna drive this town over 'til midnight 'til we find her and I don't wanna hear your moanin' today." She moved his feet off the couch. "Get up!"

"Woman, stop!"

"Don't argue with me, Quitman. I ain't in the mood."

He grabbed his baseball cap off the chair, tugged at his jeans. "You're goin' off the edge is what you're doin'. If the cops can't find her, what's to say we can do any dif'rent?"

"I'll be in the car. If you're not out there in two minutes, I'm leaving. If you wanna help, you'll get your ass out there in two minutes. Otherwise, when I get back, you have your shit packed and be gone."

—⁓—

The kids had found the key to Principal Wells's office and sat in the plush purple chairs. Danny rocked in the high-back office chair at Ardon's desk, toyed with a Christmas paper weight, turned it over in his hands, amused as snow flakes jumbled around a tiny village, his face a picture of discontent.

"Y'all think they make these things outta real snow?" he asked, and shook it once more.

Melissa opened her mouth to speak and Sadie cut her eyes, gave her a displeased look before she could talk smart. Danny's heart had crumbled. There was no need to hurt his feelings that much more.

"No, Danny. It's fake snow," Melissa said.

Sadie hooked her leg over the arm of the chair. "So, what do we do today?"

"Nothing. There's nothing to do in this dumb place." Melissa paced the room, rubbed the side of her shoes along the carpet.

"We can go play in the audi'torum. Play on that machine," Danny offered. The Yearbook Activities Group had raised money for a Karaoke machine last November for the "Fun Days" that began at noon on the last Friday of every month—a late afternoon filled with games, pizza, cake and ice cream, dodge ball in the gym, movies and singing in the auditorium. Melissa had sung LeAnne Rimes' hit, "Blue," in front of the entire school, and though she'd done a good job, a rumor spread that she lip-synched. "I didn't fake that. Why'd they say that?" Melissa asked one of her friends when the show was over. "Jealous. Everybody's just jealous is all. I was the best."

"That'd be too loud." Sadie stood, the bundle of keys in her hand. She pitched them in the air, caught them by the ring, twirled them on two fingers. "Or, we can—"

"Shh! What's that?" Danny interrupted.

Behind the walls, somewhere down the hallway, a door opened and closed, its creak heavy and solid.

Sadie hurried through the adjoining teacher's lounge, peered down the hall.

With his head down, coming their way in khakis and a button-up, was Principal Wells.

Sadie's voice sank, the authority and urgency still there, as she locked the door, turned to her friends, and with her face lit up in fear, whispered, "Hide!"

On their knees behind the couch, they heard the key fit the pad, and disengage the lock.

Ardon went directly to his office, then stopped between the room and lounge. At the threshold, he searched as if something was wrong, out of place, then sat in his padded leather chair, and picked up the phone. He dialed four digits, replaced the receiver, and rested his head on his palm.

"What's he doing?" Danny whispered.

Sadie gestured with one finger to her lips for him to stay quiet. She sneaked a peek around the corner of the couch, her throat dry, her heart pounding with the ferocity of a sledgehammer's fall.

Ardon picked up the phone and rubbed his fingers together the way someone feels of paper money, and dialed the number. His eyes were alert when someone answered on the other line. As though being watched, he looked over his shoulder, pressed the phone to his ear, turned from the door, and lowered his voice, one hand cupping the mouthpiece.

"Sheriff Combs?" he said. "There's something you need to know."

Chapter 19

−m− 8:21 A.M.

Terry lay the article to the side. He'd eaten a piece of leftover cornbread with butter pats and was working on his second cup of coffee. Monica was still gone.

He rubbed his temples, trying to subdue the tangled web of pain in his head. The rain came down more fiercely now, louder, clicks and clacks at the windows. The morning remained dark and dreary, deadening any hope for sunlight. For a moment, he feared something had happened to Monica. The image of her stuck in a water-filled ditch popped into his mind, the car's caution lights flashing, the wipers going full speed across streaked glass so that she could see clearly to wave down help.

He ignored the thought, and shifted in his seat.

She's fine, T.R.

Bobby Rampart's murder had only been the beginning, and as an active law enforcer, at the height of the media circus and the cover-page stories, he had a feeling that whoever had taken the mechanic's uneventful life was still out there watching and waiting like so many hungry wolves in a cove on the hunt for new blood.

His fingers walked over another article clipping:

Sutter Springs Press. June 10, 1997.

"KILLER STRIKES AGAIN"

Another murder in the area is currently under investigation. Sheriff T.R. Combs is being assisted by local deputies from Abbey and Tidwell Parishes to locate the suspect, who is described from an unidentified source to be a white male, early twenties, believed to be driving a red SUV.

Brady and Lisa Giles, parents of the missing girl, Melissa Giles, were found dead at the Mill Ponds in what officials have described as a crucified position. Details of their deaths are being withheld at the moment.

"We're still searching for the three missing kids," Sheriff Combs quoted yesterday. "As strange as it sounds, it doesn't appear that the murders are connected with their disappearance. We have teams scouring the edge of town as well as the northern region, all the way to the Texas border. If you have any information, please call the Sutter Springs Sheriff Department."

The second pair of murders had frightened Terry more than he'd ever known possible. He didn't know who was out there disrupting the social structure of his small town, and there were no clues, no suspects on the horizon, but he had been determined to get to the bottom of the case.

His future had depended on it. And so had his well being.

Chapter 20

–ᴡ–It had been days since the murder, and gossip rang that Bobby's death had been an accident and that there was no murderer to be found. Some even believed he'd gotten drunk and tried to cut a 2x4 piece of plywood, then tripped and fell on the blade.

But Sheriff Combs knew someone was out there hiding, their cold, hardened heart angry for more. On humid nights, the sky the color of dark marble, he cruised the streets, and tried to gain information from teenagers sitting on tailgates drinking beer in the parking lot. When they saw him aim the marked cruiser toward their trucks that were scattered front to rear, they hustled to hide bottles and plastic cups, chucked them in the air, snuffed out the weed with spit between two fingers so that they could relight the party once he moved on. Their answers were always the same.

"Haven't heard anything, Sheriff."

He'd roll away, loose gravel bouncing off the car's underside, his face motionless, and wait for something to break, or the man they'd been searching for to make a mistake. Just one.

–ᴡ–

Olivia Drake was a Hispanic woman who read palms and gave fortunes for twenty dollars each. She told of upcoming love, the gift of money, good health, and everything in between.

Town folk resented her sometimes labored and often rude behavior as she sat before a table of tarot cards or behind a crystal ball, over which she moved her hands, never grazing the surface. She said things like, "I can see," and "you will come upon," in her tiny shack off Highway 109. It was absurd and ridiculous. No one believed in her, yet she still paid rent and bills like everyone else, and seldom was there not a nice car parked in her gravel lot whose owner was inside getting advice on a cheating husband, or the old pickup with the rebel flag across the back windshield whose owner was in there wondering if he would win the Powerball Lottery. "Palm Readings" was written in black letters on a bulky yellow arrow sign that stood at the end of the narrow drive she'd salvaged from the Go-Go Mart.

The shack was scaling with chipped paint and the roofing tiles were bent and raw from Louisiana's tricky weather. A small flower garden ran the length of the walk that led to her front door, and people thought it strange that her flowers were always bright and healthy, no matter what time of year, in sun or rain or a bitch of a thunderstorm.

She had a terrible lisp, and spoke as though her tongue were attached to the roof of her mouth, her lips cracked and rubbery when she spoke. She wore old, sparkly clothes one might see in the Krewe of Gemini at a Mardi Gras Parade. Sequined blouses, beaded pants and dresses. She had an ugly brown shawl she was seldom seen without, even during warm seasons. Her hair was long, black, and straight, secured with a white headband. Those wide, penetrating blue eyes possessed the gaze of a serpent, with a sex appeal people might find odd and interesting—the kind you weren't apt to admit. She sported a nose ring, her neck bunched with beaded necklaces, her wrists stacked with assorted colored bracelets, and on her pinky finger was a huge ring that resembled a human eye. She was missing three teeth on the bottom row, and her cheeks flared when she laughed. It was a hearty, blood-curdling laugh that stuck with you, the kind you hear in nightmares or at the state fair. Sometimes she walked the streets, supporting her weight with a wooden cane she'd found in a ditch. She would scope the streets or scrounge through trash barrels behind convenience stores in search of a lampshade, hangers for clothes, or whatever she found that, to her, was of value.

Once homeless, she drifted into town, and with the help of the city's commerce, got a job cleaning office buildings and small businesses on graveyard shifts. Life on the street had taught her one thing. Others' trash was her treasure. She saved money and rented the tiny house, then began her own business when she was fired for stealing twenty dollars out of petty cash at an insurance place on a Friday evening, three years ago last March.

She now charged the same amount to give people hope, make them smile, watch their faces light up as she read their future. Every now and then, when business was slow, she'd take to her homeless ways again.

The afternoon sky was the color of driftwood when she arrived downtown Sutter Springs. Her tennis shoes squeaked underneath her, her arm tucked into her chest. She carried a roll of heavy-duty plastic bags in her hand, the flimsy black skirt patterned with tiny stars ruffled by the wind.

She came to Rachel's Massage, looked to the sky, and walked inside, the automatic bell tone ringing above her.

A young girl with short blonde hair behind the marbled front desk picked up a broom and dustpan, set them under the desk, and lay her hands on top of one another, a genuine smile appropriate on her thick lips, her greeting that of magic. "Welcome to Rachel's Massage," she said. "May I help you?"

Olivia raised her velvet-gloved finger, pointed. "You have a lady boss, no? Eh, the name eez Rashol?"

"My boss? Yes. Rachel."

A grin formed on her dry lips that were dotted with protrusions of blue veins. "She, eh, you know of the killing?"

"Ma'am?"

"That man had his head cut off!" She pulled a finger across her throat, made a Ko-*wick* sound. "The man es bad. You tell her! Go."

The girl backed away. Keeping her eyes on Olivia, she said, "Rachel? Rachel, you need to get in here. There's someone who wants to talk to—" she checked the hallway that led to the therapy rooms and spas, and when she turned around, the old woman was out the door, "–you."

Rachel came around the corner, took off a pair of latex gloves. "What's up, Connie?"

"That gypsy woman that does those palm readings was here just now.

She was, I—"

"What?"

"Said something about a guy's head was cut off and something about a bad man. Didn't make any sense. I called for you and when I turned around, she was gone. I think she meant that guy the cops found in his garage the other day."

Rachel bit her bottom lip, and her hands found their way to her hips. "Strange. Don't worry about it. I heard she used to be homeless. Probably strung out. Have you taken your lunch break?"

"I don't think I'll eat anything today."

"I'll be in back if you need me."

"She left this," Connie said, and picked up a white business card on the counter, handed it to Rachel.

It read: "Olivia Drake, Palm Reader."

"If she comes back, call the cops." Rachel returned to work as if she hadn't been interrupted and checked her wristwatch. 2:45. From her cell phone she dialed home. Mason picked up on the third ring.

"Hey, Honey. It's me. Watcha doin'?"

"Waxin' my car," Mason said, his voice flat.

"That's nice. Thought I'd call."

"Is something wrong?"

"Uh, no. Nothing. Remember to take those steaks out of the freezer and set 'em in the sink to thaw."

"Way ahead of ya. Sure you okay? Something bothering you?"

"I'm fine, baby. See ya this evening." Click! A feeling bounced in her chest like that of a weight dropping to a concrete floor. She looked out the window as Olivia Drake struggled up the sidewalk, her cane clutched tight in her hand, a breeze moving the shawl in ripples.

Chapter 21

—m— "That crazy woman came to my place today." Rachel brushed out kinks in her long brunette hair before the bathroom mirror. "Scared the hell out of Connie. Said something about the murder was bad, or that guy Bobby Rampart was a bad man. I have no idea what she was talking about, but it kinda put me on edge." She splashed cold water on her face, grabbed a towel off the shelf, patted her skin dry.

Mason lay in the bathtub, lathered shampoo in his hair. He submerged a wash rag, squeezed out the water over his head, felt the tickling sensation as it ran over his face and shoulders and he sucked in a few drops. "Any more news? Do they know who did it?"

She combed a tangle out of the tips, her face pinched in light pain. "Some are sayin' it was an accident. Can you believe that? How can you accidentally cut off your head?"

He made a grunting sound, twisted his legs and swished the pool of water to stand, turned on the shower, and rinsed. He stepped out and water fell in a flush to the rubber mat. "Stranger things have happened than decapitating yourself. Hand me a towel."

They ate steak and stuffed baked potatoes on the porch, the air the smell of pine and summer. Trees bordering his property were prickly shadowed tops against a sky peppered with stars, the moon above a white dented ball. Fireflies snapped in the air, a soft lighted dance of the night.

He stabbed tender potato, shoveled a fork-load of ham, chili, and cheese into his mouth and chewed slowly, his sight moving across the floor. Mason focused on Rachel's bare thigh and reached over and squeezed her skin. "I know you're tired of analyzing this," he said, his voice as scorched as a habitual whiskey drinker, "but if Bobby was murdered, why do you suppose someone did it? Why do you think his son ran away?"

She brought one leg underneath her butt, tapped her fork on the plate, its contact making a solid *ting!* She moved her hair away from her face, her lips frozen. "Was he a friend of yours?"

"Why do you say that?"

"He's dead. You called him by his first name. That's considered disrespectful, unless you knew him."

Mason opened his hands, palms up. "I didn't know the man, okay? So, do you think there was a reason Mr. Rampart was killed? Jesus."

"Lemme put it this way. Someone had it in for that guy if they went through the trouble to slam his head into a circle saw."

"Table saw."

"Same thing."

"No it isn't.

"Whatever. The fact remains. He's dead, and yes, I think he was murdered. He didn't trip and land on it like those idiots at the Press are trying to make everyone believe. Lotta BS if you ask me."

He looked at her in a way that was present when they first met, with an admiration and curiosity that had brought him closer to her, with the insight to know that he would one day marry her for the woman she revealed to his world, for being the person he could see himself with for a long, long time; it was love, but also respect, and even a hint of envy. He didn't possess the innate ability to speak his opinion as well as Rachel, had not been one for debates in school. He lost arguments in polite conversation, fights in confrontations back in the day, and watching her facial expressions, listening to her words and tone of voice, he wished, in that sense, he could be just as strong. "You're a wonderful woman, Honey."

She gave him a crooked smile and shot him those half-lidded bedroom eyes that never failed to melt his heart, the shine on her face resembling a woman who had just experienced a deafening orgasm.

A peaceful hour went by. While Rachel slept, he sat in his office reading the notebook, his attention on Melissa Giles' past under the roof of an abusive household. On page thirty-seven, Missy seemed to speak only to him:

> I don't hate my parents. I love them. I wish they loved me. Sometimes momma gets mad at me for some things. The other day, she slapped me when I tried on one of her shirts. I didn't cry. Momma doesn't make me cry. My daddy does. He wanted me to touch his thing one night and I didn't want to do it so I did it when he got mad at me and he told me not to tell anybody. I don't care. I told Sadie anyway.   Melissa

On the desk lay his nine-millimeter in a nylon holster. In the drawer, he pulled out a box of bullets, set them on the calendar streaked with dates and his "Things To Do" list, removed the top, and plucked one out, its feel cold. He held it up to the light, the tip sparkling, and filled the clip, pushed it into the handle. Then he pulled back the slide and loaded it.

A ball of sweat trickled down his cheek, curled underneath his chin in a halfmoon. He flexed his jaw, the knobs of muscle fisted against the skin, moved back the chair, extended his arm, and aimed the gun at the lamp across the room.

"Boom," Mason said. He moved his aim to the chair in the corner. "Boom." And his hand gently jerked backward as if jolted from a squeezed-off shot. He turned, his arm still and straight, then came to his reflection in the hanging mirror on the wall. His sight narrowed, his finger found the trigger guard, then the trigger, and his lips bent inward, sickly, as he whispered it again.

"Boom."

Melissa was careful not to wake her friends curled in spoon shapes on the four big beanbags nudged together to form a large bedding pallet. She slipped out into the gray/white hall, her book bag over her shoulder, and walked to the nearest exit.

She'd feared for her parents' safety long enough. It was time to leave. No longer did she care about Sadie's leadership, or the club's stupid woven rules, or being here, or the fruitless venture they thought would save them from additional years of physical pain and mental abuse.

Running away. Yeah. What had she been thinking?

Dumb idea, she thought. Look what happened to Danny's dad.

She got her bike out of the greenhouse, and with the night's chill at her back, tonguing her arms, she pedaled to the black top and coasted down the slope that would take her home. Her hair blew with the wind like cotton string tied to the face of a fan. Melissa's intuitions were strong and this made her pedal harder into the cool darkness. She was scared of what her parents would say when she arrived. Would they hug her? Hurt her? Both? It didn't matter. She shouldn't be at the school, she should be at home. There was something bad out there.

Coming.

—⁓—

Mason left home at ten o'clock. On the edge of town he hot-wired a 1990 Ford Bronco left in an open lot behind an abandoned warehouse. A full moon was out, spreading silver light over the rolling land. The Doors played "Roadhouse Blues" on the stereo as he drove through town and merged onto Highway 109 toward the state line. Melissa's passage in the notebook stayed on his mind. The image of her lying beside her father in her very own bed, refusing to comply with him and actually having succumbed to his sick demands, hit him in his child's heart.

Across the median, in the mall parking lot, teenagers gathered on tailgates and laps, laughing and destroying themselves with pot and double-shot mixed drinks they bought in styrofoam cups at the Bayou Drive Buy Liquor store in the neighboring town of Abbey. Rednecks hauled ass to Lilly's Lounge to down pitchers of draft beer and sing Karaoke, and the rich were at the Sutter Springs Country Club sipping on tumblers filled to the rim with Crown and water, talking up the new Sea-Doo so-and-so bought for his son. Nothing more than a wild night in a small town.

Mason pulled into an empty paved drive between the neighborhood's opening and the wood's edge, thirty yards from the Giles's brick home. Crickets chirped in the clearing. A train blared miles to his left. Voices echoed from the parking lot.

He flexed his hands, and made a promise to himself that he would use his firearm only if necessary.

The fresh smell of watered grass came to him as he fitted on a pair of leather gloves, got out, and lit a cigarette. His nerves were on edge. Concerned about Principal Wells. Would he talk? He had tried to call him from the cell phone, but there was no answer. What if his friend turned on him? What if he told the cops? If that happened, Mason had a feeling there'd be another person on his list, but he didn't want that. He liked Ardon. They'd been friends too long for something stupid to come between them.

You're killing people, Mason, a voice echoed in his mind. Isn't that enough to have a friend betray you?

No.

He crushed the cigarette on the ground. Moonlight poured onto the road, lighting it to the color of ice.

He walked in between the stone lions set on either side of the driveway's end, his imagination getting the best of him. He saw the lions move their heads, growl, and hunch to pounce, but that was fantasy. Nothing would protect the parents at 1808 Chandler Street. They might as well be in a coffin.

Shadowed by the black he sneaked behind the house, peering into a bay window on the patio.

Brady Giles stood at the kitchen sink. The man popped two aspirins in his mouth and drank from the tap. In the corner of the room, Lisa Giles folded dried towels and placed them aside in a plastic container to be put away.

Standing outside Melissa's bedroom, Mason checked the window, slid it up, and climbed inside. Adrenaline rushed through his veins, gripped tight.

He walked down the dim hall. In the living room, Brady sat in his recliner watching a late show. Lisa was out of sight.

Mason got the pistol, turned it around and crept to the back of the chair.

A noisy clatter came from the laundry room. Mason looked, Brady looked. Their eyes met. Brady opened his mouth to react, lunged, and Mason pistol-whipped him in the face. The man dropped over the chair, his gangly arms reaching to the carpet.

"Brady?" came the voice from the other room. "Bray?" Lisa walked through the dining area, saw her husband lying on the carpet, blood trickling from the side of his forehead. "Brady! Brady, oh no—my God! What's wrong!" She dropped beside her husband and touched his back, tried to move him.

Mason came out of the darkness and kicked. His foot connected with Lisa's face. Her head flew back from the force and a line of crimson shot through the air. He kicked again and her nose flattened, cheekbone cracked. She fell to the floor, legs closed, her arms placed apart above her head in a broken circle. He went to the mantle above the fireplace where a dozen portraits were organized. He chose one of Brady and Lisa posing together dressed in their Sunday best. He stood behind her, his hands on her shoulders, she with a wide, happy smile. He knocked the face of the frame against the mantle's corner. Glass fell to the floor. The scattered pieces crunched under his boots as he turned to them. He pulled out the picture and slid it into his back pocket. Shoved the gun into the holster. One by one he dragged them to the Bronco and loaded them into the rear like bundles of laundry. They were still breathing.

—⁓—

As the truck climbed out of the driveway, its lights disappearing around the curve, hiding in the bushes outside the front windows, Melissa fought to catch her breath, stop her wide, fearful eyes from darting from the house to the street and back again, her heart slamming into her chest, shocked at what she'd witnessed. If she had arrived ten minutes earlier, she would have come upon Mason ducking out in the same line of bushes.

She'd seen his face. The look of anguish on her father as he took the jaw-breaking hit, saw the blood on her mother's nose.

Her first thought was to call the police. But what would they do? she could hear Sadie ask. What would they do, what could they do, what!

Melissa steadied the bike and aimed it toward the school.

And, as she put her legs to work, she realized that her concerns for her parents' safety had been correct, her suspicions that something was wrong punctuated in the last few minutes as the man in the black shirt and dark sunglasses stepped out of her house. There was no doubt in her mind. A killer had arrived in Sutter Springs.

Chapter 22

The only time I'm happy is when I'm asleep. But I keep waking up to the same nightmare.

Melissa Giles
Notebook entry #31

They lay in the back of the Bronco bound with nylon rope and their mouths covered with duct tape, wrapped in sheets Lisa had washed and dried, but were now spotted with blood from her husband's head wound and her broken nose.

Mason drove down a red dirt road leaving heavy dust pockets high in the air, traveling through the Mill Ponds—a lay of woodlands populated by duck ponds and winding back roads behind the paper manufacturing mill that had shut down in the early Eighties. He parked alongside a rippling pond underneath an enormous cypress that stretched its thick branches over the water like loving arms. Night noises sprung up in the patch of woods when he stepped out and lifted the rear window, then lowered the tailgate.

Lisa was coming to, moving her head in the sheet. He pitched her over his shoulder and carried her slim body to the tree, her thin fingers pinching the sleeves of his shirt. He positioned her facing the water. He then placed another piece of nylon around her neck, pulled her against the bark, and tied it off. Tight, but not so that she could not breathe. Her eyes grew, her chest heaved up and down in frantic despair when she realized what was happening. She screamed, but the sound could not penetrate the tape, and it only came off as a low, struggled muffle.

The Bronco's headlights lit up Mason's face and he tilted his head, looked at her, his eyes wandering over her high neck and porcelain skin, into the fear embedded in her face.

"If you need to pray, pray. I don't think God will have sympathy for what you and your husband have done to Melissa." He leaned close to her ear, his lips grazing the microscopic hairs. "If He does, that's His problem."

Lisa's eyes fluttered, rolled into her skull, her tongue dented the tape, and she fainted on the spot.

For a moment he felt as if he were standing beside himself, watching someone else act out the scene, carry out the deed, and he didn't feel evil in his soul, or hatred toward them, but pictured himself as an entity, as though he'd been here before, done this numerous times, and he couldn't for the life of him understand why it was this easy, this carefree. It wasn't planned, but he almost decided to drop Brady on the ground, get in the truck and forget it. What stopped him from saving their lives—*you're their god, decide, live or die*—was a paragraph in the notebook about Melissa. Her mother had tried to suffocate her. On a Saturday in the spring, she handcuffed Melissa to the drainage pipe under the sink, opened all the cabinets, and set off a bug fumigation can in the middle of the room. Brady and Lisa spent the day at the park while Melissa fainted in the foggy fumes of her own house. Why? She'd gotten angry with her parents and had threatened to call the police on them for their cruelty.

Mason stood at the truck and looked at Brady. The man was tall and weighed more than expected. Did he have to go through with this? No. Did he *want* to go through with it?

Tear out their hearts . . . stuff them in their . . . sorry motherfuckers.

He had a tough time dragging Brady to the tree, leaving two lines where his bare feet scraped along the ground. Strange. It was as if he'd gained weight on the drive over.

No, Mason was just tired. He should have been home in bed with Rachel, not here, not doing this. His arms and legs ached, and if he were not so driven to offer justice to Melissa Giles, he would be home, asleep, without a care in the world.

But this was better than boogie-boarding on Red Lake, he thought.

Without hesitation, he tied Brady against the tree and tied his bobbing head with rope.

It wasn't until Mason returned with a hammer and two concrete nails that Brady awakened and squirmed on his feet, anxious, fearful. The gash along his face was like red jelly, provided a view inside the muscle structure of his cheeks, and secured with dried blood. Behind the tape, the man whimpered and begged for his life.

Mason grabbed his jaw, slammed the back of his head against the bark. "Quit." He placed Brady's hand over his wife's, then touched the man's skin with the tip of the nail. Brady tried to pull away. Mason punched him twice, and his head swung low as he went unconscious. The hammer fell. A fast, powerful swing. The large nail drove through skin, muscle, and bone. Blood spewed. Their eyes batted open as they were yanked from their black worlds, alive with pain. Mason spat in Brady's face, moved to the other side of the tree, and nailed their bodies together before they regained enough strength to free themselves. Hand covering hand crunched and was painted red. A bit of the red stuff splattered onto the rim of his sunglasses. He took them off, cleaned them on Lisa's shirt, replaced them.

He stared at her pitiful face. "I wish your daughter could see you now. I don't think she liked those cigarette burns. And I'm pretty sure she didn't care to be hit with a spatula or punched in the face just for using your makeup. What the hell's wrong with people like you? What were you thinking? How could you do that kind of thing to your own flesh and blood?" Mason pulled a Buck knife from his back pocket. He motioned around her body, toward Brady. "That goes for you too, you sick son of a bitch." A careful grin spread over his lips, and he touched Lisa's shoulder with the gloved hand. "All I want is for the two of you to feel Melissa's pain."

Brady saw light glint off the sharp blade and twisted against the tree.

Mason worked quickly. He had to get home, be with Rachel.

The last thing Brady and Lisa Giles saw before they reaped an agonizing death were the Bronco's red tail lights as it passed a pond the color of a dime.

—⁓—

Melissa pounded on the doors to the junior high section, the sound on the other side echoing down the hallway. Frightened, she kicked it. "Sadie!" she screamed. "Sadie, open the door!" Gritting her teeth, she stepped back, and the heel of her foot tapped the bicycle's tire, spun it gently. She gazed up at the oval window, picked up a handful of gravel, and slung it to the surface. "It's me!"

The door creaked open, and Sadie's long blonde bangs slipped out. "Missy, what're you doing? Hurry, get in here. "

Melissa picked up her bike and walked it into the hall, parked it beside a potted plant.

She'd been crying—this Sadie noticed before anything else—and her eyes were swollen red, her face red and white, puffed. She swallowed, gasped, then touched Sadie's shoulder. "I saw him. He killed them, Sadie. God, he killed them, I know he did!" She turned and faced her as if she'd been accused of lying. "I saw him do it!"

"Who'd you see?"

"Him!"

"Missy! Why'd you leave?" Danny ran to them in shorts and socks, holding a canned Coke.

"I didn't wanna be here. I thought about what happened to your dad, then what might happen to my parents. I was scared for them. Went home. But," she sniffed, "when I got there, some guy was there. He hit my dad with a gun and kicked my momma in the face, right here, with his boot." She touched her own nose. "He took them away, just drove off in a red truck, so I came back here, it was crazy, y'all!"

Sadie hugged her, and Melissa covered her face with her hands. She leaned her head against Sadie's shoulder, her lips a deep frown.

"Get some blankets, Danny," Sadie ordered. "She's shaking." She patted her sweaty back. "It's ok, Missy. It'll be all right. "

Sadie thought she'd done the right thing by consoling her friend, but it only seemed to heighten Melissa's anger.

"No. It's not okay! It's everything but all right! That man took my parents. He kidnapped my parents!" Melissa stumbled back, her eyes half opened, hands closed into tiny fists. "Don't you get it? Are y'all stupid or somethin'?"

Danny returned with a yellow blanket, a dumbfounded look on his face from his friend's actions.

Melissa pointed. "Take that blanket and shove it up your butt, Danny! I don't need a blanket! I need—I need to get outta here. I'll go to the cops, that's what I'll do. They need to know. They can still help."

"Missy!"

"Shut up, Sadie! I'm not listening to you anymore. You think you're bein' my friend, but you're not. If I never ran away, my parents would be at home, and they'd be okay—*I'd* be okay. I knew something bad would happen, I knew it! Whoever that was, he's got my mom and dad." She looked off aimlessly and her eyes crinkled into blue, wet circles. "And he might come for me. "

—·—

Mason wiped clean the steering wheel and driver's seat and ditched the Bronco at the warehouse five miles out of town where he'd left his Porsche. He made sure no one had followed, then hid the gun inside the console, hopped in, and spun away into the moon's smoky glow. Sweat dotted his forehead. He clicked on the air conditioner, his body melting under the blocks of cool jets attacking his skin. He'd done it again. There was no remorse, no pain, nor did he pay any attention to the red flames in his brain, or his mother's voice scream, "You're a killer," or the little angel in white perched on his right shoulder cry softly, or the devil on his left laugh out loud—he only stared ahead, calm, cool, silent.

When he got home, he dug the Giles' photo out of his pocket and turned on the car's interior light. Looking at their contentment gave him a strange feeling. The two people staring back at him were no longer smiling, they would never hurt their daughter again, and it gave him a rush. He ripped the glossy paper in two and put the pieces under the driver's seat with Bobby Rampart's news article and photo.

That night he and Rachel made love against the wall, his hands cupped underneath her heart-shaped butt, her tongue on his neck, their bodies pressed together in the heat. He lost all touch with reality, caught up in her passion, and felt her wetness snake down his bare legs in clear, sticky lines as she parted her mouth and moaned.

They slept naked on the living room floor, her head on his chest, his arm pulled snug around her. The ceiling fan cut the air that pumped from slanted vents and the drapes over the bay window ruffled like grass in a field.

He dreamed of the sky, the sea, and everything in between. As a child he'd suffered through a nightmare. Now he was in the process of taking away from three kids he'd never met the fear in their lives.

Lying there on a chestnut rug beside the one he loved, a bent smile came across his face.

Chapter 23

The next day, Sheriff T.R. Combs arrived at the station at a quarter to one. He placed his Stetson hat on a nail on the wall and slid a wooden chair from underneath the desk strewn with piles of papers and faxes. Under the desk was a star-shaped metal ashtray constructed by a worker in a minimum security prison thirty miles south of town in the middle of nowhere. He emptied ashes into the wastebasket. Among the clutter he found a box of white-tipped matches from the Bayou Boy Bar & Grill in Curry. Man, he'd gotten toasted that night, a week after his divorce from Linda.

It seemed the shit-pile was never high enough. Pressure was being applied. The mayor, the citizens who voted him to office. Impatient, having to live in fear until the man was brought down. They waited for Terry to find the person responsible for Bobby Rampart's murder and the sheriff had taken to drinking hard liquor again in the aching, never-ending whirlwind of the media storm in which he'd been caught. Damned reporters. Camera crews. Microphones shoved in his face, questions buzzing by his head. It had been over four days since the horror that was the Bobby Rampart story, and he still hadn't brought in a suspect.

He dug into his tanned shirt pocket for an unlit cigar, placed it between his cracked lips and fired a match on the side of the desk. Shook out the flame, took the first puff of sweet relief. His cold blue eyes moved from the window to the street as the midday traffic passed slowly by. Heavy gray smoke spiraled up in fat curls, masking his face, and he rolled up his sleeves to reveal his hairy arms. In January he'd celebrated his fiftieth birthday and his face began to show his age like an ugly monster that couldn't be stopped. Tiny cracks outlined his mouth and puffed, reddened cheeks. His gray hair went uncombed, left sprouting in all directions when uncovered, and crow's feet clung to the corners of both eyes, stretching back toward his temples.

He thought of the person he'd been tracking. His man left behind no fingerprints, no clues, not even a clever note to flag his presence for some feign act to become infamous. What unnerved him the most was talk that he'd lose the election if he didn't bring someone to justice, and he could hear his own words, smoky and far away, again, in his mind, when he sat with Monica in her car at her house, and told her, "People don't care who's arrested, as long as somebody's arrested."

He poured a cup of coffee into a mug that had Yosemite Sam printed on the side, pistols blazing, the cartoon character's red beard faded yellow. Dashed it with a shot of Jack Daniel's to give it that sharp, needling buzz he'd grown to love since his divorce. Took a sip. It went down smooth, warmed his insides.

Commotion and voices rang out in the next room. Someone yelled. A chair toppled over. Footsteps hurried down the hall.

The door burst open and Pace Nugent stumbled through. Deputy Steve Hanna, a folded newspaper in his hand, followed.

Terry set his cup on a Post-It in the center of the desk, rose from his chair.

"I tried to stop him, Sheriff," Hanna said, "but the hard-headed son of a bitch won't listen. He's drunk."

"Go jump up a whore's ass, you shit!" Pace growled.

"It's all right, Steve. Close the door." Terry motioned for Pace to sit.

"I'm fine, I'll stand, Terry Robert. You better not sit, either. Y'all gotta come with me." He pointed out the window to the cloudless day. "I saw him out at the Mill Ponds. He's dead."

Sheriff Combs lowered his eyebrows, spoke evenly, as if measuring his tone, and frightened by each word. "Who's dead?"

"I don't know who it is! Can't even recognize him."

"Calm down, Pace," the sheriff warned. "I won't think twice 'bout throwin' you in a cell."

Pace ignored the warning and went on. Sweat drenched his face and arms. His black hair was matted and stringy and hung from the sides from under the baseball cap with Kaleen Construction written on the forehead in cursive lettering. He looked like a marathon runner nearing the finish line, chest heaving, breath coming in thick gasps. They thought he might faint.

"The man's just nailed there," Pace said. "I ain't never seen nothin' like it. Can I have a drink of cold water? This heat's gonna cause me a stroke."

Terry Robert nodded, cut his eyes to Hanna. The young man fetched a cone-shaped paper cup and filled it at the cooler. He handed it to Pace.

He gulped the water, smacked his lips, and ran the back of his skinny arm over his mouth. "Thanks." He stood in place, looked from Hanna to the Sheriff. "Well, come on! Aren't y'all gonna do anything?"

Terry folded his hands. Sunlight glinted off the wedding band on his right finger. "Did you see anybody else out there? Was someone else with you?" Terry asked.

"No. I was goin' bream fishin'. Ya know they're bitin'. I was makin' my way around there, and there he was at the Mill Ponds. Arms wrapped around a big ol' cypress, his hands nailed to it. And his . . . well, sheriff, you just gotta see it."

"Pace, how much have you had to drink?"

"What that got to do with anything?"

"How much?"

"I don't know. Case. Case and a half since last night. Went to Lilly's."

Terry steepled his fingers, making a sucking sound through his mouth. "So, you've been drinking since then up 'til now. Do you think, Pace, do you think you might've just seen something that wasn't there? I mean, like a deer carcass or something of that nature?"

"Oh, no, sheriff. When you gut a deer, you string him up by his hind legs and saw him from ass to neck." He gulped, his throat carrying down a wet knot the size of an unshelled pecan. "This one was nailed to a tree."

—⚏—

Sadie brushed her teeth in the girl's restroom at the west end of the school, washed and dried her face with a hand towel, and changed into a pair of faded jeans, a white cotton shirt, and her favorite sandals that had formed from sweat and wear to fit the curl of her toes. On her way back to the classroom to wake her friends, she heard the soft whispers, and craned her head toward the voices as she moved closer to the opened door.

"I don't care what she thinks Danny. I'm leaving. Are you coming or not?" Melissa asked.

"I want to, but—"

"But what? We can go to the police, tell them we know what happened to our parents. It's gotta be the same guy."

"We don't know who he is, though."

"I know he had blond hair and he was wearin' a black shirt. He had on some boots, too. Looked like a cowboy. We can tell the police that."

"If we do that, where will we go then? They ain't gonna let us go home. My dad's gone and so is your parents. Where we gonna stay?"

Danny smacked on a piece of bubble gum. Sadie was so close she could smell the watermelon scent.

"What about Sadie?" he asked.

"We'll tell her we're leavin' and ask her to come, too. If she don't, so what? I wanna get outta this place. I just wanna go."

"If that's what you want, then do it."

They both looked up from the desk seats as Sadie walked in, the shine in her blonde hair dulled by the gray room. She folded her arms, shifted her stance, one foot pointed away from her body.

"Danny, is that what you wanna do?"

"Yes, he does," Melissa answered, getting to her feet. "He's coming with me. We're leavin' today." She peered over her shoulder but did not make eye contact. "Ain't that right, Danny?"

The chair squeaked as he slipped out. "Uh—"

"Let him talk for himself. He's a big boy," Sadie said.

Melissa dropped her hands on her hips. "You know what, Sadie? It's not just me that thinks you're a bitch." She thumbed back. "He does, too, ya know. He's leavin' with me."

"You're the bitch," Sadie retorted, jabbing her finger in the air. "Answer me, Danny. Do you want to leave?" Her eyes didn't leave Melissa's face.

Danny pressed his fingers together until they turned white, looked out the window to the sunlight. "I gotta aunt lives in Abbey. She's nice and she owns a haircut shop. I stayed with her for a little while last year and she let me stay up late and watch HBO. She buys those big buckets of ice cream, keeps 'em in a freezer where the washin' machine is. Strawberry and chocolate, and she let me have all I wanted." He stared at the floor, his face innocent. "I could pro'ly stay with her again. Y'all, too." His eyes moved to the back of Melissa's head. "I'd go there to see her, Missy, but I don't think we oughta go to the cops."

"Fine," Sadie said, noticing the I-told-you-so smirk Melissa displayed. "Fine, leave then. Both of y'all. I'm stayin' here."

She left the room and walked the hall, her eyes filled with tears, and feared that her friends would hear her cry.

Chapter 24

Gravel popped wildly beneath the police cruiser. Deputy Hanna drove through the Mill Ponds, passing the trees and shrubs and high weeds that bent to the edge of the road and grew from wet, overgrown ditches. Terry asked Pace more questions, but the man couldn't answer them. Did he see tire tracks? Any missing articles of clothing? Anyone else? Pace told him he'd been alone. The sheriff had dispatched an ambulance before leaving the office, and while on the road, the coroner, Gary Self, called in and said he was en route.

But by the way Pace had described the body, paramedics would be too late.

A clearing abounded up ahead, scrolling into the valley and forest, the sun reflecting glowing rays off the water's mirrored surface.

Hanna stomped the brake, shifted into park. All three men stared at the lonely cypress tree rooted just off the bank where the land ended and the rippled water began. No one said a word.

Terry stepped out. He walked slowly and felt a sudden urge to draw his gun. He gazed upon the body, and as he moved closer, his insides twisted, bile rushed to his throat, giving him the sensation to vomit. He circled the tree, paused before he reached the water. A turtle dived off a sunken branch stem and blackbirds fluttered away, darkening the sky.

The man's arms were broken, having been forced backward to hug the massive tree—a movement God had not intended for the human body to make. Gashes were ripped open along his face—over his forehead, his eyes, nose, cheeks, and mouth. His belly had been sliced open and his intestines lay at his feet, the dark hole invaded with flies. Blood had run down his blue jogging pants, coloring them black.

Terry recognized him immediately. Brady Giles. He went around the tree to see yet another body, this one Brady's wife, Lisa, in the same position, her bluish, black guts hanging from her opened stomach and forming a loose bundle beneath the silt. He squinted. A water moccasin about three feet long chewed away at the remains. The sheriff stepped closer, wary of the snake and the bank's edge. Alarmed, the reptile darted away, disappearing into the pond's liquor gloom.

"Jesus H. Christ," Terry whispered. He took off his Stetson and moved his hand over his gray hair. Their hands had been merged together, one atop the other, a concrete nail embedded through the layer of meat. Only the chrome-colored head surfaced, bunched by day-old dead skin. Brady's left eye had been gouged out and the stench fuming from the area was awful, enough to make Terry lose his lunch, but the sheriff forced himself to be strong. He had a million questions and no answers. There had been no other witnesses. He would have to start from scratch since Pace was no longer any help.

Then it hit him. Melissa. What had happened to her? If Danny's father was gone, and now both of Melissa's parents, where were those kids? Were they even alive?

He replaced his hat and turned around, his boots cutting into the rutted, graveled ground. Terry noticed zigzagged patterned tire tracks stamped into the dirt.

Deputy Hanna and Pace stood on the clearing beside fire embers that were still smoking from a gathering last night. Most area teenagers came out here to drink and let loose. Could the person he was searching for have been here stoking that same fire? Ludicrous. A teenager, no matter how angry and frustrated they were for being a teenager, in this town, at least, could not have possessed the sick courage and ruthless abandon to have performed actions of such evil. Terry had a strong feeling this was the work of a troubled, yet clever individual.

Hanna excused himself, hurried to a deep ditch where he stepped in the remains of a possum, and threw up. The red and white chunks splattered at the ground.

Pace reached into his pocket, uncapped a can of dip and pushed a pinch between his cheek and gum. He put it in his back pocket where there was a permanent faded circle of its existence. "What do ya think, Sheriff? Hey, I didn't know they was two of 'em."

Terry went to the cruiser, leaned on the hood and folded his arms over his barrel chest. "It don't make any sense. Why Brady and his wife? What'd they ever do to anybody?" He shook his head, listened as Hanna grunted, paused, and threw up again. "There's one sick son of a bitch out there and we gotta find him. Hanna!"

"Yeah!"

Without looking his way, Terry said, "You all right?"

"Uh-huh, yessir. Just, it's just I ain't never seen nothin' like this."

The most he'd ever seen was when Cal Taylor, a black bar owner in Trenton—a low-class suburb east of town—had carved up a customer with a straight-razor for not paying an evening tab.

Maybe he's not cut out for this line of work, Terry thought. "Where is that goddamn ambulance?" He chewed on a limp, splintered toothpick, watching as the sun sank behind a purple cloud.

"There it is," Pace said, pointing beyond the cruiser.

The orange and white van with "Sutter Springs Medical" imprinted on the right and left sides, drove to a stop beside the cruiser. Two paramedics hopped out, a white man in his early thirties and a younger black woman.

"'Bout time," Terry said. "Hanna, I want you to call the paper, give them enough, but don't answer any questions. I'll talk with the editor later. Pace, we don't need your assistance anymore. You can go ahead and leave."

"My truck's at the police station," Pace replied quietly.

"We'll take you back to town. What you've seen here today, keep it quiet, keep the story straight. I don't want to read that McGraw interviewed you and you happened to see more than what you're telling me just so you can have something to talk about next Saturday night. Got that?"

"No problem, T.R. Don't worry. I won't say a word. Let the newspaper and TV handle it."

Gary D. Self arrived in a new white Cadillac. He walked with a limp that seemed to have been with him since childhood, back in a time when he and T.R. spent endless summer days catching bream off Dorchoux River in Curry and sharing dreams of becoming astronauts and race car drivers and getting the hell out of this town. He shook the sheriff's hand. "What do we got here, Fats?"

"Brady and Lisa Giles. Dead."

"It's my job to decide that," he said with a casual nod.

"Whatever you say, but I don't see them breathin'."

The young woman approached. A gurney was positioned by the tree. "We're going to need a claw hammer to separate them."

Gary noticed the bodies in full view. "Oh my Holy God." He coughed into his fist, examined the cuts on their faces, their abdominal cavity opened, their frozen mouths and blank expressions of death. "Check with Sheriff Combs," he told her. "Maybe he has one."

Forensics pulled up to the scene and parked behind the yellow tape Terry had strung between two trees. A man with a small black case and plastic gloves combed the area, dusted the bodies. The man opened the case and retrieved a camera, took photographs of the tire tracks.

"Any prints on them?" Terry asked, pointing to Brady Giles.

"Clean. Whoever it was must've worn gloves and backed over their steps," the man said. He snapped close-up shots of Lisa's face and stomach. "Other than those tire tracks, we got nothin'."

Deputy Hanna and Pace waited in the car. Terry went to the trunk where he kept spare tools to help when people locked themselves out of their vehicles and retrieved a hammer. During the process of prying the couples' hands free, he broke both of Brady's wrists from the pressure, but he knew there was no other way. When Lisa was freed, she fell face first into the water.

"Grab her feet!" the woman yelled. "Hurry! She's going in the water!" The other paramedic reached out and caught Lisa's foot before she got too far out, pulled her body to the bank. They got on both sides of the woman and lifted her onto the gurney, her insides stringing along the hard, red dirt like purple rope.

Brady stood erect, the tree supporting his weight. His face was dead, his muscles were dead, his bones were dead. But he was locked into the stance, the expression in his eyes almost alive, staring off in an abyss as if wishing he wasn't gone. Terry and the woman helped him onto another gurney, and Gary, performing his job before God and six witnesses, examined the bodies, and declared them deceased.

"No shit," Pace said through a crack in the cruiser's window.

The black body bags were zipped tight and loaded onto the van in the midst of the awful, uneasy silence that surrounded them.

Terry returned to the cruiser, spit out the toothpick and lit a cigar. "Let's take Pace back to Lilly's, drop me off at the station. Call the press." He rolled down the window as Hanna drove off behind the Cadillac and thumped ashes at the glass.

"What're you gonna do?" Hanna asked.

"Find those kids," he said.

Chapter 25

Sadie watched as Danny and Melissa pedaled away. She ran her finger over the office window, tracing their bodies as they disappeared around a sharp curve and coasted downhill. She felt the familiar sting of loneliness sneak up and squeeze. In an attempt to gather herself, she lowered her head, wiped her hands on the sides of her jeans, and reached for the phone on Ardon's desk, put the receiver to her ear, dialed a number.

"It's Sadie," she said. "They're gone. They're going to the police and I couldn't stop them. What now?"

"Hide," the voice said. "If the cops find you, they'll send you home. You don't want that."

"Okay," she said, and hung up the phone, her skin tinged with goose bumps.

That afternoon, Sheriff Combs held a press conference on the front steps of the municipal building. He stood behind the podium, staring at four microphones, his shirt collar too tight around his neck. He tried not to appear nervous, but couldn't help it. A camera crew from Channel 6 out of Beaux

River had set camp and the heated lamps beaming down on him warmed his face. Photographers snapped away. A close group of reporters in suits and ties and loose khakis and tight skirts gathered before him. The questions flew from all angles.

"Do you know how this happened?"

"Any information on the missing kids?"

"What were her parents like?"

"Sheriff Combs! Do you have any leads on who has come to be known as the 'parent killer'?"

Terry touched his chin, moved his hand to the back of his neck and scratched. The Parent Killer. He let the words sink in. The circus was back in town. He hushed the crowd with a wave of his hands. "Folks, an investigation has been launched to find the kids and the person responsible for the deaths of Bobby Rampart and Mr. and Mrs. Brady Giles. We have no suspects, but Abbey and Tidwell parishes have agreed to assist us in the search. I cannot disclose any further information on the details of this case, I'm sorry. Funeral services for the Gileses will be held tomorrow at two o'clock. No more questions, please."

He stepped down from the podium and the herd of reporters moved with him as he and Deputy Hanna walked across the road to Lilly's Lounge. The day was hot and dry, bringing sweat to faces and exhaustion to brains. Ye Old Ice Cream Shoppe was having good business and people walked the town with cups of ice, wearing shorts and tank tops. Streets sizzled and kids played in the park, splashing each other with water from stone fountains.

Terry opened the heavy wooden door to Lilly's. The place was dim, the only light coming from pool lamps and neon Budweiser signs, and it smelled of fresh beer. Smoke hung in the air in fat waves. Johnny Cash poured out of the jukebox in the corner and three video poker machines moaned their losing tone. Cool air hit him and he put his hand on the bar, ordered a Coke. Over the rim of the cold can, he saw Hanna lock the door. The reporters rapped on the outside of the building, tapped the small windows, talked out loud and beckoned him to give them more. But that was the problem. He had nothing else to say. All he knew was that Brady Giles and his wife Lisa had been brutally murdered and the kids were still missing, their young faces in black-and-white photos stapled to every telephone pole in town and printed in newspapers from here to Texas and across Mississippi. Who committed the crimes was the closest thing to his mind and yet he wished it would transform into a memory. He wanted to forget it all and get a good night's sleep for a change, instead of seeing the images of blood and gore and suffering from a world of pain a stranger had created that he now lived in. He and his men had searched the Giles's home, and the only thing that was out of order besides the blood on the living room carpet was a broken frame and its glass on the fireplace mantle. Whoever had murdered Bobby Rampart and Brady and Lisa Giles was collecting their photographs. But *why?* It made no sense.

"The parent killer," he mumbled to himself, and slapped a dollar on the bar, shook his head. "Buncha crap if you ask me."

"You can't do this!" a female reporter shouted outside the opened window. "We have the right! It's freedom of speech. We have a right to visit this establishment and as Sheriff, you are committed to the people, to their concerns. You can't dictate what the people have a right to know!"

Hanna sucked a tooth. "Wish them sons of bitches would leave."

Lilly took the dollar for Terry's Coke, and slipped it in her tip jar. She was a skinny woman, with a long nose and a wrinkled face, her bulging eyes big as silver dollars. She wiped her hands on a small white towel, looked at the entrance. "They're vultures, every one of 'em," she said, lifting the wooden separator between the bar and her customers. She went to the door, staring at the several faces and moving mouths. "Go away! This is a private business." She pulled down the skin-colored drape, blocking their view into the smoke-dark room, and returned to the bar.

"Thanks," Terry said. "You're quite a host."

She opened the cash register and plucked out two twenties. Slammed it shut, went to the middle video poker machine, and inched her rear onto the padded stool. "Don't mention it. Just remember that when I'm home asleep and I hear something out in my backyard. When I call 911, I expect you to be there before I punch the last number."

"You have my word." He finished the Coke, rubbed his sand-papered chin. "C'mon, Hanna, let's go out the back."

"Terry Robert?" Lilly said, her voice reaching out. Hanna pushed himself from the wall. "You're gonna catch that maniac, aren't you?"

The sheriff grinned, gave her a curt look. "Yeah, Lilly, don't you worry." He waved his hand. "Let's head out, Steve." The two officers walked by a couple kissing in a booth, through a small hallway, past the rest rooms, and found the exit.

Outside, they got into their cruisers and drove back to the office, the horde of reporters still trying to get inside the lounge like an angry mob with torches searching for Frankenstein's monster.

Moving down Main, Terry got on his CB. "Steve?"

"Yeah, Fats?"

"See those people back there?"

"Yeah."

"Don't tell them anything unless you speak with me first. They'll be here for awhile. They're diggin' for somethin'." Terry turned on the air conditioner and cut his eyes to the rearview. "It's our job to keep our mouths shut until we get to the bottom of this. It's hairy."

"No problem, Sheriff. Hear ya loud and clear."

—⁓—

Mason drove fast. His thoughts were jumbled, mixed as his emotions were from the latest murders. He'd heard about it on the morning news, and again on the radio, and was sure to hear about it for the next few days, if not for weeks.

He compared his past, when he'd sabotaged his parents, to the present. It was ironic that the media had labeled him the "parent killer" . . .

But oh, if only they knew.

He combed his fingers through his hair and took a sip from a Coke in a plastic to-go cup, passing the sun-kissed fields and dry, yellow pastures where farmers dug up the earth on bush hogs. The workers out there sweating away the day looked like what freedom meant: the ability to taste the air under a clear blue sky, with no one biting at your back, and your bags of worry left on the front porch steps. Mason had to search himself for his freedom. He didn't know how he'd survived this long. By all rights, he should have never seen the age of twenty-four after what he'd been through. But here he was, safe and sound. The memories still lingered, though, and burned his thoughts, caught up with him during sleep, laughed at him from the nether reaches of his mind. The evil never ceased.

Mason Xavier looked like a kid, and felt like an old man. His focus today was bright and blue, filled with an inner sense that what he'd been doing was both the right and the wrong things to have done. Sympathy for the Devil. He had killed, and that was morally wrong, but he'd killed people who deserved it, and that, he felt, was as right as rain.

His blond bangs fell over his face in loose, sharp needles. These days, when he saw himself in the mirror, the man staring back at him was a complete stranger, someone he thought he left behind in the years when everything had been so complicated, blurred, so undeniably painful. Back then, he tried it all to escape. Drugs, alcohol, even running away. Running away from home at thirteen was only a fantasy. He had no money, no food, no transportation. It sucked. And he had to go back to that prison he called home. When he did return that cold, windy night in November, his mother beat him with a palm-sized billy-jack so many times, the leather scraped off to show the weapon's lead-filled head. The assault left him with a broken arm and three missing teeth, along with several bruises.

Just as the kids had written their experiences and fears in the spiral notebook, he hated his parents for doing things like that.

Chapter 26

"**S**heriff! Come up front. You're not gonna believe this." Deputy Hanna pushed open the office door.

Terry eased out of the chair, dropped his pen on a clipboard, and met Hanna and two other officers in the holding room. There, sitting side by side at the end of a long wooden table, the sunlight slanted across their faces, were Danny Rampart and Melissa Giles.

Hanna leaned into Terry's ear. "They rode their bicycles up here. Said they'd been hiding out in an abandoned house somewhere on the outskirts. Asked them 'bout the other one, that Bellis kid, but they won't talk."

Terry took off his cowboy hat and set it on the edge of the table beside a tape recorder. He planted his fat hands on the chair, turned it around and sat back to front. "Get 'em somethin' to drink, Hanna. They look thirsty." He tipped his head toward them. "Y'all thirsty?"

"Want some coffee or something?"

"A Coke, Hanna, a damn—" he held out his hand, "some water or a Coke, man. They're just kids." He looked at the other two officers, and nodded to the door, his face stretched red. "Can y'all give us some privacy?"

They left, and a minute later, Hanna returned with the sodas and two cups filled with ice. Terry pressed the red button on the recorder.

187

"We don't know where Sadie is, so don't ask," Melissa said.

Danny shifted in his seat, stared at his feet, picked at his fingernails.

"I'm sure you've seen her, though, right?" Terry asked.

"Nope." Melissa crossed her arms over her chest.

"Nu-uh," Danny said, his eyebrows raised high.

"You kids have been gone for almost the whole week. A lotta things have happened in that time." He opened his mouth to say something else, maybe to offer comforting words for their deceased parents, but instead, his eyes followed the cracks in the floor, back to the maze of veins in his hands. "Why did you two run away?"

"'Cause we didn't like livin' with our parents," Melissa told him straight-faced, clearly unnerved by the probing questions.

"Oh yeah? Why's that?" Terry asked.

Danny and Melissa exchanged looks, knowing that they were about to spill the beans and give him all the information he needed—except for the whereabouts of Sadie. Why ruin it for her?

"It's a long story," Danny said, his voice rugged and tired. He looked at Melissa again, his face begging for support.

"It's somethin' you guys shoulda heard a long time ago," Melissa told them, and the room fell silent as she began her rendition of the abusive world she'd lived in for as long as she could remember.

When she finished, she wiped the wetness away with her hands.

Terry hugged her tight, feeling a pool of hot tears soak through his tanned shirt, onto his skin.

They had been at the station for almost two hours, and when Melissa asked if they would go to jail for having ran away, Terry felt his eyes water, and he looked out the window and told her "no" in the most gentle tone he could pull from his hefty body.

"We can stay at my aunt's house," Danny offered, his voice quick, as though he'd only left home an hour ago and really needed to get back.

"Sorry, son, but whether you kids know it or not, you guys have been hot news for quite awhile. Letting you go would be like filleting a ten pound bass. Just can't do it. We'll need to ask y'all a few questions first." He crossed one leg over the other, rubbed his wristwatch with the side of his thumb, a thought coming to his eyes. "It's not definite, but you two might stay in the state's custody."

"What does that mean?" Danny asked.

"It means we're goin' to like, an orphan-ijj," Missy said, and turned her hard stare to Terry. "Then we'll wait to be adopted by people that cain't have kids on their own or somethin', or stay there 'til we grow up."

"You're a bright kid, but no, that won't happen," Terry announced, and stood. "Hanna, I'll be right back. If they're hungry, get 'em whatever they want."

"Pizza," Danny said.

—⁓—

Rachel got home at three o'clock. She told Connie to close up since she wouldn't return to the parlor today. The gypsy woman had spooked her, yet she was curious why she'd stopped by, and was well aware of the business card that lay in her white coat pocket, its presence like a living entity, burning through the thread and into her hip.

She set her purse on the kitchen table, and clicked on the stereo from across the room. Kim Richey came from the speakers. A plate with scraps of gnawed pork chop bones and the remains of baked beans lay on the table. An empty glass of sweet tea had been stuck in the sink's drain. She moved to the window above the sink and saw Mason waxing his Porsche in the shade of a white oak.

She walked outside, down the back porch steps, her arms folded over her chest as if it were cold even though the temperature was in the middle eighties. "So, did you hear what happened last night?"

Mason whipped a white towel over his shoulder, lowered his head and peered at her over the sunglasses. "I had animalistic sex with a gorgeous Italian woman, but don't tell anyone. If my girlfriend found out she'd kill me." He buffed the hood, worked his way up to the windshield wipers, sprayed glass cleaner on the windshield, and wiped it in with a piece of brown paper towel.

"This is serious, Honey." She reached out, grabbed his wrist, and tightened her grip.

He turned, looked into her eyes, splayed his hand so that the crumpled paper fell to the grass.

"Police found those people at the Mill Ponds. There's something bad wrong in this town, Mason."

"I heard."

She fingered a lace of hair over her left ear. From the south, a steady breeze caught their faces. She snubbed the ground with the edge of her sneakers. "I don't like it. Have you heard what they're callin' this guy?"

"What?"

"The parent killer," she answered.

"That's a stupid name." He whisked the back of his wrist across his upper lip that was dotted with sweat. "Look, I know the story, Rachel. Some crazy fucker out there's goin' around gettin' his rocks off. Summer Blues music festival starts in Beaux River next weekend. There's a seventy-percent chance of thunderstorms for the rest of the week. I just took the best shit before you pulled up. And tonight, there's supposed to be four episodes of COPS back to back, and I ain't missin' none of 'em." He shrugged. "What's your point? I've heard about what's goin' on in this town, I know about the murders, but life goes on. What do you want me to do about it? The cops'll get their man."

"Why are you being so argumentative? I just asked a question."

He put his palm on her bare arm, felt the cord of muscle, and massaged it. "I'm sorry, Hon. Gimme a kiss."

"Whatever, asshole. Get away from me." Rachel blew out a puff of air, craned her neck into the wind, and focused on the ground. Her face went blank as she swallowed. "I'm scared, Mason. There's a killer in this town. Sutter Springs of all places. Why don't we go to Colorado for a week or two? How about another cruise?" She lay both hands on his shoulder, the first hint of a smile coming to her mouth. "We can make love on the beach in Miami like we did that one Christmas. We'll get tanned, scuba dive. C'mon, Honey, I know how much you enjoy scuba diving. Let's do it." She hugged him, the back of her head against the side of his neck. "Say something, Mason. I don't want to stay here with some psycho out there. I want to be alone, with you."

A strand of her hair caught in the corner slit of his eye. He pushed her away. "Now's not a good time, Rachel. If you're scared, you know I'll protect you. Believe me. Nobody's gonna hurt you."

"Dammit, Mason. Can't you see? I don't want to stay here. I just wanna leave town. I wanna see something other than trees and back roads and old men sucking on wet tobacco, okay? Is that too much to ask?"

"We'll plan a trip next month. Stay gone for two weeks if that's what you want. I'm not up to it right now. Okay?"

"A month," she said tersely.

"One month."

"Mason, I went to the doctor the other day." She raised her head and her words came slowly. She stared at the tops of her shoes and said, "It didn't happen. I'm not pregnant." She placed her hand on his toned chest. "Why don't you go to the hospital? Just get a check-up to see if—"

"What? Do you think I'm sterile or somethin'?"

"Baby, it can't hurt to check. If you are, maybe we can adopt, and—"

"Bull*shit*. I am not goin' to a doctor and I sure as hell ain't adoptin' a kid. If I can't make a baby, I don't want a baby." He noticed the hurt on her face and in her eyes, and he blinked behind the shades, leaned against the car, rubbed against the wax, and slipped shoulder first to the toe of her shoe. He looked up, flecks of dirt and grass on his shoulder and arm. "I'm sorry, Honey. I'm so sorry."

She laughed and cried at the same time, the sound beautiful. "It's okay," she said in a soothing voice. "We'll try again tonight."

Chapter 27

Sadie had never felt more lonely than she did today, at a half past four, in the empty skeleton that was Sutter Springs High, lying on her back in the teacher's lounge, staring up at a soap opera she gained interest in, then lost interest shortly after, her gaze moving from the screen to her watch.

Where was he? He was supposed to have been here an hour ago. What was keeping him?

Never did she think she'd be in this kind of situation. The thought of leaving home was always there, but she imagined another world, one where her friends were at her side, and God willing, there would always be the safety factor of their company. Not this. Not being lonely and frightened and wondering who was out there taking lives and scaring every citizen in town. She felt as though she were floating inside a dream, sideways, like in a hammock, and she could see Danny and Melissa in her mind's eye, hear their laughter echo along the halls, and on a hill, standing defiant against morals and humanity itself, she saw the stranger, and, for a brief moment could have sworn he smiled. Who was he? Why was he in her subconscious?

In Principal Wells' office, she picked up the phone, put it to her ear, and dialed home. Anne answered on the second ring.

"Hello?"

Her mother's voice was urgent. Did it stem from waiting to hear from the police that they had found her little girl?

Yeah, Sadie thought, the look in her eyes empty. That's it.

"Hello?" Anne asked again. "Who is this?"

"Momma?"

"Sadie? Sadie where are you! Are you okay?"

Those words stuck in her mind. After all these years, after the river of tears and wave of blood and inches of scraped skin, this was the first time she'd heard her mother ask that question, and with so much kindness. It touched Sadie in a way she'd never felt, or had probably forgotten, and as her legs went weak behind the desk, she wanted to tell her mother that she loved her.

She sank into the office chair and focused on the paperweight Danny had played with the other day. "I'm okay, Momma. They're treating me fine. I've gotta go now," she said, and lowered the handset to the cradle, all the while Anne screaming for her to talk.

Sadie snapped her head up when a door slammed shut down the hall. She jumped to her feet, fidgeted with her hands, moving one over the other, and checked outside the room.

Ardon Wells walked into the teacher's lounge dressed in khaki shorts, a loud Hawaiian shirt, and loafers polished to a dull shine. He smelled of expensive cologne and fresh deodorant, and stared at her as a father would, pushed open the door with two fingers. "What happened, Sadie?"

"They left. I couldn't make Missy stay, but I think if I tried harder, Danny would have. She must have talked him up about how stupid it was runnin' away and all, and he never could stand up to her anyway. Said they were goin' to the police."

"It's fine." He folded his hands across his chest, blew out air straight up his face. "Let's pay attention to one thing at a time. How are you doing?"

"I'm scared of what might happen to my parents. Danny and Melissa, their parents are gone. Sometimes, I even wish I hadn't run away."

Ardon touched her shoulder, a light growing in his dark eyes. "Sadie, you came to me for help. I told you it'd be all right for you and your friends to stay here. This other mess with Danny and Melissa's parents, I wasn't prepared for anything like that to happen. It's horrible."

"The plan we made up didn't do very good, either," she said, and went to the Coke machine, dropped in thirty cents, opened a can. "You know that notebook I had? With all those secrets I wrote in it about all us?"

Ardon nodded.

"It's been missing since the last day of school. I don't know what happened. Maybe someone took it, I don't know."

He moved his tongue around inside his mouth. "Sit down, Sadie, there's something I need to remind you of."

She moved to the couch, sat near the arm, her legs together.

He sat on his haunches, elbows on knees, looked up, his raised eyebrows digging creases into his forehead that resembled three wide M's. "Remember a few weeks ago when you came to me and told me all this stuff about how your parents treated you? Now, understand me, because I could get in trouble for this, okay?"

"Yes."

"I'm an important man in this town. If the police knew what I've done for you, letting you stay here for the summer like we planned, I'd go to jail. You wouldn't want that, now would you?" She said no, and he smiled, his dimples like a thumbprint embedded in biscuit dough. "Good." He patted her knee. "You know, if it wasn't for me, you kids would have already been caught."

"What do you mean?"

He pressed the tips of his fingers together to each hand. "You see, usually, once a school year comes to an end, the faculty's job is not done. We can't call the last day of school our last day because we've still got to clean rooms, tear down posters, polish floors, do office work, move furniture if need be, get ready to send out report cards—things like that. It's not like we can start enjoying our summer vacation right off the bat like the students. And all that takes at least a couple of days. I still have about two weeks' work ahead of me, but I can get all that done during the next few days or so as long as the superintendent doesn't come around and find out. But when you told me you were really going to do this, that you and your friends were planning to run away when school let out, I told our faculty to get started earlier than usual. It wasn't very fishy I don't think, but it wasn't the norm. I wanted you to call me the minute someone showed up. A teacher, a janitor, whoever. Has anyone showed unexpected?"

"I saw the janitors, but they didn't see us. Couldn't find a phone to call you because your office was locked."

"So, how'd you get in here, then?"

"Stole the keys from that mean one, what's his name."

"Hancock."

"Yeah."

"Well, as long as we're clear on that, I think we're gonna be all right. I'm going to try and help you the best I can." He pushed his finger to his lips as if to shush her. "It's our secret, okay?" A beat. "Are you hungry?"

"I ate a sausage biscuit this mornin' before my friends took off and left." She hunched her shoulders forward. "Mr. Wells, there's something I needa ask you."

"Shoot."

She swallowed a sip of Coke, clicked her fingernails against the can. "Who did all that to Danny and Missy's parents?"

He sucked in a breath, stood, dropped his opened hands at his pockets, the look on his face like that of a warrior who had recently lost a prize fight. "A very bad man. Someone you would never want to meet."

"Do you know him?" she asked, her voice small and far away.

"No, Sadie. I don't." He eased onto the wide leather recliner, the cushions exploding with a *floof!*

"I think I know him. I've had dreams about him. He wears a black shirt and cowboy boots. He's got blond hair, like Brad Pitt, and he wears sunglasses. Dark ones. Like someone out of the movies."

Ardon blinked, his eyes drifting to the venetian blinds, and he looked out at the yellow rays of sunlight flooding a chrome sky. His memory brought back the knowledge of Mason Xavier. He saw his face, those sunglasses he wore day and night—even as a student years ago, and always wondered why ("you don't wanna know," Mason had told him)—saw the muscle of his forearms and buff in his shoulders. The image was a grotesque creature from a darkness that was all too real when he thought about what his ex-student was doing at late hours in Sutter Springs.

That day in April rushed to Ardon, its memory more of a dream than every day life.

Rain fell in a ghost-white curtain against a purple and yellow sky when he shook the water off his umbrella, unlocked it into a compact position, sat in his car, and started the engine. He applied the gas pedal and the brake at the same time, the car lurching forward, before the instant he almost slammed into a girl in a clear slicker, her face wet and blush, her black and gray baseball hat snug on her head, the strands of hair stringy and damp and plastered to her face. Sadie Bellis.

She looked thin and pale, as if she hadn't eaten or slept in days. She walked around to his driver's side door, and tapped on the glass with her knuckle, the rain cascading over her skin in long, curling slivers. Ardon pressed a button and the motorized window rolled down. Water slapped against her coat and face, flew into his car, hit the seats. He spoke above the sudden whip-crack sound of thunder around them. "Sadie! What're you doing? You're soaked through. Get to the bus stop before they leave, Darlin'!"

She loosened the book bag off her shoulder, reached inside, and pulled out the blue notebook. "I want you to read this!"

"What is it?"

"Take it home." She handed it to him. "You read it and you tell me what I need to do. Just don't tell my momma!" she shouted over the pelting rain.

He fanned away the water drops, and read the header: "The Club." When he looked up, she had disappeared.

That night, he didn't rest until he had read the last page, and even then, sleep did not come quickly. Starry-eyed, in a trance-like state of mind, he lay beside his dozing wife, his hands locked behind his neck on the pillow, the sound of the cold, harsh wind buffing the windows at every corner of his house. Sadie needed guidance and had sought his help. He could not deny her, would not let her down. He could have called the police, gotten them involved, but he knew he had to solve this problem alone, if not for the kids, for his own reasons.

This feeling, that knowing, these reasons, went back to Jay Percel. Jay came from the quintessential white-trash, low-income family that every town had. He lived in a shabby trailer close to Trenton, practiced poor hygiene, smoked pot before class and drank with rowdy friends in the evenings, and wore the same dirty, smelly clothes to school almost every day. There was one black and white AC/DC shirt with a tear in the armpit that Ardon vividly remembered. Jay bragged about how his cousin had won tickets to the Rock concert in Houston and bought it for him as a birthday gift. Jay was proud of the shirt, and he let people know where it came from every chance he got. Yeah, he remembered that kid all right.

At sixteen, the boy sat across from him years before Ardon even knew Mason Xavier. He told the principal about how his parents treated him. Whipped him with a garden hose, struck him with fists while he slept, pulled out his hair, ripped out a few select fingernails with rusty pliers. They did everything within their power to make him hate them, and they succeeded. He wanted to kill them, he told Ardon. "I wanna paint my bedroom walls with their blood," he said, and the look in his eyes was empty and cold, the creases along the corners of his nose and mouth adding remarkable years to his age.

What did principal Ardon Wells do then? He called the police, had Jay's house searched, his parents questioned, then sent him to a psychiatrist, where he was diagnosed as "Borderline Schizophrenic." Mental notes for the school's psychiatrist at the bottom of her blue-lined notebook: "Unstable. Reserved. Angry. Disconnected."

After being transplanted to an adoption facility in Abbey, police found his body in a coat closet, a leather dress belt buckled around his neck, his eyes dead to the world, and his face swearing, "I told you so, I told you so, I told you. . . ."

Once Ardon read those notebook entries, he promised himself that he would not make the same mistake with Sadie, Danny, and Melissa, as he had with Jay Percel.

Kids nowadays. You never know, ya know?

She had sauntered into his office after her first class dressed in a white blouse, jeans, and a pair of tennis shoes. She held her books out in front of her like a piece of light luggage.

"Sadie, how are you? Have a seat," he said, and when she instead stood in place and refused to dive into cardboard formalities, he offered her a cherry-flavored sucker.

She scratched her arm and mumbled something under her breath, waved her hand that she did not want it.

He lay the sucker on the edge of the desk. "What was that?"

"I said, did you read it? If you did, why aren't the cops here?" She plopped down in the plush chair across from him, let her books fall to her lap. "I'll run away if you go to the cops, won't think twice about it. You prol'y think I don't know about Jay Percel, but I do. Read about him on the Internet, under some child abuse cases here in Lou'siana. He came to you for help." She licked her lips. "Look what happened to him. You coulda helped, and you was prol'y tryin' to, but look what happened." She raised her head, and Ardon smelled wildflower perfume on her skin, the bubble gum nestled between her teeth and tongue like a piece of wadded pink paper. "He died."

In the silence that followed, Ardon discussed an alternative to their problems. He wasted no time in trying to create an escape for them and encouraged them to run away. She liked his idea. It made sense. Hide at the school during the summer until he came up with a better plan, and he assured Sadie that no one would interfere. However, there was one condition: it was only their secret. She could not inform Danny and Melissa that he had a hand in this. Too much information among too many ears might clip his throat, and she agreed to keep quiet. It was during that moment the trust was formed, the venture sought out.

Now, a month later, sitting before him in the teacher's lounge, Sadie felt like running away again, and hugging him, both emotions gripping her in unison, and she looked into his eyes, saw him melt. He had tried. So had she. What had they really accomplished, though? Had their actions really relieved her problem? She could be swiped away, returned home in a heartbeat. What if Missy and Danny squealed, told the police where she was hiding?

Get real, Sadie. That won't happen.

"Where do I go from here?" she asked.

"If you still feel like it'd be dangerous for you to go home, and you're not scared, you can stay until I figure out something. That's up to you." He placed his large hand on the top of her head, smoothed his palm over her silky hair. "Don't worry. No one will come after you."

As he left her alone, in a weird sense, that was her worst fear.

—∞—

Danny and Melissa ate a large pepperoni pizza and drank Dr Peppers in plastic containers, their faces smeared with sauce, stomachs full.

Deputy Hanna had been assigned to keep watch on them, and at the far end of the table, he read today's copy of the Sutter Springs Press, his face hidden by the paper. He looked like a big brother babysitting while Mom was off to town.

"I'm sleepy," Danny said, extending his arm across the table's grainy surface. "Where we gonna sleep tonight, Missy?"

She sloshed her drink in her hand, slurped from the straw. "Probly in jail."

Hanna chuckled, folded the paper, and put it aside. "We ain't gonna put you two in jail. That's reserved for bad people. Y'all ain't done nothin' to be slammed behind bars. Just ran away." He lifted his finger toward them. "Not that that ain't bad. You kids shoulda stayed home."

"I guess you weren't in here earlier when we talked to the sheriff, huh?" Melissa asked.

"Well? Why did you run away?"

"Would you like to stay somewhere where your momma hits you with a wooden spoon if you don't fold clothes the way she does it? Or your dad makes you—" Melissa winced, rubbed her hands together. "Forget it, I ain't sayin'."

"Or what about gettin' the crap knocked outta ya just because you was in the way of the TV? Or if you lose a screwdriver, your dad hits you 'cross the mouth with a book? I'm talkin' 'bout one of those hard books that don't bend. The kind that cost twenty bucks each," said Danny.

Melissa cocked her head to one side. "If things like that happened to you, wouldn't you run away, Mr. Hanna?"

He didn't answer, crossed one leg over the other and checked the time. He took off his baseball cap and whacked it against his other palm, his head held low. "So, y'all don't know where the other girl is, is that right?"

"Nope," they chimed.

"Ain't seen her," Danny quipped, shoving the red and white pizza box a few inches away from them.

The door opened and Sheriff Combs walked in, his features as big as a moving brick wall. He tipped his hat at the kids, then looked at Hanna. "Press knows. McGraw wants to take pictures." He swatted his Stetson against his thigh as the phone on the table rang. He answered it. "Sheriff Combs."

One of the dispatchers told him Quitman and Anne Mase were in the front office. "She says her daughter just called her, but hung up," the officer said. In the phone's background, Terry heard Anne say "They been treatin' her fine sheriff! She was kidnapped, I knew it."

He left the room, walked up the hall, readying himself for the worst.

Anne ambled toward him, her mouth moving on autopilot, throwing out her arms around her upper body. "She got kidnapped, I said, Terry! You find my daughter, damn it!" She passed him, and shoved her way into the holding room, saw Danny and Melissa at the end of the table. "I knew it, I heard them boys talkin' 'bout these two up in front."

"Shit," Terry said.

"Shit's right, Terry," she said.

"Honey, calm down."

She poked her finger at Quitman, shook it. "Don't you tell me that again or I'll bloody your face and you know it. Terry!" She motioned to the kids. "How'd they get here?" She faced them, her eyes solid red glass. "How'd you kids get here all a sudden?" She slammed her palm against the wall. "Where's my daughter?! Where is Sadie?!"

Terry grabbed the back of her arms, tried to move her away. Anne wriggled from his grasp, hurried into the room. She grabbed Danny at his shirt collar.

"Tell me you little bastard! Where is she?!"

Melissa jumped out of her chair and punched the woman in the stomach. "Get off him!"

"Sheriff Terry!"

"Anne, let him go. Anne!" Terry pulled and pushed her against the wall, leaned into her ear. "If you don't settle it right now, I'll have you cuffed and printed, got it? We got coffee in the other room, so we'll talk in there."

The break room held a small refrigerator, a table, and three hard-backed chairs. The walls were painted a dull white and it smelled of dirty ashtrays and disinfectant. When she was calmed, Anne sat between Terry and

Quitman, her hands wrapped around a steaming cup of fresh coffee. A half-empty box of Lucky's donuts was at her fingertips.

"I'm sorry. I'm so sorry. I'm just—I don't know, I'm scared." She plucked a powdered donut, bit and chewed as she went on. "I talked to her for only a few seconds, and then she was gone. It was like she never called me at all, like it was a dream." She put her hand to her head, closed her eyes, and two lines of tears fell over her puffy peach-colored cheeks.

Terry pulled a pen out of his shirt pocket, clicked it, and wrote on his legal pad. A lace of sweat beads glistened around his wrinkled neck.

Hanna walked in with a portable phone, his hand covering the mouthpiece.

"Fats? It's the mayor." He held out the phone.

Terry looked at Anne and Quitman, told them where to get more coffee if they desired it, excused himself, and offered to take the call in the corridor that led to the jail cells.

"Frank, it's Terry."

"Goddamn it Terry, if you was gonna just get two of them kids, why not just let 'em go?"

"They came here on their own, Frank. They won't give up no info on the other missing kid." He took in a deep, wet breath, and his heart beat jumped. Was it fear that this event could prove his future failure to regain his reign as Sheriff of Sutter Springs? Or was it fear of the mayor's temper? "The kids we got, they know where the other one is. We'll find her, don't worry."

"Be sure you do, Terry. November'll be here real quick-like, just remember that, Fats. I'd like to see you keep your position. See ya at the fish fry next week."

Terry pressed the "end" button and swung one arm low to his side, rubbed his neck with the other, and in the next room, he heard Anne curse Quitman for something. Farther down the hall, there were the muttered voices of Danny and Melissa and Hanna in the holding room, the kids probably laughing at one of the deputy's redneck jokes.

The air was cool and slicked with the smell of rain when Terry stepped out the side exit and folded his arms over his chest. The mayor's words stuck in his mind.

Frank Darabont was short and stout—a hotheaded Cajun from Lafayette who never took "no" for an answer. He was shrewd, loud-mouthed, and loved to mingle with his political friends. Year round, they met for golf tournaments, fund-raising fish-fries, and trips out of town to bag eight-point bucks on a wave of woodlands that rolled through the out-skirts of Abbey, a place, some have said, possessed the best hunting property in Louisiana.

Terry and Frank were not enemies, but they were not the best of friends, either. He knew the mayor could have his balls cut off and mailed to him in a gunnysack if he so wished. It was why the sheriff was always standoffish, on guard. Frank had the power to either destroy him, or further his career, and they both knew it. Fats had to find the parent killer.

At the building's corner, a mangy black mutt growled low, exposed its teeth, and after his conversation with the mayor, Terry was as inclined to shoot the animal as to look at it.

Chapter 28

Danny's aunt, Joyce Bledsoe, his deceased mother's sister, was an aerobics instructor at Prime Gym in Curry— the town that had witnessed the rage of Chad Hawkins, a local mechanic gone mad when he discovered his girlfriend had been sleeping with his best friend.

Joyce was forty-one, fit and toned, her face clean and smooth, clear of the cracks and chips that begin showing at that age, her short cropped brown hair always tied in a ponytail that jumped from side to side when she walked, her eyes squinted, hiding the neon blue within the slits.

Sheriff Combs called her at six o'clock and told her about her nephew and his friend, Melissa. Anne and Quitman had left without a "thanks" for the coffee. Anne's face was scuffed and heated and she knew that Terry could lose his job over his inept attempt to bring her daughter to safety. "This ain't right, Terry. You find her, I am serious. I want her back in one piece and you find those sons of bitches who took her, too, and make sure they pay. Needle 'em up at Angola, do it that way, 'cause if I find 'em first, I'm gonna break off their heads," she told him, and thumbed at her heavy, sagging chest to punctuate her point.

When Joyce picked up the kids at the station, she cried on Danny's shoulder, assured him it would be okay, sweat peppered on her tanned neck sticky against their skin. She took them to her home in a brand new Chevy Tahoe she'd gotten from an insurance claim when a drunk sideswiped her in Tyler, Texas, a month ago.

The orange glow of the sun behind strips of clouds lit the day when they arrived at her house. It was light-colored brick, a two-car garage, a swimming pool in back, pushed into a wooded area off the main highway.

Joyce showered while Danny showed Melissa the game room that adjoined the guest quarters. Inside was Pac-Man on arcade, a pinball machine, a jukebox, a Ping-Pong table, a racquetball court, a dartboard, and a billiard table.

Melissa walked to the pinball machine, her hand digging into her pocket for a quarter.

"You don't need money," Danny said, aiming at the dartboard. He threw and the dart hit the wall, the point jutted up through the wood grain. "Just push the button on the side. You thirsty? There's some Cokes in that ice chest over there. Prol'y only a couple 'cause Aunt Joyce don't keep too many Cokes here. She drinks water and milk and crap like that."

Melissa played her game and walked away, the pinball bouncing between rubber bands, the frame flashing metallic lightning.

Danny noticed her apprehension and pulled the dart from the wall.

"What's wrong?"

"I don't want to be here."

"Where else you gonna go?" As quickly as he'd said it, he wished he could take it back. She had no other family in town—none that he knew of, at least, and whether she liked it or not, this was the safest place for both of them.

"I wanna see my parents."

"You mean go to the graveyard?"

"Danny?"

The kids turned around. Joyce stood at the doorway in shorts and a tee-shirt, her hair put up in a blue towel, her face damp and breezey.

"Yes ma'am?"

"I've got some lunch meat in the fridge if you kids are hungry."

"No thanks, Ms. Bledsoe," Melissa said, and backed into the edge of the pool table. She folded her arms, eyed the ceiling where three fans cut the wind. "I'm okay."

"You still wanna go to the graveyard?" Danny asked.

Melissa dropped her hands to her sides, shifted her feet, and opened her mouth in disbelief. "Dan-nee!"

"I'm sor-ree!"

"It's okay, son," Joyce said, and moved up behind him, placed her hands on his small shoulders. Her voice dropped to a soft, comforting tone. "Melissa, we can't do that. Your parents haven't been... I'm afraid your mom and... Danny get her some water."

Melissa lowered her head and covered her mouth with one hand. Tears popped from her eyes and fell to the carpet and her chest heaved upward as she fought to catch her breath. "I want to." She turned away, and then felt Joyce's warm hand on her neck. She stepped backward into her opened arms. "I do, yeah."

—⁂—

Sheriff Combs showered and shaved, changed into jeans and a button-up, and drove to Monica's for supper. The cream moon hung in the sky like a torn hangnail and the setting sun glinted off the oval windows of her brick house at the end of Harper Lane. The yard was manicured thanks to a couple of junior high kids who worked the area every weekend. They only asked for twenty dollars—money, she figured, that went toward video games and movies and to the one friend in every teenage group whose older brother bought them beer. Mimosas, rose bushes, and Louisiana iris lined the end of the paved drive. A cobbled stone walk led from the carport to the swimming pool and deck, where the water was as clear as her car's windshield.

She met him at the door in shorts and an oversized flaming red blouse and a tanned suede leather vest. "There you are. I hope you like spaghetti with meatballs." She took him by the arm and walked with him to the bar. She smelled of lathered soap. "They're not the frozen kind, either. I made them myself and put red and green peppers in them. Want some sweet tea?"

"That'd be wonderful, Darlin'." Terry sat on a barstool, twisted away from the counter, and looked at the antique furniture and owls that filled the living room. Monica loved them. On the mantle above the fireplace were a dozen or so ceramic and stone owls. Miniature owls on the windowsill. On the refrigerator she even kept a cartoon owl her four-year-old nephew had drawn for her last Valentine's Day, held in place by a Mickey Mouse magnet. A red heart circled the animal's feathered body and in the center of the heart, he'd written "I love you ant Monaca."

"You look tired. Is it your stomach again? I've got some Pepto."

"No, thanks. Could use some as'prin, though. Head's killin' me."

She set a glass of iced tea and two Tylenol before him. "Any luck with the investigation?"

"A little bit. Come to find out, the tire tracks at the scene were from a 1990 Ford Bronco. That young girl, Melissa Giles, told me she saw this guy put her parents in it and drive off. Terrible. I mean, it's something, but to tell the truth, it doesn't help much. Her description of him points to half the town's young male population. My men came up with nothing else, but we did find a red Bronco behind the old chicken processing plant over toward Abbey. It had fresh mud on the tires and sides. The only prints that came back from the lab belonged to Brady and his wife. So did the hair samples and the blood. This thing's just wearin' me down. Irate reporters in my face every time I try to make a statement to the press. Got the mayor breathin' down my neck. I'm tellin' ya, Monica, if I don't find this guy, the State boys'll be in here on this before too long, then I'll be up the creek."

"I believe in you, Terry Robert. Besides, you're not one to give up so easily."

He took her hand in his and ran his fingers over her palm, patted it and smiled, a crystal light in his eyes. "That means a lot, Darlin'. Thanks."

—⁂—

Mason knew the consequences if he told Rachel the secret of his past. He'd been dating her for years, and she didn't know that side of him, that chapter of his life, and the main reason was his fear of losing her. He could see it now. "I murdered my own parents, Rachel, baby. Do you still love me?" He imagined she'd give him a hardened stare, the kind she cast when he said something smart, and she'd curl into herself, be wound up in shock. Emotions of anger and fright and love would gather like a storm in her veins. She'd lash out in harsh words, calm again, apologize for her actions, and finally console his hurt with a kiss, a rub on the back, a tight hug against her body. This, if he was lucky. But, would she stay? That was his concern. *Could* she stay with him if she knew of what he'd done to his mother and father at such a young age?

He was unable to eat the seafood gumbo she made an hour after their light argument under the oak tree. He stretched out on the back porch swing, thumping cigarette ashes over the back onto the grass. Above his head, he looked at the wooden beams, and saw the image of three kids and wondered where they were, if they were okay, if they had read their names in the newspapers, seen their faces on television.

It was a sad state of affairs when you lived in the smoky red nightmare he called home. Sometimes he thought about how it might have been had he allowed his parents to live. Was there a chance they would have stopped hurting him? The thought made him feel like a god. He had taken control, dealt with the situation, but sometimes at night while lying in bed, he wondered if he should have allowed life to take its course without trying to alter his own fate. If he'd have done that, he'd be dead by now.

Rachel walked outside with two glasses of lemonade and handed him one. She squeezed sliced lemon into his, swirled it with her finger.

"Are you okay?" Mason asked. He could see she was upset. They had been trying for over three months to get pregnant and every sexual encounter might as well have been chalked up to nothing but heated fun. He was positive the problem had more of an affect on her than himself.

"Yes. We're getting married, Mason. I'm happy. Very." She leaned against the white porch railing and tried a smile.

He lifted his head, caught her eyes. "Have you set a date yet?"

She looked off, her face full of thought. "October sometime. How about the twenty-third?"

"Aren't people supposed to get married in June?" he asked.

"There are no rules in the game, baby."

"Have you picked out a dress?"

"Not yet. Thought about going to Katherine's Formal this weekend. They have a wonderful selection."

"Get a see-through," he joked.

She stuck out her tongue. "You'll have to wait 'til our wedding night for the goods, big boy."

He stood, held her hands in his, and led her down the porch steps. "Rachel, there's something you need to know. This is a big step in our lives. What I'm gonna tell you is difficult for me because it all depends on how you take it. I've gotta get this off my chest, I've carried it for too long. Since you're going to be my wife, there's no use in hiding it anymore. You deserve the truth." He walked with her over the grass, past his car and the oak tree, toward the sprawling land, and stopped beside a fallen limb, focused on her. "I have a confession to make."

Rachel's face lost its glow and she moved her weight to one hip, placed her hand on a twisted branch, and rested her neck on her shoulder as she looked at him. Her lips were seamed with saliva, and she parted them, her eyes lost, scared. "What is it, Mason?"

He kicked at a clump of dirt with his boot, patted the thick branch as if it were a bench. "Sit down."

She sat, and without knowing exactly why, scooted as far away from him as possible. He hadn't even said a word. She tapped the back of her wrist with her engagement ring, swallowed, and raised her head to the sky. "You don't have to say anything, Mason. It's my worst fear come true. I knew it, I just knew it."

"Knew what?"

"It's another girl, isn't it?"

"Another girl? Are you insane?"

"What?"

"Is that why you ducked into yourself? You think I'm going to tell you I've been cheating?"

"Well . . . have you?"

"No." He held her face with both hands, caught her jelly eyes. "No, okay? *No.*"

"Then what? We're still getting married, aren't we?"

"I assured you that we were, not even a minute ago. Aren't you listening to me?"

"Yes. Dammit, I am."

He took in a deep breath. "It has nothing to do with our relationship, but," he held up one finger, and gazed out over the pasture that resembled green construction paper, "it might affect your feelings about me."

"Tell me," she insisted, her voice void of feeling.

He told her how his parents died. But he gave her his motive. The abuse year after year from a very young age. The unstoppable chaos that he felt and breathed every day in his childhood.

When she got to her feet, ran to the house, and slammed the back door, a quietness came over him.

Was this the end? Had he lost her?

That night, he slept alone on the couch. He listened. Down the hall, past the framed pictures of memories he'd shared with her that seemed to fade and melt, as did his image and all the things he was as a man, the blackness swirled at his brain while she lay on their bed sheets, crying, and wishing she'd never met him.

The ceiling fan whirled above him, and he prayed the blades would suddenly transform into the biting, steel teeth of a machine and fall and slice him in two halves.

Chapter 29

—ᴡ— The next morning, Rachel stood before antique-white drapes doubled and knotted in brass hooks at mid-frame, staring out the window as dawn broke across the sky in a white scar. Her satin gown was opened in the middle, revealing the inner halves of her swelled breasts and her small belly and silver belly ring that she never removed. She curled one set of toes on the carpet, twisted the plastic-coated cord to close the blinds, and stepped backward, sat on the side of the bed, folded her hands in her lap, her face blank. Last night, Mason didn't sleep beside her. One half of the bed was strewn with sheets, a pillow was on the floor, and the other one was pressed in between the headboard and mattress where she'd lay her head. She didn't know where he'd gone or what time he'd decided to split. She'd been asleep when he showered and dressed, having left the sink speckled with hair when he shaved, the mirror fogged and revealing swayed hand prints where he wiped away the moisture.

She'd been angry when she discovered his past. Rachel had the urge to leave and never return. But that wasn't the smartest thing to do and she knew it. She loved him and she couldn't doubt that, no matter what he'd done as a teenager.

In the bathroom, she washed her face, applied deodorant, and stuffed her hair under a baseball cap, dressed in spandex shorts, a tank top, and tied on tennis shoes.

The sun shot a block of orange through the trees and bathed her face as she glided down the front steps and began her usual morning jog of two miles through back roads that stretched past an above-ground cemetery, an apple orchard, Doctor Sam Helf's antebellum home, a pipeline, and the duck pond where kids fished for bream and white perch under a live oak that looked like a wretched claw clutching the sky. The voice came back again as she passed the orchard. It told her to leave, to get as far away as she could, without Mason, or anyone being the wiser, and the more she thought about it, the more she felt it was the right thing to do. Before she fell asleep last night, she thought of what he had told her.

Murdered his very own parents. When they first began dating, he told her they died in a car wreck, sure, but failed to mention his part in it. Why didn't he tell her the truth all those years ago? Why now? It was like his conscience had been on vacation for eleven years.

Get out.

Her body heated by the run, and she took a shortcut through a patch of woods and ran alongside the railroad tracks north, toward town. The muscles in her calves and thighs burned and a sheen of wetness gathered underneath her eyes and on her cheeks. When jogging, she never stopped— unless she had to urinate, and then she'd find a pine grove or a line of bushes at the base of a pasture to do her business—but she stopped this time, and it wasn't because her bladder was full. A car honked from the highway to her left and she looked. There, through an old, bent honeycomb fence, she saw Olivia Drake's little shack and the yellow advertising sign that read "Palm Readings." She'd left the old woman's business card on the dresser at home, but knew there was a reason the old woman had given it to her, knew why she still had it in her possession. Olivia wanted to see her.

Rachel put her hands on her knees and concentrated on breathing, her hair down around her face in a perfect swoop. She wiped her cheeks with her shirt and walked around the lot that separated the shack from the side road, her muscles aching in a wonderful way. Olivia's house. She strolled down a jagged, well-worn path bedded with gray rock through the back yard, trying to keep her footing as the land slanted upward and led around the shell of a 1934 Oldsmobile Sedan. She stopped and looked at the place. The wooden walls were in need of replacing and the roof tiles were split and bent backward from weather damage. Near the road, a stray cat ran through the ditch, noticed her, and zipped across the yard. As she watched the animal and the dead highway, wind whipped past her ears in a howl.

Fear rolled through her. Rachel gripped her hands into fists, then relaxed them. Why was she frightened? She rapped on the door.

Olivia opened it wearing a black dress. The old woman immediately turned her back. "You sit." She pointed at a sturdy round table covered with a white cloth. There was no crystal ball in the middle, nor was there a stack of tarot cards in her wrinkled hands. The room was bare, lit by a lone shaded lamp in the corner and a group of candles.

Rachel hesitated, then stepped into the coolness. "I wanted to—"

"Sit. Sit," Olivia demanded. She held a glass of water in the air as if to toast her visitor, then drank it down. Drops fell through the cracks in her chin, down her neck, and she didn't bother wiping away the mess. "You want to talk, yes?"

"I do. What did you mean the other day when you came to my business? You said 'He is a bad man.' Who were you talking about? The guy that died in his garage?"

"Your boyfriend!" Olivia screamed. She slammed the glass on the table and plopped down in the chair opposite Rachel. "The one you want to marry, yes?" She leaned forward, her eyes tiny black slits. "What is his name? Tell me his name."

"Mason. Mason Xavier."

"I see him. Two nights ago." She fingered the center of her palm. "A hammer in his hand." She mock swung her fist at nothing. "Beating a man to a tree, a gigantic tree. I still walk at night, still do, and there he walked, your boyfriend. Eggs-avier."

"OhmyGod." Rachel covered her mouth with one hand. She stood. "I—I'm sorry to have bothered you. I gotta go."

"He is the killer. Police are looking for the killer in this town and he is the one," Olivia said anxiously. "He kills the parents, no?"

Rachel spun on her heels. "I don't believe you. Did you hear that, you old bag? You don't know what you're talkin' about!" She rushed out into the light, ran to and across the railroad tracks. From the shack's opened front door, Olivia laughed out loud and Rachel put her legs to work, not wanting to turn, refusing to believe the lie.

Oh, but there was power even in lies. Somewhere in the pit of her stomach, whether or not Olivia Drake was the real McCoy, Rachel had a horrible feeling that the woman was right, and it dawned on her that she could very well be living with a murderer.

—◊◊◊—

"I told her," Mason said. He stood on Ardon's wraparound porch with his back to the sun and his car. He folded his arms over his chest. "I left early this mornin' for breakfast and when I looked in the bedroom, she was still asleep. But I screwed up tellin' her about what I did to my parents. She'll be gone when I get home, I just know it."

Ardon sat in a white wicker chair, his hand in the shape of an L against the side of his face. He moved his lips inward and blew out a long stream of air. "Do you think she'll go to the police?"

Mason frowned. "Not Rachel. She wouldn't do that. Besides, it's been over ten years ago and nothing can be proved." He shoved his hands in his pockets and put one leg on the coffee table between them. "I told her because I thought it was the right thing to do. She's talkin' marriage, she wants a baby. We've set a date for October sometime. I think I've already lost a little bit of her, though. She might leave, and that's what kills me."

"You've committed three unthinkable crimes in the past two weeks and you're still walking free. If I were you, I'd look at the positive side of all this."

"Life might as well be a prison without her, Ardon."

"There is something I haven't told you, Mr. Mello-Dramatic."

"What?"

"Sheriff Combs is getting close. I bumped into him yesterday at the Auto Shop when I was gettin' my radiator looked at. He asked about you."

"Why?"

"He wanted to know if you owned a red Ford Bronco. Those were the kind of tire tracks they found at the Mill Ponds after the Giles murder."

"How can you tell what kind of car it was just by examining tire tracks?"

"Melissa Giles told him. You know she and Danny turned themselves in yesterday."

"You make it sound like they're criminals. What led him to ask about me, anyway? That Melissa girl doesn't know me."

"What I hear, she was hiding outside the house. Saw a man with sunglasses put her parents into a Bronco and speed off." Ardon examined a fingernail. "Not too many people wear those things at night. Except you. Apparently, Terry thought about that, took a chance, and asked if you owned a Bronco."

"And what did you tell him?"

"Told him I didn't know."

"That was a scrap job. Hot-wired it, used it that one time, dropped it off in Abbey. Nineteen ninety-five plates. Last issued to Donald Moore. He lived in Arkansas, and now he's dead. Remember that real bad wreck on the bridge when that oil tanker hit a motorcycle head-on? He was the one on the Harley." Mason went down the steps, stopped at the hood of his car. "I've covered my tracks, Ardon. But if Terry Robert asks you anything else, you tell him you don't know shit."

Ardon got to his feet. "Mason, wait."

"What?"

"Tell me this is the end. Tell me you've stopped."

Mason cracked his knuckles with a fist-squeeze, flexed his hand. "There's still Sadie's parents. Once that's taken care of, it'll be over."

"You're already in too deep. Read today's paper. Danny and Melissa made the front page. They went to live with Danny's aunt, but Sadie's still missing."

"How do you know that? You'd think with all the shit that's hit the fan, the newspapers would keep their whereabouts hush-hush."

"That part wasn't printed. Terry Robert and I go way back. He trusts me."

Mason adjusted his sunglasses. "Can I trust you?"

"Of course. Remember what I told you, though," Ardon warned. He lifted his coffee cup. "Combs is getting close."

Chapter 30

The newspapers announced that two of the three missing kids had been found, but failed to mention that Danny and Melissa had sought help on their own behalf, instead giving glory to the Sutter Springs Police Department on their fine, diligent work.

Mason sat on the back porch drinking whiskey and ice in a tumbler when Rachel opened and closed the front door, then padded through the living room. He folded the newspaper and set it aside. The sliding glass door opened. The wooden plank floors creaked as she approached and stood in front of him, her hands on her hips, her face flushed pink from her run home.

"I didn't mean to scare you last night," Mason said, without facing her. His sight grew small and gray, and he slapped at a mosquito swarming at his head. "You'll never know what I went through as a kid and—

"Mason, stop." She held up her hand, closed her eyes, slid onto the bench across from him at the picnic table. Her face vibrated with a healthy glow and her leg muscles were hard and toned and trembling. She rested her arms on the table, pressed her palms together. "I have one question and we'll never bring this up again. Are you glad you did it?" she asked. "Are you proud?"

Tongue in cheek, he thought about the question, slapped the mosquito into a blood spot on his arm and thumped it away. "Rachel, I wish I'd had regular parents. I remember nights when I stayed up until dawn because I was afraid they'd come in and do something to me while I slept. They were monsters. Once it all went down, I was glad they couldn't hurt me anymore more, but I didn't expect to win a prize to show off on a mantle for their death."

"I remember when that made the papers," Rachel said. "I was living with my grandmother at the time. It was summer. A bad car wreck at the Devil's Elbow. Closed casket funeral." She held out her hands and touched his wrists. "I've been thinking about it all night and all morning. I'm sorry, Mason. I'm sorry for what they put you through. Baby, I had no idea. I'm not condoning what you did. It wasn't right. But—"

"Hey, it was a long time ago," he interrupted. "Before I met you. Before I was happy." He lifted his hands and spread his arms. "Before I had all this." He shook his head. "But all of this means nothing without you. I thought I'd lose you if I ever told you that. When you slammed that door last night, I thought you were gone."

She smiled. It was weak, but a smile nonetheless, and gripped his wrists tighter between her fingers. "I still want you. Forever. Mason, I'd never do anything to hurt you. Okay?"

"Thanks, Hon."

They hugged and Mason looked out over the vast land to the line of trees and the shadows leveled over his house. Deep inside, he wanted to cry, but it seemed he'd forgotten how, couldn't remember the last time he even shed a tear. He just looked at her and thanked God they met and that she was still his.

For dinner, Rachel prepared chicken fried steaks, garlic mashed potatoes, homemade buttermilk biscuits, and a green salad tossed with olive oil. They ate at the kitchen table when dusk touched down. It was an unspoken decision not to dwell on the local murders, Mason's past, or even the wedding. The atmosphere between them was the kind a parent and child share after the kid gets in trouble and is quickly forgiven—stale, but bearable. Later, when they watched the ten o'clock news, Danny and Melissa's faces appeared onscreen. With his arm wrapped loosely around Rachel's shoulders while they sat together on the couch, Mason moved a toothpick between his lips and looked into the kids' blank, but knowing expressions, and he wondered where their friend, Sadie, was hiding.

That's what she's doing, he thought. Hiding. If she were in danger, her friends would have talked by now. Danny and Melissa are protecting her.

Rachel kept quiet. When the television reporter announced that "the Parent Killer was still at large," she swallowed and her heart skipped. Mason's arms felt so warm, so right. Did Olivia's words hold any truth? Was Mason a murderer? Was he the BAD MAN? She tuned out the world around her as the thought circled her mind, and focused at the corner of the TV where her vision fell into oblivion and the room went black.

Mason's voice was at her ear. She gasped.

"What, baby?" She raised her head from the couch, the side of her face etched with the pillow's jagged patterns. Blinked, rubbed her cheeks. She was alone. The television screen had transformed to a snowy blur. She called out to the dark room. "Mason? Mason, where are you?" She swung to her feet and stumbled into the coffee table. "Shit!" Her fingers curled into her shin. She checked the door. Locked.

Out the window she saw that the Porsche was gone.

—⚬—

Terry didn't eat Chinese food. It upset his stomach and gave him gas, but he wasn't going to decline the Chicken Low Mein Monica prepared tonight. He scooped and twirled the noodles with a fork, and stared aimlessly at his full plate. Uneasy, he felt Monica's eyes upon him, as if prodding his mind, questioning his actions. It was too quiet in here.

The murders weighed him down, applying stress to an otherwise routine job of law enforcement. Being a cop in a small town didn't call for much. Be nice, give the correct tickets to the right people, shake hands with the rich and sometimes give the poor a break. If he wanted to be re-elected that's how it was done, no questions asked.

Now, he didn't know the difference between his friends and his enemies. It all began with the Rampart murder, then escalated when the Giles' bodies were found.

Big news and he had arrested no one. The public eye stared down on him in heat, waited for someone to be brought to justice, the case solved, and Terry, despite his efforts, couldn't satisfy them. The only clue came from the tire tracks at the Mill Ponds, and that proved no help even when he found the Bronco five miles out of town.

"Terry? Are you okay?" Monica's sweet voice asked. She sipped warm coffee. "Would you like to lay down for awhile and take a nap?"

He lifted his head, held her chocolate brown eyes and tried for a smile, the muscles in his face pulling off a crooked grin. "Yeah, yeah, I'm okay. The food's delicious."

"You sure you're okay?"

He closed his eyes and rubbed the lids with his thumb and finger. "I am. I'm just thinking."

"I know it's hard, Terry." She cupped her chin in her palm. "Who would do such horrible things?"

"Got me puzzled." He took another bite of noodles, felt his guts loosen. "Those kids, Danny and Melissa, at least they're safe. The press, they've been on my back about finding that other kid, Sadie Bellis. It made all the channels in Beaux River. I tell ya, they're gonna suck this dry, and I'm right in the middle of it."

"Sounds like you've become a popular man overnight," she said.

"If I wanted popularity, I sure didn't want it this way." He scooted the chair back and shoved his hands in his jeans, jangled loose change. The dining room seemed to close in on him. The hair on the back of his neck erected, sending a surge of steel spikes down his spine.

He clicked his eyes across the room and through the bay window, he saw a movement. "Are you expecting company?" he asked.

"No." She set her drink on the table. "Why?"

"Stay here." He left the dining room, went through the foyer, opened the carport door, peeked outside. Hot wind hit him, the sky black and filled with puffed purple clouds in the silver-tinged moonlight. He turned on the carport lights and sent a yellow beam to his truck, Monica's car, and the gate that separated her neighbor's house.

From the kitchen, he heard her ask, "What is it?" He ignored her and closed the door behind him as he walked to the truck.

Something didn't feel right.

His gun was in the glove compartment.

Through the truck window's gray reflection, he saw the figure again, and spun on his heels. His heart jump-started, rammed his chest. A pearl of sweat pierced his scalp and fell over one eye, caught in a lash. He blinked it away, rubbed his face as if he were hallucinating.

Terry opened the door, popped the glove compartment and fumbled for his personal firearm, a .357 Magnum. It was a fitting weapon for a man his size and with the gun at his side, he returned to the carport where it opened to the back yard. He took the side entrance through a small gate, passing Monica's rose bushes and flower garden. He moved up the sidewalk, his breath coming in short gasps to the night air, the summer heat bearing down on him like a thick wool coat. He grasped the gun with both hands, held it by his ear, the way he was trained years ago. This was the first time since Rodney Simmons' joy ride through the Go-Go Truck Stop that he had to take on the stance.

The movement came again.

He braced himself. A child's swing-set between two pine trees broke his concentration. The plastic seat sagged and shook drunkenly as if someone had been sitting on it seconds before he approached. Over his shoulder, he saw Monica at the kitchen table, hands in her lap, a look of concern on her face. He wanted to tell her to lock the doors and hide.

Something's not fucking right.

Terry lowered the gun and wished he'd worn his holster.

When it happened, the night was the same black blanket of oddly placed clouds, the wind the same course wave at his cheeks. There was no sound, no warning, no time to react to protect himself. He pulled in a breath. The knife's sharp edge touched his throat and a gloved hand covered his own fingers, pulling the gun out of his palm. Mint breath spread over his face. Curved lips grazed his ear. He heard an unfamiliar cigarette-roasted voice.

"You tried, T.R., but you failed. Don't keep going, or I'll find you again. Bobby Rampart deserved to die. The Giles needed to die. And Sadie's parents *will* die. Leave it alone. You have no idea what world you're walking into."

The knife left his skin. Footsteps echoed through the carport, faded in the darkness.

Terry whirled around, his own hand to his throat to make sure the steel didn't penetrate. No cut, no blood. His silver Magnum lay on the brick underneath the kitchen's windowsill. He searched the drive, listened for a car drive off, or footsteps stomp the pavement. He saw no one, and there was no sound.

Monica opened the front door and peeked out. "Terry? What's going on?" She saw the gun in his hand and covered her mouth with her hand. "Why do you have that?"

"Get back inside! Go!" He followed her in, bolted the door, set the gun on the bar's counter and checked through the window blinds. Someone knew he was here. Someone knew his name. Terry realized then and there that the Parent Killer had been standing behind him at his girlfriend's house with a blade at his flesh. It took a moment for him to understand the danger, that he could have been seriously hurt, maybe even killed. "Lock all the doors!"

"They are. Yes, they are locked."

He grabbed the phone, dialed the station. At the other end, Deputy Hanna picked up.

"Steve, it's Terry. Is Randy there?"

"Yeah, sheriff. He's in the office. Just clocked in, why?"

"I want you to come out to Monica's."

"Your girlfriend's house?"

"Bring an extra shotgun and hurry." He hung up.

She walked to the counter, a worried look on her face, touched his shoulder. "Terry?"

"I'd feel much safer if Hanna kept watch here tonight. You need some protection," he said.

"Terry Robert, you're scaring me. Why do I need protection?"

He wanted to tell her about the man with the knife, the ghost, the killer who could have ended his life only minutes ago. But out of respect and for the sake of keeping peace, he didn't mention it. It would only force her to ask more questions—questions he couldn't answer.

"Since the Rampart and the Giles murders are fresh and the man we're looking for is still out there, I'd just feel better if Hanna stayed the night. He'll be in his patrol car with a pump shotgun. If anything happens, he'll be on it."

"Terry, if you're insinuating that the person responsible for hurting those people will come after me, you're being silly. What have I ever done?"

"Don't argue with me, Monica. This is the best thing to do."

"It's nonsense!"

He grabbed her arms. "Monica, listen to me! I saw what this guy did—no, listen to me, be still, listen!"

She twisted in his arms. "You're hurting me!"

"I saw what he did to those people! There was blood everywhere."

"I don't wanna hear it."

"Bobby's head was gone, Lisa's throat was cut," he jerked her toward him, his mouth close to hers, "Brady's stomach was—"

"Terry, quit it!"

"I want you to be safe! I'd feel a helluva lot better. I don't want anything to happen to you."

"I don't either. I just don't like the idea that I must have a cop outside my door to protect me from a killer you can't even catch!"

Terry let her free, stepped backward into the refrigerator. He brushed the surface and a couple of magnets fell to the floor. His eyes hurt, face drawn down. "Is that how it is? Do you see me as a failure?"

"Terry, no. I didn't mean that and you know it. Come here." She pulled him to her and hugged him. "I'm scared is all."

"It's only for a couple of nights, Monica."

She saw red veins pulsate in his bulging eyes. "Okay, but Terry?"

"Yes?"

"Why don't *you* stay? You can protect me," she offered. Her actions and sudden ebullience in speech were those of a teenage girl waiting for her first French kiss under the bleachers of a high school football game in the middle of September.

Car lights illuminated the kitchen walls, crossed their faces. "That's Hanna." He kissed her cheek and went outside to bring the officer up to date.

Monica stood with her back against the wall when he left, fixed the top button of her blouse that had somehow come undone, and exhaled a sigh full of concern, excitement, but mostly fear. She scanned the table where Terry had sat, noticed the plate of noodles that had barely been touched, and she thought of being in his arms, being kissed by his lips, holding him tight, without concerning themselves with who or what was out there.

Chapter 31

The road was a white-lined stream with no end as Mason drove west to Joyce Bledsoe's home in Abbey. He knew of Joyce from when Rachel used to take her aerobics class. He'd even visited once or twice and knew of no one else who could make a tastier meatloaf, or had better homemade mulberry wine. It was the drink of the gods, cut and mashed in a metal ice bucket by her and a couple of her students, college coeds with the prettiest feet he'd ever seen—except, of course, for Rachel's.

Thoughts of Sadie swirled in his brain. In his mind, he envisioned Ardon's undulating face, those small, knowing eyes that fell upon him and accused him of doing and being wrong. But Ardon could not impose guilt no matter how much blood Mason shed. The ex-student was well aware of the principal's demons, and he would find no sympathy for him. He would feel no remorse by bringing up that awful day—a hot, blistering August day in the summer of '67 when Ardon took a twelve-year-old Vietnamese girl behind a green tent in the middle of the night while his buddies played cards and laughed and cursed and drank canned beer sent over from the States. He had bound the girl's mouth with strips of first-aid tape, then shucked her white cotton panties and put himself inside her again and again.

"We all have secrets," Mason whispered aloud, and pulled into Joyce's paved drive, cut the lights. Out of habit, he reached underneath the seat and retrieved his nine-millimeter Glock.

When he approached the kitchen window, then the living room, he spied Melissa Giles lying stomach-down on a blanket in the middle of the floor, her legs bent at the knees, pointed high in the air and hooked together at the heels. The phone cord was stretched from the wall and set in front of her. In her right hand, she played with the remote, switching the TV channels in a bored, monotonous manner. While looking through the glass—although it was thin and Mason could hear the TV stations as they flew by, or even Melissa if she spoke—he questioned why he was even here.

Did he really expect to discover where Sadie was hiding by standing in the hot night with his ear against the window? He reasoned that sooner or later, Danny would walk into the room and he and Missy would talk about their friend. But the boy was nowhere to be found. And Melissa looked tired, on the verge of sleep.

He nudged a shrub and ripe red thorns pricked the back of his hand, and he decided to move through the garden and onto the back patio for a better look.

As soon as he stepped on the concrete, he came face to face with Danny Rampart, frozen in place with two Cokes stacked on top of one another.

The kid's lips were open, a string of saliva hanging from the roof of his mouth, and his eyes remained on Mason, who, in the darkness reminded him of a vampire from "The Lost Boys" rather than a human being. Danny dropped the Cokes. The cans burst on the concrete floor, spewed out brown, fizzy liquid that formed a pool and edged to Mason's boots. He breathed faster, pissed his pants.

Mason touched one finger to his lips and knelt before him. "What are you doing outside?" he asked.

Danny was quiet.

Mason looked at the pool of Coke and picked up one of the cans. "You dropped your drink."

The kid nodded. "Yeah." His voice was small, underlining the fear in his words.

"Are you scared of me?" Mason placed both hands on Danny's shoulders.

The boy flinched. "Uh-huh."

"I'm not gonna hurt you. I need your help, Danny."

"How'd you know my name?" he asked, his nose and lips blue in the moon's glow.

"Everybody in Sutter Springs knows who you are," Mason whispered. "You and your friends are like movie stars. Ever wanted to be a star?"

Danny shook his head, kept his eyes focused on the stranger's face.

"Do you know who I am?"

"I think I do. No, no I don't."

"I want you to listen real good. I'm gonna help your friend, Sadie, but you've gotta tell me where she is. Where is it the three of you been hiding?"

"At the school." The reflex in his hand to cover his mouth was lightning sharp, his eyes wide and apologetic. He wished he could take back the words. As always, he spoke before thinking—a handicap he had yet to master and a flaw that Melissa had always used to insult him in arguments. He looked to the east where the clouds sustained a metallic gray in the sky and had never been more angry with himself. Would this man in the black shirt hurt Sadie? Did Danny just inadvertently murder one of his friends? He removed his hand and rubbed it against the side of his shorts. "Don't hurt her, if you go there. Sadie's my best friend. She's always been my friend." Wetness gathered in his innocent eyes and he scraped the edge of his shoe along the rock embedded in the patio foundation.

Mason stood, the bottom of the shirt slapping the sides of his hips. "Don't worry. I won't hurt her. And don't you tell anyone you saw me. Okay? Do we have a deal?"

Danny nodded, again at a loss for words. He reached down to pick up the emptied Coke cans and when he looked up, the stranger was gone.

—⁂—

Sadie was curled up on the couch in the teacher's lounge watching a B-movie on TV, dressed in shorts and socks and a white tank top she bought at The Corner in Curry a few weeks after spring fell across the land. She thought about her mother and her friends. Since she was still safe at the school, she figured Danny and Melissa hadn't whined to the police. That was comforting, but being alone here was no day at the park. It was spooky. Shadows lined the corners and flashed through the hallways when cars came around the curve by the old store at the bottom of the hill. She'd hear things.

Creepy things. A creak. The wind. A leaf scaling the outside of a window like a skeletal spider. Once, she thought she heard a whistle, but it was only the cooler in the cafeteria pumping alive sometime after midnight.

When the phone rang in the principal's office, she could have jumped out of her skin. Hesitant, she slipped off the couch and set her Dr Pepper on the coffee table, then walked to Ardon's desk. Her reflection against the black window kick-started more electric fear in her and she clutched her chest, thinking that she'd come face to face with someone else. At night, she slept on the couch and had gotten into the habit of locking all three doors that exited the room, though she kept telling herself there was nothing to fear. Ardon was keeping close tabs on her and he made a promise the wall between her and the police was concrete thick. They would never find her here. The phone rang and rang and she picked up the handset, held it to her ear. If by some miracle the person on the other end recognized her voice, she'd pretend they had gotten a wrong number. A light-weight male voice came over the line, and in the background Sadie heard a female say, "She's not gonna answer!" The male voice returned a quick "Shh!"

"Danny?"

"Sadie! Melissa, it's her!" He spoke up into the mouthpiece. "Sadie, he's coming! You gotta get outta there!"

"Who's coming?" she asked, and her heart lurched to her throat when she heard footsteps down the hall, around the corridor, at the parking lot's entrance. And then, the metal doors slammed shut with the cruel damnation of a prison cell.

"Sadie, are you there?"

She dropped the phone, turned, and looked into the dim hallway, her eyes wide. A man's shadow appeared, glided along the floors and walls, the lockers, and vanished as if it were never there. Chills ran up her spine to her neck. The telephone's handset dangled from its cord, tapping the center of the desk, and she could hear Danny on the other end yelling her name: "Sadie! Sadie! Get out of there now!"

The TV screen flooded the teacher's lounge in blue and silver. She shut it off with the remote and listened to the silence grow strong, invading her ears like cold wind. She'd seen a hundred scary movies and was one of those people who screamed at the screen to run—the killer's around the corner! don't take a shower at midnight! grab the gun, shoot him, shoot him!—but she felt the same fear those actors portrayed, and to think rationally was more difficult than she expected.

It was a ball and chain, it froze her, and she dared not move, not even to breathe. But she *did* move. She took two steps, stopped, and searched for something to use as a weapon. She hurried into the adjoining room and picked up a letter opener on Ardon's desk and looked through the thick network of glass wedged between the cinder-block walls and the door. The office doors did not make a sound on their small hydraulic pump fixtures, and she turned the knob, pulled it open.

The halls were empty, the tan-colored floors shown in a brilliant gloss. The circular lamps above hung in a steady row like that of the old psychiatric ward at Woodlands Care in Summerset where her Uncle Carl had worked during the 1950s. She held the weapon tight in her palm. Despite all the abuse she'd endured, Sadie was healthy. She'd eaten at least one meal a day, was not starved, slept in an actual bed, not in a garage, was not stuffed into a shed or an attic in which some abused children have been forced, and overall, her case was not that horrific when you took a closer look at it. But, at the moment, she felt the instrument in her hand was something she couldn't survive without.

Footsteps echoed at the end of the hall.

Her better judgment told her to run to the nearest exit and scream out to the open night, but her legs did not work, and her voice was numbed. All that moved her were fear and curiosity. This was no onstage portrayal, she was not pretending in front of a camera, her life at that very second was not a movie.

Maybe Melissa had been right. Running away was a dumb idea.

Sadie saw the locker rows and the water fountain, nothing else, and heard the clicking of the metal black-and-white clock behind her head. A loneliness crept into her. She wished Danny and Melissa were here. Hell, she would have been happy to see her own mother at this point. The silence around her grew intense, the ticking clock loud and pounding her ears. The footsteps faded, and then, she felt the presence of someone behind her.

She turned and stabbed the air.

A man grabbed her wrist, squeezed. The letter opener fell to the floor.

She did not make a sound, but wanted to scream. She opened her mouth just as he reached out and placed a gloved hand over her lips.

He leaned into her ear. "Quiet."

Her eyes were blue and watered, begging for him not to strike, and he acknowledged the expression.

"Don't scream. I'm not here to hurt you."

She stared at her reflection in his tar-black sunglasses. It was just like in her dreams. His blond hair was a wavy, coffee-stained color; the dress shirt starched and straight, circled perfectly at his waist. His cheeks were cropped with five o'clock shadow, making him handsome, and he stood with his shoulders erect.

"Sadie, I know all about you and your friends. I know about what you went through at home. Everything, all the bad stuff. And I know the cops are looking for two people in this town. You. And me. If you stay here, they will catch you, and after the news dies down, you'll be sent home. You don't want that, do you?"

She scratched her arm, turned her face.

"Do you?"

"No."

"Then, come with me. I'll take care of you, put you in a safe place."

"You're the one who killed Danny and Missy's parents," she said, almost as an afterthought to a lengthy conversation.

"Do you want to go with me, or not?"

"No."

"You can't stay here."

"Just don't hurt me."

"I'm not."

"I'll stay—what you did, it wasn't right. I don't wanna go with you."

"Fine," Mason said, and walked toward the lobby windows. Before he stepped outside, he hooked his chin over his shoulder, caught her eyes, and said, "I've got your blue notebook. If you want it back, you'll come with me. If you stay, I'll turn it over to the police." A beat. "With that much information, they'll think your friends were the ones who did all that to their parents." A grin formed across his lips. "Imagine that." Both lobby doors banged shut as he walked away, the untucked dress shirt flapping in the wind.

He reached his Porsche and heard her at the front entrance.

"Wait!" she cried, and stepped into the sizzling night.

Chapter 32

"We've gotta go to the school!" Melissa flung a thin blanket off her legs. Excited, she moved her arms rapidly, and walked around an octagon-shaped coffee table in the middle of the living room. "Sadie's in trouble. Does your aunt have a gun?"

"Man! Calm down. I'm not gonna shoot nobody. You mean you want to go all the way to the school? What if that mean bastard's there?"

She smacked her fist into her opened palm. "Then we pound his face in!"

"Like that's gonna happen. Are you crazy?"

"We'll call the cops." She reached for the phone.

Danny grabbed her arm, moved her hand from the handset. "Not the cops. I told him I wouldn't tell them, and if he finds out.... Missy, he could come back for me, for you. Don't call them, please. Okay? Don't do it."

"If we don't do *something*, Sadie could get hurt."

"If you call the cops, we'll all get hurt!" Danny kicked the couch, folded his arms over his chest and blew out a stressful breath. "If we leave, Aunt Joyce'll kill me. I ain't goin' nowhere and you can't make me. My ass is stayin' here."

"Whatever. I'll call the cops and I'll go with them to the school. You stay here, ya chicken."

Danny stared off with angry eyes. "I ain't chicken."

Melissa picked up the phone, dialed 911. "We'll see."

—⁘—

Sheriff Combs was sitting in a recliner watching the late news. Monica was in bed asleep and she'd asked him to join her an hour ago, but he couldn't rest. He had agreed to stay with her, but first he cruised the neighborhood in search of the stranger. Deputy Hanna was still in the driveway, asleep in his car. The idea that someone was at his back a couple hours ago haunted Terry to no end. The psycho could show any second. But, he knew that if someone out there wanted him dead, they'd have finished him off when that knife was put to his throat.

The killer...where was he? Who was he?

He muted the TV when he got the call from the station. He put on his boots, grabbed his gun and Stetson off the kitchen table and took the highway to Joyce Bledsoe's residence, red and blue lights flashing, the siren whining out.

Joyce met him at the door wrapped in a lavender bathrobe and slippers, her hair matted from sleep. "Sheriff, thank God."

"What's going on? I just got an emergency call from the station. What happened?"

"I came in the kitchen about ten minutes ago to get some water and Danny and Melissa weren't here. Checked all over the house, in the yard, looked in the playroom. Couldn't find them anywhere. Wait a second, I didn't call the police."

"Did you hear anything? A car, maybe?" he asked, and moved her aside, walked in.

"Danny?" Joyce yelled outside.

"Missy!" Terry followed.

From the back sliding glass door, Melissa emerged with Danny. She broke into a powerful stride. "We've gotta get to the school! Sadie's in trouble."

Joyce's eyes narrowed. "Danny, I've been looking all over for you two. Where were you?"

"Outside," Melissa told her, "in the garage."

Terry knelt, placed a large hand on the girl's shoulder. "Slow down, Darlin'. Is that where Sadie is? The school?"

"Yes, and we've gotta get there fast," Danny broke in.

"Okay," Terry agreed. "I'll get her."

"We're goin' with you," Melissa demanded.

"I'm afraid the two of you will have to stay with Ms. Bledsoe. Don't worry, I'll make sure Sadie's safe."

Melissa tugged at his sleeve. "You don't understand! You've got to take us with you! If the man sees you, he'll get you just like he got my parents. We're going. He won't hurt us, he won't!"

"The man?"

"The one with the sunglasses y'all been lookin' for," Danny said, his voice barely audible. "You know. The Parent Killer."

—⚹—

Sadie had only seen a Porsche in movies and in the few Hot Rod magazines Danny had stolen from his father and brought to the tree house. She sank down in the tight, conforming leather seat, and gripped the sides, watching out the window as the world flew by. Where was he taking her? She wanted to ask his name, but had a feeling he wouldn't tell her, so she remained silent, fully aware that she was seated next to a killer. The man the entire town was talking about, the one Sheriff Combs and his deputies were trying to track down was right beside her, close enough to touch.

Ten minutes and two Red Hot Chili Peppers songs later, Mason pulled into the Owl motel. A sign at the front office read: "Free HBO and free XXX—4.99 for one hour." He shook his head. You had to love this country.

"If you're hungry, there's a candy bar in the glove compartment," he said before getting out. "And there's a Dr Pepper in that little ice chest in the back. You can have it." He watched her face for a reaction to his kind words.

She hesitated, turned in the seat.

"Go ahead, take it."

She popped the ice chest open and watched him walk into the front office and pay the front desk clerk who looked like a teenager out of the movie *Dazed and Confused*. He returned shelling money in his hands and drove the car to Room 18.

"Why're we here?"

Mason ignored her question and led her into the motel room. From across the parking lot, a cat ran by. He scanned the lot for anyone, but they were alone, and he hurried inside and locked the door. In the corner he clicked the air conditioner to high and closed the curtains over the bed.

Sadie sat in one of the two chairs beside the air conditioning vents, the canned soda between her legs, chilling her crotch. "Afraid of being followed?" she asked.

"No." He sat across from her, placed his hands on his thighs and took in a deep breath. "You'll be safe here. I'll bring you some food tomorrow. In the meantime, watch TV, sleep, read, whatever. Pick out as many movies as you want. They're paid for." He dug inside his shirt pocket and pulled out a pack of cigarettes, shuffled one out, stuck it between his lips, and fired his Zippo.

A cloud of gray smoke drifted to Sadie and she winced, waved her hand in front of her face. Mason noticed this and quickly stubbed the white stick in a clay ashtray.

"Sorry, I'm not used to being around kids."

"Why are you doing this?"

"What? Helping you?"

"No. Why did you—" She lowered her head and focused on the floor. "You know what happened to my friends' parents. Why did you do that?"

"I don't think that's something I need to explain. I've got your notebook and I read everything that happened to you kids. Y'all practically wished they would die of heart failure." He scooted toward her on the bed. "I've got secrets, too, ya know. But you don't wanna hear 'em. They make what happened to you look like a day at DisneyLand. Let's just say I did those kids a favor." Tired and groggy, he stretched his arms above his head, and yawned. Rachel was probably worried sick. Enough of the Good Samaritan act. He had to get back home. "Before I leave, there is one question I have to ask. Can I trust you?"

"Yeh, sure."

"Can I?"

She nodded fast, moved a long bang from her face. "Yes."

She watched him go and stood at the window for a few minutes, wondering if this was some kind of trick, a way for the police to catch her and send her home—and he was right, that's exactly what they'd do if she got caught. Send her home. She'd rather stay in this motel room forever than to go back. She didn't want to face her mother. Sadie wondered if she could trust the stranger. Above all, that was the real question.

She drank the rest of her Dr Pepper and nibbled on the chocolate bar, then curled under thin sheets and doubled over her pillow to go to sleep before the digital clock on the end table flashed midnight.

—∞—

Sheriff Combs parked beside a shrubbery that lined the school's front lobby and shined a Q-beam mounted on the driver's side window into the building, from front office to each classroom, in search of any movement. The moon poured onto the lot so that he could see clearly. He had wanted to bring Melissa and Danny—their insistence was cute, yet a bit unnerving—but he'd come alone. Help find their friend before a killer beat them to her. Amazing.

Terry harbored his own reasons in catching the criminal: one, to rid the town of the problem, and two, to win the election in November. If he brought the man who had claimed three lives to justice, he had the election in a velvet bag. Selfish but necessary, it was more important to him than anything else. Even marrying Monica, and that was something he planned to fulfill once the town was quiet again, and his nerves were settled, and when he remained Sheriff of Sutter Springs.

A half-hour later, he walked out of the school and to his patrol car, having found nothing. No sign of foul play, forced entry, blood or bodies, and he drove off, depressed as hell.

When he arrived at Monica's, a note was tacked to the door. He ripped it from the wood and held it under the carport light. It read: "You're next."

—∞—

After cruising the back roads, a cold beer in hand, Mason got home at one o'clock. He thought about the press and what they had labeled him. The title should've been called the Nice Killer. For Christ's sake, if only people knew the real reason behind his actions, they'd understand why he sliced open Bobby Rampart's head, why he gutted Brady and Lisa Giles, why he planned to end Sadie's misery. Or would they?

Mason didn't care. It had been a real bitch trying to rid himself of the demons of his past that clouded his mind. The note he'd left for the sheriff was nothing more than a warning. It was to let the man know that he was completing a circle, making things right for three kids who had done no wrong. If Fats had any sense at all, he'd put the pieces together and know the game, and why Mason, if the sheriff kept pursuing him, was about to park a homerun in his ass.

You can't stop a machine this hard. I've set a goal, and I plan to reach it, Fats. I'm a goddamn caregiver.

The only sound in his house was the air conditioner's calming hum when he stepped onto the carpet. Moonlight fell in slants across Rachel's body in the bedroom, the sight stirring his crotch. She looked innocent and beautiful as she slept, and Mason lightly stroked her cheek with the back of his hand, then kissed her forehead. And sexy. She looked sexy as she lay with half her body under the blankets, the other half hidden by the darkness. Her swollen breasts peeked out from her satin nightgown and he touched them, cupped one in his hand, put his head on her. He moved his hand over the curves of her body to her hip, pressed his palm into her soft butt, and felt the heat rise from the middle of her legs. It got him hot, and he was instantly hard. With all the headlines swarming the papers and TV, with him behind the scene terrorizing the town, and the fact that he should be worried about his own future, it was strange, remarkable, and downright wrong that at this very minute, all he could think about was Rachel's tanned, delicate body, and himself deep inside her.

He was staring out the window, lost in his thoughts, when she kissed his cheek and traced her tongue to the curve of his mouth.

Chapter 33

Sadie woke to the sounds of a jack-hammer at the far end of the lot. She threw the covers off her body and looked out the window, her vision blurred from sleep. A heavy-set foreman in a tanned Carhart long-sleeve shirt, stained blue jeans and steel-toed boots yelled orders to a group of men slaving on the ground and tying rebar to a concrete foundation, telling them that the cement truck would be here in twenty minutes, so they'd better hurry the hell up.

The curtains dropped from her hand and she checked the digital clock on the nightstand. 9:36. Later than usual. For an eleven-year-old, she was accustomed to getting up early, around six or seven. Besides watching TV, there was nothing much to do in a motel room, except sleep the morning away, and she wished she hadn't. It had been two long days without anyone to talk to, without a thing to keep herself occupied. During those crazy nights at home, she would have jumped at the chance to stay up and watch TV in her bedroom, but Anne always made her go to sleep around nine o'clock every night—even on weekends. But here, she'd watched enough to make her sick. Sadie wished she could go outside and play, see Danny and Melissa at the tree house, get on the computer and email her friends, or even walk up the street, carefree, whistling a lullaby. She was so bored, she'd even had trouble sleeping.

To bide her time last night, she watched an action movie on HBO and realized for the first time since riding in the Porsche that the killer the police were trying to capture was her personal hero. He was keeping her away from her parents, from the cops, making sure she was safe, and that made her feel special.

When she stepped into a warm bath, there was a knock at the door, and she immediately jumped up, grabbed a towel off the back of the toilet, and wrapped it around her body. Her hurried actions were silly, a fear that whoever was at the door could also see through the walls and view her naked. She dared not ask who it was, imagined the police were on the other side, or worse, her mother, and that it was not the stranger who drove a black Porsche.

She remained silent, and reached the door, looked through the peephole.

But it was him, dressed in a blue T-shirt, faded jeans, tennis shoes, and an LSU Tigers baseball cap, holding a paper sack splattered with grease spots.

He rushed inside, set the food on the bed, and ordered her to lock the door. He turned off the TV and got a plastic cup off the sink, filled it with cold water, and drank.

Sadie stood in silence, holding the towel around her waist, and though she was covered up, she felt naked, so completely unveiled.

"I brought you some magazines. You like *People?*" He dropped it on the bed. "Got a six pack of Dr Pepper here, and a cheeseburger and fries."

"Thank you." She ran her hand over the seam securing the towel to make sure it was tight. Why was he doing this? she wondered. Why was he being so nice? He didn't even know her. A question she'd been brooding over ever since Melissa had seen him at her house the night her parents were murdered, then when she described the stranger to her, popped into her mind. "Why do you always wear those sunglasses? Like, at night and everything?"

He lowered the water from his lips and his mouth was red from the sun through the gap in the curtains. "My eyes are sensitive, that's all. Don't worry about it."

"Okay," she agreed, and there was a defensiveness in her voice. She backed away, her head down, and sat on the chair sideways so that the towel covered her legs down to her knees.

"You're afraid of me."

She nodded.

"Don't be. Like I said, I'm not gonna hurt you." He shifted his position on the bed and cupped his hand around the back of his head as if he were on the living room floor at home with Rachel, chest to back against the contour of her body and they had just settled into a movie. The air conditioner was on full blast and the cool flow dried the sweat off his face. He lit a cigarette, wary of her actions the last time he tried to smoke in front of her, but he didn't care, and she, sitting silent, didn't make a fuss. "You want your notebook back?"

"Uh-huh. That'd be nice."

"I'll give it back to you soon. Another question: do you want to go home?"

"No!" She didn't mean to shout, didn't want to alarm him, but the word came out with a fury, and her eyebrows furrowed at the illogical suggestion, giving her face an expression of evil, as if she were the one in charge in this room, and not him. "I'm sorry—no, I don't wanna go back there. Not ever."

He took a long drag on the cigarette and the cherry glowed bright red at his face. "I'm gonna tell you a story." He held up one finger, caught her eyes. "It's part of the reason why I'm helping you and why I've done these other things. But it's our secret. You don't talk about it. Deal?"

"Sure. I've got lots of secrets. I can keep them, too," Sadie said, and her muscles relaxed, her body loosened in the chair. Her focus never left his face. For all she knew, she could end up at the Mill Ponds with her throat cut and her guts hanging to the ground like Lisa Giles'. She assumed no friendship and kept her guard. She couldn't fight to win—she was too young, not quite strong enough—but she knew how to defend herself, and even the TV remote on the table could be used as a weapon to inflict damage before she managed to run outside and find help.

He told her he wasn't going to hurt her.

She knew that. She believed it.

Sadie listened as he began talking about his childhood, how his parents had treated him, and when and how he'd met a wonderful girl named

Rachel.

Mason failed to mention the part about inheriting millions of dollars—Xavier Oil was a household name across the South, and with that nugget of information, she'd instantly know who was behind those dark shades.

—∞—

Rachel didn't feel like exercising that afternoon. She'd been drained since having sex in the middle of the night, then trying to regain rest. She washed her Lexus under a maple tree in the back yard, grateful there was a steady breeze out, and thought about grabbing one of Mason's shotguns from the hall closet and using it to blow a group of blackbirds off a limb that kept dropping a white surprise on her hood. "Freakin' birds," she cursed, and looked up into the tree. The animals fluttered away. From the front drive, she heard a car door slam, and saw Mason walk through the house, caught a glimpse of him pass each window, like a shadow was there, not a human. She dropped the rag into the white bucket of soapy water and met him on the back porch.

"Hey, Hon." He gave her a quick, impartial kiss on the lips, and eased onto the porch swing. "Car looks good."

She sat at the end of the picnic table, hunched forward, and clawed her fingers through her brunette hair. The sweat covering her forehead and cheeks gave her a clean, wet look. She sighed against the wind, pursed her thick lips. "Mason, where've you been?"

"Town. Paid some bills, dropped by the hardware store. Why?"

"Because I'm getting tired of waking up in the morning without you beside me," she admitted. "It's not like you have a job. I know we're not married, but it'd be nice to let me know where you're going."

"Are you keeping tabs on me already?" he asked, a slight smartness in his voice. "I don't see a ring on this finger."

By the look on her face, she didn't take the remark too well. "You don't have to cop an attitude. And stop with the jokes. It was just a question."

"I answered it."

"Mason, why are we arguing?"

"We're not."

"Yes we are!"

"You are," he said in a flat tone. "I didn't come back here to argue, okay?"

"Shit! Why are you doing this?"

"Doing what?"

"Staying out all hours of the night, leaving early in the morning, dropping by here when you feel like it, then bolting again? It's not right—I just wish, I wish you'd tell me what you're doing, where you're going, who you're with."

"Oh my God. Not this again. If I've told you once, I've told you a thousand fuckin' times! I'm not cheating on you, there isn't another woman, okay?"

She turned a deaf ear, lifted her head to the ceiling. "Fine." She stomped away and disappeared into the house.

Rachel was putting away dishes when he came inside and went into his office. Mason seemed to spend most of his time in there when he was actually home, and she figured the fuel for his absence during the last week might be inside that little room. It wasn't that she was angry with him, but it did disturb her. Before now, whenever he left home, he told her where he was going and when he'd return, as if by habit, and she was filled with a sort of girlish happiness from his consideration of her feelings. Since the middle of last week, he'd been out at night doing God knows what (with God knows whom, a voice echoed in her mind) and he seemed distant, not at all his normal self. Was it her? Was he getting tired of her? There was something else. Something wrong.

Rachel thought about the murders, those kids who had run away, and the one girl who was still out there. What was her name? Sadie Bellis.

And the Parent Killer. She thought of who that might be.

"It is him, it is your boyfriend," Olivia's voice sounded out in her head.

No. It was wrong to dwell on a stranger's foolish thoughts. Mason had committed murder against his own parents, but that happened years ago, and after he'd told her what they'd done to him, how they treated him with such cruelty, she accepted it and continued on, agreeing that there was nothing else he could have done to escape that type of life.

She told herself her future husband had nothing to do with the crimes in Sutter Springs. Mason had too much to live for, too much at risk, and she knew him well enough that he wouldn't gamble it all away in order to carry out some meaningless psychotic plan in order to . . . to what? To kill?

The person responsible for the deaths of those people. . . it was someone else . . .not Mason . . . it couldn't be.

He ignored her when he walked out of the house, got in his Porsche, and drove away, dust clouds billowing up from the tires. He didn't even say goodbye to her and the entire time she'd been sitting at the kitchen table reading a magazine. That gave her reason to be concerned.

She looked out the window to make sure he was gone, then bolted the front door, and went to his office. As usual, the door was locked. Her first instinct was to let it go, turn and walk away, but the feeling that he was keeping a secret was too strong. She grabbed the knob, twisted, and leaned her shoulder into the hardwood without success. If she broke in, he'd find out, then what would she tell him? More importantly, what would he do? Go into a rage? Lash out at her? Forgive her? Think nothing of it? She felt ill. This wasn't right, this wasn't her. She was a grown woman and here she was playing sneak-around with her fiancee.

Rachel had to get in there. She had to know what he'd been hiding.

For the next few minutes, she toyed with the lock, slid credit cards and butter knives between the wall paneling and the lock fixture, like she'd seen done in the movies. Nothing worked. Her MacGyver skills seemed frail, and just when she was about to give up, something clicked in the workings of the door, and it inched opened.

She walked in, looked on the desk, and her hand flew to her mouth as she pulled in a deep breath of shock.

Chapter 34

Sheriff Combs bought strawberry slushes for both children and talked with them on Joyce's patio under an overhanging oak tree in her side yard. His newfound energy came when they revealed where Sadie had been. When he mentioned there was no one at the school last night, the kids couldn't believe it, and they began talking about the young man in the black sunglasses.

"Have you two seen this man?" Terry asked, interested in their association of him.

"I saw him take my parents and I can't stop thinkin' about it." Melissa sipped the slushy drink. "I don't know if I should've gotten there earlier or later, but either way would've been better than showing up at the end. It's a lotta bullcrap." She set her cup on the wrought-iron table.

"Do you know his real name? It would help the police if I had a name," Terry said.

The kids shook their heads at the same time. Danny was scared, remembered what the man in black had told him on the patio last night. He hesitated to say or agree to anything Melissa was spewing forth. What did they have to do with this anyway? Why was Sheriff Combs here? Danny understood the police wanted to get more information on the killer, and even find out where

Sadie was hiding out now, but he had told him everything he knew. Melissa had only recently told Terry that her parents were knocked unconscious and then shoved into the rear of a Ford Bronco for a ride to sure death, if that helped. She even saved the fact that Danny had cried his eyes out when he saw his father's picture on the late news at the school because it was a hard truth the kid had to face. After the murders, there was no question that inner demons would forever haunt their lives.

Terry bit the end of a cigar and moved it between his lips, looking from Melissa to Danny and to the treetops set against the mid-morning sun. He didn't understand why they hadn't come forward with this information sooner. He'd been thinking of the Parent Killer since Bobby Rampart's death, had been trying to pinpoint a suspect, wanted nothing more than to find and destroy the son of a bitch, but he'd been chasing a ghost, and the outlook on this venture seemed more bleak to him now than ever before.

"Besides the black sunglasses and blond hair, is there any other distinguishing characteristics you saw? A scar? A birthmark? Maybe an earring or a tattoo?"

Melissa and Danny exchanged a glance.

"No, but you forgot one thing about those sunglasses," Melissa said. "He wears them at night. He had them on when he kidnapped my parents and the night he came here when Danny saw him. Kinda strange. Why would anybody have on those at night?"

Terry placed his Stetson on his head and stood. "Good question and I don't know the answer. It is strange." He noticed Joyce behind the sliding glass door in jeans and a T-shirt, and he gave her a comforting nod. She returned a weak wave, placed her palm against the wall paneling. "You kids be safe," he said. "Thanks a lot."

As he walked off, Danny and Melissa turned to Joyce, and she smiled and went into the house.

—∞—

Sadie now understood what her grandfather once told her about a condition called "cabin fever" and how it felt. Though she was only the width of a door away from the outside world, it felt more like a hundred miles, and the loneliness and boredom began to set in as heavy as concrete. The stranger hadn't been by today and it was getting late, the sun blazing hot in the sky. She was worried that he'd forgotten about her, or maybe her worst fears had come true: maybe he put her here and told the cops where she was hiding. Since he had blood on his hands, it wasn't so difficult to believe.

How can you trust a killer? she wondered.

She'd inhaled the cheeseburger he brought her this morning while laid up in bed watching the early news, where, again, she'd been reminded that she was still missing and the hunt for the Parent Killer was still going strong, yet she was growing hungry, her stomach groaning low every few minutes.

The police won't find him, she thought. Their search still going strong? Give me a break. They'll never find who's helping me.

She'd seen evil's face. She'd heard its voice, knew its actions, and she could destroy it if she wanted. But he'd helped her, and she wasn't a tattle-tell, even if it meant bringing a cold-blooded murderer to his knees.

The motel room was small and grew smaller every day. She hadn't been able to play, or go outside, or get any kind of exercise, and the lethargy hung on her bones like damp cloth. In the bathroom, she rinsed her mouth and chewed on a peppermint to suppress her hunger until her food arrived. Her body needed energy. The hunger pains were growing powerful. She needed something to eat and she planned to eat and she didn't care who saw her on the outside. This was ridiculous.

She dressed in a T-shirt and shorts, and tied on her New Balance shoes, pulled on a GAP baseball cap, then cracked the door to survey the parking lot. All her fears and worries were tossed aside momentarily when she stepped out into the sun's bright flare and headed down the sidewalk toward a corner grocery store that was wedged between a shoe repair shop and a gas station with beer advertisements spray-painted on the frosted glass.

Inside there weren't many people, and none of them seemed to take notice or even recognize her face. Taped to the counter beside a chip stand was her photograph. She turned and took the candy aisle until she came to her reflection in the beer cooler, checking to make sure no one spotted her. Melissa had taken off with most of their money, so when she emptied her pockets, she came up with two dollars and change. When the last customer left, she tugged on the cap to cover her face and approached the clerk behind the register, steadily feeding out quarters in her hand. It was enough. She bought four chicken fingers from the deli with hot sauce and a Dr Pepper.

Having a sweet tooth was sometimes a burden. She wanted to buy a package of donuts, but she didn't have the money, and she'd seen Anne scarf them down by the dozen before, and if it was one thing she feared, it was becoming as fat as her mother.

She didn't even want to see Anne Mase. Ever.

A smile played on her lips. Things weren't all that bad. At night she slept in peace without having to worry about that woman bursting into her room with a broom or a belt and lash out across her skin.

Sadie prayed silently as she walked out of the store and stepped onto the sticky asphalt, thanked God for this time, for this change.

She ate a golden chicken fillet from the white sack as she walked around the corner, past the gas station, toward the sidewalk that led to the motel. She took her time. It was only a block and a half. It was good to feel the grass under her feet, breathe in the fresh, cool scent of summer, hear the birds in the trees, see other kids play in waving water sprinklers in the church side yard across the railroad tracks.

What happened next came without warning, so quick and so painful that she didn't know what to do. Her body froze. Her palms became sweaty, her mouth filled with saliva. The world around her went on as usual, nothing different, and she thought that was unfair. She wanted the world to feel her insides, suck on the sour taste in her mouth, know how fast her heart was beating. Felt as though she'd stepped into an alternate plane where her nightmares returned with a vengeance. Legs went weak, her hands trembled. Sadie was frightened to see her, so frightened that her cold drink slipped through her hand and burst on the sidewalk, her lunch landing with a thick, audible thud at her feet.

Anne stood at the gas pumps, filling her car. Their eyes locked and the tension between them was quick and abrasive. Sadie had never been more scared of her mother than she was now.

She wanted to run, but her legs couldn't move, and she wanted to look away, but her mother's gaze was too captivating.

Anne popped the gas pump handle out of the car and opened her mouth. The words she spoke were soft, loving, those whispered by couples under star-spangled summer nights. "Sadie?" She hurried around the car. "Sadie!"

"Oh God." Sadie remained on the sidewalk. Customers walking to and from their cars and out of the store stopped to catch the commotion.

Anne was in front of her and she hugged her quickly, almost smothering her in her massive chest. She planted a kiss on Sadie's forehead. "Baby, ohmyGod, you're safe. I found you, oh thank heavens I found you!"

Sadie was numb. She wished she had listened to Mason. She should have stayed at the motel.

The ride was pleasant. Sadie sat with her hands in her lap, legs straight, silent. She was skeptical in believing this reunion meant her mother had possibly changed. She kept scratching her palms, watchful of Anne's movements and that smile—*she was smiling.* Sadie thought there was a chance running away had been the answer to her prayers: that Anne Mase realized she loved her daughter.

Anne showed her love when they got home.

—ɯ—

Inside Mason's office, Rachel picked up the articles one by one, scanned the dates and headers and looked over the children's photos. Two front-page headlines told about the murders of Bobby "Champ" Rampart at 138 King Street and of the Giles at the Mill Ponds. There were also personal photographs of these same people, in what looked like more innocent times, torn apart like so much trash. Olivia Drake entered her head and she heard the old woman's voice. "I see him. Had a knife! I still walk at night, still do." The Mill Ponds. She remembered that Mason had not been home with her when either murder occurred. She thought he'd been cheating on her with another girl.

Rachel would rather that have happened than to accept this.

Still, her heart wouldn't allow her to believe Mason was that man, this monster, the Parent Killer. Her love, so warm and strong, would not retreat as the result of some coincidence, because some old hag with an empty life and the smarts to scare the hell out of people had told her she'd seen Mason Xavier gutting two bodies at the edge of a pond.

No. She couldn't believe it—she wouldn't believe it. There was no way Mason could be the—

She found the gun in the drawer. At first it seemed like a toy, or a novelty, not the real thing, but there it was, and she picked it up, felt its solid weight in her hands, and a pang of sickness climbed through her stomach, into her chest, needled her heart. It couldn't be true. Then, she found the notebook and opened it to the first page. She read two paragraphs. That's all she could take. Rachel rushed out of the office, ran to the kitchen sink, and semi-digested food tumbled out of her mouth in a chunky, chalk-white stream.

"Oh no. No, no, no. No!" She wrapped her arms around herself, turned and slid down the side of the wall to the floor, her feet coming out from under her in a lazy snap. Stared off in a zombie-like trance. Her imagination reacted and she envisioned Mason with a knife, saw the gun in his hand, looked into his sunglasses and saw malevolence that surpassed every awful thing she'd ever felt or seen or heard in this life. Tears fell down her cheeks, leaving dampened spots on her shirt. She shivered.

"What now?" she whispered. "What if it is him? What if he comes after me?"

It was all so clear to her now. She'd discovered the truth. The late hours, the gun in the drawer, the notebook. That notebook.

And his past. When he was thirteen and rigged his parents' car and they skidded off the Devil's Elbow and were sent sailing through cypress branches, into Beauvoir River.

"There was nothing else I could do. It was either me or them," he'd told her.

Me or them. Them or me.

Was there really ever a choice? she thought.

She got to her feet and went to her car. Still in a daze, she started the engine and drove away. There was no final destination in mind. She didn't know where she was going or why, she just wanted to get as far away from there as possible. She'd even left the back door open. The realization gripped her. *Damn him!*

She needed time to think, to collect her thoughts, control her actions.

Heart pounding, the truth set ablaze in her head, she drove in silence, and felt her soul crumble into a million pieces.

It was true. She'd been living with a killer.

Chapter 35

"You little bitch!" Anne slapped her cheek and Sadie's head jerked. "Who do you think you are, runnin' away like that? Huh? Answer me!"

The house was like a prison, and when the front door closed, she knew she was locked down. Sadie's shirt was torn and now the girl's head throbbed from where Anne knocked her skull with a mini-flashlight on her key chain the moment she'd gotten out of the car.

"Do you think this is a goddamn game? Have you forgotten who I am, what I can do? Don't you ever defy me, Miss Priss, or I'll bury you in the back-yard. Do you hear me? Look at me when I'm talking to you!"

Sadie lifted her head. Her face was puffed, her eyes small and beady as she tried to focus. Clean lines of bright blood ran from the corners of her mouth. Her left eye was swollen shut, a dark bruise forming under the lid. She had a loose tooth on the bottom right section of her jaw she was supposed to have pulled at the dentist next week—she remembered her appointment, it was tacked on the refrigerator, and she remembered Anne bitching that she'd better be grateful Quitman was paying for it, or they would have to consult a door knob with a piece of tied string and wrap it around the tooth in order to yank that sucker out the old-fashioned way—but the appointment would no longer be necessary. Sadie had already swallowed it during her reunion with her mother, and the copper-tasting blood ran down her throat in a slow leak, the small tooth scratching the inner walls of her stomach like jagged pebble-rock.

She hated her mother. Oh, how she hated that woman.

"I'm sorry, Momma, I'm sorry. Don't hit me. Please! I'm hurtin'. My face hurts."

Anne just stood there, silent, her fists perched on her hips, her mouth pressed into a hard frown. She wagged a finger. "I ought to do more than hit you. Wait 'til your father comes home. Then you'll know the meaning of hurt, you got that?" The house vibrated with her footfalls as she stomped into the kitchen.

Sadie touched her face, and just like the night her mother had swung the belt buckle into her crotch, she winced.

It was almost seven o'clock. She thought of the stranger in the black short-sleeve shirt. Had he been by the motel with her food? Nervous, she gazed outside at the daylight, heard birds singing in the trees, the hum of an occasional car on the road, and a rather devilish smile played on her lips as she thought of what might happen when he discovered her missing.

—⁂—

Mason knocked twice on Room 18, but there was no answer. He cupped his hands against the window. Venetian blinds walled his sight, so he knocked again, repeated Sadie's name. The door was locked, but not chained, and that worried him. From around the corner, a maid pushing a cleaning cart stopped three doors down.

She was Spanish, and she smiled as he approached. "Help you, sir?"

"I lost the key to my room and I left a bag in there," he lied. "Can you let me in?"

She opened the door and walked away.

Mason didn't like this. He stepped inside, checked the bathroom, but there was no sign of Sadie. Where was she? Why did she leave? He specifically told her *not* to leave. There was no sign of her, and a shot of fear for her sprang in his gut.

He slammed the door on the way out, got into his Porsche, and spun off across the loose gravel scattered about the parking lot. Dreaded thoughts invaded his head. The first one was that police had found Sadie and she was singing like a canary, telling them all about the man who found her at the school. But he didn't believe that. Though they had only known each other personally for a couple of days, a bond had materialized and stuck. He knew her better than she knew him, though, and that relaxed him. She, on the other hand, didn't even have his name. He knew everything about her from studying the notebook, examined her darkest nightmares and thoughts— what made her cry, what made her laugh—and she didn't know any more than the fact that he had a history of child abuse, wore his shades at night, had blond hair, and drove a hundred-thousand dollar car.

Shit.

He lit a cigarette, cracked the window, and drove to the outskirts of town. Ardon Wells would probably know what to do. He needed to tell his friend what he'd done, that he tried to help the missing girl, but that now she was gone and he'd screwed up. Sadie might have willingly gone to the police, and that would suck, it would put him away for a very long time. He'd end up in Angola for life, or worse, be served with a date of execution, and the days leading up to that would be worse than death itself.

A sea of clouds blocked the sun and turned the day gray. He parked and found the principal watering his back yard, dressed in shorts and an unbuttoned shirt to show his dark chest and protruding stomach.

"Looks like rain," Mason said, as he walked around the corner of the house. He leaned his butt against a stone birdbath, crossed his arms over his chest, his legs over one another.

Keep your cool. You should be in a hurry, excited and agitated that Sadie's not there, but you've got to be cool. Ardon may be able to help.

"Rains off the Gulf. Supposed to be a big Voodoo bitch comin' to town." Ardon sprayed the lawn, and a gust of wind carried the mist into Mason's direction, onto his skin.

"Why're you waterin' your plants if it's comin' a storm?"

"Call it impatience. Guess you've heard about the other missing kid, Sadie."

Mason's arms dropped lazily to his sides. His lips moved, but no sound followed. Behind the sunglasses, he felt like crying. *Just break down and cry,* let it all out. It had been too long since he felt tears, felt the relief of good hurt. It was happening again. Mixed, troubled emotions from the past were sneaking up on him. The murders, of having stranger's blood on his hands—it was all spiraling down on him, and it hurt so much, he was beginning to care. Care? Yes. Damn. His feelings cut deep, were getting to him. But he did care. Cared about Sadie. She reminded him of himself at eleven, and he couldn't bear the thought of anything horrible happening to her. If she got hurt, then he'd failed his job. He hadn't reached his goal of taking out the parents of those three abused children. He would be no hero to them—real or imagined—and in his mind, he would be as worthless as the parents who called for his actions. Mason had risked everything he had to accomplish his cause. All he ever wanted was to see Sadie and Melissa and Danny smile and laugh and play like kids do, not see them cry and run away, and wind up lost.

He'd murdered three people in cold blood, with no insight of what the future might hold for their children. Christ, what had he been thinking? Had he done the right thing? Or was he just a madman? Was he the brutal psychopath the media had portrayed?

Yes, he was, and no, his feelings for the kids ran strong. He was watching out for them, not their parents. Fuck the parents. Now, he had to make things right. They needed someone to look up to. They needed security, stability, guidance, and a future. Soon, Melissa and Danny would be placed in foster homes, he was sure of that, and he couldn't stand by and watch them wait for months, even years for the right couple to come along and whisk them away into a Ward Cleaver dream home. Foster parents could be wealthy, average, or poor—the latter scaring the hell out of him. Somehow, Mason had to find them a good home and ensure their livelihood.

He was apprehensive in asking Ardon what happened to Sadie, but kept his fears at bay. As long as Sadie was alive, he'd save her again, wherever she may be. He promised himself that.

"What happened to her?" he asked.

Ardon shut off the water hose and bit into a half-gnawed apple. "She's fine," he said. "Her mother found her and took her home."

"You gotta be kiddin' me."

"It's true. It was on the scanner about twenty minutes ago. Sheriff

Combs was on his way over to talk to the girl, see how she was doing."

"This is insane. She can't stay there! I told her to stay at the Owl Motel until—" he trailed off, saw the blank expression on Ardon's face, and hardened his words. "What?"

"The Owl?"

"I found her at the school and took her there. Told her not to leave," he threw his arm into the air, "begged her not to leave! Now look what happened. God damn it!" He kicked at the wet grass with the toe of his boot.

"How did you know she was at the school?" Ardon said.

"That kid Danny told me."

"You showed your face?"

"He won't say anything."

Ardon dropped his eyes to the ground. A pool of water from the garden hose surrounded his feet, ran underneath his soles.

The water snaked its way to Mason, who looked off at the edge of the horizon where a group of blackbirds flew from the treetops, their tiny sharp bodies ink-black against the golden sun. A purple thundercloud, thick and huge and far off, was rolling in.

"I know how you feel, Mason. I tried to help those kids, too." Ardon bent to his knees and scooped up an empty beer bottle that had been thrown into his yard, twirled it in his hands.

"What're you talkin' about?"

"Sadie came to me for help over a month ago. She told me about the notebook you have. I read it too, ya know. I told her she and her friends could stay at the school over summer break. Thought it was harmless at first. I knew about what happened to them, what with their parents and all."

"Someone in your position should have gone to the cops with that kind of information. What kept you?"

"Jay Percel. A kid that came to me for help one time years ago. He told me how his father sexually abused him, how his mother beat him anywhere below the face with anything she could find, and it just, hell, it just made me sick." He shook his head, his eyes distant and aimless. "Someone in my position, yeah. I thought I did the right thing. Called the police. Got Social Services involved. The boy was sent to the Wilcox Children's Home up in Abbey nevertheless. Jay, he hung himself with a dress belt in a coat closet.

When the police found him, he was barefoot in jeans, no shirt on, either. Across his chest in a black magic marker, the words were all screwed up because he'd written the message himself. It was one fragmented word and that word, Mason, got to me in a bad way."

"What was it?" Mason asked, holding his breath. "What did the message say?"

"Free."

"What?"

"We found a note in his back pocket and it described the shit he went through while living with his parents. He said in the note that the pain he felt engulfed him. The madness in his head was enough to make him go insane, and I truly believe that if he didn't do himself in, he would have hurt someone else. The pain he felt—all that ate away at Jay, it drove him to the edge, and he ended his life because of it." Ardon caught his reflection in Mason's sunglasses. "That's why this time, when Sadie Bellis came to me and told me about her troubles, I offered to help. I didn't know exactly what I was going to do, I just knew I wasn't going to the cops this time or get government agencies involved. Didn't plan on making the same mistake twice. Call it childish, but I feared Sadie would do something stupid like Jay."

Mason ran his tongue between the slit of his mouth. "Was it really stupid?"

Ardon disregarded the question. "I did what I had to do. Those kids, they could have been sent back home, or worse, into foster care."

"That's what'll happen to Danny and Melissa if someone doesn't step up to the plate, and it's one of the reasons why I dropped by. Strange question. Do you know anyone who needs a couple of kids?" His serious proposal came off more like a joke he'd heard at a bar. "You sound pretty calm about Sadie. She did return home."

"By force, not voluntarily."

"So, how are you gonna help her now?"

Ardon shrugged. "It's beyond me. There's really nothing I can do for her."

"There's something I can do."

"Mason, you've . . . taken lives, man. Five, if you count your own parents. Stop now, it's not right. You've come too far and you and I both know it. Ease off. Go back to Rachel, go back to your life. God forgive me, but if

I had met you only a month ago and knew what you've done, I'd have turned you over to the authorities myself."

Mason licked his lips again. "At least you're honest. Ardon, it'll haunt me knowing Sadie's back in the same situation she tried to run from. I can't let that happen." He walked off, and what he heard next made his blood boil.

"I can still turn you in, Mason." Ardon's voice was hard-edged. "I'll tell them everything if you kill Sadie's parents. I'll tell the cops what you did to the Giles, how you slammed Bobby's head on a table saw. I'll even throw in the fact that you sabotaged your parent's car, and it doesn't matter if it happened over ten years ago, they will care, and I will get on the witness stand and testify in a court of law if you don't believe me."

"You're my friend. You wouldn't do that. What, is it money you want?"

"I don't need your money, it's not about money. It's about not shedding any more blood." The veins in Ardon's neck bulged against his skin, his face went beet red. "Don't you have a conscience? Ever heard of that? What happened to you, son? You keep on going this way, you're gonna freakin' snap, buddy, lemme tell ya. You'll end up like Jay Percel. The pain in you will sneak up, dig its claws in deep, and suffocate you—just like it did him!" He chunked the beer bottle down on the patio and glass shattered at the barbecue grill. "You're not a good person, Mason. I'm here to tell you that. You're not helping those kids, you're killing them, man. Don't you understand that? Killing them!"

Mason stepped forward. The air around him felt thick on his skin, the tension between them rising. "I'll bring you down with me, don't think I won't."

"I'm not gonna stand here and listen to this shit. I'll deny I ever helped Sadie stay at the school. You have nothing on me, and—"

"Raping a twelve-year-old child in Vietnam is nothing? I think the police would care about that. Your family, your friends. They'd all care." He noticed the muscles in Ardon's arms flex, and he considered the possibility of them in a physical fight, and though he was strong as an ox, he knew he was no match against this man he'd called his friend all these years. Ardon would wipe the concrete with his head, and from the look in the principal's eyes, he knew this, too. "How about some advice before you get hurt?"

"Is that a threat?" Ardon said.

"In the soul's witching hour, everyone sleeps. Even you. It might be next week, or next month, even next year, but I will find you, and what happens happens, that's all I can say. That is, if you go to the cops." He sucked in a breath, pressed his palms together. "I have two words for you, Principal Wells. Back. Off."

Mason got into his car, started the engine. He had a feeling his threat did nothing but piss Ardon off, and it would take time to see if his friend would actually turn his back on him, or keep quiet.

Chapter 36

Sadie was in her bedroom checking her email when Quitman came home. One of her AOL buddies was a girl by the name of May Halter, from Mount Olive, Arkansas, whose mother passed from heart failure a year ago when she was sixteen. Sadie told May several times that if she needed a mother so badly, she could have Anne—ha ha ha. But truth be known, she wouldn't wish her mother on even her worst enemy.

Downstairs in the kitchen, she heard them talking about her. The conversation went on for at least an hour. Anne said things like, "I found her, she's here, thought she could run away, stay gone forever, but the idiot was bad wrong." A pan dropped to the floor and footsteps fled up the stairway. The hustle stopped outside her room.

Sadie waited. She imagined the door being torn off its hinges at Quitman's force, but nothing happened, and she let out a breath of relief.

She hadn't cried since Anne last hit her, but her face was still red and wet from tears. Her lips trembled. She had stuffed toilet tissue into the hole where her tooth had been, could still taste the blood, and the pain was unbearable. Her left eye looked like a flesh-covered marble. Anne had yanked her out of the car with such force, Sadie thought her wrist had dislocated. Unbelievable. What was it? Why was this happening to her? How had she managed to return to this? She thought about her friends. Were they in jail? With aunts or uncles? In a foster home? She feared they'd been adopted and moved out of town forever with nice parents, people who attended church on a regular basis, went for picnics out at Red Lake, nurtured, cared, loved them. *Jeez.* She'd never see them again. Then, she pictured the stranger in black. If his earlier actions showed any truth that he was on her side, surely he'd found her missing by now and was on the search.

The long cold blade of loneliness crept back into her bones and made her sick. If only that stranger were here right now. He would come into the house, shoot her parents, take her away, and she'd be safe.

That's all she ever wanted.

She lay in bed, on top of the sheets, and set the clock for six-thirty. Yellow moonlight flooded the room in a pool and the pine trees outside her window swayed in the wind. Sadie held a stuffed teddy bear to her chest for the first time since she was seven and heard nothing in the room but an eerie silence. Her mother had recently put up storm screens on the window, so there was no way out unless she went downstairs. Out of the question. She believed that Anne was crazy enough to injure her so badly that she would die. It was almost as if the woman was aching to do it, waiting in the shadows for the perfect moment when Sadie screwed up so that she had a reason to knock off her own daughter.

"God? Why does my momma hate me?" she asked out loud. "Why does she do this to me? If she don't love me, who does? Do you?" A tear rolled down her cheek and she closed her eyes, turned over and squeezed the soft teddy bear. She left the computer on for the security of light. The scary thing was that it showed her dolls that aligned her dresser in squat, fat shadows, their faces illuminated by the glow, some smiling, others frowning. It brought back visions of scary movies and tales of the supernatural Melissa used to read about. Dolls coming to life, killing off entire households. In her own defense, she begged for sleep, but she could sleep in the dark no longer.

When it happened, she cried. His large hands moved over her body as if touching an antique sculpture, there was the sweat from his lips on her tender skin, his body odor at her nose, the rage she felt. She just cried.

Around two in the morning, Quitman opened her bedroom door and staggered in, his breath stinking of beer, his skin coated with sweat. He was barefoot, in a tank top and ripped jeans.

She didn't feel his touch in her sleep until it was too late. He shoved one finger up her vagina, and wiggled it around.

She woke in shock, screamed—or tried to scream—but his hand was faster than her voice, and covered her mouth, pushed her head into the pillow.

"Mmph!"

"Be quiet, you hear me? You deserve this, you know you deserve it, so shut your mouth," he whispered.

Sadie's eyes widened, as big as newly minted quarters, and her heart accelerated. She wanted to jump up and run, but his strength overpowered her. In his hand, she saw the knife, the blade shiny in the pale, blue light, and her muscles locked.

He grunted as he sucked and kissed her skin, moving from her stomach to her neck, groping her breasts in his hands.

She tried to think of nice thoughts, of something else—anything but what was happening here and now—but she drew a blank and was angry at herself for not being more imaginative, angry that she had been given to these sadistic people. She wished the stranger were here, wished he could see what was happening to her and put a bullet straight through Quitman's head. That was a long shot, she knew, and Sadie cried when she realized that her entire life had come to this—to being degraded and touched and viewed as nothing but a piece of meat, a flesh machine only breathing in order to entertain drunkards like Quitman, and serve as a punching bag for abusive parents like Anne.

Kill them. Take them away.

His fingers dug in deeper, and it hurt more than when Anne had knocked out her tooth. At the same time, whether she welcomed the feeling or not, a sense of pleasure overcame her.

Forgive me.

She felt guilty, dirty. It wasn't right, but she couldn't stop it. In school, she'd never even French-kissed a boy, much less had a man's hand near her crotch, so how could she have known what it felt like, or if she would enjoy it?

God forgive me. Please. Kill him. Kill him and kill her.

She closed her eyes as his kisses became harder, his grip around her hips more firm, his fingers more aggressive.

Son of a bitch asshole jerkoff fucker!

"Augh!" Sadie squirmed from under his grip, managed to remove his hand from over her mouth, and she shrieked at the top of her lungs.

The knife sliced through her skin so quickly that it felt more like a numbing hit than a cut. She looked down, gasped at the blood spilling out of her forearm.

The bedroom light flicked on, and Anne stepped inside.

—◊—

Rachel was sitting on the couch with her feet up on the coffee table when Mason got home. She composed herself and acted as though she'd seen nothing in his office, and tried to make herself believe that he was the same man she'd met when she was eighteen—that sweet, innocent teenager who wouldn't have hurt anyone or anything. Instead, beyond her mask, she viewed him as a complete and total stranger. She couldn't help it.

"Hey, baby." He kissed her lips and strolled into the kitchen, opened the freezer and popped ice into a glass, filled it with sweet tea. From underneath the sink, he grabbed a bottle of Jack Daniel's and doused the drink with a couple of shots. He raised the glass toward her. "How was your day? Want a drink?"

She tried to hide the truth that she knew about him. It showed in her actions, on her face. Still, she wasn't positive he was the man the entire town was searching for. On his desk, she'd found only articles from recent newspapers. Anyone had access to that kind of information. The ripped photographs played an important part in her decision. They were personal, so how did he get them? But what spun her head was the gun. Why did he have that gun in his desk, and had he used it before? If so, on what . . . or whom?

"I don't feel like drinking," she lied. She did. She wanted to drown her mind in a bottle of Vanilla Schnapps until she again recognized the man she'd grown to love. She watched him lean against the sink's counter and sip the drink like there was nothing wrong. In her mind, she connected the possibilities that he was the killer; the articles of the recent murders, his interest in the kids' disappearances, how he'd finished off his own parents, those torn photos, why he'd been gone on select evenings for varying lengths of time and arrived home late—like tonight—and she remembered what Olivia had said to her.

It can't be true.

And the notebook.

The gun in the drawer materialized in her head.

He approached, knelt at her feet. His hair was damp with sweat and his skin felt hot against her bare thigh where he placed his cheek. She combed her nails through his hair, clawed his scalp. He hummed in pleasure.

"Mason?"

"Yes?"

"How much do you love me?"

He closed his eyes and snuggled up to her midsection, kissed her stomach. "More than you'll ever know."

"Would you ever hurt me?"

"I told you," he said, without meeting her eyes, "there isn't another woman."

"No." Her peppermint breath fell gently onto his shoulder. "Would you ever *physically* hurt me?"

That got Mason's attention and he lifted his head, caressed her skin, his touch warm. "What're you saying? Why're you asking me this? Of course not. I'd never hurt you."

She pretended to smile, and thought of the day she'd been standing in front of the curtains in her bedroom before she took her morning jog and ended up at Olivia's shack. It was that day she'd first began feeling neglected by him, and not being needed was the saddest thing in the world. Rachel needed him to need her. She wanted to wrap her arms around him and hug him until his head exploded, kiss him, make love to him, whisper in his ear that he was the one for her, the only one, and that they'd be together forever. But being in his presence was now disconcerting. It didn't seem real. She could not bring herself to look him in the eye, let alone talk, and something held her back from saying and doing all those things, though they burned bright red in her heart.

Rachel saw the confusion in Mason's face and pulled off his sunglasses, lay them on the couch's cushion. "I'm sorry—I don't know why I said that."

He tilted his head. "What's wrong? Why are you acting like this?"

"Like what?"

"You're just not yourself this evening." He tipped the glass to her lips and demanded she drink. "Taste this, it'll make you feel better." She shook her head. "Go ahead. For me."

"I don't want a drink."

"C'mon, baby. Tell me what's on your mind. Drink this, it'll help." He pressed the cold glass to her cheek and she craned her neck away from him.

"Mason, no!" She punched the air and caught his arm. Ice and spiked tea flew into his face, soaked his hair. Her chest heaved with fright and her fingers dug into the back of the couch for support as she realized what she'd done.

He spit, wiped his mouth with the back of his hand, and stood. Mason looked down on her, his face lit by the lamp on the end table. In this view, his glance took on a hard, sharpened move, and his tongue shot out, struck a drop of whiskey running down his cheek. "Why're you acting like this? I just wanted to talk to my girl. It seems like you're . . . scared of something."

Two tears crept from the corners of Rachel's eyes, her nose clogged up, her cheeks swelled, grew damp. She positioned her feet along the carpet underneath Mason's stance. "I found the gun. I found it in your office, baby. Tell me it's not true."

He backed off, shoved his hands in his pockets, and walked around the coffee table. The emptied glass lay on the plush white carpet. He picked it up, turned it in his hand, and inspected the specks of dirt and hair stuck to its surface. His jaws locked, his grip tightened, and veins popped over his skin. "I need to vacuum this carpet."

"I thought we agreed you'd keep your guns at the lake house. You know I hate those things. The articles of those children. I found them, too."

"I'm a good person, Rachel."

"How'd you get those people's personal photos? And why are they ripped?"

"You wouldn't understand," he whispered. "Just be cool."

"The late nights. Tell me it's not true."

He swallowed, set the empty glass and ice on the bar's counter.

"The headlines about their parents' deaths. Those, too. The notebook.

I found the notebook and the stories those kids wrote. What's that all about?"

"I'd never hurt you."

"Mason, every time you leave this house, somebody ends up dead!"

"Rachel? Calm down. You're getting—"

"I wish it *was* another girl!" She bolted to her feet. "I wish you were downtown fucking some slut's brains out! I wish you could tell me what her cunt tastes like! Anything, Mason! Anything other than—"

"Enough!" Mason spun and sent the tumbler flying across the room. It shattered against the mirror, the impact causing a blunt, spiderweb crack that stretched to the edges. He got his sunglasses off the edge of the couch, swiped his keys off the counter, and slammed the front door on the way out into the night. His thoughts went into disarray, snaking through his head like jolts of lightning, telling him he'd made a mistake, telling him that his plans that had gone so smoothly, had suddenly taken a sharp, definite turn, and he had to do something before things got out of hand, and he was discovered.

Rachel knew.

Chapter 37

8:42 a.m.

Terry refilled his coffee cup. The kitchen table looked like a playground for an investigation, what with the articles and newspaper headlines scattered about. It reminded him of being back at the office, being Sheriff of Sutter Springs. But that was history and he wished he could change the past. What would he be doing if he'd kept the position?

After the Parent Killer?

It had been the most horrible crime that ever hit the town, and nothing would ever compare. He thought of Principal Wells and the kids, and Mason Xavier, and his girlfriend, Rachel Borello.

Where did it all go wrong?

He stopped worrying when Monica would be home. She'd called from the pharmacy and said she'd bumped into Ms. Ezona Wilcox from the Wilcox Children's Home in Abbey. Knowing Ms. Wilcox, the woman didn't shut her mouth for an hour, and he saw that as the reason it was taking his wife so long to return with his medicine.

The Giles' murder had been the big one, but what came next was an explosion. Even after the Parent Killer was tracked down, Terry lost his job thanks to the mayor, that son of a bitch. Ultimately, he had to look at it from Frank's point of view.

Murder is murder, no matter how you look at it.

He searched through the articles and found the black-and-white photos of Quitman and Anne Mase, the people who had physically, mentally and sexually abused eleven-year-old Sadie Bellis for who knows how long.

Terry remembered the splintering rain, the harsh winds, the roaring thunder on the dark day that ended it all. He did not arrive on the scene until it was too late.

Chapter 38

If my mom ever hits me again, I'm just going to hit her back. Who cares anyway?

Sadie Belli's
Notebook entry #47

—ᴍ— A sense of calm came over her, and she was relieved when she saw her mother standing at the threshold of her bedroom. She never thought she'd be this happy to see her. They locked eyes. Sadie's face punctuated every fear she'd known, and it was in this light, at this moment, when the woman approached and Quitman pulled his finger out of her, his skin slicked with her wetness, that she knew her mother was a product of pure evil.

Anne noticed the gaping cut on her forearm. The big-bodied woman sat on the bed and the springs creaked from her weight. She moved her hand over Sadie's hair, gazed into her eyes.

Sadie tried to talk—got out the word help—and her eyelashes fluttered. Drops of blood covered the sheets, spotted her chest.

Anne patted her cheek with assurance. "It's okay," she said. "Shhh, everything's okay."

"Moh-ma." The child closed her eyes, her face perplexed with hurt.

Anne held Sadie's arms above her head, and kissed her cheek, then looked up at Quitman. She nodded, and he shucked his dirty, oil-stained jeans, pulled himself out, and held his penis firmly in his right hand.

"It's time to teach you who's in charge around here," Anne said.

271

Sadie squirmed beneath her. "Momma? Momma, stop it, make him stop. Don't, don't, pleeeeeze!" She screamed when he put himself inside her, widening her walls, driving deep. She cried out, fought to free Anne's grip, but couldn't break the woman's strength.

Her mother laughed out loud, told Quitman to "give it to her good."

Hell. The most intense pain she'd ever felt coursed through her body. She'd given up fighting them off and prayed she'd pass out.

Heated and sweaty, Quitman pulled out and squirted on her stomach.

Anne's lips were at her ears. "Did it feel good? I bet it felt real good, didn't it you little slut?" She slapped her cheek. "You hear me!" When she got off the bed, it bounced upward. "Let that be a lesson. Handle that?"

Sadie turned away and buried her face in the pillow. She caught the dolls lining the ledge of her windowsill. Out of habit she stuck her thumb in her mouth and sucked, like she'd done so many years ago when her mother would scorn her for soiling herself. She felt full of sin.

Why had her mother done this?

I hate her. Hope Quitman burns.

She was weak, lying there with her panties around her ankles and her shirt pushed up underneath her soft breasts. Tears streamed over her nose, tickled her skin, spread in tiny drops on the pillowcase. She didn't care what she looked like right now, all she wanted was rest.

As if in a trance, she whispered, "Help me . . . help me . . . God . . . help me," then closed her eyes, still repeating the words, and begged for contentment, her cut forearm wrapped in the bed sheet, the middle of her legs throbbing.

—⁂—

Rachel got the key to their lake house from a hide-a-key rock in the flower bed at the foot of the steps. She threw her purse on the counter and drank bottled water while staring out over Red Lake. Moonlight bathed the pier that ran underneath a scattered row of tall, ghostly cypress trees and wind licked the hanging Spanish moss that resembled limp, skeletal feathers.

With a drunk's reflexes, she held the bottle to her lips, allowed the perfect plastic circle to move at her wet, pink skin left to right in a seductive move. She thought about what she'd done to Mason only a half hour ago. What was he thinking at this moment? Of her? How was he reacting? More importantly, where was he?

She held a picture of them at the lake in the winter. Their faces were red and chapped, reflecting the season, but they were smiling. That's all that mattered. Comfortable, loving one another. Smiling. What had happened to them? Rachel couldn't figure it out. There was an emptiness in her heart, a void that needed filling, but all she focused on was that Mason Xavier could actually be a criminal, and that possibility made her shiver.

The lake house was adorned with several stuffed animals that Mason had killed on hunting expeditions. Deer, elk, duck, a cougar. A Kodiak bearskin rug was laid out in the center of the den, stamped to the floor by a glass coffee table the shape of a diamond. She set her drink on the table and dropped to the floor. While thumbing through a magazine, trying to get her mind off Mason, she spotted something in the next room that made her jump. It was her own reflection in the light that panned off the frontal glass of a gun case. She inspected. Inside the case were three high-powered rifles, a pistol, and an 18-inch barrel, short stock scatter gun. The case's handle was locked.

She got to her knees, slipped her hand underneath the two-inch crack of its base and retrieved a small key that might have fitted a padlock. She opened it, and felt like a little girl about to get in trouble for doing something she knew was wrong. She picked up the rifle, shouldered it, and peered through the scope. In the cross-hairs, she moved her sight into the kitchen, the den, into the guest room, and finally settled on the front plank porch shining neon blue from two zapping bug lights.

Her breath was stale in her mouth, and all color drained from her face. The tip of her tongue touched her dry lips. A beat. Was she crazy? No, she wasn't. It felt good to hold a gun. Powerful, in control. Control. She had physical power in her hands, and she believed, if need be, she could unleash that kind of fury.

Rachel let out the breath, and lowered the rifle. Then, she grabbed the pistol. It was about the same size as the one she'd seen in Mason's office. That's what had caught her off guard—the gun she'd found at home. Mason had been so trustworthy over the years, so why had he broken the rules? It was unlike him. Lake house? Fine. She just didn't want them in her home.

She was aware of how to use a firearm. Her father had taught her when she was younger. Aim and shoot. Not so difficult.

It's what you're shooting, a voice said.

She checked the clip. Full. Disengaged the chamber. A hollow-point fell to the carpet. She picked it up and eyed it in the bright light. She slid out a drawer in the gun cabinet, searched through extra clips, found a pair of mini-binoculars with infrared capability, and then a white box containing more bullets.

"Holy shit." The sound of her voice in the silence unnerved her. The loads were powerful enough to penetrate a steel wall.

She put the guns into the cabinet and returned to the living room, lit a scented candle on the mantle. In the blackness at the beginning of a TV program, she saw a movement reflected by the screen. Her heart lurched to her throat. It was true she hated guns, but she would have felt safer with the pistol in her hands. Rachel moved her neck, looked at the front porch through the window. Nothing. Her heart didn't slow as she rose to her feet. A sheet of sweat covered her palms. She hurried into the bedroom to the gun cabinet and retrieved the pistol, walked sideways into the den, the weapon locked in her hands.

With a flick of a switch, the yellow lamps poured over the front walk. There was no movement, but she could've sworn she'd seen a shadow. Maybe a stray cat, a possum. Something told her that was not it.

What she'd seen resembled a person.

Damn it, now she was scaring herself. She searched the front yard and the walk, looked out over the shimmering lake, and before she turned off the light, she noticed the porch swing breaking sideways where no one sat. A gentle breeze could not muster enough force to shake it so—only a human being, someone in a rush.

—⁓—

Mason never looked upon himself as a fool. Tonight proved him wrong. He should have had his office door bulletproof so that no one could manipulate their way inside. When Rachel went into her little fit, he should have done a lot of things. Instead, he stopped the words before they came out, and hurried into the night like a frightened child.

He drove slowly. Differently. Usually he was a speed demon. He had unfinished business to attend to. The lake house was in the rearview. He felt a flush of anger overcome his body. Just there, sitting on the porch swing, watching her on the couch. He loved her, loved her with all his heart, and if only he could tell her that, he'd feel a world better. Rachel had discovered the truth and it was going to be difficult to face her again. The gun, the articles, the torn photographs . . . the notebook. That's what gave him away.

A question he couldn't answer entered his mind, and he combed his hand over his hair, frustrated. *Would she go to the police?*

No. She was smarter than that. She knew of his capabilities. But he wasn't absolutely positive. When you put a person in danger and fearing for their lives, there are no rules to follow, no foreseen action someone might try in order to protect themselves. He thumped the cigarette out the window in haste, angrily, as if it had burned his finger. He blew the white smoke into the dashboard, and parked the Porsche a block from Sadie's house.

Unfinished. *Business.*

The night air was damp and humid, the sky clean and clear, the color of silver and ocean blue high above. The moon blinked behind thick rain clouds and a row of trees that lined Bahama Street bent in the coming rains. His boots grew unusually hard on the concrete, clomped along, echoed out. Through the thicket and power lines, Mason saw red taillights dance past each other on the highway. He sniffed the air, smelled the sweet, heavy scent of honeysuckle glide by his head. As he walked the cracked sidewalk through the old Bradmoore neighborhood, the one hundred-year-old Victorian-style homes stared eerily down upon him from their pillars and wraparound porches. He was in open view of any onlookers, cautious of the street lamps shedding faded light at the corner of every block. Standing at the end of the paved drive and manicured lawn, he looked up at the brick home nestled in a clump of tall healthy pines. He lit a cigarette and pulled in a deep breath and approached. The dress shirt and sunglasses were on the move. His hands were steady, his sight crisp. Inside, it was a different story. His nerves jumped and shot through his system with the intensity of an electrical storm.

Mason spit on the sidewalk. The forefront of Sadie's house was blocked by a large, blossoming oak and when he stepped onto the dew-covered grass, he thought about what Principal Wells had said.

Stop now while you're ahead.

He shouldn't be here, he shouldn't be doing this. It wasn't right.

Sadie entered his mind. He thought about the short time they had spent together, and his memory brought back those terrible stories in her notebook. How her mother once slammed her face on the stove and busted her lip and loosened a tooth; when Quitman walked in the bathroom as she was taking a shower and had tried to touch her. His jaw clenched tight as he imagined her mistreated, living in a fear without end, and he had to feel sorry for her, had no choice but to keep on, reach his goal.

To hell with morality. Real justice had costs.

As the madness filled his veins, Mason was again hungry. Revenge. Sweet.

In the window, he caught a glimpse of Quitman's silhouette in the TV's inky, blue cast. He went to the next window. Nothing. On the second floor, he saw Anne walk out of a bathroom with a towel over her head, and a large pink robe around her obese body. She opened it, revealing her naked form, and Mason looked away, disgusted by the sight. He moved to the back patio, tried the sliding glass door. Upstairs, a light clicked on. He found a stack of wooden crates edged against a tree and climbed aboard. The crates were unsteady as he stood, but he kept his balance, and saw Sadie in the bedroom, her hair matted, face long and sleepy.

On the bed, she looked into a mirror mounted above the headboard. She touched her eye, then jaw, and flinched. A dark red line scarred her forearm.

When she turned toward the window, Mason saw that her face was red, her eye was bruised. For a second, he thought she'd seen him. She went into a bathroom.

He jumped down from the crates, sneaked around the corner. His heart pounded hard in his chest. Nervous energy flooded him. It was almost as if he were excited with what he was about to accomplish. He'd cared for Danny, and Melissa, but the bond with Sadie seemed different, like he was protecting himself in the process. He unscrewed the front porch light bulb, pitched it into the bushes. The nine-millimeter was down the back of his jeans. By now, he would've had it out, poised high, ready to fire. But here he felt more like an observer, not an intruder. He touched the doorknob and it clicked open. He pushed it farther and the TV glare flashed at his feet.

I saw her last night in the moonlight haze. Her skin was ripped away from bone, the muscles deteriorated to hair-like fragments, the dents sunken in her forehead purple and black and slick. A long gash that ran the length of her cheek melted into and over her eye like a . . . .

Her eye.

Above, he heard Anne's heavy footfalls move from room to room. Quitman was no longer on the couch. The smell of cigarettes and alcohol, dirty laundry, and a hint of potpourri air-freshener hit him at once.

He stepped softly, cat-like, aware of the hardwood floor adjacent to the living room and dining room. A refrigerator opened and closed. Snap of a canned beer, pish! He peered around the corner, saw Quitman at the counter hand-rolling a joint. A flimsy plastic bag of marijuana lay open on the cutting board. He was in boxers, no shirt. His underarm hair flared, and he looked like a crack smoker on a bad day.

Mason reached for the gun, popped the safety. A series of thumps sounded out. He backed into the open hall closet, and hid.

Anne took the stairs, her bustling weight shaking the house. She dragged Sadie kicking and screaming into the kitchen. "You see this little shit? Caught her tryin' to climb out the bathroom window! Gonna hafta put up storm windows in there, too. All because of her sorry ass. Won't listen, she'll never learn."

"Stop it, that hurts! Quit it! Get off me you fat hog!"

"Nothin' but a got-damn crybaby," Quitman said, lighting the joint. Smoke puffed into his face. Through the cloud, his eyes were black. "Shut her damn mouth!" He took a drag.

"To hell with you!" Sadie yelled. "You fuckin' bum!" She jumped out of her mother's grip, ran for a broom leaning against the laundry room wall. She swung it heavy in the air. The hard tip caught Quitman's nose. "You ugly . . . bastard! I hate you!"

Quitman's head did a double take. He caught himself on the counter. His hand flew to his face, and when he pulled his fingers away, they were spotted with bright red blood.

"I hate you! I hate both of you! I—"

Anne's hand went across her face. The "slap" sound was sharp and solid. "That's enough out of you, Ms. Priss! I'm runnin' this show now, you hear me? Who do you think you are?!"

Sadie was quiet. Her eyes grew, and filled with tears. Her cheek stung, and she wanted to punch her mother in the face as hard as she could, but no matter how hard she tried, no matter how strong the urge to lash out, she simply couldn't do it. Anne could hurt her as much as she wanted, and Sadie was so weak against her that she'd take it every time.

She couldn't believe what she saw. A black dress shirt. The tail-end whipped out from around the corner like dark wind. Was it her imagination?

Heart pounding steady, Mason stepped into view, his boots touched the tile floor, his arm and the gun extended. He gritted his teeth.

The air thickened, felt tense, as all eyes were drawn to him.

The joint between Quitman's lips dropped, tumbled down his chest, as if in slow motion, knocking lit ashes into his skin. He tuned his attention to the stranger before him.

Anne's throat clenched, her body tightened. She looked, Sadie noticed, *scared*.

Sadie sucked in a breath, relieved and excited and frightened all the same as the stranger stopped underneath the kitchen's glow, and moved the gun from Quitman to Anne.

The room fell silent.

Mason controlled the play, his presence that of cold hate. Each person felt it. Especially him.

Sadie looked up, a clear, unconditioned welcome in her eyes. "You came," she said.

Anne's voice was weak and frail. "Who . . . are you?"

Quitman was broken. He froze, didn't know what to do.

Mason swallowed, his lips parted. "The Parent Killer," he said. The notebook and its written contents flashed through his mind, and it angered him all over again, as if he was just now discovering the nightmare Sadie had endured for so long. His heart skipped a beat. He caught a bead on Quitman's forehead.

And he pulled the trigger.

The sound of silence was deafening. The weapon in his hand might as well have been a water pistol. No blast, no earth-shattering thunder. Just a fast, dry *click*.

Quitman's chest exhaled and he glanced at Anne. The desperate expression on his face asked what he should do.

Seated on the floor, Sadie covered her face with both hands, peeked between her fingers.

"You son of a bitch." It was Quitman's crawling-country voice. "You damn son of a bitch!" He slid out the counter drawer, reached in, and pulled out a steak knife.

Sadie sensed the fear in the Parent Killer. He crumbled right in front of her. What could he do now? How could he save her, save himself? She noticed the innocence in Mason—after all, he was still only a young man himself, not a hardened criminal—and in the kitchen light, he seemed no older than Sadie. A young man without the strength to carry on.

"Get him," Anne ordered. She faced Quitman. "For Christ's sake! Get him!"

At her command, he lurched forward, the steel blade held out at his side. He swung. Mason shifted to avoid the attack, but the sharp, corrugated steel sliced into his side. Dark blood poured over his skin in a wave. He held his breath in shock, struggled to get a grip, then grabbed Quitman's arm, and punched his face. The man slammed into the refrigerator.

Mason looked down at the knife jutting out of his side. He grabbed the handle, pulled it out, and rushed Quitman.

"No!" Quitman yelled. "God, Jesus! No!"

"Quitman!" Anne yelled. "No! Stop it! Don't hurt him!"

Mason put the blade to his throat. The edge sank into skin, touched cartilage, and he was about to pull it across and end the man's life when a blast sounded out. A tiny hole appeared in Quitman's forehead. The back of his head exploded and brain matter and blood sprayed the refrigerator's white surface as if splattered there with a paintbrush.

Anne screamed. It was the most horrible, most single frightening sound Mason had ever heard.

He turned to see Sadie standing at the threshold of the living room, a pistol in her hand, smoke drifting in circles from the barrel.

She licked her lips, and turned the gun on her mother.

"Sadie, no. No, baby. Put the gun down, please."

"You hurt me," Sadie said. "You've always hurt me."

"I love you, Honey. Don't do this, don't be stupid."

"You're doing it again!"

Anne waved her hands. "I'm sorry! Okay, now. Just listen to me, Sadie. I don't want this to go any farther than it already has. Please put the gun down."

"You let him touch me, Momma. He did that awful thing to me in my bed and you let him!"

"Please don't, please, oh God . . . don't do it, baby. I'm sorry, I'm so sorry."

"I have to, Momma." Sadie pulled down the hammer, and the sound spiked the room.

"Why Sadie? Why? Why are you doing this?"

"Because I love you."

Mason took one step back and covered his ears with gloved hands.

Chapter 39

In her dream, Rachel walked through a snow-covered field. The snow produced orgasmic sounds when her foot sank into its mass. Over the horizon, she gazed at a thousand silver moons. Sweat drenched her face as if someone had dumped a bucket of water over her head, and her muscles throbbed with a strange, pleasurable ache. A breeze swept her hair from her face. Cold chills passed through her body, stabbed at her bones, and she noticed her reflection in a silver pond. Naked. Looked down. Wished she hadn't. A red wave flushed out of her vagina, crawled down her legs in bright, wet clumps, stirred around her bare feet, and then bubbled into a steaming pool. In the mess she saw a finger, an eye, strands of brown hair.

She clasped her hand over her face, and let out a held breath. She cried out, but her throat was stiff. She clutched at her neck, gagged herself, closed her eyes, and when she vomited, the faint, innocent laughter of a child echoed in the distance—over the hills, into her ringing ears.

She sat bolt upright, searched the living room, disillusioned. Her chest heaved, heart rolled. The TV had gone snowy.

Still here. Alone. Inside the lake house.

She felt the hard, numbing bulge in her back pocket she'd been lying on, and pulled out the clip to Mason's nine-millimeter. She'd taken it for fear he'd turn against her—extreme, she supposed, but the dragon on his back had awakened, he was capable, and in the whirlwind of their argument, she'd forgotten it had been in her possession. Without a clip, he could not use the gun, and maybe there wasn't a loaded chamber. Another life perhaps had been spared.

As the seconds ticked away and the idea became clear in her mind that she believed Mason was the one the police were searching for, it hurt her so much, she really did want to puke.

She settled into the couch. The ceiling fan whipped through the air, and pressed a comforting blanket on top of her body. Taking caution, Rachel looked down and felt her legs. There was no blood and no wetness. No laughter in her head, or from the back walls of the cabin. What did it mean? Was she going crazy? The scene clutched her brain. Blood from her crotch? What the hell was that all about?

She locked herself into the bathroom, opened a box, and pulled out a small plastic item that resembled a kazoo. She dropped her jeans to her ankles, arched her back forward, and stood over the toilet rim as best she could, then peed.

Pregnancy tests were never easy, especially for a couple who had been trying for over four months. For her, the anticipation was as important to her as receiving junk mail. Was it her? Mason? Were they both at fault? She finished. Still tired, still worried, and she staggered back to the couch. Maybe this was it. Maybe she would become pregnant and her life would change for the better. She and Mason's. Could she keep on loving him?

Her eyes fell at the thought, and she slipped into a deep sleep.

—⁓—

Four rounds. Sadie had emptied the gun into Anne's chest. Blood covered the floors, the cabinets, her hair and skin. Her mother's stare was alive, or rather, disgusting, but her body was dead.

Sadie had done it. She'd killed her.

Her tiny arm was kept extended. Tiny smoke curls still flipped out of the gun barrel. Her face was stony, her eyes heavy. She couldn't move, do, or say anything for the fear that gripped her.

Mason touched her skin, and took the gun from her hand.

"Let's go," he whispered. "We've gotta get outta here."

"I found it under their bed. Heard Quitman talking about it one night. I was afraid they'd use it on me sooner or later." Her arms fell to her sides. She looked at Mason, blinked out a tear.

Mason reached out and wiped the liquid salt from her skin, took her by the hand, like a doll's in a baseball glove, and led her to his car. He put his nine-millimeter, and the gun Sadie had underneath the passenger seat. "Stay here," he told her and returned inside the house.

He stepped over Quitman's body, careful of the red pool surrounding him, and ripped a picture off the refrigerator. It was a computer enlargement. Grainy, with a slicked surface. It showed Anne and Quitman sitting on a bench at a lake, beers in their hands, Anne's arm over his hairy thigh, him wearing cheap shades, both with weekend smiles. He looked at the bodies. He couldn't grasp that an eleven-year-old child had just murdered her very own parents.

Her face was pale and bluish, her lips cracked and peeled from lying in a coffin.

Anne's eyes were still open even though hot lead had torn through her heart, and he dropped the picture in her blood on his way out the door.

When he reached his car, he dialed a number from his cell phone. Sheriff Combs answered on the second ring.

"Sheriff?" Mason said. "There's been a murder at Five-Twenty, Bahama. Get over here before the bodies start to smell."

"Who is this?!"

"I've finished the game."

"What? Who is this!"

"Fuck, it's over. End of conversation."

Static came over the line in a sharp wave. Terry's voice was small, wary, each word pronounced, spoken carefully, with the authority normally attached to a man of his stature. "Who. Is. This."

Mason moved his tongue over his bottom lip, started the car. Sadie looked upon him with wondering eyes.

"The man you can't catch." Click.

He drove west. The night was a vast black sea, the moonlight slatted across the windshield the color of vanilla, the air streaking into the cracked windows hot against their skin. He fired a cigarette, and clicked on the air conditioner.

Sadie shifted in her seat, hesitated to turn his way. "Where're we goin'?"

"I'm taking you to your friends."

"Who?"

"Danny and Melissa. You wanna see them, don't you?"

She was quiet, tapped the ends of her fingers together. "What's going to happen now? I mean, after—?"

He put his hand on top of hers and squeezed. It was the warmest, most caring touch she'd ever felt.

"Don't worry. You'll be just fine." Mason turned his head quick to pop his neck. A million thoughts ran through his mind. He had finished the game. His self-initiated murder spree had come to an end. The investigation would probably continue for another month or so, but would soon die down, and he'd leave it all in the past where it belonged. He'd risked too much—his life, Rachel's future, the kids' safety—but there was no going back, neither now, nor ten years from now, was the time to reconsider his actions and decide if he had done the right thing.

Murder was never the answer.

But his mind always switched back to the kids and what they had experienced.

He pulled alongside the end of the gravel drive and looked over Sadie's shoulder at the darkened brick house edged back from the highway. The first few drops of rain fell to the earth. Mason unlocked the passenger side door.

"Why are you doing this?" Sadie asked.

"Doing what?"

She threw out her hand. "Just dropping me off."

"There's nowhere else for you to go. This is the safest place for you right now."

She turned to the rain-soaked window and wiped her nose with the back of her hand. "You're feelin' sorry for me. I don't need nobody to feel sorry for me. I know what I did. After what they did to me, it was easy. Easiest thing I've ever done."

"Do you regret it?"

A beat. She faced him, a curl of hair covering the left side of her angelic face. "I just want to know what to do now. Where—where will I live? Here? I can't live *here*. It's not my house. They're gonna send me to some kinda children's home or somethin', and—"

"Don't worry about your future." He shifted into park. "You're gonna be all right."

"So, this is it?"

"It is."

"Okay. Before I go, can I ask you something? I prol'y won't ever see you again, okay?"

He nodded.

"Why do you wear those sunglasses? Even at night," she licked the sweat from her lips, "you wear them." Shook her head. The confusion grew on her face. "Some people might think you look stupid wearin' sunglasses all day long."

"You're probably right," he said, and lifted his hand to his shades, flicked them off.

Sadie gasped, and covered her mouth with her hand. "OhmyGod!"

His left eye was gone. It appeared as if it had been hollowed out and sewn shut with a single thread. Skin had grown tight over the hole.

"It happened when I was twelve. My dad was drunk. He got an ice pick, held me down, and dug out my eye like he was digging for a pearl in an oyster shell. I hated him for it. That goes without sayin', I guess. Why do I wear these shades? To hide from a world that still follows me." He lowered his head, pressed his palms together and rubbed them. "Those are bad thoughts. You don't need to think of things like that. You need to be thinking of the cutest boy in school, or going to the mall with your friends. What you did tonight, it'll follow you. It will haunt you. The trick is . . . well, there is no trick. Just try not to let it get to you. You got me, Sadie?"

She nodded. Hesitant, she stepped out into the wind and rain, her skin silver in the moonlight. She closed the door, her hands pressed against the wet windshield. Water snaked over her fingers, down her arm, into her shirt.

He could see that she had something to say, so with the press of a button, the window rolled.

"Who are you?" she asked, and amid the rainwater, a tear crept out the corner of her puffed, purple eye.

"My name doesn't matter," he said, smoke drifting from between his lips and in streams out both nostrils. "What does matter is that I'm a believer. I believe in good and I believe in evil." He took one last drag from the cigarette and snubbed it in the ashtray, put on his sunglasses and shifted gears. "You decide for yourself which side I'm on." He turned from her, the sky filled with midnight thunderheads, and he drove into the falling rain.

The Porsche faded in the distance. Somehow, a smile crossed Sadie's lips. Whatever happened from this point on, no matter what life threw her way—good or bad—she'd never have to return to the nightmare.

And that made life so much more precious.

Chapter 40

Night of misery. That's how Sheriff Combs described it as he stood in the kitchen, his hands on his hips. Blood painted the room. He watched while Quitman and Anne Mase's bodies were zipped in black bags and loaded into the ambulance. Forensics again combed the area for clues, any trace of evidence. Even a hair would prove productive. They found nothing.

Whoever it was—the son of a bitch had phoned him—was gone.

"Sheriff?" Hanna. His shirt was soaked, and he looked like he could use a day's worth of sleep. "Mayor's on the phone."

"Jesus H." Terry went to the porch with the cell phone, put it to his ear, and covered his other with his left hand to shield a rumble of thunder rolling over the hills. "Hello, Frank?"

"Goddamn if this don't beat all."

"You've heard."

"We've gotta find us a nigger to hang, Fats. I don't give a good country fuck if the man's stopped for speeding. Once this news gets out, the town's gonna go down. People done got scared. They don't wanna be next, and I don't blame 'em. I need votes, you need votes. If everybody moves out because of the murders, we're up shit creek with the paddle up our ass, man. You gotta think about this!"

"I've got the town covered, Frank. These things take time. I can't arrest an innocent man. Might be a woman, ya know? Who knows?"

"My hairy ass it's a woman, sheriff. No woman I've ever known has had the guts to nail two people to a tree, then slice 'em open. Hear me now, Terry Robert, and you hear me good. Find this motherfucker. Find him and bring me his nut sac. Or, you can hang it up come election time." A beat. "Go!"

Terry folded the clamshell phone and returned it to Hanna. The man-child was leaning against the back of the couch with tears in his eyes. "What's wrong, son?" Terry placed a hand on his shoulder.

The deputy shook his head, pressed his thumb and forefinger into the corner of his eyes, coughed into his fist. "I can't see how anyone could do such a thing. I mean, this is screwed up. You'd think somethin' like this only happens in New York or LA or Dallas, but it happened here, in a town no bigger than my front yard. I can't understand it, Fats, it's crazy, I—"

"Hey, I know it's tough, but this is how it is. Can't change it. It's a cruel job but it's the only one we have, so you've gotta make the best of it. Remember that and you'll never forget what you're made of. Go clean yourself up before someone sees you." Terry leaned in, shoved the stub of an unlit cigar between his lips. "Bein' an officer of the law don't carry with it a box of tissue. You'll be fine."

Hanna left. Terry returned to the scene of the crime. As he looked at the blood stains and thought of the mayor's words in his mind, he couldn't help but think that someone, somewhere was getting away with murder, and laughing. Laughing loud, and laughing out loud at him.

—ɷ—

Sadie knocked at the door. The front lamp came on, and shed a white light across the drive. Danny opened it, dressed in shorts and socks, his hair messed and waved sideways from sleep, one knuckle held firm at his right eye.

"Sadie?" he said weakly.

"Hey, Danny."

"Sadie!" He hugged her.

From the end of the hall, Melissa emerged. She was holding the TV remote and dressed in a pair of Joyce's black jogging pants and an oversized shirt.

"Look, Missy!" Danny shouted, pointing out the door. "Sadie's here."

The girls embraced. It took all they had to keep from crying, but their best wasn't good enough. Tears rolled.

Ten minutes later, the three of them sat on a blanket in the living room, each holding canned drinks and mysterious smiles.

It was Danny who first asked the question they were all anticipating.

"Where have you been?"

"Yeah, Sadie," Melissa said, popping a piece of gum in her mouth, "got tired of the school?"

"No. Somebody took me away from there, and then my mom saw me at the store, she took me home, and they hit me, then—" she trailed off, unable to tell the truth. "It's a long story."

"Who took you away from the school?" Melissa asked. "The cops?"

"That guy with the sunglasses."

"Holy crap!" Danny wheeled on his butt. "You seen him, too?"

"Yeah." Sadie searched the room, then her two friends. "I guess now we all have."

"What happened?" Melissa took a sip of the soft drink. "Tell us everything."

When it was over, Sadie's two-person audience said nothing. Their blank expressions told all. They were both excited and frightened for her. But she didn't tell them about her part in Anne and Quitman's death. She gave the stranger credit for that. It was the sensible way to finish the story without having to explain herself. Many would persecute her for what she'd done. Others—those who had grown up in the same situation—would have applauded her. She prayed no one discovered the truth. God only knew what would happen to a girl her age.

She dismissed the thought. Sitting with her friends in the comfort of a real house without the threat of Anne or Quitman was wonderful. She listened to Danny tell how he'd met the stranger on the back porch, and how Melissa had gone to see her parents' graves. Soon, the conversation faded into the meaningless mumbo-jumbo that focused on music and movies and which new PlayStation game had hit the market.

"Did you ever find out why he wears those sunglasses all the time?" Danny asked.

"Yeah," Melissa chimed in, "why does he?"

As Sadie looked at her friends, she knew they were going to be fine. No one would ever hurt them again. Her life felt as if it were becoming a routine, a child's life, a simple life—the life she'd never had and always wanted.

"He told me he has sensitive eyes," Sadie said.

Chapter 41

Early Tuesday morning, Mason went to Tara's Salon and paid nine dollars for a haircut. He left, his hair darker now, closer to the roots, scalp visible, cooler, the feel of it stiffened with gel. Maybe it was his way to shed the evil crawling under his skin, or maybe he did it because change is locked inside the human heart and as death, it is inevitable.

At one o'clock he walked into the First National Bank of Sutter Springs and sat across from a balding man in his early forties with chapped lips and a mole on the corner of his nose near his left nostril. The bronze nameplate read William H. Marble, President. Most customers were indeed intimidated by the man's presence, but considering that Mason had more money in five separate accounts than the bank owned, he was unruffled by the title.

Marble leaned back in his high-back mahogany chair and pressed his hands together, stared into Mason's unmoving face. "Mr. Xavier, before we continue, let me get this straight. You would like to deposit a total amount of $1.5 million into three separate trust funds, under names known only to you. Correct?"

"I'll sign whatever documents need to be signed. The recipients will be designated in them," Mason said. "They're underage, and won't be able to get the money until they're eighteen. I want the identity of these three people to remain anonymous until their birthdays come around. I've appointed two adults to come in and sign over the funds when the time is right. No one will be able to change the precautions or guidelines of the documents, either. And no one will be able to withdraw the money except for those specified. That includes myself."

Mr. Marble nodded, pursed his lips. "Five hundred thousand dollars each. Somebody's going to have a relatively pleasant introduction to the rest of their lives, don't you think Mr. Xavier?" he asked with a coy smile.

Mason coughed into his fist. "It's more like an explosion."

"Yes, well, if you'll give me just a moment, sir, I'll have my secretary draw up the necessary paperwork. It'll take about a day to—"

"I don't have a day."

"Oh, well, hold on a second, Mr. Xavier, and I'll see what I can do. Please, if you would like some coffee, there's a fresh batch in the corner. Help yourself."

"Thanks."

When he left, the day had grown hot and dry, the season bleeding into his skin. The smell of the paper mill in the distance mixed with the fishy stench of Bayou Sans drifted through the town air. He reached his car and was startled to find a lady hunched down by the right tire, the edge of her black dress pulled up to her ankles, and a shawl dancing with the wind wrapped loosely around her neck. Her skin was bronze, hair the color of burnt coal.

"Can I help you?" Mason said rudely.

The lady looked up. Her face was clear and oval, but a darkness was buried deep within the pores that Mason found disturbing. In her hand, she held a squashed candy bar, pressed cruelly out of its package. Tire tracks made a perfect groove through the chocolate. She brought it to her lips, but did not eat.

"I still walk at night, still do. I roam and roam and roam." She bit into the candy. Gooey caramel stretched from her rotted teeth as she pulled it away and smacked out loud. "I see you at the water, down by the river, at the tree. I did, ah yes. With a knife. And two souls you took for your own." Her eyes glowed with a mysterious spark. *"Murderer."*

"Get outta my way. You don't know what you're talkin' about." He fit his key into the door lock and realized his hand was trembling.

She sneaked behind him, tapped his shoulder. "What does Rachel think about staying the future with a murderer? Does it put smile on her face, no? Get her wet down there so it easy to feel, better to taste? Ah?"

Mason whirled around. "Who are you?"

"Olivia Drake," she said, and bowed, one hand over her heart.

"Gypsy bitch."

"I put curse on you for that," she said, waving her finger at him, "but something far worse than curse will come your way, Mr. Xavier. You see. It will come soon."

Mason watched her walk away and did not get behind the steering wheel until she disappeared around the corner of the bank. He sat there for a few minutes, the dashboard lights blinking, the engine idling, before he drove off.

What was that all about?

He shook his head. Insane. Just an old woman with nothing better to do than to annoy people. What really bothered him was her rendition of the Giles' murder. How did she know? Had she really been there? He tried to forget about it. For him, it seemed today was full of surprises.

When he got home, Ardon was sitting on his front porch beside a dying fern that Rachel had been nurturing since May even though the thing still bled brown, withered leaves.

"Want a drink?" Ardon asked, as Mason stepped out of his car.

"Sure."

Ardon had arrived prepared. He dipped into a tiny red Igloo filled with crushed ice, and pulled out a Budwieser, handed it over.

Mason cracked the top, took a long, satisfying drink. "What's up?"

His friend stared down at the tips of his shoes. "Oh, nothing. Just two more murders in town. Haven't you heard?"

"Didn't know you could be such a smartass, Ardon." Mason took a seat beside him. He looked out over the winding roads that sloped and disappeared into the rolling hills.

"There's a rainmaker out there, son, and he's brewing a cloud for you." Ardon downed his beer, let out a sigh, and crushed the can.

"I told you not to call me 'son'."

"It's a shame, it really is. You just don't see what you've got. Every man's fantasy. More money than God, a beautiful woman who loves you, no worries. None at all. And you're betting it all on a horse with a broken leg, lemme tell ya. You will lose."

"I don't need you to tell me what's right or wrong. I know what I did. I'd do it again if it would help a kid, any kid who can't defend himself. You don't understand my motive because you don't know what it's like to grow up as an abused child. So, I'm not gonna explain myself to you. Besides, it's over. No more."

Ardon popped another beer. "Why do I get the feeling I don't believe you?"

"I don't give a shit if you don't believe me. My life's back to normal. Thinkin' about takin' Rachel to the Bahamas. Maybe Cancun. That's always fun."

"I thought she left."

Mason nodded, spit on the wooden rail. "Yep."

"So where is she?"

"I got an idea. I might even drop by and see her later." Mason turned, his blond bangs in his face. "Look at me." He took off his sunglasses, pointed to the pale, dead eye that looked like a puffy piece of dough. "This is why I killed those people. It's why I risked everything. I can't go back and make it right with my own past, but hopefully what I did can relieve any future pain those kids would have gone through. There. I've said my peace. You don't have to agree with me. It's just how I think, and that's how it is." A breeze lifted his hair and he replaced his sight as the orange ball in the sky burned a giant hole into the earth.

"I respect you, Mason. Always have. You're a strong kid with a kind heart. But behind all that, you're dangerous. You can be a mean person. You hide that better than your past, bud."

"I'll take that as a compliment, Ardon," Mason said, and lit a cigarette.

A wave of smoke hit the principal and he coughed. "You know those things'll kill ya."

Mason took another drag. "My mom used to tell me that."

—◊◊◊—

Terry told Monica he'd pick up milk and eggs on his way over to her house, but said he would not be able to make it for dinner until seven o'clock. He sat behind his desk cleaning his boots with a soft cloth, a cigar an inch long shoved in his mouth. Questions ran through his head. Anne and Quitman's death had been less complex than the others. Someone finished them off with a bullet, and their daughter was again missing. He'd come to a dead end. The Parent Killer was definitely a sleek son of a bitch.

The windows were cracked in his office and the fan was on high. Air conditioner was still down, and he was sweating like a farmhand in the field. He wiped away the moisture from his face with a dirty cloth when Hanna poked his head around the door, his hat in his hand.

"Fats? The mayor's here to see ya."

"Great." Terry scooted his chair back and walked to the window. He lit the cigar and smoke floated over his face. "Show him in."

Frank Darabont walked through the door—all five-feet-six of him. His face was wrinkled by the sun and his hands were gripped by arthritis, making his fingers knotted and twisted. He wore a white collared shirt, no tie, and black jeans with dress shoes, his hair the color of a rain cloud, and he was bathed in cheap cologne he bought in vials at gas stations. He sat in the chair and propped his feet on the desk. "Helluva day, huh? Got goddamn athlete's feet–gonna kill me, son."

Terry paced the floor in a broken circle. "Frank," he greeted.

"Tell me, Fats. How is it you think you're gonna keep your job when you ain't done nothin' about our ghost?"

Terry didn't answer. He puffed away.

"It's the juice, son. Votes. We need 'em. You find me that sombitch and I'll make sure you're sheriff of this town again." Frank smacked his lips aloud. "People are scared, Terry. They want justice, they want peace. They're lookin' at me and you to make things right around here, and I don't give a hot red shit how you do it, you find me somebody, and bring him down. I've been gettin' calls from all over. Beaux River, Abbey, hell even as far as New Orleans. Nobody thinks you can do your job, man. Word is the FBI's gonna crawl up our ass pretty soon. The things happenin' in this town, you can't keep to yourself for long. We're gonna be the laughin' stock of the whole state, maybe the whole country. Can you see yourself on *Larry King*

Live goin', 'Hell, he just slipped through my fingers,' and think ol' Larry's gonna respect ya? You read me here, Chief?"

"I hear ya," Terry said, "but you can't find a duck under water."

"That's when you toss in some dynamite and blow up the fuckin' pond!" Frank jumped out of the chair, whacked his hand on the desk. The sound reverberated off the walls. "You got 'til the end of the week, Sheriff Combs." He waved his finger in the air as if scolding a child. "Or I'll take your badge and wipe my ass with it. Hear that?"

"Loud and clear," Terry said, his eyes squinted to two black slits.

Frank stormed out. He slammed the door and the shutters banged hard against the inset window.

Outside his office, Terry heard his men talking, and thought for a second someone giggled like a fifteen-year-old schoolgirl.

"Jerkoff," he whispered, and snubbed the cigar in the star-shaped ashtray.

Chapter 42

At two o'clock, thunderheads gathered in the west and threatened to burst. High winds fell and thrust through the pines mapping the front lawn. The log house was quiet again. Ardon was gone.

Mason sat in silence with a bourbon and Coke in his hand and a half-drunken smile on his face, deep in thought. After all he'd done, after all the emotion he'd weathered, nothing hurt him more than having lost Rachel. He would have rather lost his fortune, his house, his cars, his freedom—anything and everything—than see her slam the door on their relationship.

A searing hole burned deep into his heart, filled with emptiness and a touch of hate.

"What if?" was the question of the day.

What if Rachel went to the cops? Since she'd learned the truth, he had to assume she'd do this. For all he knew, there could be a plot against him. There could be an army of officers equipped with rifles and pistols and Terry Combs leading them to raid his house at this very moment. Paranoid, he checked the window blinds. Nothing.

"What have I done?" he asked the room, his voice strained. He scraped his fingers over the back of his head and accidentally dropped his drink. The tumbler nicked the coffee table and bounced along the floor, liquor splashing over the cuff of his jeans. Thunder rumbled overhead and a flash of lightning brightened the darkened room. He remained in one place, stared at the front door and envisioned Rachel walking inside. She'd sit across his lap, breathe a minty sigh over his face, and kiss his lips, hug him and tell him she was sorry, and that she was here to stay. She'd forgive him and promise she'd never leave again.

Mason touched his stomach. A series of cramps pounded against his sweaty palm where he'd been stabbed. It was patched with discolored white gauze. "What in Christ's name have I done?"

Nice time to grow a conscience, he thought.

He rushed through the kitchen, around the corridor, into the bathroom and put his head under the water faucet. Cool water cascaded over his skin and through his hair and it felt good. He stayed under for one minute, trying to sober up, trying to clear his hazy mind. He shut off the faucet and faced the mirror.

"You screwed up," he told himself. His eyes burned hot and bright, spit flew from his mouth, and out of view, at his sides, his hands folded into rock-hard fists. He screamed when he punched the glass. Blood popped out over his knuckles, splotched the back of his hand, ran down his wrist. He flexed his fingers in pain, watching the skin manipulate the lines of bright red. He flung his throbbing hand out to the side. The red stuff slapped and speckled the tile walls. From above the toilet, he took a wash rag off the towel rack and wrapped his wound, pulled it into his stomach as if he were caring for a newborn child. A tear dropped from his eye. His mouth was parched. "God . . . *help me!*" He kicked the door with such force, the bottom hinge ripped off the wall, and the hard wood slammed against a picture of Rachel and him in Palm Springs last March, their skin tanned, hair stringy from the ocean, dried and shiny in the sun. The picture fell to the floor, the frame broke in three places.

Mason purposely stepped on it as he made his way down the hall toward the living room, leaning against the wall for support as he walked, knocking more pictures to the ground with his shoulder. He didn't care. To hell with it. Rachel was gone, his life was over. He ached. Was this what depression felt like? Or the ticket to suicidal tendencies?

Yeah, just put the gun in your mouth and pull the . . . .

He fell onto the couch, put a throw pillow over his face, and tried to concentrate on something else—anything besides the hurt in his hand, and the pain that doubled inside him from knowing that from this day forward, he was without Rachel Borello, and her love.

—⁂—

Rachel got her keys off the hanger by the door and walked outside into a drizzle of wind and rain. It was only three-thirty, but the day had turned black as night, the sun hidden by a sheet of dark clouds that tore across the sky. On the morning news, she'd heard a storm would be moving through, but had not expected it to be this dank and depressing. Summer was here, but it might as well have been a gray, windy afternoon in the fall.

She drove. Her mind was going ninety miles an hour. She had to do something, she had to make things right. She still loved Mason. That was her problem. Loved him and wanted him. The downside to her feelings was the voice inside her that told her to run. He'd killed. For that, she could never forgive, and she had to tell him—whether it meant ending their relationship, or making it that much stronger, she had to face him, and let him know how she felt. They'd been together too long, survived too much in life's path to throw it all away. Some might say that she had a good reason to end it, so she had to ask herself the most important question of all: could she marry a murderer?

She popped a Prozac to help numb her rattled nerves. She'd been up since four this morning, lying on the couch watching infomercials and day-time shows, boredom attacking her brain, a sickness gripping her heart. "Jerk," she had then scolded Mason. She tried to see things through his point of view. She'd never been hurt as a child—except for the time she and Macy Ferrah tied into a fight in the cafeteria over whose dress was prettier in grade school, and even then, she'd lost. She went home with a black eye and busted lip, and stayed in bed for the rest of the week. Didn't want to show up in homeroom with scars and have all the children laugh at her. That was part of growing up. Her parents were wonderful people, always giving, always caring, never abusive–mentally or physically. Who was she to prosecute Mason and how he handled his childhood? Or his present actions?

"Jesus, just help me through this," she whispered. She wore shorts and a blue T-shirt with sandals, but now realized how awful the weather had turned, and she wished she'd have worn jeans and hiking boots. Her skin smelled of Tommy Girl perfume—Mason's favorite. As the road rose long and wet, her vision more distorted from the rainy blur outside the Lexus, she didn't know whether to curse his name in his face, or try to rekindle their love in some vain attempt to rescue lost feelings. Sometimes she wished she had never met the man.

The turn was up ahead and for a second, she thought about passing it. Turn chicken and drive until she arrived in the next town or ran out of gas at the Texas border.

She could do it and he'd never know. She had over forty grand in her bank account alone, so money was no problem. But he had millions. Maybe it was money that made her click on her signal and swerve onto the blacktop. Most girls she knew would stay for money. The stupid ones wouldn't. She took the curvy road until she came upon the log house on the hill. Through the black rain, the yellow porch lights illuminated their front yard and Mason's car.

She pulled into the driveway. Stepped out. Rain pricked her skin. Mud splashed under her sandals and onto her feet. She tucked her head under a newspaper and hit the stairway running. Heart pounding harder and harder, she stopped at the front door.

—⚇—

Mason woke to the ceiling fan's slow, droning whir. Sleep crust glued the inner corners of his eye closed and he rubbed it with his knuckles. For about five seconds, he was temporarily blind. His hair was disheveled, jutting out in every direction, and his right hand cramped with solid pain from where he'd slammed his fist into the mirror. He hadn't cleaned the mess in the bathroom. Rachel was always on him to clean up after himself, but he was lazy and they both knew it. The wash rag was now blotched red, the last three fingers swollen to twice their size.

Wearing only his jeans, unbuttoned and loosened around his waist, he dropped the hand-woven afghan to the ground and went to the kitchen for a beer. He spun off the top, lightly cutting his palm, and tipped the bottle to his lips. Cold and crisp, the beer refreshed his senses, relaxed his stomach. He'd only been asleep for thirty minutes, but it felt like hours. Power nap. That's what his friends in high school had called them before they spent an entire Friday night zipping up and down Main Street, heads hanging out the windows of pickup trucks, the stereo cranked loud, and alcohol floating in their veins in hopeless hopes of finding willing teenage girls by dawn's light.

And he thought of Rachel. God he missed her.

He looked at the door with arrogance, as if he could see through its oak structure.

You killed them, a voice said deep within his mind—the wastelands where the darkness gathered, and a rage pulsated—where childhood memories of being beaten resided, rested, were buried. Where he slept as a monster. Where he was that evil person the police had been trying to hunt down and the town folk were hiding from.

There's a rainmaker out there brewing a cloud for you.

A fear like none other he'd ever felt bubbled over him, shook his nerves, and rattled his bones. Bobby Rampart's head split open by a table saw flashed before him. The blood that gushed and covered his clothes, the floor, the walls. His screams.

Brady and Lisa Giles, nailed to a tree. Their skin baked by the merciless summer sun. He saw how their eyes popped open when he stabbed them, their cries and the anguish in their faces more real and more horrifying than any movie he'd seen, or any book he'd read, or any experience he'd ever braved.

There was Anne, Quitman—the gun. Sadie.

Now the cops—they were here, standing on his porch, in the rain—had finally found him, and were planning to take him down.

They deserved it. It's true. Those people deserved what they got for what they did.

His gun was in his car, not in his desk. Although, that didn't matter since the clip was empty—he proved that last night when he stood in that kitchen like a fool. He'd searched for it earlier, but had not found it. Was he losing his mind?

He stared at the floor as the door opened. Mason dared not move. A heavy roll of breath escaped his lungs when he saw mud-stained feet on the mat outside.

"It was you, wasn't it?" Rachel stood at the threshold of the door and in the background, rain hammered the earth in sheets. Tall pines swayed. A car somewhere around the bend braked, screeched over the road. "What? What did you do?" she said, her eyes wandering to his head.

He raked his palm over the sharp needles, an uncertain look on his face, one that told her he wished he hadn't cut his hair. "Rachel. My God, Rachel, you're here." Mason wanted to reach out and touch her, but from the look in her eyes and the stance she took, he knew she didn't want to feel him against her. He could see she was angry with him and she had every right to be. The distance between them was only a few feet, though it felt like a mile. He held his ground.

"It's you. The one the news is talking about. The one the cops are trying to find." She swallowed the hardness down her throat. "You are the Parent Killer."

"Rachel," he said, his head shaking from side to side. "You're not making any sense."

"Oh no?" She slapped a manila folder on the counter. The children's photos slid across the hard wood. Sadie, Danny, and Melissa. She blinked and a tear rolled over her cheek. The air seemed stiff, making it difficult for her to breathe. "I found these at the lake house. The police're lookin' for a blond-headed man, early twenties, known to wear sunglasses often. Where are your Ray Bans, Mason? Or are you wearing your Oakleys this week?"

He craned his neck, eyed the window. Said nothing. She knew.

God, she knew.

A shady haze of light fell through the slits of the venetian blinds, pierced the black room and lined the white carpet like jailhouse bars. Off in the distance, a dog barked loud enough for them to hear its noise inside the house.

Sweat beaded her forehead, her eyes glowed with the intensity of a diamond, mixed with the fear that settled and thrived there. She loved him. She truly loved him. He could even see that. After discovering the truth, knowing what he'd done—the blood that had gloved his hands, the screams he'd heard, the faces he'd drained from the beating pulse that was God-given life—she wasn't so sure anymore.

Rachel eased into Mason with the elegance of an exotic dancer, her toned, bronzed skin now touching his bare chest. Her eyes never left his face. She slipped her thumbs into his jean's waistline, held him tight, moved her wet, pouty lips to his, and opened her mouth. Tender, gentle. She bit his bottom lip, sucked it in, and paraded it between her teeth and gum line as a child would chewy candy. Tasted salt and sweat and saw the terror in his face—the cold, hard face a madman possessed—complicated by the sensual presence of the man she once knew and loved.

It was love, it was hate, only a dance. And bad, so very bad.

Catching his stare, the fear they shared erupted on her face, made her heart tremble, and ordered icy beads down her arms. Ran over the backs of her legs. Covered her palms. Forced her armpits to surface wet. Angry, her cheeks turned cherry red, her arched eyebrows dipped, and her breathing staggered, coming now in rapid gasps that washed over him. From the insatiable rage, she gripped his sides, pulled him close, bit down on his lip.

"Hmph!" Mason's eye shot wide open. He tried to step away. She held him with force. Blood seeped from his skin as air hit the cut and stung the exposed jelly-like muscle. He breathed in her intoxicating perfume—the scent of her pure, sweet skin—and the thick coppery taste of blood and saliva trickled down his throat.

Rachel set him free, stepped back. From her front pocket, she pulled out the gun she'd taken from the lake house, gripped it tight in her hands—at the moment more attractive than a bouquet of red roses.

"How could you do this?" she sobbed, her reddened face alive and alert. She jabbed her finger at the air, two quick motions like she was trying to poke out his only eye. "Who are you to play God?! To take a life. To kill?" She screamed in his face, the sound ear-splitting and terrifying. Flecks of spit landed on his skin. "You killed those people, Mason. I'm in love with a killer!"

"You don't understand!" he yelled, jerking away. In that instant, he felt alive. No longer in a trance, back in control, back to himself. "You think you know all the pieces to this puzzle? You don't know a goddamn thing! Don't start with your assumptions. There's more to this than people's lives." He flung out his arms and the wash rag wrapped around his hand flew into the kitchen, came to rest underneath the refrigerator. "Those people deserved to die!"

The conviction in his voice was almost enough for her to agree.

She closed her eyes, opened them, almost as if she'd transformed into another person. The gun in her hand beckoned. It was a Colt .45 automatic, chrome-plated with a walnut handle. The firearm Mason had bought at a Gun and Knife show two years ago—the year they had cruised the Caribbean and gambled away almost a quarter-million dollars, and had drank until the sun went down, then had danced until it rose over the ocean's crest—was turned on him, that one dark hole aimed at his face, and her delicate finger touching the trigger.

He raised his hands in protest. "Rachel! Please," he shook his head, "put that thing down!"

"I bet a lot of people would have liked to have seen you do that, too." Crying, teardrops seeped into the corners of her mouth, and she sucked on the stream. "I love you Mason. I love you so much." She sniffed, blinked, her eyelashes soaked and crinkled from the wetness. Licked her lips. "But what you did, it wasn't right. You're not the same man. Not the one I knew. Not the same man at all."

"Honey, don't. Just put the gun down. We can work through this."

"The police found those people nailed to a tree, Mason. Their stomachs were cut open, guts and shit all over the place. What did they do that was so bad that they had to die like that? Like dogs! And the others. There were others! That guy, Bobby Rampart. I thought that crazy old gypsy lady was telling me that he was a bad man, but Mason, she was talking about *you!* You're the bad man! And yesterday, it happened again. Two people shot dead in their own home."

"Remember Hailey Carpenter?"

"Shut. Up."

"Do you?"

"Don't you say it!"

"You used to baby-sit her. That night you saw her mother wiping strawberry jam from her cheek when you went back to get your purse."

"Shut up!"

"Remember? You forgot your purse. That wasn't strawberry jam, it was blood. You had the feeling it was blood all the way home, and you didn't say anything to me until the next day when Hailey Carpenter, who would've turned seven years old...Rachel! Quit shaking your head, listen to me—you didn't say anything to me! Didn't do anything about it. You even had the suspicion all along that her parents were hurting her. What did you do? Buried it, kept it a secret because you couldn't prove it. That little girl could be alive today." Mason reached for the manila folder on the floor, held up a girl's photo. "Meet Melissa Giles, Honey. Beaten with a piece of pipe, molested by her father. Look here, look! This is Danny Rampart. Knocked out with a two-by-four for coming home late from school when the school bus broke down and there was nothing he could do about it. Slapped around like a punching bag. And here, here, look at this. Look at this one. This is Sadie Bellis. Her mother hit her with belts, coat hangers, burned her with cigarettes, put hot sauce in her eyes, even pulled out a tooth with a pair of pliers. All this, Rachel. I got all this information from that blue notebook. It was the only proof I needed to carry out my plan. I took their problems seriously because unlike you, I won't stand by and watch this shit happen." Mason threw the photos into the air and the fan's powerful breeze sent them scattering around the room.

Rachel's lips peeled over her teeth. "Are you insinuating that I murdered that child? That I had a hand in ending Hailey Carpenter's life?"

"Insinuating? You might as well have choked her with your bare hands."

"I can't believe you just said that."

"If you had come to me, I could have done something about it. I grew up in that kind of environment. I understand it. It wasn't always millions of dollars, baby. I was dirt poor and hurt. See my eye? This didn't happen when I was born. I never had cancer in my eye like I told you when we met. It happened when my dad got drunk and rammed an ice pick in it! I did those kids a favor."

"And you should be so proud, Mason."

"I am." Though it was a whisper, the stone came back to his voice, and he wasn't afraid. He'd never been afraid. In the past month, he'd been the giver of misery. Since the cards had turned on him, he wasn't going to gripe and cry about it now. He stared at the gun. All facts aside, he hoped Rachel didn't summon the courage he knew she had deep within her to pull the trigger. "But you don't care about why those people had to die, do you?"

"I'm leaving, Mason. I just wanted to tell you. I'm getting away. From you!"

"Rachel, listen to me."

"I don't want to listen. I don't want to hear anything else you have to say."

He touched her shoulder. She pulled away.

"Why did you come back here!"

She wiped her cheeks with both wrists, at one point the gun aimed directly at him.

"Those people were evil. They're the bad guys. Don't you see why I did those things? Hurt their kids, Rachel, molested them. I killed those people to save their children. It may not be right, it may not be wrong, but it happened, and I'm responsible. Have sympathy for the devil 'cause the motherfucker just left town. It's over. That's all I can say, and if that's not good enough for you, then do what that little voice in the back of your mind says." He tapped his skull. A grin passed across his mouth, stretching the cut where fresh blood slipped out and ran down his chin in a broken line. The rage in his mind and body had returned, and she saw it, and it scared her. "Go ahead. Pull that trigger."

Just looking at his smooth, childlike face reminded her of all the times he'd kissed her, made love to her, showed her the world, showed her his heart, and it frightened her to the bone to know that she'd been sleeping with a killer night after night.

She lifted the gun with both hands, steadied it. Rachel closed her eyes, and thunder rumbled outside, shook the house. The breeze from the ceiling fan pressed down on their bodies in the still log house as their eyes met, giving in to the knowledge that both their worlds were about to take an abrupt turn.

"Rachel?"

She fired.

—ɯ— **8**:53 A.M.

Monica called and said she was on her way home from town. The cellular reception wasn't great, so Terry had to speak beyond the static and muffled sound. She'd been late because the Piggly Wiggly had specials on almost everything, and she cleaned house.

The coffee in his favorite mug had turned cold, so he warmed it in the microwave. He remembered Frank's visit to his office. He could've ranted and raved and caused all hell to break loose between them, but that's what he was trying to avoid. Politicians were a greedy bunch, and so were sheriffs up for re-election. He kept peace with the Mayor for the hopes of being elected and decided to work the case alone.

One night during the investigation Ardon had called him from the school and his information had put him on the right track. Even though Terry knew the true identity of the Parent Killer, and why this man was spilling blood, he never said a word until he knew an innocent person was about to be harmed.

He lit a cigar. He only smoked when he was nervous, and reading the article in front of him always made his skin crawl. It was like reliving the entire ordeal, scene by scene in his head, with him as the only audience, and again,

He could do nothing to stop what transpired that dark, rainy afternoon at the edge of town.

Mason and Rachel were there. So was that Mercedes.

Chapter 44

The blast was deafening. Mason froze. He'd seen fire explode out of the gun barrel, saw Rachel's wrist jerk backward from the force. Glass shattered. He slowly turned to see what was left of the window.

She'd only fired once. If lead had hit him, he felt nothing. He checked himself. No wound. If she had wanted to frighten him, she succeeded. If she had wanted to harm him, she needed lessons.

Mason felt the sudden urge to smile. He was alive and it was the greatest feeling in the world. His lips made no effort, his body tightened. He opened his mouth to speak.

"Rachel?" he whispered. "I love you."

She was crying, her hand over her mouth, another trying to steady the .45. "Don't say that. Don't say things you don't mean!"

"I'd never hurt you," he said. "I'd never—"

The door burst open in the middle of his sentence, and Sheriff Combs stepped inside, his gun drawn.

"All right, now. Nobody move!" His tan uniform was rain-soaked and pressed to his large body. He kept his eyes on Mason, and reached out to Rachel. "Gimme that, Darlin'."

Rachel's finger lightly tap danced on the trigger guard. She couldn't let go. She had power over the most dangerous man in north Louisiana and it felt good. "I can't. I can't do it. He killed them all. Every one of them. He might try to hurt me."

"Nobody's gonna get hurt. Just put the gun away." His eyes moved to Mason. "You need to calm down."

"Why are you here?" He looked from Rachel to Terry.

"Ardon told me y'all were havin' problems. Let's just say I've been keeping watch." Terry held up a pair of handcuffs.

"This is bullshit!" Mason said.

"He wanted me to look out for Rachel. Who fired the gun?"

"She did, Fats. I didn't touch her!"

"Spread 'em against the wall real cool-like, Mason. We don't need any problems."

Mason turned, walked around the coffee table, and placed his hands against the cracked mirror, his bangs in his eye. His reflection in the glass was cut and deformed, split in shards. The image reminded him of how he felt inside.

Rachel lowered the gun, handed it to the sheriff.

"Stay turned, son. Make it easy on yourself. We'll just go down to the station for the night and talk, so you can calm down."

Mason stared at the floor.

Terry placed the Colt .45 on the bar, then frisked his suspect. He grabbed Mason's wrist, pulled it around to his lower back and clapped a cuff on him. When he reached for the kid's right hand, he was unprepared for what happened. Seemed like years of training would have taught him to see things like this coming.

Mason elbowed him in the chin, whirled around, and punched him in the face. Terry's .38 fumbled from his hands. Mason grabbed it off the floor. "You want me? Let's do it." He flipped the coffee table to its side, lifted it into the air and dropped it on Terry's chest and looked up. The door was wide open. Rachel was gone. Rain hustled beyond the front porch as the Lexus' headlights panned across the wood line.

He ran and jumped the front porch railing. When he came to the police cruiser, he fired shots at the tires and one into the windshield. It imploded with a loud, vibrant blast. The cuffs were not tightened, and he slipped them off, jumped in the Porsche. Thunder roared as he accelerated into the mist, his heart running wild. His life had taken such a drastic turn, he didn't know how to resolve the very misery he'd caused. He had to find her. The taste of revenge wet his tongue. He couldn't believe Ardon had betrayed him and told Fats to keep an eye on Rachel. In case he hurt her? For all he knew, Rachel probably called the cops herself before she walked inside his house.

As far as he was concerned, his life was over. The news would get out that Mason Xavier was the dark face of Sutter Springs, that the millionaire who had it all, who had risked everything for a group of kids he'd never met, had managed to lose his mind.

But before he went out, he was going out with a bang, and the love of his life was coming along for the ride.

—ⲱ—

Rachel switched on the windshield wipers as she drove into the white-wash mist, feeling the hum of tires beneath her on the slicked tongue of road, the moon soft and pale in the sky. The green dashboard lights illuminated her face and she gripped the leather-encased steering wheel with both hands with such strength, she believed she could break it in half. In the rearview, she saw headlights speed toward her, the sound of thunder in the gray-black clouds like earthen rock scraping together. Her hands trembled and she bit her bottom lip, shifted in the seat, and picked up her cell phone to call Ardon Wells, fumbled it between the seat and console, listening to the wind pass her ears as the flat tone of an automated voice sing-songed "We're sorry, your call cannot be completed as dialed." She screamed out terror at the top of her lungs. A cold, white fear erupted in her eyes and her skin dampened with sweat.

She turned onto a service road that dead-ended at a tennis court and a construction site for a new lightweight shopping center. She swerved the car in a flash, tires squealing. Steam billowed up in transparent curls. The Lexus skidded toward the honeycomb fence that bordered the courts and came to a grinding halt. The engine died, and over her shoulder, Rachel faced Mason's car, saw him—the heat and curves that were all too real, and the gun outside the driver's window, the engine growling low like a calmed

Hellhound. Her instinct took over and she locked the doors with a press of a button. She saw him get out of the car, walk toward her, almost lethargic, dress shirt snapping in the wind, the gun pointed at the ground.

Mason stood before her car window and looked down at her, then tapped the glass with a gold nugget. "Get out, Rachel."

She shook her head, and from inside the car, her voice came off muffled. "Go away Mason! Just leave me alone!"

"I did what I had to do to protect those kids. I won't be ruined because you think it's wrong. Get out of the car."

She looked into his black eyes.

"Get out of the car!" His words echoed over the hillside, coupled with another rumble of thunder. He swung and broke the glass with the gun.

Rachel moved to the passenger side, slid out the door and fell to the ground. Ran. She felt as if the world would collapse around her, and she didn't care if it did, or swallowed her up. Anything would be better than this—running from her lover, her man, the "Parent Killer" of Sutter Springs, Louisiana.

Chapter 45

Sheriff Combs opened his eyes. A sharp pain attacked his spine and surged to the nape of his neck. Felt like he'd just woke from an all-nighter down at Lilly's. He pushed the coffee table over and helped himself to his feet with the couch's arm. Had to give Mason credit. The boy had guts and a nice right hook.

His gun was missing.

It wasn't in his holster, on the floor, or in his sight, and he didn't remember it being taken. Out of the corner of his eye, he saw the Colt .45 Rachel had had, on the bar. Heavy, bigger than his, and fully loaded.

Terry went to his cruiser. The back two tires were flattened. He opened the car door, grabbed his CB. Something inside forced him not to press the button and call for backup. He realized his future as Sheriff depended on his finding Mason, and taking him down single-handedly. The accomplishment would secure his job and his reputation, not to mention staying on the mayor's good side.

In the garage, he spied a tan car. Mason's convertible Mercedes. He checked the ignition for the keys, under the seat, under the body, but found nothing. He didn't know how to hot-wire, so he was out of luck in that area. Then, he spied a white cabinet, rushed through it and found several sets of keys hanging from hooks. One had the Mercedes symbol stamped into it.

—⁓—

The muscles in her legs and back ached, pounded into her bones. She could run no farther.

At the base of a pine tree, she fell to her knees and gasped for air. The wind moved in sharp wisps at her ears and rose in curls across her cheeks. Rachel heard the footsteps behind her. Her knees pressed into soft mud, her palms lay flat on her thighs. The rain soaked her clothes to transparent cotton. She turned, but did not meet his face. He was so close, she could smell his sweat.

"I'm angry," she said, the hurt throbbing in her voice. "I don't know what to think anymore." She fingered a tear away from her cheek, sniffed, let out a heavy sigh. "I've never forgiven myself for what happened to Hailey Carpenter. You're right, I might as well have murdered that child myself." She clawed her fingertips gently over her face. "If you wanna talk about a horrible feeling, there's your story."

"We had a life." Mason stood only a couple of feet from her. "It stopped, what else can I say? I'm about to lose everything I have. Even you."

"Who's fault is that? I didn't go to the cops!"

"I'm not talking about that. I'm talking about you pulling that gun."

"I thought you'd hurt me. I was scared. Protecting myself."

"Christ! You never have listened to me. You thought I was cheating on you all this time, and I wasn't. I told you I wasn't going to hurt you and I didn't. But that changed—did that ever change when you tried to put a bullet in my head." He knew as the words came tumbling out of his mouth that he couldn't hurt her. He loved her too much. There were memories, and in those memories lay the truth that Rachel was his, and would be his forever, long after he lost her touch and her kiss, the little sweet nothings she teased him with at night, and those pampered caresses when he woke with her pink lips grazing the skin of his neck on those rain-slicked mornings when all he cared to do was stay still and feel as though he were one of God's favorite sons.

"You've got a cruel heart," she said, and got to her feet, the red bruise at her left knee throbbing like a runner's heartbeat. Tears glazed her eyes and her mouth curved down. "It's black and burned and scarred like a goddamn coal." She looked up, his shadow across her face. "So, now what? You're going to shoot me? Is that your way of solving this problem?"

His grip tightened on the gun's handle. "Why didn't you trust me? Why couldn't you have just kept to your own business? Do you think it's going to be the same between us? All I tried to do was help those kids. I never wanted to hurt you, Rachel." He watched her face for a reaction, but there was only her blank expression. Bittersweet memories from years past floated through his mind. She was so beautiful, so smart and caring. And though these were perfect qualities, a madness he couldn't stop crept through him. He saw in her eyes the faces of the people he murdered from his mother to Bobby Rampart to Lisa Giles, and he hated her for it.

"You're crazy, Mason. You have no reason to touch me. I didn't turn you in. Ardon did!"

He did the only thing he knew how to do.

It won't work. You don't have that kind of evil inside.

He lifted the gun to her chest as the blinding flash of a jagged bolt of lightning touched down on the riverbank to the east, and thumb-cocked the revolver he'd taken from Sheriff Combs. "You shot and missed. You wanted me dead."

Not true. She loves you, Mason. Listen to your soul. It dances for you. Don't do it.

"You say you didn't go to the cops, and that's fine. But you had the nerve to shoot at me. It don't set well. Unlike you, I won't miss."

She stared at him, feeling him all over again.

There was no siren, only the Mercedes' white headlights that crested the hill.

He did not turn around. Rachel stood there, her eyes closed. The next thing they heard was Terry's voice through the rain.

"Mason!" He trudged through the mud, the lights from the tennis courts at his face. "Put the gun down! It's over!" He held the .45 at arm's length, took aim at Mason's back.

"This ain't none of your business, Terry!" Mason shouted over his shoulder. "Just walk away."

"I know what you did! I've known all along! You killed those people for a reason. Ardon Wells is my friend, too," Terry said. "He called me at home, told me everything. The only reason you're still alive is 'cause I've allowed it!

Do you understand me? Rachel has done nothing. She's innocent."

Mason blinked back tears, strengthened his arm to hold the steel on Rachel. "She tried to kill me, Fats!" He looked into her face. "After all I've done for you, how could you do that? How could you be so cruel? Can I have a new car, baby? You got it. I want my own business, honey. Where do you want the foundation built?" He raised his voice in the wind. "I can't go back, sheriff! You know this. My life's over!"

"You're wrong, Mason," Terry yelled. "I don't blame you for what you've done. God knows there'll never be an end to child abuse and anyone has my vote to rid this society of it. That's why I haven't arrested you yet. I agreed with you. I let you slide. But when Ardon told me that Rachel left you, he was scared for her. He called me to make sure nothing happened to her. She's innocent, Mason, let her go. Don't be a fool! We can all walk away right now like this never happened and be nice about it, or if you don't put that gun down, I will shoot you, no hesitation. Not because you killed those people. Because I won't let you hurt that girl! Do you hear me?"

"Listen to him, Mason," Rachel pleaded. "Please, baby. Listen to what he's saying. You can go back to your life. It'll be like it was before."

"I allowed you to live, by God!" Terry said. "I put my life and my job on the line. For you! Ardon didn't want me to bring you down. I know those kids deserved better, but this has gone too far. It ends here, it ends now." He approached with caution. "Mason Xavier, give me the gun."

"Honey, please!" Rachel said, the barrel only inches from her shirt. "Do what he says. I love you. I always have." Her wet hair fell below her shoulders. "Do it for us. Do it for our baby."

"What?" Mason's hand moved.

"Put the gun down now!" Terry demanded. He was ten yards away, his sight obstructed in the dreary weather.

"I'm pregnant, Mason. I did a home-test at the lake house. Came out positive. We did it. I'm finally pregnant. We're gonna have a—"

Terry fired one shot.

The hollow-point bullet plowed into Mason, burst on impact through meat and bone. His arm jerked backward, the gun loose in his hand. His eyebrows raised, his mouth dropped. A line of blood dripped from his shoulder blade, down his back and gathered with the rain and sweat in his shirt. Fear caught him—a danger that gripped his insides, shed no mercy for his heart. He fell sideways into the grass and mud, his stare never leaving Rachel's face. The sunglasses snapped in half when his head hit the ground, exposing his dead eye, and the gun loosened from his grip and landed at her feet.

Rachel raised her head. She did not cry out or run or kneel to help. Her face went ghost-gray. The man she'd spent years with lay still on the muddy ground, his chest working hard to expand for one more breath—and she saw in him the love she once had, the times they spent together over the years, the clear memories that came back in her mind, the music they'd danced to, the chambers of her heart beating for him—and she wanted to say something, anything, but there were no other words.

Terry approached, looked down at Mason. He turned to her, placed his hand on her shoulder. "I'm sorry," he said.

Rachel spaced out. The sheriff's words were far off, coming from another world. His mouth moved, but she heard no sound.

"You're gonna be all right," Terry assured. "Come with me." He gripped tight. She did not move.

Rachel placed her hand over her chest as if she were standing at attention for the Pledge of Allegiance.

The sheriff beckoned her again. This time, his grasp loosened, and he stepped away, horrified.

Her neck moved limp to the side. Her face dragged as she peered out over the pink and purple horizon infested with thunderheads. Blood flooded her chest cavity as if being pumped there by a machine, turning the blue shirt black. She fell to her knees, slid in the mud and shook her head from left to right.

This couldn't have happened, shouldn't have happened, why did this—

She landed beside Mason in a heap, and the sweet breath she sucked in spread out over his face like a deep, loving kiss that only lovers share.

Terry looked at his own .38 Mason had used.

Mason's eye popped open. He felt of his shoulder where he'd been hit, stared up in disbelief at the sheriff. He put his hand on Rachel's head, smoothed down her hair, and touched her wet skin, pulled her up like a doll, and held her, his face buried in her hair, as the rain and thunder fell and rolled over the sky. And he cried, his voice squeezed tight, his face wrinkled, as he touched her for the last time.

From beyond the hill came sirens. When an ambulance and another police unit arrived, they found Sheriff Combs standing over Rachel's body under the tree with the .45, his cheeks creased and reddened by tears. He watched lightning shake the sky, and through the rain, Mason drove away, the Porsche's red taillights a signal that the game was over.

Terry looked down at the sunglasses, broken and bent, one plastic hold curled into the soft mud. He saw his reflection in the lenses.

9:01 a.m.

On that fatal afternoon a year ago, thunder covered the sound of the sheriff's .38 in Mason's hand. Or maybe it was his own clouded thoughts. He'd heard the blast but didn't want to believe it. It was almost like watching a cartoon character jerk back, stumble and grope until he slipped and fell. Later, Terry also discovered Rachel was pregnant. And what haunted him was why he even pulled the trigger. Mason had been in a crazed fit, but did the young man really have it in him to intentionally murder Rachel? Terry explained to his fellow officers that from where he'd been standing, it looked as though the kid wasn't going to give up, and that put everyone in danger. The way he looked at it, he had no choice but to fire. Looks, he decided, could be deceiving. He always wondered that if he had held off for only a few more seconds, would Mason have lowered his arm? Tossed the gun? Or put a bullet through Rachel's head in the circus of madness those last couple of weeks had fed him?

Terry was forced to resign his gun and badge. Just as well. He no longer cared for the election to office. Frank said he'd never work in Sutter Springs again—at least not under the government's payroll—and he had no problem with that. He had inadvertently killed an innocent woman, after which, police work did not seem that interesting to him. Terry got up the nerve at the fish fry later that week and just told Frank to shove it.

A month rolled by, and he married Monica south of Alexandria at a little brick church that dead-ended down a dusty, golden road that ran through the middle of a sugarcane field. They honeymooned in Branson, Missouri, for a week. During the entire trip, Terry did not once mention his time with the Sutter Springs Sheriff's Department, or that he knew the Parent Killer's identity before the man was caught. He did not reveal his sympathy for Mason, that deep down, he did not want to arrest him because behind the townsfolk's masks and their Southern morals, there were people who wanted to see black-market justice, there were demons that still raged—and Terry had been one of them. He had no use for someone who would treat their kids the way Sadie, Melissa, and Danny were treated.

From underneath a maple dresser in his bedroom, he pulled out a folder bound with leather straps. Inside, he pulled out a blue notebook. Across the cover read "The Club." He smiled, his lips melting into a crinkle in his cheeks as he thought of those three children.

Danny was adopted by his Aunt Joyce, erasing any fear of having to endure time at the Wilcox Children's Home. It was a place for children from broken homes whose parents could not afford to raise them and for those with parents who didn't care for them at all. The last Terry heard was that Danny had become the best bat on his Little League team.

Along with Terry Robert, Ardon Wells stood in the shadows as the murders took place. But Ardon had a special place in his heart for Sadie and Melissa. When he knew that Danny would be raised in a normal environment, he decided to do the right thing. He adopted the girls. They needed a father figure, and in his mind, he imagined it would ease the grief in the death of their parents, and also shave his guilt in having allowed the murders to come full circle. The children's livelihood did not depend solely on a good home. A few days after Terry's run-in with Mason on that hill, Ardon received a letter telling him to find the kids a decent family. The letter also stated that each of them had a substantial amount of money in the First National Bank of Sutter Springs, and that he and Joyce Bledsoe were announced as beneficiaries until they came of age.

Terry knew about the money, but he never questioned the principal. It was none of his business. He was just thankful those kids would be able to experience a better life. When police officials and a forensic team searched Mason's sprawling log house, Terry found the notebook. Ardon had mentioned it, and Terry swiped it from the crime scene—if nothing but to remind himself why he never stopped one of the most dangerous men the South had ever known.

Mason thought he'd accidentally murdered Rachel and his unborn child when the sheriff allowed him to go. And maybe, in a sense, he had. To that young man, the title of the Parent Killer went deeper than Terry would ever know. That night, Mason left his house, his car, and all belongings and caught a flight out of town. In the year since, no one had seen him.

Terry dropped the article of Rachel Borello's recovery into the notebook, closed it gently, and stuffed it into the folder, then bound it with the straps, and pushed it back under the dresser. She had suffered a chest wound, where the bullet tore left of her heart, and through her lung. After surgery and two weeks in a hospital bed, she returned home for a short time. She soon left the log house she'd shared with Mason. Staying at the lake house wasn't even an option. Both places reminded her of what they had had together. She bought a small brick home in the middle of a Cul de sac south of town, closer to the interstate, and the roads that gave her freedom. On late afternoons, or lazy Sundays, she'd hop into her Lexus and drive to nowhere in particular. Free. Just drive. And think. About what happened and what might have been.

Eight months passed. She gave birth to a blond-headed boy, with blue eyes, and a smile that squeezed her heart. She named him Adam.

The doorbell rang.

His breath smelled of coffee and cigar smoke, so he picked up a stick of chewing gum on his way out and met Monica at the back door. She walked in with grocery sacks in both arms.

Terry popped the gum in his mouth, stopped her, and kissed her lips.

She stared up at him. "What was that for?" she asked.

"I love you," he said, running his fingers through her hair. "I want you to know that."

"You're sweet, Fats." She put a little white sack on the counter. "I got your medicine. So, what've you been doing since I've been gone?"

The Old Man and Little Girl

December, 1995. Bayou Boy Bar & Grill.
Curry, Louisiana. 6:15 p.m.

The bartender set a Seven and Seven on a napkin and gave the man in the sunglasses a wink. She wiped her hands on a towel, tossed it over her shoulder, and walked to the end of the bar. Some teenage kids were at the jukebox and Coolio's "Fantastic Voyage" thumped from the speakers at low volume.

Mason lifted the drink to his lips and sipped. It felt good. But he'd felt good since he'd returned from Florida last week. Ecstatic, in fact. The blue/green ocean stayed a perfect picture in his mind. He saw Rachel in a new blue bikini and a fresh tan. Her hair over her face, the smile and those lips, the way she touched him at midnight while the surf sang a romantic song, the cool sand they routed out with their heated bodies. He'd always remember that vacation. Hell, he wished he'd have caught it on videotape. Maybe he could have sold it. Yeah, right. Now, it was back home, back to routine. What was he going to do this week? Fishing came to mind. Or he could drive down to New Orleans and hit the casinos for a few grand. Rachel had gone back to work baby-sitting and was still bugging him about getting her own business. "I am a certified Massage Therapist," she told him. "I should have my own business."

But he'd been a smartass. "What? You're going to contribute thirty grand a year to our bank account? Think we'll be able to make it, Hon?"

He drank.

"Turn that up." The old man sitting beside him pointed to a small television high in the corner.

Mason turned to him. His face was wrinkled from too many hours in hay fields, his overalls ripped at the seams, loose cotton strands fringed over the material. His bearded face placed him as a perfect candidate for a member of ZZ Top. He had nicotine stains on his fingers and a fever blister on his bottom lip, his skin burned with cancer spots.

The old man swirled his draft beer. "It's a shame, ain't it?"

Mason looked up at the TV. A little girl's grade school photograph appeared onscreen. She had brown hair, she was cute, and there was a spark in her eyes, the kind that made you feel warm inside. Her arms were straight down, hands folded in her lap.

A brunette reporter spoke up. "Six-year-old Hailey Carpenter, of Sutter Springs, was taken to Abbey Medical Center late last night in a fight to save the child's life. Police reports say her parents, Phillip and Barbara Carpenter, noticed she was having difficulty breathing around eight o'clock and rushed her to the ER. Hailey suffered massive injuries to the head and neck, and the child was critical upon arrival. Doctors worked to stabilize her condition, but to no avail. She died at approximately 9:30." A pause. "In two days, she would have celebrated her seventh birthday."

Mason clawed his pinkie over the water beads on the glass.

"Services for Hailey Carpenter will be held Saturday at one o'clock at the Sutter Springs Baptist Church. Her parents are being detained for questioning at this time. There is reason to believe the child had been mistreated and an investigation is currently underway."

"Look at that. Parents don't even wanna take care of their kids no more. Look what happened to that little girl," the old man said.

"It is a shame," Mason said, and moved his butt uncomfortably on the padded stool.

"Got-damn right." The old man finished his beer and brought the glass down on the counter with a loud, empty thud. He lit another cigarette and blew the smoke directly in Mason's face. "Somebody oughta just kill those sons of bitches."